KILL
OR CURE

Suspense Stories about
the World of Medicine

KILL
OR CURE

EDITED BY

MARCIA MULLER

AND

BILL PRONZINI

BONANZA BOOKS
New York

This 1989 edition is published by Bonanza Books, distributed by
Crown Publishers, Inc., 225 Park Avenue South, New York, New
York 10003, by arrangement with Macmillan Publishing Co., Inc.

Printed and Bound in the United States of America

Library of Congress Cataloging-in-Publication Data
Kill or cure / edited by Marcia Muller and Bill Pronzini.
    p.   cm.
    ISBN 0-517-68135-8
    1. Detective and mystery stories, American.   2. Detective and
mystery stories, English.   3. Medicine—Fiction.   I. Muller,
Marcia.   II. Pronzini, Bill.
PS648.D4K54   1989
813'.0872'08356—dc19   89-557
                                                            CIP

h g f e d c b a

Contents

Acknowledgments

The editors gratefully acknowledge permission to reprint the following:

"Easter Devil," by Mignon Eberhart. From *The Cases of Susan Dare* by Mignon Eberhart. Copyright 1934 by Mignon G. Eberhart. Reprinted by permission of Doubleday & Company, Inc.

"But the Patient Died," by Lawrence G. Blochman. From *Diagnosis: Homicide* by Lawrence G. Blochman. Copyright 1947, 1948, 1949, 1950 by Lawrence G. Blochman. Reprinted by permission of Anita Diamant, agent for the estate of Lawrence G. Blochman.

"The Problem of the Covered Bridge," by Edward D. Hoch. Copyright © 1974 by Edward D. Hoch. First published in *Ellery Queen's Mystery Magazine*. Reprinted by permission of the author.

"Hurting Much?" by Cornell Woolrich. Copyright © 1934 by The Red Star News Company. First published in *Detective Fiction Weekly* as "Death Sits in the Dentist's Chair." Reprinted by permission of Scott Meredith Literary Agency, Inc., 845 Third Avenue, New York, N.Y. 10022.

"The Memorial Hour," by Wade Miller. Copyright © 1960 by Wade Miller. First published in *Ellery Queen's Mystery Magazine*. Reprinted by permission of Robert Wade.

"Guilty Witness," by Morris Hershman. Copyright © 1949 by Street & Smith Publications, Inc. Originally published as "Innocent Bystander." Reprinted by permission of the author and Larry Sternig Literary Agency, Inc.

"The Doctor Takes a Case," by George Harmon Coxe. Copyright 1942 by George Harmon Coxe; copyright renewed © 1970 by George Harmon Coxe. Reprinted by permission of Brandt & Brandt Literary Agents, Inc.

"Doctor's Orders," by John F. Suter. Copyright © 1959 by Davis Publications, Inc. First published in *Ellery Queen's Mystery Magazine*. Reprinted by permission of the author.

"Sound Alibi," by Jack Ritchie. Copyright © 1957 by H.S.D. Publications, Inc. First published in *Alfred Hitchcock's Mystery Magazine*.

KILL
OR CURE

Introduction

THE WORLD of medicine has long held a fascination for most people. We are not only interested in such larger issues as surgical techniques and the use of sophisticated modern medical equipment but in the personal lives of medical people and even in such bits of esoterica as the reason doctors wear white coats (because white is a "clean" color) and where modern surgery developed (on the battlefields of war). We are also very much in awe of the one great mystique of the medical profession: the practitioner's supposed power of life and death.

That power is one of the reasons the physician is such a prominent character in stories of crime and detection—from Sherlock Holmes's friend, Dr. Watson, to TV's detecting pathologist, Quincy. Another reason is that the perceived romance of the medical setting lends itself to matters of intrigue. Yet another is that medical personnel, with their specialized knowledge and intelligence, make excellent sleuths who uncover obscure clues that others might all too easily overlook.

Of course, not all medical protagonists in crime fiction are paragons of virtue or intellect. Watson, bless him, misses clues that are obvious to Holmes and (perhaps) to the astute reader; and we all remember what Dr. Jekyll did as Mr. Hyde. Nevertheless, whether bumbler or villain, the doctor, nurse, or other member of the profession retains his or her fascination for the lay reader.

[1]

Sleuths and villains alike come from all areas of medical specialization. The pathologist, for instance, by the very nature of his work, is an ideal fictional detective. The first pathologist sleuth was Lawrence G. Blochman's Dr. Daniel Webster Coffee; he appears in one novel and numerous short stories (one of the best of which appears in these pages), as well as in a short-lived television series, *Diagnosis: Unknown*, that lasted one season (1960) and starred Patrick O'Neal as Dr. Coffee. Another notable series pathologist (retired but well versed in current medical knowledge) is Margaret Scherf's Dr. Grace Severance, who is featured in four novels set in both a small Montana town and Las Vegas—*The Banker's Bones* (1968), *The Beautiful Birthday Cake* (1971), *To Cache a Millionaire* (1972), and *The Beaded Banana* (1978). In the 1968 Edgar-winning *A Case of Need*, Jeffrey Hudson (a pseudonym of Michael Crichton) portrays a doctor, John Berry, who strays far from the pathology lab in order to prove a friend innocent of murder by illegal abortion. Not only is this a fine whodunit, it makes a powerful and informed case for the legalization of abortion. Finally, P. D. James's 1977 mystery, *Death of an Expert Witness*, demonstrates the danger to a medical examiner who testifies at trials or inquests in cases of unusual death.

Psychiatrists and psychologists are also popular subjects of mystery and suspense fiction. One of the earliest of this type of series detective is Anthony Wynne's Dr. Eustace Hailey, a Harley Street (London) "specialist in mental diseases," who solves baffling murders in novels such as *The Green Knife* (1932), *The Case of the Gold Coins* (1934), and *Emergency Exit* (1941)—and in short stories such as "The Cyprian Bees," which has been reprinted here. A more memorable creation, one who uses sound psychiatric and psychological principles to solve *his* baffling cases, is erudite and cosmopolitan Dr. Basil Willing; Helen McCloy's psychiatrist detective appears in a dozen novels, as well as in such outstanding short stories as the one you'll find later in these pages. In Lynn Meyer's 1975 mystery, *Paperback Thriller*, a therapist reads about herself and the crime about to be perpetrated against her in a cheap paperback novel and must then try to rationally explain—and prevent the consequences of—such a bizarre occurrence. In Robert Bloch's *Psycho II*, a 1983 sequel to his chilling 1959 classic, *Psycho*, a psychiatrist follows the trail of Norman Bates when that homicidal slayer escapes from the mental institution where he has been incarcerated for some twenty years. Laura Munder's *Therapy for Murder* (1984) has a therapist heroine and deals with murder and family problems in a psychiatric clinic. There have also been numerous novels set in insane asylums, private sanitoriums, and hospitals for the mentally and emotionally disturbed—among them Jonathan Latimer's *Murder in the Madhouse* (1935), Carter Cullen's *The Deadly Chase* (1957), Winfred van Atta's *Shock Treatment* (1961), Robert Bloch's *Night World* (1972), and two Lew Archer novels by Ross Macdonald, *The Drowning Pool* (1950) and *The Goodbye Look* (1969).

Nurses, generally thought of as support personnel for physicians or private parties, tend to take command when murder and mayhem invade the hospital wards or residences in which these protagonists are employed. An early nurse sleuth was Mary Roberts Rinehart's Hilda Adams, dubbed "Miss Pinkerton" for her detective savvy; she appears in *Miss Pinkerton* (1932) and *Haunted Lady* (1942), as well as in two long novelettes, "The Buckled Bag" and "Locked Doors" (collected in *Mary Roberts Rinehart's Crime Book*, 1933). Nurse Sarah Keate, a creation of Mignon Eberhart, teams with detective Lance O'Leary to solve five crime puzzles, then goes on to solve two more on her own; representative titles are *The Patient in Room 18* (1929), *Murder by an Aristocrat* (1932), and *Man Missing* (1954). Christianna Brand gives us a fascinating look at wartime nursing (and nurse-doctor relationships) in *Green for Danger* (1944), which is set in a hospital beleaguered by both murder and the blitz. A more contemporary nurse protagonist investigates the death of her physician husband in Miriam Borgenicht's *Fall from Grace* (1984). And P. D. James once again uses the knowledge gleaned from many years of hospital administration in *Shroud for a*

Nightingale (1971), in which Adam Dalgleish investigates murder in a nurses' training school.

Medical researchers are usually thought of as quiet, contemplative souls content to be left alone with their test tubes, but quite often they venture outside the laboratory—with dynamic results. One such fictional character is John Rhode's Dr. Lancelot Priestley, the hero of more than fifty novels, among them *The Paddington Mystery* (1925), *The Claverton Mystery* (1933), *Death at the Helm* (1941), *Death at the Inn* (1954), and *The Vanishing Diary* (1961). Michael Crichton once again uses his medical expertise in his 1969 best-seller about a strange malady that threatens world health, *The Andromeda Strain*; and Thomas L. Dunne's heroes and heroines at the National Institutes of Health and the disease-control center in Atlanta face a similarly disastrous problem and similarly overwhelming odds in battling it in *The Scourge* (1978).

The ordinary doctor, slaving away in general practice, is also well represented in crime fiction. Edward D. Hoch's country physician, Dr. Sam Hawthorne, solves "impossible crimes" in the 1920s in a distinguished series of short stories, one of the best of which appears here. Willo Davis Roberts's Dr. Herbert Scott must find the murderer of his bride of two months when he is framed for that gruesome crime in *Didn't Anybody Know My Wife?* (1974). In two notable fictional cases, such "ordinary" doctors are also made to wear the villain's mantle. The anti-hero of Richard Gordon's 1981 novel, *A Question of Guilt*, is none other than the notorious wife-murderer Dr. Crippen. Driven to desperation by his spendthrift spouse and a flagging career, Crippen borrowed a *Gray's Anatomy* from a doctor friend (the narrator and hero of the novel) and proceeded to take a do-it-yourself approach to the disposal of a body. The other villainous doctor, tired of his genteel country practice in England and angry with his nagging wife, resorts to poison in Francis Iles's widely praised *Malice Aforethought* (1931).

Neither have those specialized members of the medical profession—pharmacists, dentists, veterinarians—been forgotten. Marvin Kaye's pharmacist Marty Gold has more than his share of criminous problems in *My Son, the Druggist* (1977) and *My Brother, the Druggist* (1979), as do the protagonists of two stories in this volume, Joe L. Hensley's "Paint Doctor" and Morris Hershman's "Guilty Witness." Dentists have been featured prominently in a number of short stories—Cornell Woolrich's entry here is one of the best—but to date in no major novel in the mystery field. And Barbara Moore gives us a veterinarian sleuth (who detects with the help of a dog named Gala) in *The Doberman Wore Black* (1983), while Mary Roberts Rinehart does the same in her fine short story "The Splinter."

The stories that follow offer the broadest possible range of medical mysteries and medical personnel, representing both good and evil, both "kill or cure." In fact you may not know the difference until you finish each story, and even then you may not be sure.

What you *can* be sure of, from start to finish, is that these tales are authentic in their medical lore, and well calculated to amuse, entertain, inform, and mystify.

—Marcia Muller and Bill Pronzini

San Francisco, California
February 1985

The Resident Patient

SIR ARTHUR CONAN DOYLE

Sir Arthur Conan Doyle (1859–1930) is the most famous of those physicians who established major careers as fiction writers. And, of course, retired army surgeon Dr. John H. Watson is the most famous of all fictional doctors, narrating as he does the fabulous feats of deduction performed by the world's greatest detective, Sherlock Holmes. "The Resident Patient" is one of the earlier and lesser known Holmes and Watson stories (from The Memoirs of Sherlock Holmes, *1894); but the pleasures to be found in this tale of the resident patient at the Brook Street home of nerve specialist Percy Trevelyan are nonetheless considerable. Return with us now to gaslit Victorian London and 221-B Baker Street, where the game is once again afoot. . . .*

IN GLANCING over the somewhat incoherent series of Memoirs with which I have endeavoured to illustrate a few of the mental peculiarities of my friend Mr. Sherlock Holmes, I have been struck by the difficulty which I have experienced in picking out examples which shall in every way answer my purpose. For in those cases in which Holmes has performed some *tour de force* of analytical reasoning, and has demonstrated the value of his peculiar methods of investigation, the facts themselves have often been so slight or so commonplace that I could not feel justified in laying them before the public. On the other hand, it has frequently happened that he has been concerned in some research where the facts have been of the most remarkable and dramatic character, but where the share which he has himself taken in determining their causes has been less pronounced than I, as his biographer, could wish. The small matter which I have chronicled under the heading of "A Study in Scarlet," and that other later one connected with the loss of the *Gloria Scott*, may serve as examples of this Scylla and Charybdis which are forever threatening the historian. It may be that in the business of which I am now about to write the part which my friend played is not sufficiently accentuated; and yet the whole train of circumstances is so remarkable that I cannot bring myself to omit it entirely from this series.

It had been a close, rainy day in October. Our blinds were half-drawn, and Holmes lay curled upon the sofa, reading and rereading a letter which he had received by the morning post. For myself, my term of service in India had trained me to stand heat better than cold, and a thermometer of ninety was no hardship. But the paper was uninteresting. Parliament had risen. Everybody was out of town, and I yearned for the glades of the New Forest or the shingle of Southsea. A depleted bank account had caused me to postpone my holiday, and as to my companion, neither the country nor the sea presented the slightest attraction to him. He loved to lie in the very centre of five millions of people, with his filaments stretching out and running through them, responsive to every little rumour or suspicion of unsolved crime. Appreciation of nature found no place among his many gifts, and his only change was when he turned his mind from the evildoer of the town to track down his brother of the country.

Finding that Holmes was too absorbed for conversation, I had tossed aside the barren paper, and, leaning back in my chair I fell into a brown study. Suddenly my companion's voice broke in upon my thoughts.

"You are right, Watson," said he. "It does seem a very preposterous way of settling a dispute."

"Most preposterous!" I exclaimed, and then, suddenly realizing how he had echoed the inmost thought of my soul, I sat up in my chair and stared at him in blank amazement.

"What is this, Holmes?" I cried. "This is beyond anything which I could have imagined."

He laughed heartily at my perplexity.

"You remember," said he, "that some little time ago, when I read you the passage in one of Poe's sketches, in which a close reasoner follows the unspoken thoughts of his companion, you were inclined to treat the matter as a mere *tour de force* of the author. On my remarking that I was constantly in the habit of doing the same thing you expressed incredulity."

"Oh, no!"

"Perhaps not with your tongue, my dear Watson, but certainly with your eyebrows. So when I saw you throw down your paper and enter upon a train of thought, I was very happy to have the opportunity of reading it off, and eventually of breaking into it, as a proof that I had been in rapport with you."

But I was still far from satisfied. "In the example which you read to me," said I, "the reasoner drew his conclusions from the actions of the man whom he observed. If I remember right, he stumbled over a heap of stones, looked up at the stars, and so on. But I have been seated quietly in my chair, and what clues can I have given you?"

"You do yourself an injustice. The features are given to man as the means by which he shall express his emotions, and yours are faithful servants."

"Do you mean to say that you read my train of thoughts from my features?"

"Your features, and especially your eyes. Perhaps you cannot yourself recall how your reverie commenced?"

"No, I cannot."

"Then I will tell you. After throwing down your paper, which was the action which drew my attention to you, you sat for half a minute with a vacant expression. Then your eyes fixed themselves upon your newly framed picture of General Gordon, and I saw by the alteration in your face that a train of thought had been started. But it did not lead very far. Your eyes turned across to the unframed portrait of Henry Ward Beecher, which stands upon the top of your books. You then glanced up at the wall, and of course your meaning was obvious.You were thinking that if the portrait were framed it would just cover that bare space and correspond with Gordon's picture over there."

"You have followed me wonderfully!" I exclaimed.

"So far I could hardly have gone astray. But now your thoughts went back to Beecher, and you looked hard across as if you were studying the character in his features. Then your eyes ceased to pucker, but you continued to look across, and your face was thoughtful. You were recalling the incidents of Beecher's career. I was well aware that you could not do this without thinking of the mission which he undertook on behalf of the North at the time of the Civil War, for I remember you expressing your passionate indignation at the way in which he was received by the more turbulent of our people. You felt so strongly about it that I knew you could not think of Beecher without thinking of that also. When a moment later I saw your eyes wander away from the picture, I suspected that your mind had now turned to the Civil War, and when I observed that your lips set, your eyes sparkled, and your hands clenched, I was positive that you were indeed thinking of the gallantry which was shown by both sides in that desperate struggle. But then, again, your face grew sadder; you shook your head. You were dwelling upon the sadness and horror and useless waste of life. Your hand stole towards your own old wound, and a smile quivered on your lips, which showed me that the ridiculous side of this method of settling international questions forced itself upon your mind. At this point I agreed with you that it was preposterous, and was glad to find that all my deductions had been correct."

"Absolutely!" said I. "And now that you have explained it, I confess that I am as amazed as before."

"It was very superficial, my dear Watson, I assure you. I should not have intruded it upon your attention had you not shown some incredulity the other day. But the evening has brought a breeze with it. What do you say to a ramble through London?"

I was weary of our little sitting-room and gladly acquiesced. For three hours we strolled about together, watching the ever-changing kaleidoscope of life as it ebbs and flows through Fleet Street and the Strand. His characteristic talk, with its keen observance of detail and subtle power of inference, held me amused and enthralled. It was ten o'clock before we reached Baker Street again. A brougham was waiting at our door.

"Hum! A doctor's—general practitioner, I perceive," said Holmes. "Not been long in practice, but has a good deal to do. Come to consult us, I fancy! Lucky we came back!"

I was sufficiently conversant with Holmes's methods to be able to follow his reasoning, and to see that the nature and state of the various medical instruments in the wicker basket which hung in the lamp-light inside the brougham had given him the data for his swift deduction. The light in our window above showed that this late visit was indeed intended for us. With some curiosity as to what could have sent a brother medico to us at such an hour, I followed Holmes into our sanctum.

A pale, taper-faced man with sandy whiskers rose up from a chair by the fire as we entered. His age may not have been more than three or four and thirty, but his haggard expression and unhealthy hue told of a life which had sapped his strength and robbed him of his youth. His manner was nervous and shy, like that of a sensitive gentleman, and the thin white hand which he laid on the mantelpiece as he rose was that of an artist rather than of a surgeon. His dress was quiet and sombre—a black frock-coat, dark trousers, and a touch of colour about his necktie.

"Good-evening, Doctor," said Holmes cheerily. "I am glad to see that you have only been waiting a very few minutes."

"You spoke to my coachman, then?"

"No, it was the candle on the side-table that told me. Pray resume your seat and let me know how I can serve you."

"My name is Dr. Percy Trevelyan," said our visitor, "and I live at 403 Brook Street."

"Are you not the author of a monograph upon obscure nervous lesions?" I asked.

His pale cheeks flushed with pleasure at hearing that his work was known to me.

"I so seldom hear of the work that I thought it was quite dead," said he. "My publishers gave me a most discouraging account of its sale. You are yourself, I presume, a medical man?"

"A retired army surgeon."

"My own hobby has always been nervous disease. I should wish to make it an absolute specialty, but of course a man must take what he can get at first. This, however, is beside the question, Mr. Sherlock Holmes, and I quite appreciate how valuable your time is. The fact is that a very singular train of events has occurred recently at my house in Brook Street, and tonight they came to such a head that I felt it was quite impossible for me to wait another hour before asking for your advice and assistance."

Sherlock Holmes sat down and lit his pipe. "You are very welcome to both," said he. "Pray let me have a detailed account of what the circumstances are which have disturbed you."

"One or two of them are so trivial," said Dr. Trevelyan, "that really I am almost ashamed to mention them. But the matter is so inexplicable, and the recent turn which it has taken is so elaborate, that I shall lay it all before you, and you shall judge what is essential and what is not.

"I am compelled, to begin with, to say something of my own college career. I am a London University man, you know, and I am sure that you will not think that I am unduly singing my own praises if I say that my student career was considered by my professors to be a very promising one. After I had graduated I continued to devote myself to research, occupying a minor position in King's College Hospital, and I was fortunate enough to excite considerable interest by my research into the pathology of catalepsy, and finally to win the Bruce Pinkerton prize and medal by the monograph on nervous lesions to which your friend has just alluded. I should not go too far if I were to say that there was a general impression at that time that a distinguished career lay before me.

"But the one great stumbling-block lay in my want of capital. As you will readily understand, a specialist who aims high is compelled to start in one of a dozen streets in the Cavendish Square quarter, all of which entail enormous rents and furnishing expenses. Besides this preliminary outlay, he must be prepared to keep himself for some years, and to hire a presentable carriage and horse. To do this was quite beyond my power, and I could only hope that by economy I might in ten years' time save enough to enable me to put up my plate. Suddenly, however, an unexpected incident opened up quite a new prospect to me.

"This was a visit from a gentleman of the name of Blessington, who was a complete stranger to me. He came up into my room one morning, and plunged into business in an instant.

" 'You are the same Percy Trevelyan who has had so distinguished a career and won a great prize lately?' said he.

"I bowed.

" 'Answer me frankly,' he continued, 'for you will find it to your interest to do so. You have all the cleverness which makes a successful man. Have you the tact?'

"I could not help smiling at the abruptness of the question.

" 'I trust that I have my share,' I said.

" 'Any bad habits? Not drawn towards drink, eh?'

" 'Really, sir!' I cried.

" 'Quite right! That's all right! But I was bound to ask. With all these qualities, why are you not in practice?'

"I shrugged my shoulders.

" 'Come, come!' said he in his bustling way. 'It's the old story. More in your brains than in your pocket, eh? What would you say if I were to start you in Brook Street?'

"I stared at him in astonishment.

" 'Oh, it's for my sake, not for yours,' he cried. 'I'll be perfectly frank with you, and if it suits you it will suit me very well. I have a few thousands to invest, d'ye see, and I think I'll sink them in you.'

" 'But why?' I gasped.

" 'Well, it's just like any other speculation, and safer than most.'

" 'What am I to do, then?'

" 'I'll tell you. I'll take the house, furnish it, pay the maids, and run the whole place. All you have to do is just to wear out your chair in the consulting-room. I'll let you have pocket-money and everything. Then you hand over to me three quarters of what you earn, and you keep the other quarter for yourself.'

"This was the strange proposal, Mr. Holmes, with which the man Blessington approached me. I won't weary you with the account of how we bargained and negotiated. It ended in my moving into the house next Lady Day, and starting in practice on very much the same conditions as he had suggested. He came himself to live with me in the character of a resident patient. His heart was weak, it appears, and he needed constant medical supervision. He turned the two best rooms of the first floor into a sitting-room and bedroom for himself. He was a man of singular habits, shunning company and very seldom going out. His life was irregular, but in one respect he was regularity itself. Every evening, at the same hour, he walked into the consulting-room, examined the books, put down five and three-pence for every guinea that I had earned, and carried the rest off to the strong-box in his own room.

"I may say with confidence that he never had occasion to regret his speculation. From the first it was a success. A few good cases and the reputation which I had won in the hospital brought me rapidly to the front, and during the last few years I have made him a rich man.

"So much, Mr. Holmes, for my past history and my relations with Mr. Blessington. It only remains for me now to tell you what has occurred to bring me here tonight.

"Some weeks ago Mr. Blessington came down to me in, as it seemed to me, a state of considerable agitation. He spoke of some burglary which, he said, had been committed in the West End, and he appeared, I remember, to be quite unnecessarily excited about it, declaring that a day should not pass before we should add stronger bolts to our windows and doors. For a week he continued to be in a peculiar state of restlessness, peering continually out of the windows, and ceasing to take the short walk which had usually been the prelude to his dinner. From his manner it struck me that he was in mortal dread of something or somebody, but when I questioned him upon the point he became so offensive that I was compelled to drop the subject. Gradually, as time passed, his fears appeared to die away, and he renewed his former habits, when a fresh event reduced him to the pitiable state of prostration in which he now lies.

"What happened was this. Two days ago I received the letter which I now read to you. Neither address nor date is attached to it.

'A Russian nobleman who is now resident in England [it runs], would be glad to avail himself of the professional assistance of Dr. Percy Trevelyan. He has been for some years a victim to cataleptic attacks, on which, as is well known, Dr. Trevelyan is an authority. He proposes to call at about a quarter-past six tomorrow evening, if Dr. Trevelyan will make it convenient to be at home.'

"This letter interested me deeply, because the chief difficulty in the study of catalepsy is the rareness of the disease. You may believe, then, that I was in my consulting-room when, at the appointed hour, the page showed in the patient.

"He was an elderly man, thin, demure, and commonplace—by no means the conception one forms of a Russian nobleman. I was much more struck by the appearance of his companion. This was a tall young man, surprisingly handsome, with a dark, fierce face, and the limbs and chest of a Hercules. He had his hand under the other's arm as they entered, and helped him to a chair with a tenderness which one would hardly have expected from his appearance.

" 'You will excuse my coming in, Doctor,' said he to me, speaking English with a slight lisp. 'This is my father, and his health is a matter of the most overwhelming importance to me.'

"I was touched by this filial anxiety. 'You would, perhaps, care to remain during the consultation?' said I.

" 'Not for the world,' he cried with a gesture of horror. 'It is more painful to me than I can express. If I were to see my father in one of these dreadful seizures I am convinced that I should never survive it. My own nervous system is an exceptionally sensitive one. With your permission, I will remain in the waiting-room while you go into my father's case.'

"To this, of course, I assented, and the young man withdrew. The patient and I then plunged into a discussion of his case, of which I took exhaustive notes. He was not remarkable for intelligence, and his answers were frequently obscure, which I attributed to his limited acquaintance with our language. Suddenly, however, as I sat writing, he ceased to give any answer at all to my inquiries, and on my turning towards him I was shocked to see that he was sitting bolt upright in his chair, staring at me with a perfectly blank and rigid face. He was again in the grip of his mysterious malady.

"My first feeling, as I have just said, was one of pity and horror. My second, I fear, was rather one of professional satisfaction. I made notes of my patient's pulse and temperature, tested the rigidity of his muscles, and examined his reflexes. There was nothing markedly abnormal in any of these conditions, which harmonized with my former experiences. I had obtained good results in such cases by the inhalation of nitrite of amyl, and the present seemed an admirable opportunity of testing its virtues. The bottle was downstairs in my laboratory, so, leaving my patient seated in his chair, I ran down to get it. There was some little delay in finding it—five minutes, let us say—and then I returned. Imagine my amazement to find the room empty and the patient gone.

"Of course, my first act was to run into the waiting-room. The son had gone also. The hall door had been closed, but not shut. My page who admits patients is a new boy and by no means quick. He waits downstairs and runs up to show patients out when I ring the consulting-room bell. He had heard nothing, and the affair remained a complete mystery. Mr. Blessington came in from his walk shortly afterwards, but I did not say anything to him upon the subject, for, to tell the truth, I have got in the way of late of holding as little communication with him as possible.

"Well, I never thought that I should see anything more of the Russian and his son, so you can imagine my amazement when, at the very same hour this evening, they both came marching into my consulting-room, just as they had done before.

" 'I feel that I owe you a great many apologies for my abrupt departure yesterday, Doctor,' said my patient.

" 'I confess that I was very much surprised at it,' said I.

" 'Well, the fact is,' he remarked, 'that when I recover from these attacks my mind is always very clouded as to all that has gone before. I woke up in a strange room, as it seemed to me, and made my way out into the street in a sort of dazed way when you were absent.'

" 'And I,' said the son, 'seeing my father pass the door of the waiting-room, naturally thought that the consultation had come to an end. It was not until we had reached home that I began to realize the true state of affairs.'

" 'Well,' said I, laughing, 'there is no harm done except that you puzzled me terribly; so if you, sir, would kindly step into the waiting-room I shall be happy to continue our consultation which was brought to so abrupt an ending.'

"For half an hour or so I discussed the old gentleman's symptoms with him, and then, having prescribed for him, I saw him go off upon the arm of his son.

"I have told you that Mr. Blessington generally chose this hour of the day for his exercise. He came in shortly afterwards and passed upstairs. An instant later I heard him running down, and he burst into my consulting-room like a man who is mad with panic.

" 'Who has been in my room?' he cried.

" 'No one,' said I.

" 'It's a lie!' he yelled. 'Come up and look!'

"I passed over the grossness of his language, as he seemed half out of his mind with fear. When I went upstairs with him he pointed to several footprints upon the light carpet.

" 'Do you mean to say those are mine?' he cried.

"They were certainly very much larger than any which he could have made, and were evidently quite fresh. It rained hard this afternoon, as you know, and my patients were the only people who called. It must have been the case, then, that the man in the waiting-room had, for some unknown reason, while I was busy with the other, ascended to the room of my resident patient. Nothing had been touched or taken, but there were the footprints to prove that the intrusion was an undoubted fact.

"Mr. Blessington seemed more excited over the matter than I should have thought possible, though of course it was enough to disturb anybody's peace of mind. He actually sat crying in an armchair, and I could hardly get him to speak coherently. It was his suggestion that I should come round to you, and of course I at once saw the propriety of it, for certainly the incident is a very singular one, though he appears to completely overrate its importance. If you would only come back with me in my brougham, you would at least be able to soothe him, though I can hardly hope that you will be able to explain this remarkable occurrence.''

Sherlock Holmes had listened to this long narrative with an intentness which showed me that his interest was keenly aroused. His face was as impassive as ever, but his lids had drooped more heavily over his eyes, and his smoke had curled up more thickly from his pipe to emphasize each curious episode in the doctor's tale. As our visitor concluded, Holmes sprang up without a word, handed me my hat, picked his own from the table, and followed Dr. Trevelyan to the door. Within a quarter of an hour we had been dropped at the door of the physician's residence in Brook Street, one of those sombre, flat-faced houses which one associates with a West End practice. A small page admitted us, and we began at once to ascend the broad, well-carpeted stair.

But a singular interruption brought us to a standstill. The light at the top was suddenly whisked out, and from the darkness came a reedy, quavering voice.

''I have a pistol,'' it cried. ''I give you my word that I'll fire if you come any nearer.''

''This really grows outrageous, Mr. Blessington,'' cried Dr. Trevelyan.

''Oh, then it is you, Doctor,'' said the voice with a great heave of relief. ''But those other gentlemen, are they what they pretend to be?''

We were conscious of a long scrutiny out of the darkness.

''Yes, yes, it's all right,'' said the voice at last. ''You can come up, and I am sorry if my precautions have annoyed you.''

He relit the stair gas as he spoke, and we saw before us a singular-looking man, whose appearance, as well as his voice, testified to his jangled nerves. He was very fat, but had apparently at some time been much fatter, so that the skin hung about his face in loose pouches, like the cheeks of a bloodhound. He was of a sickly colour, and his thin, sandy hair seemed to bristle up with the intensity of his emotion. In his hand he held a pistol, but he thrust it into his pocket as we advanced.

"Good-evening, Mr. Holmes," said he. "I am sure I am very much obliged to you for coming round. No one ever needed your advice more than I do. I suppose that Dr. Trevelyan has told you of this most unwarrantable intrusion into my rooms."

"Quite so," said Holmes. "Who are these two men, Mr. Blessington, and why do they wish to molest you?"

"Well, well," said the resident patient in a nervous fashion, "of course it is hard to say that. You can hardly expect me to answer that, Mr. Holmes."

"Do you mean that you don't know?"

"Come in here, if you please. Just have the kindness to step in here."

He led the way into his bedroom, which was large and comfortably furnished.

"You see that," said he, pointing to a big black box at the end of his bed. "I have never been a very rich man, Mr. Holmes— never made but one investment in my life, as Dr. Trevelyan would tell you. But I don't believe in bankers. I would never trust a banker, Mr. Holmes. Between ourselves, what little I have is in that box, so you can understand what it means to me when unknown people force themselves into my rooms."

Holmes looked at Blessington in his questioning way and shook his head.

"I cannot possibly advise you if you try to deceive me," said he.

"But I have told you everything."

Holmes turned on his heel with a gesture of disgust. "Good-night, Dr. Trevelyan," said he.

"And no advice for me?" cried Blessington in a breaking voice.

"My advice to you, sir, is to speak the truth."

A minute later we were in the street and walking for home. We had crossed Oxford Street and were halfway down Harley Street before I could get a word from my companion.

"Sorry to bring you out on such a fool's errand, Watson," he said at last. "It is an interesting case, too, at the bottom of it."

"I can make little of it," I confessed.

"Well, it is quite evident that there are two men—more, per-haps, but at least two—who are determined for some reason to get at this fellow Blessington. I have no doubt in my mind that both on the first and on the second occasion that young man penetrated to Blessington's room, while his confederate, by an ingenious device, kept the doctor from interfering."

"And the catalepsy?"

"A fraudulent imitation, Watson, though I should hardly dare to hint as much to our specialist. It is a very easy complaint to imitate. I have done it myself."

"And then?"

"By the purest chance Blessington was out on each occasion. Their reason for choosing so unusual an hour for a consultation was obviously to insure that there should be no other patient in the waiting-room. It just happened, however, that this hour co-incided with Blessington's constitutional, which seems to show that they were not very well acquainted with his daily routine. Of course, if they had been merely after plunder they would at least have made some attempt to search for it. Besides, I can read in a man's eye when it is his own skin that he is frightened for. It is inconceivable that this fellow could have made two such vin-dictive enemies as these appear to be without knowing of it. I hold it, therefore, to be certain that he does know who these men are, and that for reasons of his own he suppresses it. It is just possible that tomorrow may find him in a more communicative mood."

"Is there not one alternative," I suggested, "grotesquely im-probable, no doubt, but still just conceivable? Might the whole story of the cataleptic Russian and his son be a concoction of Dr. Trevelyan's, who has, for his own purposes, been in Blessington's rooms?"

I saw in the gas-light that Holmes wore an amused smile at this brilliant departure of mine.

"My dear fellow," said he, "it was one of the first solutions

which occurred to me, but I was soon able to corroborate the
doctor's tale. This young man has left prints upon the stair-
carpet which made it quite superfluous for me to ask to see those
which he had made in the room. When I tell you that his shoes
were square-toed instead of being pointed like Blessington's,
and were quite an inch and a third longer than the doctor's, you
will acknowledge that there can be no doubt as to his individual-
ity. But we may sleep on it now, for I shall be surprised if we do
not hear something further from Brook Street in the morning."

Sherlock Holmes's prophecy was soon fulfilled, and in a dramatic fashion. At half-past seven next morning, in the first dim
glimmer of daylight, I found him standing by my bedside in his
dressing-gown.

"There's a brougham waiting for us, Watson," said he.

"What's the matter, then?"

"The Brook Street business."

"Any fresh news?"

"Tragic, but ambiguous," said he, pulling up the blind.
"Look at this—a sheet from a notebook, with 'For God's sake
come at once. P.T.,' scrawled upon it in pencil. Our friend, the
doctor, was hard put to it when he wrote this. Come along, my
dear fellow, for it's an urgent call."

In a quarter of an hour or so we were back at the physician's
house. He came running out to meet us with a face of horror.

"Oh, such a business!" he cried with his hands to his temples.

"What then?"

"Blessington has committed suicide!"

Holmes whistled.

"Yes, he hanged himself during the night."

We had entered, and the doctor had preceded us into what
was evidently his waiting-room.

"I really hardly know what I am doing," he cried. "The police
are already upstairs. It has shaken me most dreadfully."

"When did you find it out?"

"He has a cup of tea taken in to him early every morning. When the maid entered, about seven, there the unfortunate fellow was hanging in the middle of the room. He had tied his cord to the hook on which the heavy lamp used to hang, and he had jumped off from the top of the very box that he showed us yesterday."

Holmes stood for a moment in deep thought.

"With your permission," said he at last, "I should like to go upstairs and look into the matter."

We both ascended, followed by the doctor.

It was a dreadful sight which met us as we entered the bedroom door. I have spoken of the impression of flabbiness which this man Blessington conveyed. As he dangled from the hook it was exaggerated and intensified until he was scarce human in his appearance. The neck was drawn out like a plucked chicken's, making the rest of him seem the more obese and unnatural by the contrast. He was clad only in his long night-dress, and his swollen ankles and ungainly feet protruded starkly from beneath it. Beside him stood a smart-looking police-inspector, who was taking notes in a pocketbook.

"Ah, Mr. Holmes," said he heartily as my friend entered, "I am delighted to see you."

"Good-morning, Lanner," answered Holmes; "you won't think me an intruder, I am sure. Have you heard of the events which led up to this affair?"

"Yes, I heard something of them."

"Have you formed any opinion?"

"As far as I can see, the man has been driven out of his senses by fright. The bed has been well slept in, you see. There's his impression, deep enough. It's about five in the morning, you know, that suicides are most common. That would be about his time for hanging himself. It seems to have been a very deliberate affair."

"I should say that he has been dead about three hours, judging by the rigidity of the muscles," said I.

"Noticed anything peculiar about the room?" asked Holmes.

"Found a screw-driver and some screws on the wash-hand stand. Seems to have smoked heavily during the night, too. Here are four cigar-ends that I picked out of the fireplace."

"Hum!" said Holmes, "have you got his cigar-holder?"

"No, I have seen none."

"His cigar-case, then?"

"Yes, it was in his coat-pocket."

Holmes opened it and smelled the single cigar which it contained.

"Oh, this is a Havana, and these others are cigars of the peculiar sort which are imported by the Dutch from their East Indian colonies. They are usually wrapped in straw, you know, and are thinner for their length than any other brand." He picked up the four ends and examined them with his pocket-lens.

"Two of these have been smoked from a holder and two without," said he. "Two have been cut by a not very sharp knife, and two have had the ends bitten off by a set of excellent teeth. This is no suicide, Mr. Lanner. It is a very deeply planned and cold-blooded murder."

"Impossible!" cried the inspector.

"And why?"

"Why should anyone murder a man in so clumsy a fashion as by hanging him?"

"That is what we have to find out."

"How could they get in?"

"Through the front door."

"It was barred in the morning."

"Then it was barred after them."

"How do you know?"

"I saw their traces. Excuse me a moment, and I may be able to give you some further information about it."

He went over to the door, and turning the lock he examined it in his methodical way. Then he took out the key, which was on the inside, and inspected that also. The bed, the carpet, the chairs, the mantelpiece, the dead body, and the rope were each in turn examined, until at last he professed himself satisfied, and with my aid and that of the inspector cut down the wretched object and laid it reverently under a sheet.

"How about this rope?" he asked.

"It is cut off this," said Dr. Trevelyan, drawing a large coil from under the bed. "He was morbidly nervous of fire, and always kept this beside him, so that he might escape by the window in case the stairs were burning."

"That must have saved them trouble," said Holmes thoughtfully. "Yes, the actual facts are very plain, and I shall be surprised if by the afternoon I cannot give you the reasons for them as well. I will take this photograph of Blessington, which I see upon the mantelpiece, as it may help me in my inquiries."

"But you have told us nothing!" cried the doctor.

"Oh, there can be no doubt as to the sequence of events," said Holmes. "There were three of them in it: the young man, the old man, and a third, to whose identity I have no clue. The first two, I need hardly remark, are the same who masqueraded as the Russian count and his son, so we can give a very full description of them. They were admitted by a confederate inside the house. If I might offer you a word of advice, Inspector, it would be to arrest the page, who, as I understand, has only recently come into your service, Doctor."

"The young imp cannot be found," said Dr. Trevelyan; "the maid and the cook have just been searching for him."

Holmes shrugged his shoulders.

"He has played a not unimportant part in this drama," said he. "The three men having ascended the stairs, which they did on tiptoe, the elder man first, the younger man second, and the unknown man in the rear—"

"My dear Holmes!" I ejaculated.

"Oh, there could be no question as to the superimposing of the footmarks. I had the advantage of learning which was which last night. They ascended, then, to Mr. Blessington's room, the door of which they found to be locked. With the help of a wire, however, they forced round the key. Even without the lens you will perceive, by the scratches on this ward, where the pressure was applied.

"On entering the room their first proceeding must have been to gag Mr. Blessington. He may have been asleep, or he may have been so paralyzed with terror as to have been unable to cry out. These walls are thick, and it is conceivable that his shriek, if he had time to utter one, was unheard.

"Having secured him, it is evident to me that a consultation of some sort was held. Probably it was something in the nature of a judicial proceeding. It must have lasted for some time, for it was then that these cigars were smoked. The older man sat in that wicker chair; it was he who used the cigar-holder. The younger man sat over yonder; he knocked his ash off against the chest of drawers. The third fellow paced up and down. Blessington, I think, sat upright in the bed, but of that I cannot be absolutely certain.

"Well, it ended by their taking Blessington and hanging him. The matter was so prearranged that it is my belief that they brought with them some sort of block or pulley which might serve as a gallows. That screw-driver and those screws were, as I conceive, for fixing it up. Seeing the hook, however, they naturally saved themselves the trouble. Having finished their work they made off, and the door was barred behind them by their confederate."

We had all listened with the deepest interest to this sketch of the night's doings, which Holmes had deduced from signs so subtle and minute that, even when he had pointed them out to us, we could scarcely follow him in his reasonings. The inspector hurried away on the instant to make inquiries about the page, while Holmes and I returned to Baker Street for breakfast.

"I'll be back by three," said he when we had finished our meal. "Both the inspector and the doctor will meet me here at that hour, and I hope by that time to have cleared up any little obscurity which the case may still present."

Our visitors arrived at the appointed time, but it was a quarter to four before my friend put in an appearance. From his expression as he entered, however, I could see that all had gone well with him.

"Any news, Inspector?"

"We have got the boy, sir."

"Excellent, and I have got the men."

"You have got them!" we cried, all three.

"Well, at least I have got their identity. This so-called Blessington is, as I expected, well known at headquarters, and so are his assailants. Their names are Biddle, Hayward, and Moffat."

"The Worthingdon bank gang," cried the inspector.

"Precisely," said Holmes.

"Then Blessington must have been Sutton."

"Exactly," said Holmes.

"Why, that makes it as clear as crystal," said the inspector.

But Trevelyan and I looked at each other in bewilderment.

"You must surely remember the great Worthingdon bank business," said Holmes. "Five men were in it—these four and a fifth called Cartwright. Tobin, the caretaker, was murdered, and the thieves got away with seven thousand pounds. This was in 1875. They were all five arrested, but the evidence against them was by no means conclusive. This Blessington or Sutton, who was the worst of the gang, turned informer. On his evidence Cartwright was hanged and the other three got fifteen years apiece. When they got out the other day, which was some years before their full term, they set themselves, as you perceive, to hunt down the traitor and to avenge the death of their comrade upon him. Twice they tried to get at him and failed; a third time, you see, it came off. Is there anything further which I can explain, Dr. Trevelyan?"

"I think you have made it all remarkably clear," said the doctor. "No doubt the day on which he was so perturbed was the day when he had seen of their release in the newspapers."

"Quite so. His talk about a burglary was the merest blind."

"But why could he not tell you this?"

"Well, my dear sir, knowing the vindictive character of his old associates, he was trying to hide his own identity from everybody as long as he could. His secret was a shameful one, and he could not bring himself to divulge it. However, wretch as he was, he was still living under the shield of British law, and I have no doubt, Inspector, that you will see that, though that shield may fail to guard, the sword of justice is still there to avenge."

Such were the singular circumstances in connection with the Resident Patient and the Brook Street Doctor. From that night nothing has been seen of the three murderers by the police, and it is surmised at Scotland Yard that they were among the passengers of the ill-fated steamer *Norah Creina*, which was lost some years ago with all hands upon the Portuguese coast, some leagues to the north of Oporto. The proceedings against the page broke down for want of evidence, and the Brook Street Mystery, as it was called, has never until now been fully dealt with in any public print.

The Superfluous Finger

JACQUES FUTRELLE

✸

Professor Augustus S.F.X. Van Dusen, alias The Thinking Machine, is the singular creation of Jacques Futrelle and appears in forty-three short stories, one novella (The Haunted Bell, 1915), and one novel (The Chase of the Golden Plate, 1906). Like Sherlock Holmes, the professor applies his ratiocinative powers to particularly baffling cases, and his careful deductions, combined with Futrelle's excellent characterization and crisp prose, produce tales that are sure to amuse and surprise. In "The Superfluous Finger," a surgeon who has been compelled to perform an odd operation on a beautiful young woman enlists the professor's aid in uncovering her reasons for requiring such medical attention—and the reasons are strange indeed.

SHE DREW off her left glove, a delicate, crinkled suede affair, and offered her bare hand to the surgeon.

An artist would have called it beautiful, perfect, even; the surgeon, professionally enough, set it down as an excellent structural specimen. From the polished pink nails of the tapering fingers to the firm, well moulded wrist, it was distinctly the hand of a woman of ease—one that had never known labor, a pampered hand Dr. Prescott told himself.

"The forefinger," she exclaimed calmly. "I should like to have it amputated at the first joint, please."

"Amputated?" gasped Dr. Prescott. He stared into the pretty face of his caller. It was flushed softly, and the red lips were parted in a slight smile. It seemed quite an ordinary affair to her. The surgeon bent over the hand with quick interest. "Amputated!" he repeated.

"I came to you," she went on with a nod, "because I have been informed that you are one of the most skillful men of your profession, and the cost of the operation is quite immaterial."

Dr. Prescott pressed the pink nail of the forefinger then permitted the blood to rush back into it. Several times he did this, then he turned the hand over and scrutinized it closely inside from the delicately lined palm to the tips of the fingers. When he looked up at last there was an expression of frank bewilderment on his face.

"What's the matter with it?" he asked.

"Nothing," the woman replied pleasantly. "I merely want it off from the first joint."

The surgeon leaned back in his chair with a frown of perplexity on his brow, and his visitor was subjected to a sharp, professional stare. She bore it unflinchingly and even smiled a little at his obvious perturbation.

"Why do you want it off?" he demanded.

The woman shrugged her shoulders a little impatiently.

[30]

"I can't tell you that," she replied. "It really is not necessary that you should know. You are a surgeon, I want an operation performed. That is all."

There was a long pause; the mutual stare didn't waver.

"You must understand, Miss—Miss—er—" began Dr. Prescott at last. "By the way, you have not introduced yourself?" She was silent. "May I ask your name?"

"My name is of no consequence," she replied calmly. "I might, of course, give you a name, but it would not be mine, therefore any name would be superfluous."

Again the surgeon stared.

"When do you want the operation performed?" he inquired.

"Now," she replied. "I am ready."

"You must understand," he said severely, "that surgery is a profession for the relief of human suffering, not for mutilation—willful mutilation I might say."

"I understand that perfectly," she said. "But where a person submits of her own desire to—to mutilation as you call it, I can see no valid objection on your part."

"It would be criminal to remove a finger where there is no necessity for it," continued the surgeon bluntly. "No good end could be served."

A trace of disappointment showed in the young woman's face, and again she shrugged her shoulders.

"The question after all," she said finally, "is not one of ethics but is simply whether or not you will perform the operation. Would you do it for, say, a thousand dollars?"

"Not for five thousand dollars," blurted the surgeon.

"Well, for ten thousand then?" she asked, quite casually.

All sorts of questions were pounding in Dr. Prescott's mind. Why did a young and beautiful woman desire—why was she anxious even—to sacrifice a perfectly healthy finger? What possible purpose would it serve to mar a hand which was as nearly perfect as any he had ever seen? Was it some insane caprice? Staring deeply into her steady, quiet eyes he could only be convinced of her sanity. Then what?

"No, madam," he said at last, vehemently, "I would not perform the operation for any sum you might mention, unless I was first convinced that the removal of that finger was absolutely necessary. That, I think, is all."

He arose as if to end the consultation. The woman remained seated and continued thoughtful for a minute.

"As I understand it," she said, "you *would* perform the operation if I could convince you that it was absolutely necessary?"

"Certainly," he replied promptly, almost eagerly. His curiosity was aroused. "Then it would come within the range of my professional duties."

"Won't you take my word that it is necessary, and that it is impossible for me to explain why?"

"No. I must know why."

The woman arose and stood facing him. The disappointment had gone from her face now.

"Very well," she remarked steadily. "You *will* perform the operation if it is necessary, therefore if I should shoot the finger off, perhaps—?"

"Shoot it off?" exclaimed Dr. Prescott in amazement. "Shoot it off?"

"That is what I said," she replied calmly. "If I should shoot the finger off you would consent to dress the wound? You would make any necessary amputation?"

She held up the finger under discussion and looked at it curiously. Dr. Prescott himself stared at it with a sudden new interest.

"Shoot it off?" he repeated. "Why, you must be mad to contemplate such a thing," he exploded, and his face flushed in sheer anger. "I—I will have nothing whatever to do with the affair, madam. Good day."

"I should have to be very careful, of course," she mused, "but I think perhaps one shot would be sufficient; then I should come to you and demand that you dress it?"

There was a question in the tone. Dr. Prescott stared at her for a full minute, then walked over and opened the door.

"In my profession, madam," he said coldly, "there is too much possibility of doing good and relieving actual suffering for me to consider this matter or discuss it further with you. There are three persons now waiting in the ante-room who *need* my services. I shall be compelled to ask you to excuse me."

"But you will dress the wound?" the woman insisted, undaunted by his forbidding tone and manner.

"I shall have nothing whatever to do with it," declared the surgeon, positively, finally. "If you need the services of any medical man permit me to suggest that it is an alienist and not a surgeon."

The woman didn't appear to take offense.

"Someone would have to dress it," she continued insistently. "I should much prefer that it be a man of undisputed skill—you I mean; therefore I shall call again. Good day."

There was a rustle of silken skirts and she was gone. Dr. Prescott stood for an instant gazing after her in frank wonder and annoyance in his eyes, his attitude, then he went back and sat down at the desk. The crinkled suede glove still lay where she had left it. He examined it gingerly, then with a final shake of his head dismissed the affair and turned to other things.

Early next afternoon Dr. Prescott was sitting in his office writing when the door from the ante-room where patients awaited his leisure was thrown open and the young man in attendance rushed in.

"A lady has fainted, sir," he said hurriedly. "She seems to be hurt."

Dr. Prescott arose quickly and strode out. There, lying helplessly back in her chair with white face and closed eyes, was his visitor of the day before. He stepped toward her quickly, then hesitated as he recalled their conversation. Finally, however, professional instinct, the desire to relieve suffering, and perhaps curiosity, too, caused him to go to her. The left hand was wrapped in an improvised bandage through which there was a trickle of blood. He glared at it with incredulous eyes.

"Hanged if she didn't do it," he blurted angrily.

The fainting spell, Dr. Prescott saw, was due only to loss of blood and physical pain, and he busied himself trying to restore her to consciousness. Meanwhile, he gave some hurried instructions to the young man who was in attendance in the ante-room.

"Call up Professor Van Dusen on the 'phone," he directed, "and ask him if he can assist me in a minor operation. Tell him it's rather a curious case and I am sure it will interest him."

It was in this manner that the problem of the superfluous finger first came to the attention of The Thinking Machine. He arrived just as the mysterious woman was opening her eyes to consciousness from the fainting spell. She stared at him glassily, unrecognizingly; then her glance wandered to Dr. Prescott. She smiled.

"I knew you'd have to do it," she murmured weakly.

After the ether had been administered for the operation, a simple and an easy one, Dr. Prescott stated the circumstances of the case to The Thinking Machine. The scientist stood with his long, slender fingers resting lightly on the young woman's pulse, listening in silence.

"What do you make of it?" demanded the surgeon.

The Thinking Machine didn't say. At the moment he was leaning over the unconscious woman, squinting at her forehead. With his disengaged hand he stroked the delicately pencilled eye-brows several times the wrong way, and again at close range squinted at them. Dr. Prescott saw and seeing, understood.

"No, it isn't that," he said and he shuddered a little. "I thought of it myself. Her bodily condition is excellent, splendid."

It was some time later when the young woman was sleeping lightly, placidly under the influence of a soothing potion, that The Thinking Machine spoke of the peculiar events which had preceded the operation. Then he was sitting in Dr. Prescott's private office. He had picked up a woman's glove from the desk.

"'This is the glove she left when she first called, isn't it?" he inquired.

"Yes."

"Did you happen to see her remove it?"

"Yes."

The Thinking Machine curiously examined the dainty, perfumed trifle, then, arising suddenly, went into the adjoining room where the woman lay asleep. He stood for an instant gazing down admiringly at the exquisite, slender figure; then, bending over, he looked closely at her left hand. When at last he straightened up, it seemed that some unspoken question in his mind had been answered. He rejoined Dr. Prescott.

"It's difficult to say what motive is back of her desire to have the finger amputated," he said musingly. "I could perhaps venture a conjecture but if the matter is of no importance to you beyond mere curiosity I should not like to do so. Within a few months from now, I daresay, important developments will result and I should like to find out something more about her. That I can do when she returns to wherever she is stopping in the city. I'll 'phone to Mr. Hatch and have him ascertain for me where she goes, her name and other things which may throw a light on the matter."

"He will follow her?"

"Yes, precisely. Now we only seem to know two facts in connection with her. First, she is English."

"Yes," Dr. Prescott agreed. "Her accent, her appearance, everything about her suggests that."

"And the second fact is of no consequence at the moment," resumed The Thinking Machine. "Let me use your 'phone please."

Hutchinson Hatch, reporter, was talking.

"When the young woman left Dr. Prescott's, she took the cab which had been ordered for her and told the driver to go ahead until she stopped him. I got a good look at her, by the way. I managed to pass just as she entered the cab and walking on down got into another cab, which was waiting for me. Her cab drove for three or four blocks aimlessly, and finally stopped. The driver stooped down as if to listen to someone inside, and my cab passed. Then the other cab turned across a side street and after going eight or ten blocks, pulled up in front of an apartment house. The young woman got out and went inside. Her cab went away. Inside I found out that she was Mrs. Frederick Chevedon Morey. She came there last Tuesday—this is Friday—with her husband, and they engaged—''

''Yes, I knew she had a husband,'' interrupted The Thinking Machine.

''—engaged apartments for three months. When I had learned this much I remembered your instructions as to steamers from Europe landing on the day they took apartments or possibly a day or so before. I was just going out when Mrs. Morey stepped out of the elevator and preceded me to the door. She had changed her clothing and wore a different hat.

''It didn't seem to be necessary then to find out where she was going, for I knew I could find her when I wanted to, so I went down and made inquiries at the steamship offices. I found, after a great deal of work, that none of the three steamers which arrived the day the apartments were rented had brought a Mr. and Mrs. Morey, but a steamer on the day before had brought a Mr. and Mrs. David Girardeau from Liverpool. Mrs. Girardeau answered Mrs. Morey's description to the minutest detail, even to the gown she wore when she left the steamer. It was the same gown she wore when she left Dr. Prescott's after the operation.''

That was all. The Thinking Machine sat with his enormous yellow head pillowed against a high-backed chair and his long, slender fingers pressed tip to tip. He asked no questions and made no comment for a long time, then:

''About how many minutes was it from the time she entered the house until she came out again?''

''Not more than ten or fifteen,'' was the reply. ''I was still talking casually to the people downstairs trying to find out something about her.''

''What do they pay for their apartment?'' asked the scientist, irrelevantly.

"Three hundred dollars a month."

The Thinking Machine's squint eyes were fixed immovably on a small discolored spot on the ceiling of his laboratory.

"Whatever else may develop in this matter, Mr. Hatch," he said after a time, "we must admit that we have met a woman with extraordinary courage—nerve, I daresay you'd call it. When Mrs. Morey left Dr. Prescott's operating room, she was so ill and weak from the shock that she could hardly stand, and now you tell me she changed her dress and went out immediately after she returned home."

"Well, of course—" Hatch said, apologetically.

"In that event," resumed the scientist, "we must assume also that the matter is one of the utmost importance to her, and yet the nature of the case had led me to believe that it might be months, perhaps, before there would be any particular development in it."

"What? How?" asked the reporter.

"The final development doesn't seem, from what I know, to belong on this side of the ocean at all," explained The Thinking Machine. "I imagine it is a case for Scotland Yard. The problem of course is: What made it necessary for her to get rid of that finger? If we admit her sanity, we can count the possible answers to this question on one hand, and at least three of these answers take the case back to England." He paused. "By the way, was Mrs. Morey's hand bound up in the same way when you saw her the second time?"

"Her left hand was in a muff," explained the reporter. "I couldn't see, but it seems to me that she wouldn't have had time to change the manner of its dressing."

"It's extraordinary," commented the scientist. He arose and paced back and forth across the room. "Extraordinary," he repeated. "One can't help but admire the fortitude of women under certain circumstances, Mr. Hatch. I think perhaps this particular case had better be called to the attention of Scotland Yard, but first I think it would be best for you to call on the Moreys tomorrow—you can find some pretext—and see what you can learn about them. You are an ingenious young man—I'll leave it all to you.''

Hatch did call at the Morey apartments on the morrow, but under circumstances which were not at all what he expected. He went there with Detective Mallory, and Detective Mallory went there in a cab at full speed because the manager of the apartment house had 'phoned that Mrs. Frederick Chevedon Morey had been found murdered in her apartments. The detective ran up two flights of stairs and blundered, heavy-footed, into the rooms—and there he paused in the presence of death.

The body of the woman lay on the floor and someone had mercifully covered it with a cloth from the bed. Detective Mallory drew the covering down from over the face and Hatch stared with a feeling of awe at the beautiful countenance which had, on the day before, been so radiant with life. Now it was distorted into an expression of awful agony and the limbs were drawn up convulsively. The mark of the murderer was at the white, exquisitely rounded throat—great black bruises where powerful, merciless fingers had sunk deeply into the soft flesh.

A physician in the house had preceded the police. After one glance at the woman and a swift, comprehensive look about the room Detective Mallory turned to him inquiringly.

"She has been dead for several hours," the doctor volunteered, "possibly since early last night. It appears that some virulent, burning poison was administered and then she was choked. I gather this from an examination of her mouth."

These things were readily to be seen; also it was plainly evident for many reasons that the finger marks at the throat were those of a man, but each step beyond these obvious facts only served further to bewilder the investigators. First was the statement of the night elevator boy.

"Mr. and Mrs. Morey left here last night about eleven o'clock," he said. "I know because I telephoned for a cab, and later brought them down from the third floor. They went into the manager's office, leaving two suit cases in the hall. When they came out I took the suit cases to a cab that was waiting. They got in it and drove away.''

"When did they return?" inquired the detective.

"They didn't return, sir," responded the boy. "I was on duty until six o'clock this morning. It just happened that no one came in after they went out until I was off duty at six."

The detective turned to the physician again.

"Then she couldn't have been dead since early last night," he said.

"She has been dead for several hours—at least twelve, possibly longer," said the physician firmly. "There's no possible argument about that."

The detective stared at him scornfully for an instant, then looked at the manager of the house.

"What was said when Mr. and Mrs. Morey entered your office last night?" he asked. "Were you there?"

"I was there, yes," was the reply. "Mr. Morey explained that they had been called away for a few days unexpectedly and left the keys of the apartment with me. That was all that was said; I saw the elevator boy take the suit cases out for them as they went to the cab."

"How did it come, then, if you knew they were away that someone entered here this morning, and so found the body?"

"I discovered the body myself," replied the manager. "There was some electric wiring to be done in here and I thought their absence would be a good time for it. I came up to see about it and saw—that."

He glanced at the covered body with a little shiver and a grimace. Detective Mallory was deeply thoughtful for several minutes.

"The woman is here and she's dead," he said finally. "If she is here, she came back here, dead or alive, last night between the time she went out with her husband and the time her body was found this morning. Now that's an absolute fact. But *how* did she come here?"

Of the three employees of the apartment house only the elevator boy on duty had not spoken. Now he spoke because the detective glared at him fiercely.

"I didn't see either Mr. or Mrs. Morey come in this morning," he explained hastily. "Nobody came in at all except the postman and some delivery wagon drivers up to the time the body was found."

Again Detective Mallory turned on the manager.

"Does any window of this apartment open on a fire escape?" he demanded.

"Yes—this way."

They passed through the short hallway to the back. Both the windows were locked on the inside, so it appeared that even if the woman had been brought into the room that way, the windows would not have been fastened unless her murderer went out of the house the front way. When Detective Mallory reached this stage of the investigation, he sat down and stared from one to the other of the silent little party as if he considered the entire matter some affair which they had perpetrated to annoy him.

Hutchinson Hatch started to say something, then thought better of it and, turning, went to the telephone below. Within a few minutes The Thinking Machine stepped out of a cab in front and paused in the lower hall long enough to listen to the facts developed. There was a perfect network of wrinkles in the dome-like brow when the reporter concluded.

"It's merely a transfer of the final development in the affair from England to this country," he said enigmatically. "Please 'phone for Dr. Prescott to come here immediately."

He went on to the Morey apartments. With only a curt nod for Detective Mallory, the only one of the small party who knew him, he proceeded to the body of the dead woman and squinted down without a trace of emotion into the white pallid face. After a moment he dropped on his knees beside the inert body and examined the mouth and the finger marks about the white throat.

"Carbolic acid and strangulation," he remarked tersely to Detective Mallory, who was leaning over watching him with something of hopeful eagerness in his stolid face. The Thinking Machine glanced past him to the manager of the house. "Mr. Morey is a powerful, athletic man in appearance?" he asked.

"Oh, no," was the reply. "He's short and slight, only a little larger than you are."

The scientist squinted aggressively at the manager, as if the description were not quite what he expected. Then the slightly puzzled expression passed.

"Oh, I see," he remarked. "Played the piano." This was not a question; it was a statement.

"Yes, a great deal," was the reply, "so much so in fact that twice we had complaints from other persons in the house despite the fact that they had been here only a few days."

"Of course," mused the scientist abstractedly. "Of course. Perhaps Mrs. Morey did not play at all?"

"I believe she told me she did not."

The Thinking Machine drew down the thin cloth which had been thrown over the body and glanced at the left hand.

"Dear me! Dear me!" he exclaimed suddenly, and he arose. "Dear me!" he repeated. "That's the—" He turned to the manager and the two elevator boys. "This is Mrs. Morey beyond any question?"

The answer was a chorus of affirmation accompanied by some startling facial expressions.

"Did Mr. and Mrs. Morey employ any servants?"

"No," was the reply. "They had their meals in the café below most of the time. There is no housekeeping in these apartments at all."

"How many persons live in the building?"

"A hundred, I should say."

"There is a great deal of passing to and fro, then?"

"Certainly. It was rather unusual that so few persons passed in and out last night and this morning, and certainly Mrs. Morey and her husband were not among them, if that's what you're trying to find out."

The Thinking Machine glanced at the physician, who was standing by silently.

"How long do you make it that she's been dead?" he asked.

"At least twelve hours," replied the physician. "Possibly longer."

"Yes, nearer fourteen, I imagine."

Abruptly he left the group and walked through the apartment and back again slowly. As he re-entered the room where the body lay, the door from the hall opened and Dr. Prescott entered, followed by Hutchinson Hatch. The Thinking Machine led the surgeon straight to the body and drew the cloth down from the face. Dr. Prescott started back with an exclamation of astonishment, recognition.

"There's no doubt about it at all in your mind?" inquired the scientist.

"Not the slightest," replied Dr. Prescott positively. "It's the same woman."

"Yet, look here!"

With a quick movement The Thinking Machine drew down the cloth still more. Dr. Prescott, together with those who had no idea of what to expect, peered down at the body. After one glance the surgeon dropped on his knees and examined closely the dead left hand. The forefinger was off at the first joint. Dr. Prescott stared, stared incredulously. After a moment his eyes left the maimed hand and settled again on her face.

"I have never seen—never dreamed—of such a startling—" he began.

"That settles it all, of course," interrupted The Thinking Machine. "It solves and proves the problem at once. Now, Mr. Mallory, if we can go to your office or someplace where we will be undisturbed I will—"

"But who killed her?" demanded the detective abruptly.

"Let us find a quiet place," said The Thinking Machine in his usual irritable manner.

Detective Mallory, Dr. Prescott, The Thinking Machine, Hutchinson Hatch and the apartment house physician were seated in the front room of the Morey apartments with all doors closed against prying, inquisitive eyes. At the scientist's request Dr. Prescott repeated the circumstances leading up to the removal of a woman's left forefinger, and there The Thinking Machine took up the story.

"Suppose, Mr. Mallory," and the scientist turned to the detective, "a woman should walk into *your* office and say she must have a finger cut off, what would you think?"

"I'd think she was crazy," was the prompt reply.

"Naturally, in your position," The Thinking Machine went on, "you are acquainted with many strange happenings. Wouldn't this one instantly suggest something to you? Something that was to happen months off?"

Detective Mallory considered it wisely, but was silent.

"Well, here," declared The Thinking Machine. "A woman whom we now know to be Mrs. Morey wanted her finger cut off. It instantly suggested three, four, five, a dozen possibilities. Of course, only one, or possibly two in combination, could be true. Therefore which one? A little logic now to prove that two and two always make four—not *some* times but *all* the time.

"Naturally the first supposition was insanity. We pass that as absurd on its face. Then disease—a taint of leprosy perhaps which had been visible on the left forefinger. I tested for that, and that was eliminated. Three strong reasons for desiring the finger off, either of which is strongly probable, remained. The fact that the woman was unmistakably English was obvious. From the mark of a wedding ring on her glove and a corresponding mark on her finger—she wore no such ring—we could safely surmise that she was married. These were the two first facts I learned. Substantiative evidence that she was married and not a widow came partly from her extreme youth and the lack of mourning in her attire.

"Then Mr. Hatch followed her, learned her name, where she lived and later the fact that she had arrived with her husband on a steamer a day or so before they took apartments here. This was proof that she was English, and proof that she had a husband. They came over on the steamer as Mr. and Mrs. David

Girardeau—here they were Mr. and Mrs. Frederick Chevedon Morey. Why this difference in name? The circumstance in itself pointed to irregularity—crime committed or contemplated. Other things made me think it was merely contemplated and that it could be prevented; for then absence of every fact gave me no intimation that there would be murder. Then came the murder presumably of—Mrs. Morey?''

"Isn't it Mrs. Morey?'' demanded the detective.

"Mr. Hatch recognized the woman as the one he had followed, I recognized her as the one on which there had been an operation, Dr. Prescott also recognized her,'' continued The Thinking Machine. "To convince myself, after I had found the manner of death, that it was the woman, I looked at her left hand. I found that the forefinger was gone—it had been removed by a skilled surgeon at the first joint. And this fact instantly showed me that the dead woman was not Mrs. Morey at all, but somebody else; and incidentally cleared up the entire affair.''

"How?'' demanded the detective. "I thought you just said that you had helped cut off her forefinger?''

"Dr. Prescott and I cut off that finger yesterday,'' replied The Thinking Machine calmly. "The finger of the dead woman had been cut off months, perhaps years, ago.''

There was blank amazement on Detective Mallory's face, and Hatch was staring straight into the squint eyes of the scientist. Vaguely, as through a mist, he was beginning to account for many things which had been hitherto inexplicable.

"The perfectly healed wound on the hand eliminated every possibility but one,'' The Thinking Machine resumed. "Previously I had been informed that Mrs. Morey did not—or said she did not—play the piano. I had seen the bare possibility of an immense insurance on her hands, and some trick to defraud the insurance company by marring one. Of course, against this was the fact that she had offered to pay a large sum for the operation; that their expenses here must have been enormous, so I was beginning to doubt the tenability of this supposition. The fact that the dead woman's finger was off removed that possibility completely, as it also removed the possibility of a crime of some sort in which there might have been left behind a tell-tale print of that forefinger. If there had been a serious crime with the trace of the finger as evidence, its removal would have been necessary to her.

"Then the one thing remained—that is that Mrs. Morey or whatever her name is—was in a conspiracy with her husband to get possession of certain properties, perhaps a title—remember she is English—by sacrificing that finger so that identification might be in accordance with the description of an heir whom she was to impersonate. We may well believe that she was provided with the necessary documentary evidence, and we know conclusively—we don't conjecture but we *know*—that the dead woman in there is the woman whose rights were to have been stolen by the so-called Mrs. Morey."

"But that is Mrs. Morey, isn't it?" demanded the detective again.

"No," was the sharp retort. "The perfect resemblance to Mrs. Morey and the finger removed long ago makes that clear. There is, I imagine, a relationship between them—perhaps they are cousins. I can hardly believe they are twins because the necessity, then, of one impersonating the other to obtain either money or a title, would not have existed so palpably, although it is possible that Mrs. Morey, if disinherited or disowned, would have resorted to such a course."

There was silence for several minutes. Each member of the little group was turning over the stated facts mentally.

"But how did she come here—like this?" Hatch inquired.

"You remember, Mr. Hatch, when you followed Mrs. Morey here you told me she dressed again and went out?" asked the scientist in turn. "It was not Mrs. Morey you saw then—she was ill and I knew it from the operation—it was Miss Rossmore. The manager says a hundred persons live in this house—that there is a great deal of passing in and out. Can't you see that when there is such a startling resemblance Miss Rossmore could pass in and out at will and always be mistaken for Mrs. Morey? That no one would ever notice the difference?''

"But who killed her?" asked Detective Mallory, curiously. "How? Why?"

"Morey killed her," said The Thinking Machine flatly. "How did he kill her? We can fairly presume that first he tricked her into drinking the acid, then perhaps she was screaming with the pain of it, and he choked her to death. I imagined first he was a large, powerful man, because his grip on her throat was so powerful that he ruptured the jugular inside; but instead of that he plays the piano a great deal, which would give him the hand-power to choke her. And why? We can suppose only that it was because she had in some way learned of their purpose. That would have established the motive. The crowning delicacy of the affair was Morey's act in leaving his keys with the manager here. He did not anticipate that the apartments would be entered for several days—after they were safely away—while there was a chance that if neither of them had been seen here and their disappearance was unexplained the rooms would have been opened to ascertain why. That is all, I think."

"Except to catch Morey and his wife," said the detective grimly.

"Easily done," said The Thinking Machine. "I imagine, if this murder is kept out of the newspapers for a couple of hours you can find them about to sail for Europe. Suppose you try the line they came over on?"

It was just three hours later that the accused man and wife were taken prisoner. They had just engaged passage on the steamer which sailed at half past four o'clock.

Their trial was a famous one and resulted in conviction after an astonishing story of an attempt to seize an estate and title belonging rightfully to a Miss Evelyn Rossmore, who had mysteriously disappeared years before, and was identified with the dead woman.

The Cyprian Bees

ANTHONY WYNNE

✳

*Anthony Wynne (Robert McNair Wilson, 1882–1963) was a pop-
ular writer of formal, fair-play detective stories in the 1920s and
1930s, all of which feature the deductive talents of Dr. Eustace
Hailey, specialist in mental diseases. Of the twenty-nine Dr.
Hailey books, only one is a collection of short stories:* Sinners Go
Secretly *(1927). "The Cyprian Bees" is one of the tales in that
book, and a fine one it is. Ellery Queen once called it "Dr.
Hailey's triumph—principally because he knows what anaphy-
lactic shock is. Do you?"*

INSPECTOR BILES, of Scotland Yard, placed a small wooden box on the table in front of Dr. Hailey.

"There," he remarked in cheerful tones, "is a mystery which even you, my dear Doctor, will scarcely be able to solve."

Dr. Hailey bent his great head, and examined the box with minute care. It was merely a hollowed-out block of wood, to which a lid, also of wood, was attached at one point by a nail. The lid rotated on this nail. He put out his hand to open it, but Biles checked that intention immediately.

"Take care!" he exclaimed; "there are three live bees in that box." He added, "There were four of them originally, but one stung a colleague of mine, who was incautious enough to pull the lid open without first finding out what it covered."

He leaned back in his chair, and drew a long whiff of the excellent cigar with which Dr. Hailey had supplied him. He remained silent, while a heavy vehicle went lumbering down Harley Street. Then he said:

"Last night, one of my men found the box lying in the gutter in Piccadilly Circus, just opposite the Criterion Theatre. He thought it looked peculiar, and brought it down to the Yard. We have a beekeeper of some distinction on the staff, and he declares that these insects are all workers, and that only a lunatic would carry them about in this fashion. Queens, it appears, are often transported in boxes."

Dr. Hailey raised his eyeglass and set it in his eye.

"So I have heard." He opened his snuffbox, and took a large pinch. "You know, of course, my dear Biles," he added, "what this particular box contained before the bees were put into it."

"No—I don't."

"Serum—either anti-diphtheria serum or one of the other varieties. Practically every manufacturer of these products uses this type of receptacle for them."

"H'm!" Biles leaned forward in his chair. "So that means that in all probability, the owner of the bees is a doctor. How very interesting!"

Dr. Hailey shook his head.

"It doesn't follow," he remarked. "The box was perhaps left in a patient's house after its contents had been used. The patient may have employed it for its present purpose."

Biles nodded. He appeared to hesitate a moment; then he said:

"The reason why I troubled you was that, last night, a woman was found dead at the wheel of a motor car—a closed coupé—in Leicester Square. She had been stung by a bee just before her death."

He spoke in quiet tones, but his voice nevertheless revealed the fact that the disclosure he was making had assumed great importance in his mind. He added:

"The body was examined by a doctor almost immediately. He observed the sting, which was in her forehead. The dead bee was recovered later, from the floor of the car."

As he spoke he took another box from his pocket and opened it. He held it out to the doctor.

"You will notice that there are rather unusual markings on the bee's body—these yellow rings. Our expert says that they indicate a special breed, the Cyprian, and that these insects are notoriously very ill-natured. The peculiar thing is that the bees in the wooden box are also Cyprian bees."

Dr. Hailey picked up a large magnifying glass which lay on the table beside him, and focused it on the body of the insect. His knowledge of bees was not extensive, but he recognized that this was not the ordinary brown English type. He set the glass down again, and leaned back in his chair.

"It is certainly very extraordinary," he declared. "Have you any theory?"

Biles shook his head. "None, beyond the supposition that the shock caused by the sting was probably the occasion for the woman's sudden collapse. She was seen to pull quickly to the side of the road, and stop the car, so she must have had a presentiment of what was coming. I suppose heart failure might be induced by a sting?"

"It is just possible." Dr. Hailey took more snuff. "Once, long ago," he said, "I had personal experience of a rather similar case—that of a beekeeper who was stung some years after he had given up his own apiary. He died in about five minutes. But that was a clear case of anaphylaxis."

"I don't understand."

Dr. Hailey thought a moment. "Anaphylaxis," he explained, "is the name given to one of the most amazing phenomena in the whole of medical science. If a human being receives an injection of serum or blood, or any extract or fluid from the animal body, a tremendous sensitiveness is apt to develop, afterwards, towards that particular substance. For example, an injection of the white of a duck's eye will, after the lapse of a week or so, render a man so intensely sensitive to this particular egg white that, if a further injection is given, instant death may result.

"Even if a duck's egg is eaten, there may be violent sickness and collapse, though hen's eggs will cause no ill effect. Queerly enough, however, if the injection is repeated within, say, a day of its first administration no trouble occurs. For the sensitiveness to develop, it is essential that time should elapse between the first injection and the second one. Once the sensitiveness has developed, it remains active for years. The beekeeper, whose death I happened to witness, had often been stung before: but he had not been stung for a very long time."

"Good God!" Biles's face wore an expression of new interest. "So it is possible that this may actually be a case of—murder!"

He pronounced the word in tones of awe. Dr. Hailey saw that already his instincts as a man hunter were quickening.

"It is just possible. But do not forget, my dear Biles, that the murderer using this method would require to give his victim a preliminary dose—by inoculation—of bee poison, because a single sting would scarcely be enough to produce the necessary degree of sensitiveness. That is to say, he would require to exercise an amount of force which would inevitably defeat his purpose—*unless he happened to be a doctor.*"

"Ah! the wooden serum box!" The detective's voice thrilled.

"Possibly. A doctor undoubtedly could inject bee poison, supposing he possessed it, instead of ordinary serum, or of an ordinary vaccine. It would hurt a good deal—but patients expect inoculation to hurt them."

Biles rose. "There is no test, is there," he asked, "by which it would be possible to detect the presence of this sensitiveness you speak of in a dead body?"

"None."

"So we can only proceed by means of circumstantial evidence." He drew a sharp breath. "The woman has been identified as the widow of an artist named Bardwell. She had a flat—a luxurious one—in Park Mansions, and seems to have been well off. But we have not been able to find any of her relations so far." He glanced at his watch. "I am going there now. I suppose I couldn't persuade you to accompany me?"

Dr. Hailey's rather listless eyes brightened. For answer he rose, towering above the detective in that act.

"My dear Biles, you know that you can always persuade me."

The flat in Park Mansions was rather more, and yet rather less, than luxurious. It bespoke prodigality, but it bespoke also restlessness of mind—as though its owner had felt insecure in her enjoyment of its comforts. The rooms were too full, and their contents were saved from vulgarity only by sheer carelessness of their bestowal. This woman seemed to have bought anything, and to have cared for nothing. Thus, in her dining room, an exquisite Queen Anne sideboard was set cheek by jowl with a most horrible Victorian armchair made of imitation walnut. In the drawing room there were flower glasses of the noblest period of Venetian craftsmanship, in which beauty was held captive in wonderful strands of gold, and beside these, shocking and obscene examples of "golden glass" ware from some third-rate Bohemian factory.

Dr. Hailey began to form a mental picture of the dead woman.

He saw her, changeable, greedy, gaudy, yet with a certain instinctive charm—the kind of woman who, if she is young and beautiful, gobbles a man up. Women of that sort, his experience had shown him, were apt to drive their lovers to despair with their extravagances or their infidelities. Had the owner of the bees embarked on his terrible course in order to secure himself against the mortification of being supplanted by some more attractive rival? Or was he merely removing from his path a woman of whom he had grown tired? In any case, if the murder theory was correct, he must have stood in the relationship to the dead girl of doctor to patient, and he must have possessed an apiary of his own.

A young detective, whom Biles introduced as Tadcaster, had already made a careful examination of the flat. He had found nothing, not even a photograph. Nor had the owners of neighbouring flats been able to supply any useful information. Mrs. Bardwell, it appeared, had had men friends who had usually come to see her after dark. They had not, apparently, been in the habit of writing to her, or, if they had, she had destroyed all their letters. During the last few weeks, she seemed to have been without a servant.

"So you have found nothing?" Biles's tones were full of disappointment.

"Nothing, sir—unless, indeed, this is of any importance."

Tadcaster held out a crumpled piece of paper. It was a shop receipt, bearing the name of the *Times* Book Club, for a copy of *The Love Songs of Robert Browning*. There was no name on it.

Biles handed it to Dr. Hailey, who regarded it for a few moments in silence, and then asked:

"Where did you find this?"

"In the fireplace of the bedroom."

The doctor's eyes narrowed.

"It does not strike me," he said, "that such a collection of poems would be likely to interest the owner of this flat."

He folded the slip, and put it carefully into his pocket book. He added:

"On the other hand, Browning's love songs do appeal very strongly to some women." He fixed his eyeglass and regarded the young detective. "You have not found the book itself, have you?"

"No, sir. There are a few novels in the bedroom, but no poetry of any kind."

Dr. Hailey nodded. He asked to be shown the collection, and made a detailed examination of it. The novels were all of the lurid, sex type. It was as he had anticipated. He opened each of the books, and glanced at the flyleaves. They were all blank. He turned to Biles.

"I am ready to bet that Mrs. Bardwell did not pay that bill at the Book Club," he declared. "And I am ready to bet also that this book was not bought for her."

The detective shrugged his shoulders.

"Probably not," he said unconcernedly.

"Then, why should the receipt for it be lying in this room?"

"My dear Doctor, how should I know? I suppose, because the man who possessed it chose to throw it away here."

The doctor shook his head.

"Men do not buy collections of love songs for themselves, nor, for that matter, do women. They buy them—almost invariably—to give to people they are interested in. Everybody, I think, recognizes that."

He broke off. A look of impatience came into Biles's face.

"Well?"

"Therefore, a man does not, as a rule, reveal to one woman the fact that he has made such a purchase on behalf of another. I mean, it is difficult to believe that any man on intimate terms with Mrs. Bardwell would have invited her jealousy by leaving such plain evidence of his interest in another woman lying about in her rooms. I assume, you see, that no man would give that poor lady this particular book."

Biles shrugged his shoulders. The point seemed to him immaterial. He glanced round the bedroom with troubled eyes.

"I wish," he declared, "that we had something to go on—

something definite, leading towards some individual."

His words were addressed impartially to his subordinate and to Dr. Hailey. The former looked blank, but the doctor's expression was almost eager. He raised his eyeglass, and put it into his eye.

"My dear Biles," he said, "we have something definite to go on. I was about to suggest to you when you interrupted me that the receipt for the book probably fell from the pocket of the purchaser through a hole in that pocket. Just as the little box containing the additional bees, which he had not found it necessary to release, was destined to fall later, when the man, having assured himself that an insect of unimpaired vigour was loose and on the wing, descended in Piccadilly Circus from Mrs. Bardwell's car."

He paused. The detective had turned to him, interested once more. The thought crossed Dr. Hailey's mind that it was a pity Biles had not been gifted by Providence with an appreciation of human nature as keen as his grasp of material circumstances. He allowed his eyeglass to drop, in a manner which proclaimed that he had shot his bolt. He asked:

"You have not, perhaps, taken occasion to watch a man receiving a shop receipt for goods he has just bought and paid for? Believe me, a spectacle full of instruction in human nature. The receipt is handed, as a rule, by a girl, and the man, as a rule, pushes it into his nearest pocket, because he does not desire to be so rude or so untidy as to drop it on the floor. Shyness, politeness, and tidiness, my dear Biles, are all prominent elements in our racial character."

Again he broke off, this time to take a pinch of snuff. The two detectives watched that process with some impatience.

"A man with a hole in his coat pocket—a hole not very large, yet large enough to allow a piece of crumpled paper to work its way out as the wearer of the coat strode up and down the floor of the room—is not that a clue? A doctor, perhaps, with, deep in his soul, the desire for such women as Mrs. Bardwell—cheap, yet attractive women—"

"I thought you expressed the opinion that he bought the love songs for some other woman!" Biles snapped.

"Exactly. Some other woman sufficiently like Mrs. Bardwell to attract him, though evidently possessed of a veneer of education to which Mrs. Bardwell could lay no claim." Dr. Hailey's large, kindly face grew thoughtful. "Has it not struck you," he asked, "that, though a man may not be faithful to any one woman, he is almost always faithful to a type? Again and again I have seen in first and second wives the same qualities of mind and appearance, both good and bad. Indeed, I would go so far as to say that our first loves and our last are kindred spirits, recognized and chosen by needs and desires which do not change, or change but little, throughout the course of life."

"Even so, my dear Hailey—"

Biles's look of perplexity had deepened. The doctor, however, was too eager to be discouraged.

"If Mrs. Bardwell was, in fact, murdered," he continued, "the figure of her murderer is not, I think, very difficult to visualize: a doctor in early middle life—because the dead woman is at least thirty—with a practice in the country, but the tastes of a townsman; a trifle careless of his clothes, since he tolerates holes in his pockets, a sentimental egoist, since he buys Browning's love songs while plans of murder are turning over in his mind—" He broke off, and thought a moment. "It is probable that Mrs. Bardwell was an expensive luxury. Such women, too, fight like tigers for the possession of the men they rely on. Yet, though she had undoubtedly obtained a great, perhaps a terrible, hold on him, she had failed to make him marry her."

He turned to Biles, and readjusted his eyeglass.

"Why do you suppose," he asked, "Mrs. Bardwell failed to make this doctor marry her?"

"I have no idea." The detective's tones were crisp, almost to the point of abruptness.

Dr. Hailey moved across the room to a writing table which stood near the window. He took a sheet of paper, and marked a small circle on it. Around this he drew a much larger circle. He returned to the detectives, who stood watching him.

"Here is London," he said, pointing to the small circle, "and here is the country round it up to a distance of forty miles—that is to say, up to a two-hour journey by motor car. As our doctor seems to make frequent visits to town, that is not, I think, too narrow a radius. Beyond about forty miles, London is no longer within easy reach."

He struck his pencil at two places through the circumference of the larger circle, marking off a segment.

"Here," he went on, "are the Surrey highlands, the area, within our district, where heather grows, and where, in consequence, almost everyone keeps bees."

He raised his head, and faced the two men, whose interest he seemed to have recaptured.

"It should not," he suggested, "be impossible to discover whether or not, within this area, there is a doctor in practice who keeps Cyprian bees, is constantly running up to London, wears an overcoat with a hole in one of the pockets, and lives apart from his wife."

"Good heavens!" Biles drew his breath sharply. His instincts as a man hunter had reasserted themselves. He glanced at the doctor with an enthusiasm which lacked nothing of generosity. The younger detective, however, retained his somewhat critical expression.

"Why should the doctor be living apart from his wife?" he asked.

"Because, had she not left him as soon as he tired of her, he would probably have killed her long ago, and, in that case, he would almost certainly have married Mrs. Bardwell during the first flush of his devotion to her. I know these sensualists who are also puffed up with literary vanity. Marriage possesses for them an almost incredible attractiveness."

He glanced at his watch as he spoke. The recollection of a professional appointment had come suddenly to his memory.

"If you are to follow up the clue, my dear Biles," he remarked, as he left the flat, "I hope you will let me know the result. *The Medical Directory* should serve as a useful starting point."

Dr. Hailey was kept fully occupied during the next day, and was unable, in consequence, to pursue the mystery of the Cyprian bees any further. In the later afternoon, however, he rang up Inspector Biles at Scotland Yard. A voice, the tones of which were sufficiently dispirited, informed him that the whole of the home counties did not contain a doctor answering the description with which he had furnished the police.

"Mrs. Bardwell," Biles added, "kept a maid, who has been on holiday. She returned last night, and has now told us that her mistress received very few men at her flat, and that a doctor was not among the number. Of course, it is possible that a doctor may have called during the last fortnight, in the girl's absence. But, in the circumstances, I'm afraid we must look on the murder theory as rather far fetched. After all, the dead woman possessed a car, and may have been in the country herself on the morning on which she was stung. Bees often get trapped in cars."

Dr. Hailey hung up the receiver, and took a pinch of snuff. He sat down in his big armchair, and closed his eyes that he might pass, in fresh review, the various scraps of evidence he had collected. If the dead woman had not received the doctor at her house, then the idea that they were on intimate terms could scarcely be maintained. In that case, the whole of his deductions must be invalidated. He got up and walked down Harley Street to the *Times* Book Club. He showed the receipt which he had retained, and asked if he might see the assistant who had conducted the sale. This girl remembered the incident clearly. It had occurred about a week earlier. The man who had bought the volume of poems was accompanied by a young woman.

"Did you happen to notice," Dr. Hailey asked, "what his companion looked like?"

"I think she was very much 'made up.' She had fair hair; but I can't say that I noticed her carefully."

"And the man?"

The girl shrugged her shoulders. "I'm afraid I don't remember him clearly. A business man, perhaps." She thought a moment. "He was a good deal older than she was, I should say."

Dr. Hailey left the shop, and walked back towards Harley Street. On one point, at least, he had not been mistaken. The purchaser of the *Love Songs* was a man, and he had bought them for a woman who was not Mrs. Bardwell. Biles had mentioned that this lady had auburn hair. Why should the man have visited Mrs. Bardwell so soon after making this purchase? He sighed. After all, why not? Biles was quite right in thinking that no jury in the world would listen to evidence the only basis of which was character reading at second hand. He reached his door, and was about to let himself into the house when a cab drew up beside him. The young detective, Tadcaster, to whom Biles had introduced him at Park Mansions, got out.

"Can I see you a moment, Doctor?" he asked.

They entered the house together, Tadcaster produced a letter from his pocket, and handed it to Dr. Hailey. It was a prescription, written on Mrs. Bardwell's note paper, and signed only with initials, which were nearly indecipherable.

"I found it after you had gone," the young man explained. "It was dispensed, as you can see, by a local chemist. Today I have seen him, and he says he has had other similar prescriptions to dispense. But he has no idea who the writer is. Mrs. Bardwell had the medicine a few days ago."

Dr. Hailey read the prescription, which was a simple iron tonic. The signature was illegible. He shook his head.

"This does not carry us much further, I'm afraid," he declared.

"You can't tell from the initials who the doctor is."

"No."

"In that case, I think we shall have to throw our hands in." Tadcaster's voice expressed considerable disappointment. It was obvious that he had hoped to make a reputation out of the solution of the mystery. "Your reasoning yesterday," he added, "impressed me very much, sir, if I may say so."

Dr. Hailey inclined his head, but his eyes were vacant. So a doctor had called on the dead woman recently—and also, apparently, made earlier visits—a doctor, too, whose prescriptions were unfamiliar to the local chemist. He turned to the young detective.

"I have just heard from Biles," he said, "that the maid has come back. Do you happen to know if she has any recollection of these professional visits?"

"I asked her that myself. She says that she knows nothing about them."

Again the far-away look came to the doctor's eyes. The fact that the prescriptions were written on Mrs. Bardwell's note paper showed that they had been given during an attendance at the flat. For what reason had the dead woman been at pains to hide her doctor's visits from her maid?

"Should I be troubling you very much," he said, "if I asked you to take me back to Park Mansions? I confess that I would like to ask that girl a few questions. A doctor can obtain information which is not likely to be imparted to any layman."

As they drove through the crowded streets, Dr. Hailey asked himself again the question which had caused him to embark on this fresh investigation. What reason had Mrs. Bardwell for hiding her need of medical attendance from her maid? Even supposing that her doctor was also her lover there seemed to be no sense in such a concealment. He opened his eyes and saw the stream of London's home-going population surging round the cab. Sweet-faced girls and splendid youths, mingled with women whose eyes told their story of disappointment, and men who wore pressing responsibility as an habitual expression. No wonder the police despaired of finding any one nameless human being in this vast tide of humanity, of hopes and fears, of desires and purposes!

The cab stopped. They entered the lift and came to the door of the flat. Tadcaster rang the bell. A moment later the door was opened by a young girl, who invited them to enter in tones which scarcely disguised the anxiety she apparently felt at the return of the police. She closed the door, and then led the way along the dim entrance corridor. She opened the door of the drawing room.

As the light from the windows fell on her face, Dr. Hailey repressed an exclamation of amazement. He started, as though a new idea had sprung to his mind. A slight flush mounted to his cheeks. He raised his eyeglass and inserted it quickly in his eye.

"I have troubled you," he said to the girl, "because there are a few points about Mrs. Bardwell's health, before her fatal seizure, which I think you can help us to understand. I may say that I am a doctor, assisting the police."

"Oh, yes!"

The girl's voice was low. Her pretty, heavily powdered face seemed drawn with anxiety, and her eyes moved restlessly from one man to the other. She raised her hand in a gesture of uneasiness, and clasped her brow, seeming to press her golden curls into the white flesh.

"Perhaps it might be better if I spoke to you alone?"

Dr. Hailey's tones were very gentle. He looked at Tadcaster as he spoke, and the detective immediately got up and left the room. Then he turned to the girl.

"Your mistress," he asked, "discharged you from her employment a fortnight ago?"

The girl started violently, and all the blood seemed to ebb from her cheeks. Wild fear stared at him from her big, lustrous eyes.

"No!"

"My dear girl, if I may say so, you have everything to gain, nothing to lose, by telling the truth."

He spoke coldly, yet there was a reassuring note in his voice. He saw fear give place a little to that quality of weakness which he had expected to find in her character—the quality which had attracted Mrs. Bardwell's lover, and which explained, in some subtle fashion, the gift of the *Love Songs*. He repeated his question. The girl hung her head. She consented. He let his eyeglass fall.

"Because of your intimacy with a man she had been accustomed to look on as her own particular friend."

"Oh, no, no! It is not true!"

Again her eyes challenged him; she had thrown back her head, revealing the full roundness of her throat. The light gleamed among her curls. No wonder that this beauty had been able to dispossess her mistress!

"Listen to me." Dr. Hailey's face had grown stern. "You have denied that any doctor came to this flat—at least, so far as you know. As it happens, however, a number of prescriptions were dispensed for Mrs. Bardwell by the local chemist; so that, either she took great pains to hide from you the fact that she was calling in a doctor, or—you have not been speaking the truth."

"She did not tell me."

He raised his hand. "It will be easy," he said, "to get an answer to that question. If your mistress was really hiding her doctor's visits from you, she must have taken her prescriptions herself, personally, to the chemist. I shall find out from him later on whether or not that is so."

Again the girl's mood changed. She began to whimper, pressing a tiny lace handkerchief to her eyes in coquettish fashion.

Dr. Hailey drew a deep breath. He waited a moment before framing his next remark. Then he said:

"You realise, I suppose, that if a girl helps a man to commit a crime, she is as guilty as he is, in the eyes of the law."

"What do you mean?"

All her defences now were abandoned. She stood before him, abject in her terror, with staring eyes and trembling lips.

"That your presence here today proves you have had a share in this business. Why did you return to the flat?"

"Because—because—"

"Because he—the man you are shielding—wanted to find out what the police were doing in the place?"

She tottered towards him, and laid her hands on his arm.

"Oh, God, I am so frightened," she whispered.

"You have reason—to be frightened."

He led her to a chair, but suddenly she seemed to get her strength anew. Her grasp on his arm tightened.

"I didn't want him to do it," she cried, in tones of anguish. "I swear that I didn't. And I swear that I have no idea, even yet, what he did do. We were going to be married—immediately."

"Married!" His voice seemed to underline the word.

"I swear that. It was honest and above-board, only he had her on his hands, and she had wasted so much of his money."

For the first time her voice rang true. She added:

"His wife cost a lot, too, though she was not living with him. She died a month ago."

They stood facing one another. In the silence of the room, the ticking of an ornate little clock on the mantel shelf was distinctly audible.

Dr. Hailey leaned forward.

"His name?" he asked.

"No, I shall not tell you."

She had recaptured her feeble courage. It gleamed from her eyes, for an instant transforming even her weakness. The vague knowledge that she loved this man in her paltry, immoral way, came to him. He was about to repeat his demand, when the door of the room opened. Tadcaster came in with a small, leather-bound volume in his hand.

The girl uttered a shrill cry and sprang towards him; but Dr. Hailey anticipated that move. He held her firmly.

"It is the collection of Browning's *Love Songs*," the detective said. "I found it lying open in the next room. There is an inscription signed 'Michael Cornwall.' "

He held the book out for the doctor's inspection, but Dr. Hailey's face had grown as pale, almost, as that of the girl by his side.

He repeated the name—"Michael Cornwall"—almost like a man in a dream.

The place was hidden among its trees. Dr. Hailey walked up the avenue with slow steps. The thought of the mission which had brought him to this lovely Hampstead house lay—as it had lain through all the hours of the night—like death on his spirits. Michael Cornwall, the well-known Wimpole Street bacteriologist, and he had been boys together at Uppingham. They were still acquaintances.

He came to the front door, and was about to ring the bell when the man he was looking for appeared round the side of the house, accompanied by an old man and a girl.

"Hailey—well I'm dashed!"

Dr. Cornwall advanced with outstretched hand. His deep, rather sinister eyes welcomed his colleague with an enthusiasm which was entirely unaffected. He introduced: "My uncle, Colonel Cornwall, and my cousin, Miss Patsy Cornwall, whom you must congratulate on having just become engaged," in his quick staccato manner.

"We're just going round the garden," he explained, "and you must accompany us. And, after that, to luncheon. Whereupon, my dear Hailey, if you have—as I feel you have—great business to discuss with me, we shall discuss it."

His bantering tones accorded well with his appearance, which had changed but little in the years. He was the same astute, moody, inordinately vain fellow who had earned for himself, once upon a time, the nickname of "The Lynx."

They strolled across the lawn, and came to a brick wall of that rich russet hue which only time and the seasons can provide. Dr. Cornwall opened a door in the wall, and stood back for his companions to enter.

A sight of entrancing beauty greeted them, lines of fruit trees in full blossom, as though the snows of some Alpine sunset had been spread, in all their glowing tints, on this English garden. Dr. Hailey, however, had no eyes for this loveliness. His gaze was fixed on a row of white-painted beehives which gleamed in the sunlight under the distant wall. Patsy Cornwall exclaimed in sheer wonder. Then a new cry of delight escaped her, as she detected, in a large greenhouse which flanked the wall, a magnificent display of scarlet tulips. She took Dr. Hailey, in whose eyes the melancholy expression seemed to have deepened, to inspect these, while her father and cousin strolled on up the garden path. She stood with him in the narrow gangway of the greenhouse, and feasted ecstatic eyes on the wonderful blossoms.

"Don't they make you wish to gather them all and take them away somewhere where there are no flowers?"

She turned to him, but he had sprung away from her side.

A cry, shrill and terrible, pierced the lazy silence of the morning. She saw her father and cousin fleeing back, pursued by an immense swarm of winged insects, towards the garden gate.

Blindly, frantically, they sought to ward off the dreadful onslaught. The old man stumbled, and would have fallen, had not his nephew caught him in his arms. She had a momentary glimpse of his face; it was as though she had looked on the face of Death.

"The bees!"

The words broke from Dr. Hailey's lips as a moan of despair. He had come to the closed door of the greenhouse, and seemed to be about to open it; but at the same moment one of the infuriated insects in delirious flight struck the glass pane beside him. Then another—and another—and another. He came reeling back towards the girl.

"Lie down on the gangway!" he shouted, at the highest pitch of his voice. "There may be a broken pane somewhere."

She turned her horror-stricken eyes to him.

"My father—oh, God!"

"Lie down for your life!"

He stood beside her, watching, ready to strike if one of the bees succeeded in entering the greenhouse. Only once did he remove his straining eyes from this task. The sight which then greeted them wrought a fresh cry of horror from his lips.

The terrible swarm hung like a dust cloud in the air above the garden gate, rising and falling in swift undulations, which caused the light to flash and scintillate on a myriad gilded bodies and shining wings. A faint, shrill piping came to his ears across the silence. The door in the wall was open, and the garden now quite empty.

Biles leaned forward.

"Mrs. Bardwell's maid has confessed that she rang up Dr. Cornwall immediately before luncheon this morning," he said. "She tried to communicate with him before, but he had gone to the country, to a case, overnight. He got her warning that the police suspected him of being responsible for her mistress's death just after he had carried his second victim, his uncle, in a dying condition, from the garden."

The detective struck a match, and relit his cigar. Dr. Hailey sat watching him with sorrowful eyes.

"Ten minutes later, as you know," he went on, "Cornwall blew his brains out. He had the wit to see that the game was up. He had been badly stung, of course, but his long experience of the bees made this a less serious matter than it would have been in the case of an ordinary outsider. In any case, moreover, he had to accept that risk if his plan was to succeed."

Silence fell in the big consulting room. Then the doctor remarked:

"Miss Cornwall has recently become engaged to be married?"

"Yes." Biles drew a long whiff. "That was the circumstance which made speed essential to her cousin's murderous plan. He was hopelessly in debt, as a result of Mrs. Bardwell's extravagance. Only his uncle's money, which is considerable, would have saved him. If Miss Cornwall married he must have lost all hope of obtaining it, and so of marrying the girl on whom he had set his fickle heart. I have ascertained that he insisted on inoculating both father and daughter against spring catarrh a month ago, and that the injections he gave them hurt them terribly. No doubt Mrs. Bardwell received a similar injection about the same time. Thus, for each of these three individuals, a single bee sting, on your showing, meant instant death."

Dr. Hailey inclined his head.

"The moment I saw the swarm, the truth flashed across my mind," he declared. "These Cyprian bees, as I have been at pains to find out, and as your bee-keeping friend told you, are exceedingly ill-natured. But no bees, unless they have been previously roused to frenzy, ever attack at sight people who have not even approached their hives. It was all too clear, even in that first terrible moment, that the swarm was part of a carefully prepared plan."

The detective rose, and held out his hand.

"But for you, my dear friend," he said, "Miss Cornwall must inevitably have shared her father's fate, and the most devilish murder of which I have ever so much as heard would, almost certainly, have gone unsuspected and unpunished."

Easter Devil

MIGNON EBERHART

⸸

Susan Dare is a young mystery writer whom the police frequently call upon for aid in especially puzzling cases. In this story she must pose as a nurse in order to answer the question "What possible connection was there between a piece of wood, some shattered fine glass, and a murdered butler?" Although Susan is an ersatz nurse—whose other adventures are collected in The Cases of Susan Dare *(1934)—her creator, Mignon Eberhart, is well versed in both nursing and the medical world. Her series sleuth, nurse Sarah Keate, solves cases while dispensing T.L.C. Eberhart, the author of more than fifty novels, is one of America's leading writers of romantic suspense.*

SUSAN DARE sipped her coffee and quietly contemplated devils. Outside, rain beat down upon cold, dark streets, but inside the drawn curtains of Susan's small library it was warm, with a fire cheerful in the grate, and the dog lazy upon the rug, and cigarettes and an old book beside the deepest armchair. An armchair which Susan just then decorated, for she had dressed for her dinner *à seul* in soft trailing crimson. Too bad, thought Susan regretfully, that her best moments were so often wasted: a seductive crimson gown, and no one to see it. She smashed her cigarette sadly and returned to her book.

Devils and devil-possessed souls! Of course there were no such things, but it was curious how real the old writers made both. Susan, who was a successful young writer of thrilling mystery novels, was storing up this knowledge for future use.

Then the doorbell rang. The dog barked and scrambled to his feet and bounced into the hall, and Susan followed.

Two men, beaten and wet with rain, were waiting, and one of them was Jim Byrne, with a package under his arm.

"Company?" asked Jim tersely, looking at the dress.

"No. I was alone—"

"You remember Lieutenant Mohrn?"

Of course she did! It was her volunteer work with him on a recent Chicago crime that had led the police force to regard her as a valuable consultant.

"How do you do?" said Lieutenant Mohrn. "I hope you don't mind our coming. You see, there's something—"

"Something queer," said Jim. "In point of fact, it's—"

"Murder," said Lieutenant Mohrn.

"Oh," said Susan. Her own small warm house—and these two men with sober faces looking at her. She smoothed back her hair. "Oh," she said again.

Jim pushed the package toward her.

"I got size thirty-six," he said. "Is that right?—I mean, that's what we want you to wear."

That was actually Susan's introduction to the case of the Easter Devil. Fifteen minutes later she was getting out of the glamorous crimson gown and into a brown tweed suit with a warm topcoat, and tossing a few things into a bag—the few things included the contents of the package, which proved to be several nurse's uniforms, complete with caps, and a small kit of tools which were new and shiny.

"Do you know anything about nursing?" Jim Byrne had asked.

"Nothing," said Susan. "But I've had appendicitis."

"Oh," said Jim, relieved. "Then you can—oh, take a pulse, make a show of nursing. She's not sick, you know. If she were, we could not do this."

"I can shake a thermometer without dropping it," said Susan. "If the doctor will help—"

"Oh, he'll help all right," said Lieutenant Mohrn somewhat grimly. "We have his consent and approval."

She pulled a small brown hat over her hair and then remembered to change gold slippers to brown oxfords.

In the hall Jim was waiting.

"Mohrn had to go," he said. "I'll take you out. Glenn Ash is about an hour's run from town."

"All right," said Susan. She scribbled a note to Huldah and spoke soberly to the dog, who liked to have things explained to him.

"I'm going to a house in Glenn Ash," she said gravely. "Be a good dog. And don't chase the neighbor's cat."

He pushed a cold nose against her hand. He didn't want her to go, and he thought the matter of Petruchkin the cat might better have been ignored. Then the front door closed and he heard presently two doors bang and a car drive away. He returned to the library. But he was gradually aware that the peace and snugness were gone. He felt gloomily that it would have been very much better if the woman had stayed at home.

And the woman, riding along a rain-swept road, rather agreed with him. She peered through the rain-shot light lanes ahead and reviewed in her mind the few facts that she knew. And they were brief enough.

At the home of one Gladstone Denisty in Glenn Ash a servant had been murdered. Had been shot in the back and found (where he'd fallen) in a ravine near the house. There was no weapon found, and anyway he couldn't have shot himself. There were no signs of attempted burglary. There were, indeed, no clues. He was a quiet, well-behaved man and an efficient servant and had been with the Denisty family for some time; so far as could be discovered, his life held no secrets.

Yet that morning he had been found in the ravine, murdered.

The household consisted of Gladstone Denisty and his wife, his mother and brother, and two remaining servants.

"It's Mrs. Gladstone Denisty—her first name is Felicia—whom we want you to nurse," Lieutenant Mohrn had said. "There's more to the thing than meets the eye. You see, the only lead we have leads to the Denisty home; this man was killed by a bullet of the same caliber as that of a revolver which is known to have been in the Denisty house—property of nobody in particular—and which has disappeared within the last week. But that's all we know. And we thought if we could get you inside the house—just to watch things, you know. There's no possible danger to you."

"There's always danger," said Jim brusquely, "where there's murder."

"If Miss Dare thinks there's danger, she's to leave," said Lieutenant Mohrn wearily. "All I want her to do is get a—line on things."

And Jim, somehow grudgingly, had said nothing; still said nothing.

It was a long ride to Glenn Ash, and that night a difficult one, owing to the rain and wind. But they did finally turn off the winding side road into a driveway and stop.

Susan could barely see the great dark bulk of the house looming above with only a light or two showing.

Then Jim's hand was guiding her up some brick steps and across a wide veranda. He put his mouth to her ear: "If anything happens that you don't like, leave. At once." And Susan whispered, "I will," and Jim was gone, and the wide door was opening, and a very pretty maid was taking her bag and leading her swiftly upstairs. The household had retired, said the maid, and Mrs. Denisty would see her in the morning.

"You mean Mrs. Gladstone Denisty?" asked Susan.

"Oh, no, ma'am. *Mrs.* Denisty," said the maid. "Is there anything—? Thank you. Good-night, ma'am."

Susan, after a thoughtful moment, locked her door and presently went to bed and listened to the rain against the windowpanes and wished she could sleep. However, she must have fallen asleep, for she awakened suddenly and in fright. It had stopped raining. And somewhere there had been a sound.

There had been a sound, but it was no more. She only knew that it had waked her and that she was ridiculously terrified. And then all at once her heart stopped its absurd pounding and was perfectly still. For something—out there in the long and empty hall—had brushed against her bedroom door!

She couldn't, either then or later, have persuaded herself to go to that door and open it and look into the hall. And anyway, as the moments dragged on, she was convinced that whoever or whatever had brushed against her door was gone. But she sat, huddled under blankets, stonily wide awake until slow gray dawn began to crawl into the room. Then she fell again into sleep, only to be waked this time by the maid, carrying a breakfast tray and looking what she thought of trained nurses who slept late. Mrs. Denisty, she informed Susan, wished to see her.

Not, thought Susan, getting into the unaccustomed uniform, an auspicious beginning. And she was shocked to discover that she looked incredibly young and more than a little flip in the crisply tailored white dress and white cap. She took her horn-rimmed spectacles, which improved things very little, and her thermometer, and went downstairs, endeavoring to look stern enough to offset the unfortunate effect of the cap.

But on the wide landing of the stairs she realized that the thick, white-haired woman in the hall below was interested only in the tongue-lashing she was giving two maids. They were careless, they were lying, they had broken it—all of it. She looked up just then and saw Susan and became at once bland.

"Good-morning, Miss Dare," she said. "Will you come down?" She dismissed the servants and met Susan at the foot of the stairs. "We'll go into this drawing room," she said. She wore a creamy white wool dress with blue beads and a blue handkerchief and did not ask Susan to sit down.

"The household is a little upset just now," she said. "There was an unfortunate occurrence here, night before last. Yes—unfortunate. And then yesterday or last night the maid or cook or somebody managed to break some Venetian glass—quite a lot of it—that my daughter-in-law was much attached to. Neither of them will admit it. However, about my daughter-in-law, Mrs. Gladstone Denisty, whom you are here to care for: I only wished to tell you, Miss Dare, that her nerves are bad, and the main thing, I believe, is merely to humor her. And if there is anything you wish to know, or if any—problem—arises, come to me. Do you understand?"

Susan wondered what was wrong with the room and said she understood.

"Very well," said Mrs. Denisty, rising. "That is all."

But that was not all. For there was a whirlwind of steps, and a voice sobbing broken phrases swept through the door, and a woman ran into the room clutching in both hands something bright and crimson. A queer little chill that she could never account for crept over Susan as she realized that the woman clutched, actually, broken pieces of glass.

"Did you see, Mother Denisty?" sobbed the woman. "It's all over the floor. How much more—how much more—"

"Felicia!" cried Mrs. Denisty sternly. "Hush—yes, I know. It was an accident."

"An accident! But you know—you know—"

"The nurse is here—Miss Dare."

The young woman whirled. She was—or had been—of extraordinary beauty. Slender and tall, with fine, fair hair and great, brilliant gray eyes. But the eyes were hollow and the lids swollen and pink, and her mouth pale and uncertain.

"But I don't need a nurse."

"Just for a few days," said Mrs. Denisty firmly. "The doctor advised it."

The great gray eyes met Susan's fixedly—too fixedly, indeed, for the look was actually an unwavering stare. Was there something, then, beyond Susan—near Susan—that she did not wish to see?

"*Oh*," said Felicia Denisty with a thin sharp gasp and looked at her hand, and Susan ran forward. On the slender white hand was a brighter, thicker crimson than the Venetian glass which was just then and quite slowly relinquished.

"You've cut your hand," said Susan inadequately. Felicia had turned to the older woman, who was unmoved.

"See," she said, extending her bleeding hand. "Just to be in the room with it—"

Mrs. Denisty moved forward then.

"Will you go upstairs with Mrs. Gladstone, Miss Dare," she said firmly, "and dress her hand."

Upstairs Susan blessed a brief course of Red Cross lectures which during school days she had loathed, and made a fairly workmanlike job of bandaging the wound.

But it was not so easy to spend the long hours of the slow gray day with Felicia Denisty, for she had fallen into a brooding silence, sat and stared either at her bandaged hand or out the window upon a dreary balcony, and said practically nothing.

The afternoon passed much as the morning, except that with the approach of dusk the wind rose a bit and rattled shutters, and Felicia grew restless and turned on every available light in her room.

"Dinner," she said to Susan, "is at seven-thirty." She looked fully at Susan, as if for the first time. "You've been inside all day, Miss Dare. I didn't think—would you like to take a walk before dinner?"

Susan said she would, and hoped she wasn't too eager.

But at the end of half an hour's walk through rapidly increasing gray dusk she was still no wiser than she had been, except that she had a clearer notion of the general plan of the house— built like a wide-flung T with tall white pillars running up to the second-story roof of the wide double porch, which extended across the front of the house—and of the grounds.

On two sides of the house was a placid brown lawn, stretching downward to roadway and to rolling meadows. But on the south lay the ravine, an abrupt, irregular gash, masked now and made mysterious by dripping shrubbery. Beyond it appeared the roof of a house, and at the deepest point of the ravine it was crossed by a small wooden bridge which lost itself in the trees at the farther end. It must lead, thought Susan, to the house, but she did not explore it, although she looked long at the spot where (as revealed by a discreet inquiry of the pretty housemaid) the butler had been murdered.

It was perhaps ten feet from the entrance to the small wooden bridge and just behind a large clump of sumach. It was not in view from the windows of the Denisty house.

Susan, made oddly uneasy by the fog-enshrouded shadows of the trees, made her way back.

Once inside she turned at once to the drawing room. It was dark, and she fumbled for the light and found it. The room was exactly as she remembered it from the morning; a large room of spaces and many windows and massive furniture. Not somehow a pleasant room. It was too still, perhaps, too chilly, too—she turned suddenly as if someone had spoken her name and saw the Easter image.

And she realized what was wrong with the room.

It stood there beside the fireplace—a black, narrow image of a man—a terribly emaciated man, with protruding ribs and a queer, painted face, roughly carved. It was perhaps two feet tall and there were white marks on it that looked like but were not chalk. Its emaciation and its protruding ribs suggested that it was a remnant of that strangely vanished race from mysterious, somber Easter Island. When you looked at it analytically, that was all there was to see.

But it was singularly difficult to look at it analytically. And that was because of the curiously repellent look in its face; the air of strange and secret sentience that somehow managed to surround the small figure. There was a hint of something decadent, something faintly macabre, something incredibly and hideously wise. It was intangible: it was not sensible. But, nevertheless, it was there.

Yet, Susan told herself sternly, the image itself was merely a piece of wood.

A carved piece of wood from Easter Island: a souvenir, probably, of a journey there. It had no connection with the murder of a butler, with the shattered fine fragments of Venetian glass.

Susan turned suddenly and left the drawing room. But when in the hall the door behind her opened. Susan all but screamed before she saw the man who had entered. He flung off hat and coat and reached for a stack of letters on the hall table and then finally looked at her and said: "Oh, hullo. You must be the nurse. Miss—"

"Dare," said Susan. He was thick, white-haired, brusque, with a blunt nose and bright, hard blue eyes. He wasn't over forty-five, and he must be a Denisty.

"Dare," said he. "Nice name. Well, take care of my wife." His blue eyes shot a quick glance up the stairway, and he bent and kissed at Susan; turned, humming, toward the library, and vanished.

Kissed at her; for what she felt would have been a rather expert kiss had been pretty well deflected by some quick action on her part.

Well, that was Gladstone.

And Marlowe Denisty, the brother, who turned up at dinner, was a handsome Byronic-looking youth who talked enthusiastically of practically everything.

It was Marlowe who later, in the drawing room, spoke of the Easter image.

He had brought it, he told Susan expansively, from Easter Island himself. It was a present to Gladstone.

"An akuaku," said Susan absently.

"A *what*?" said Gladstone, turning sharply to look at her.

Susan wished she had not spoken, and Marlowe flashed her a glance of bright approval.

"An akuaku," he said. "An evil god. You remember, Glad, I told you all about it when I brought the thing home. These wooden figures, or moai miro, were made first, so far as can be discovered, by Tuukoihu, who ruled the island following Hotu Matua. These small figures with protruding ribs were thought to be reminders of the imminence of death, threats of—"

"Thank you, I can read the encyclopedia myself," said Gladstone Denisty sharply. "And anyway, it's all nonsense. A piece of carved wood with white painting on it can't possibly have any sort of significance."

"It *can* have," cried Felicia with sudden unexpected violence. "It *does* have!"

Mrs. Denisty, with a glance at Gladstone, interrupted. "Felicia, dear child," she cried in a deprecating way. "How can you be so absurd!"

"Hush!" Felicia's voice was all at once taut; her eyes were wide and dark, and she flung out her hand toward the image. "Don't you realize that it hears you? Don't you realize what it has brought into this house? Misfortune—suffering—murder—"

"*Felicia!*" The interruption was loud and covered anything Felicia might have continued to say, and Mrs. Denisty went on swiftly. "You are hysterical, my dear, and not quite yourself. As to misfortune, we have lost no more than other people and are still very comfortable. And your illness couldn't possibly have been induced by a wooden image—"

"An evil god—an evil influence," muttered Felicia, staring at the image.

Mrs. Denisty swept on, though her mouth was tight.

"And William's death, which I suppose you are referring to, was the result of his discovering an attempt to burglarize the house. It is dreadful, of course. But it had no possible connection with this—this piece of wood."

Felicia was trembling. Susan put a hand upon her arm but could not stay the uneven torrent of words.

"What of the things that have happened to me?—Why, even my kitten died. Flowers die if I touch them. Something happens to everything that is mine. Why—just last night—the glass—" She was sobbing. "William—he was kind to me—he—"

Gladstone intervened.

"Take her upstairs, Miss Dare," he said quietly. "See if you can quiet her. She has some capsules the doctor gave her—try to calm yourself, Felicia."

"Oh, I'll go. I'll go."

She sobbed weakly. But she said no more, and once in her room upstairs took the sedative and afterwards lay quiet, staring at the ceiling with great tragic eyes.

"Your illness," said Susan gently. "The doctor didn't tell me—"

Felicia did not look at her.

"Nerves, he says. That's all any of them say. But I was all right until he brought the image home. About a year ago." The sedative was beginning to take effect, and she spoke calmly. "It is the image, you see, Miss Dare. It hates me. I feel it. I know it. And—I heard the story—of a woman in Tahiti, an Englishwoman who had one, and it hated her, and it brought evil and suffering and misfortune, and finally—death."

She spoke the last word in a whisper.

"Did Marlowe tell you of it?"

"Yes. He told us. We thought nothing of it—then. Mother Denisty says it is wrong of me to fear it. She's religious, you know."

"She holds very firmly to the church?"

"Oh, yes. Except in the modern trend. That is—divorce, you know. She is very much against divorce." Owing perhaps to the capsule, Felicia was beginning to talk in a rambling way. "She says my feeling about the image is superstition."

"How was William kind to you?" asked Susan.

"Oh, in so many little ways. I think he liked me. It was he who told me about the flowers. Of course, I didn't believe him. I know why they died. But he told me that, so I would feel better." She was becoming drowsy, and her words were soft and slow.

Susan felt and stifled with rather shocking ease a scruple against further questions and said: "What did he tell you?"

"Oh—something about acid in the water. I don't know—it couldn't have been true. Flowers died because they were mine. And I don't want to study French anymore."

"*French*," said Susan. "*French!*"

Felicia's drooping eyelids flared open. She stared hazily but intently at Susan and suddenly lifted herself on one elbow and leaned toward her and whispered hoarsely: "It's Dorothy. She knows about the image. I can see it in her eyes. In her eyes." She dropped back upon the pillow, repeated "In her eyes—in her eyes," and then quite suddenly was heavily asleep.

After a long time Susan tiptoed away.

But at midnight she was still broadly awake, strongly aware, as one is at night, of the house about her and all that it held— including the thing that brooded over a downstairs room.

Only a piece of wood.

And what possible connection was there between a piece of wood, some shattered fine glass, and a murdered butler? French lessons and dead flowers and an acid? A kitten—dead, also. An image that represented the imminence of death. A hysterical woman—talking of death.

That night, if anyone brushed against her door, Susan did not know it, for she fell at length into an uneasy sleep.

Her second day in the Denisty household was in many ways a

replica of the first, except that nothing at all happened.

Once during the morning she heard Mrs. Denisty telephoning to someone she called Dorothy and saying that Felicia would not be able to do French that morning, which left Susan little wiser than she had been. And once she herself was called to the telephone for what proved to be an extremely guarded conversation with Jim Byrne. She succeeded only in reassuring him as to her own personal safety, told him carefully that she did not know how long the "case" would last, and hung up.

That night, too, was quiet. But the next day things happened.

In the first place, "Dorothy" came to call. Susan, just entering Felicia's room with the morning paper, heard her voice on the stairs.

"Is Mrs. Gladstone in her room?"

"Yes, Mrs. Laasch," replied the housemaid's voice.

"So I thought. No, no—I know the way. Mrs. Gladstone won't mind."

Susan waited. In another moment the owner of the voice came along the hall, glanced at Susan, and preceded her into Felicia's room with the ease of very old and intimate acquaintance.

"Oh, good-morning, Dorothy," said Felicia.

So this was Dorothy. Dorothy Laasch. Susan gave Felicia the paper and at Felicia's gesture sat down near her.

"Mother Denisty tells me there'll be no more French until you are feeling better," Dorothy was saying. She was a handsome woman in perhaps her middle thirties; a blonde with short hair, vivacious if rather large features, and light, swift eyes. She wore a green wool suit, no hat, and suède pumps. Felicia murmured something and Dorothy went on:

"Since Mother Denisty says so, I suppose that settles it. You ought to rouse yourself, Felicia. You let that woman rule you. Just because she controls the purse strings—"

"Dorothy," said Felicia in a remonstrating way.

Dorothy shot a quick glance toward the door into the hall.

"She's outdoors. I met her down by the bridge."

"But—" said Felicia.

"Oh, you mean the nurse." Dorothy looked at Susan and laughed. "Nurses neither hear nor care, do they, Miss—"

"Dare," said Felicia. She turned briefly to Susan. "This is Mrs. Laasch. I thought you'd met. Let's put off the French lessons for a couple of weeks, Dorothy."

"Nonsense," said Dorothy vigorously. "You'll be all right in a day or two. How's Mother Denisty taking this business of William's death?"

"I—don't know," faltered Felicia.

"No, I don't suppose you do know," said Dorothy with something like exasperation. "Really, Felicia, you can't see anything. Have the police done anything?"

"About William, you mean? Nothing more. At least, nothing that I know of."

Dorothy patted Felicia's hand briskly.

"Then why do you worry? Mother Denisty can't live forever. And think of the insurance she—"

"Mother Denisty is very kind to me," said Felicia. Her hands were trembling.

"Kind," said Dorothy. She laughed abruptly. "You are all afraid of her. Every one of—"

"Ah, there you are, Dorothy," said Mrs. Denisty's bland voice from the doorway. Dorothy turned quickly, Felicia bent closer over her knitting, and Susan felt quite suddenly as if something had shifted and moved under her feet. Like quicksand, she thought, only it was nothing so perceptible.

"I hope you've cheered up Felicia," said Mrs. Denisty. Her eyes were as blank and cold as two blue beads, but her voice was pleasant. If she had heard Dorothy's words, she gave no indication of it.

"I've tried to," said Dorothy. She rose. "I must run now. Good-bye, Felicia. Good-bye, Miss Dare. Good-bye, Mother Denisty."

She kissed Felicia's white face; she kissed Mrs. Denisty. But Susan rose and walked downstairs and out the wide front door with Dorothy, who accepted her company with the breezy manner that seemed characteristic of her.

"Poor Felicia," said Dorothy. "Do walk along to the bridge with me, Miss Dare. The path goes this way. I live just across the ravine, you know. I should be so alone but for Felicia. I'm a widow, you know. Tell me, just how *is* Felicia?"

"She seems not much changed," said Susan.

"That's what I feared. It seems so queer and useless for her to brood over William. I can't imagine—" She checked herself abruptly and then continued in the same rapid way: "I don't believe any of them realize the state Felicia is in. And Miss Dare—I am afraid for her."

"Afraid! Of whom?"

Dorothy paused before she said, very slowly: "I'm afraid Felicia has Felicia to fear more than anyone else."

Suicide! Brooding over William. Was that what Dorothy meant? At their right was the patch of brown, dripping sumach. Susan said: "That's where the man was murdered, isn't it?"

"About there, I believe," said Dorothy. She met Susan's eyes for a long moment. "Take care of Felicia—watch her, Miss Dare. Good-bye."

Her heels tapped the wooden floor of the bridge. Susan watched, thinking of her last words, until Dorothy's blonde head vanished around the curve in the path beyond the bridge. Then Susan turned. As she did so something about the floor of the bridge caught her eye, and she bent to look.

Presently she rose and very thoughtfully went back to the house. But it was exactly then that terror clutched at Susan and would not be shaken off.

Yet, at the moment, there was nothing at all that she could do. Nothing but wait and listen and look.

It made it no easier when, that dreary afternoon, Felicia talked of death. Talked absently, queerly, knitting on a yellow afghan. What did Susan think it would be—did she think it would be difficult—would one regret at the last—when it was too late—would one—

"Has anyone talked to you—of death?" asked Susan sharply.

"N-no," said Felicia. "That is, Dorothy and I have talked of it. Some. And Marlowe always likes to discuss such things."

"But that is wrong," said Susan abruptly. "You are sad and depressed."

"Perhaps," said Felicia agreeably. She knitted a long row before she said:

"Dear Glad—he is so good to me. He would, really, give me anything I want. Why, he would even give me a divorce if I asked for it: he has often said so. Not that I want a divorce. It only shows that he would put my wishes, even about that, ahead of Mother Denisty's."

"Then why," said Susan very gently, "does he keep the—Easter image?"

Felicia flinched visibly, but replied:

"Why, you see, Miss Dare, he—he believes in its power. And he keeps it because he says it would be very weak to give in to his—feeling about it."

"But he talks as if—" began Susan irrepressibly and checked herself.

"Oh, yes," said Felicia. "But that's only because he doesn't like to admit it to other people."

It was that night that the thing happened in the drawing room. And that was the matter of the yellow afghan.

While they were at dinner, somehow, some time, under the very eyes of the Easter image, the knitting was unraveled.

They found it when they entered the chill and quiet drawing room immediately after dinner. It lay in an untidy heap of crinkly yellow yarn, half on the chair where Felicia had left it, half on the floor.

Felicia saw it first and screamed.

And even Mother Denisty looked gray when she saw the heap of yarn. But she turned at once commandingly to Susan and told her to take Felicia upstairs.

Gladstone took Felicia's arm, and Susan followed, and somehow they got her out of the room. As they passed the still, black Easter image Felicia shuddered.

Upstairs, however, she managed to reply to Gladstone's inquiries.

Yes, she said, she had left the knitting there on the chair just before dinner.

"You are sure, Felicia?"

"Why, of course. I knew we would come into the drawing room for coffee and I—I wanted to have my knitting there. It—keeps me from looking at the image—"

"Nonsense, Felicia. The image won't hurt you."

Felicia wrung her hands.

"Glad, don't keep up this pretense. You know you are afraid of it, too. And Miss Dare knows—"

"Miss Dare—" He turned, his eyes blue and cold and exactly like his mother's, plunged into Susan's eyes and Felicia cried:

"So there's no need to pretend because she is here."

"My wife," said Gladstone to Susan, "seems to be a bit hysterical—"

"Oh, no, no," moaned Felicia. "Don't you see? Listen to me, Glad." She was leaning forward, two scarlet spots in her cheeks and her great eyes blazing. "I left the knitting there in the chair. I was the last one in the dining room—do you remember?"

"Y-yes," said Gladstone unwillingly.

"No one left the table. No one was in the drawing room. And when I returned, it was completely raveled out. Oh, it isn't the knitting that matters: I don't care about that. But it's the—the cruelty. The—" she paused, searching for the word, wringing her hands again. Finally it came: "The persecution," said Felicia Denisty.

"Nonsense," said Gladstone heavily. "You are making too much of an absurdly trivial thing. Now, Felicia, do be sensible. Take one of your capsules and go to sleep. The image simply couldn't have pulled your knitting loose—if that's what you mean."

"The image," said Felicia slowly, "couldn't have killed William, either. But William is dead."

"Don't be morbid, Felicia," said Gladstone. He paused with his hand on the door-knob. "Miss Dare, will you help me a moment, please?"

It was, of course, an absurdly transparent excuse. Felicia said nothing and Susan followed Gladstone into the hall. He closed the door.

"Did my wife unravel the knitting herself, Miss Dare?" he said directly.

"I don't know."

His hard blue eyes, so strangely like his mother's, were plumbing her own eyes, seeking for any thought that lay behind them.

"She seems to have been talking to you a great deal," he said, slowly.

"No," said Susan quietly, "not a great deal."

He waited for her to say more. But Susan waited, too.

"I hope," he said at length, "that you realize to what her talk is due."

Susan smoothed back her hair.

"Yes," she said truthfully. "I believe I do."

He stared at her again, then suddenly turned away.

"That's good," he said. "Good-night, Miss Dare."

He went down the stairs at once. In a moment, Susan heard the heavy outside door close. He had not, then, joined his mother and Marlowe, whose voices, steadily and blandly talking, were coming from the drawing room. The room where the Easter image brooded and waited. She returned to Felicia.

"I took two capsules," said Felicia wearily. "You needn't stay, Miss Dare. I'll be asleep in no time."

Two capsules. Susan resolved to talk to the doctor the next day, did what she could for Felicia, and left. This time she met Marlowe, his arms full of yellow wool.

"Oh, hello there, Miss Dare," he said. "I was just looking for you. What shall we do with this? Mother is frightfully upset about it. Glad is the apple of her eye, you know. It's never been exactly a happy marriage—you've probably guessed it. Poor mother. And now Felicia's got this queer notion about the Easter image."

"How did she get the notion?" said Susan. "I mean—has it been long?"

"M-m—a few months. Seems to have got worse since these unlucky things have been happening. Just accidents, of course. But it is a bit queer. Isn't it?"

"Very," said Susan. "Tell me, is she interested in the French lessons?"

"With Dorothy, you mean? Oh, I don't know. She goes regularly, nine o'clock every morning. Mother sees to that. But I don't know that she likes it much. Funny thing, psychology, isn't it? I suppose you see a lot of queer things in your profession, don't you?"

"Well," said Susan guardedly, "yes and no. Good-night. Oh, I don't think it would be a good thing to give the yarn to her just now. Anyway, she's asleep."

He turned toward the stairway, his arms still full of yellow yarn.

In her room, Susan locked the door as she had done carefully every night in the silent haunted house. Haunted by a wooden image.

And then, vehemently, she rejected the thought. It was no wooden image that menaced that house and those within it. It was something far stronger.

And yet she was shaken in spite of herself by the incident of the knitting. After all, *had* Felicia herself unraveled it? The family were all at the table and no one left it even momentarily. And the pretty housemaid who was, since William's death, acting as waitress, had been busily occupied and also, naturally, the cook.

But Susan was dealing only with intangibles. There was still no definite, material clue.

She turned, smoothed back her hair, and sat down at the writing desk. And set herself to reducing intangibles to tangibles.

It was after midnight when she leaned back and looked at what she had written.

A conclusion was there, of course, implicit in those facts. But she needed one link. And, even with that one link, she had no proof. Susan turned off the light and opened the window and stood there for a moment, looking out into the starless, quiet night.

Through the darkness and quiet a small dull sound came, beating with rhythmic little thuds upon her ears. And quite suddenly it was as if a small far-away tom-tom was beating out its dark and secret message.

Easter Island and a devil.

"This," said Susan firmly to herself, "is fantastic. The sound is made by footsteps on the wooden bridge."

She listened, and faintly the footsteps came nearer. She could see nothing through the soft damp blackness. But suddenly, not far below her window, the footsteps ceased. Whoever was on the bridge then had now reached the path.

There was no way to know who had passed.

Yet quite suddenly Susan knew as surely as if she had seen.

And with the knowledge came the strangest feeling of urgency. For she knew, with a blinding flash of light, what those footsteps on the bridge meant.

She snatched a dark silk dressing gown and flung it around her shoulders, unlocked her door and fled down the hall. She waited in the dusk above the stair railing, until the door below opened and she caught a glimpse of the person who entered. It was as she expected, and she turned and was at Felicia's door by the time steps began to ascend the stairs.

If Felicia's door was locked! But it was not. She opened it and slipped inside and leaned against it, her heart pounding as if she'd been racing. Felicia was sleeping quietly and peacefully.

Now what to do? If there were only time—time to plan, time to make arrangements. But there was not.

And she had no proof.

And the feeling of urgency was stronger.

Felicia lay so sunk in sleep that only her heavy drugged breathing told Susan that she was alive.

At the bedside table was a telephone—a delicate gold and ivory thing—resting on a cradle.

Did she dare use it?

She must take the risk. She would need help.

She went to the telephone, lifted it, and called a number very softly into the ivory mouthpiece, and waited.

"Hello—hello—" It was Jim Byrne's voice and sounded sleepy and far away.

"Jim—Jim, this is Susan."

"Susan—do you want me?"

"Yes." Did she imagine it or did the floor creak very softly just below the door? If anyone were out there, if her voice, not Felicia's, were heard—

"Susan—what are you doing? *Susan*—"

Even at a distance the vibration from the telephone might be heard.

"Susan!" cried Jim and very softly Susan replaced the telephone on its cradle. Suddenly his voice was gone. And he was miles and miles away.

The floor under the door did not creak again. If she could only have told Jim what to do, what she was trying to do, where to wait until she signaled. Well, the thing now was to get Felicia out of danger.

She turned to the bed.

It was terrifically difficult to rouse Felicia. Susan was exhausted and trembling by the time she had managed to half carry and half push Felicia into the small dressing room. A chaise-longue was there, and when Felicia's slack, inert figure collapsed upon it gracelessly, she fell again into the horribly heavy slumber from which she had never fully aroused. And all the time there had been that dreadful necessity for haste.

Susan, panting from the sheer physical strain, very softly closed the door of the dressing room.

Then, with the utmost caution, she turned the shade of the

light so that it would not fall directly upon the door into the hall
and yet so that anyone entering the room would be obliged to
cross that narrow band of light.

Then, because she was shaking from cold and nerves and the
strain of the past few moments, she took Felicia's place on the
bed. And waited.

And in the waiting, as always happens, she became uncertain.
All the other possibilities crowded into her mind. She was mistaken. There was no proof. This attempt to trap the murderer
would fail. She was wrong in thinking that the attack would be
made that night.

She knew that Jim Byrne, and probably Lieutenant Mohrn and
a number of extremely active and husky policemen, were at that
very moment speeding along the road to Glenn Ash.

The thought of it was inexpressibly comforting. But it was
also fraught with dangerous possibilities. They might easily arrive too soon. They couldn't arrive too late, she thought, as,
once she had proof, that was enough.

But there were so many ways the thing could go wrong,
thought Susan rather desperately as the minutes ticked away on
the little French clock on the mantel. And her own rapidly con-
ceived plan was so weak, so full of loopholes, so dependent
upon chance. Or was it?

After all, it had been intuitional, swift, certain. And intuition
with her, Susan reminded herself firmly, was actually a matter of
subconscious reasoning. And subconscious reasoning, she went
on still firmly, was far better than conscious, rule-of-thumb
reasoning. And anyway, the rule-of-thumb reasoning was
clear, too.

The attack upon Felicia must come. It had already been prepared and ready once, but then William, poor William, had
come into it and interfered and had had to be murdered.

She was in the deep shadow, there on Felicia's bed. But the
door into the hall was in deep shadow, too. Would she hear it
when it opened?

How long was it since she had telephoned to Jim? Where was he now? What would he do when he arrived?

She became more and more convinced that the police would arrive too soon.

Yet, unless she was entirely mistaken, the attack must come soon. Although planned perhaps for months, that night it would be in one way an impulsive act.

She did not shift her eyes from the door. It was so quiet in the house—so terribly quiet and so cold. It was as if the Easter image downstairs had extended the realm of his possession. So cold—

It was then that Susan realized that the cold was coming from the window and that it was being opened, moving almost silently inward. Her eyes had jerked that way, and her heart gave a great leap of terror, but otherwise she had not moved.

She hadn't thought of the window.

A figure, black in the shadow, was moving with infinite stealth over the sill.

"From the porch, of course," thought one part of Susan's mind. "There are stairs somewhere; there must be." And then she realized coldly what a dangerous thing she had undertaken to do.

But it was done, and there she was in Felicia's place. And she must get one clear glimpse of that figure's face.

It was so dark in the shadows by the window. Susan realized she must close her eyes and did so, feigning sleep and listening with taut nerves.

A rustle and a pause.

It was more than flesh and blood could bear. Surely that figure was far enough away from the window by this time so that it could not escape before Susan had a look at its face.

She moved, and there was still silence. She flung one arm outward lazily and sat up as if sleepily and opened her eyes.

"Is that you, Mrs. Denisty?" she asked drowsily.

And looked at the figure and directly into a revolver.

There was to be no pretense then. Susan's vague plan of talk, of excuses on both sides, collapsed.

"If you shoot," she said in a clear low voice that miraculously did not tremble, "the whole house will be here before you can escape."

"I know that." The reply was equally low and clear. "But you know too much, my dear."

The last thing Susan remembered before that pandemonium of struggle began was the revolver being placed quite deliberately upon the green satin eiderdown. Then all knowledge was lost, and she was fighting—fighting for balance, fighting for breath, fighting against blackness, against faintness, against death. If she could get the revolver—but she could not. She could not even gasp for breath, for there were iron hands upon her throat. She twisted and thrust and got free and had a great gasp of air and tried to scream, and then hands were there again, choking the scream.

She kept on pulling at those hands—pulling at something— pulling—but it was easy to drop into that encircling blackness— easy to become part of it—part of it . . .

Somewhere, somehow, in some curious, dim netherworld very much time had passed. And someone was insisting that she return, forcing her to come back, making her open her eyes and listen and leave that dizzy place of blackness.

"She's opened her eyes," cried a voice with a curious break in it. Susan stirred, became curious, opened her eyes again, saw a confused circle of faces bending over her, remembered, and screamed:

"Let me go . . . *let me go* . . ."

"It's all right—it's all right, Susan. Look at me. See, I'm Jim. You are all right. Look at me."

She opened her eyes again and knew that Jim was there, and Lieutenant Mohrn and a great many other people. And she knew she was being wrapped in the eiderdown, and that Lieutenant Mohrn and Jim made a sort of a chair with their arms and carried her out of the room and down the stairs. And then all at once she was in Jim's car, warm and snug.

"I'll get the story from her when she's better," said Jim shortly to Lieutenant Mohrn, who stood at the side of the car. Susan, in a very luxury of tears, was crying her heart out.

Jim let her cry and drove very swiftly. His profile looked remarkably grim. He said nothing even when they reached Susan's house, beyond ordering Huldah to fix some hot milk.

The story of the Easter image ended, as, for Susan, it had begun, in her own small library with a fire blazing cheerfully and the dog at her feet.

"What happened?" she said abruptly.

"Don't talk."

"But I must talk."

He looked at her.

"All right," he said. "But don't talk too much. We got in at the window. Saw the open window on the upper porch and heard—sounds. Got there just in time." He looked back at the fire and was suddenly very grim again.

"Where is—*she?*" whispered Susan.

"Where she belongs. Look here, if you must talk, Sue, how did you know it was that woman? She confessed; had to. She had the gun, you know. The one that killed the butler."

"It couldn't be anyone else," Susan said slowly. "But there wasn't any evidence."

"Huh?" said Jim, in a startled manner.

"I mean," said Susan hurriedly, "there was only my own feeling, the things I saw and heard and felt about the people involved. It was all intangible, you see, until I put the things I knew on paper—chronologically, as they revealed themselves. Then all at once there was a tangible answer. But there weren't ever any direct material clues. Except the gun, there at the last. And the attack upon Felicia."

A paper rustled in Jim's hand.

"Are those my notes?" asked Susan interestedly.

"Yes—Lieutenant Mohrn wanted you to explain them—"

"Very well," she said. "But it's rather like a—a—"

"Problem in algebra," suggested Jim, smiling.

"No," said Susan hastily. She had never been happy with algebraic terms. "It was more like a—a patchwork quilt. Just small unrelated scraps, you know, and a great many of them. And then you put them together in the only way they'll all fit, and there you have a pattern."

Jim read:

" *'Noise in night that must have been crash of Venetian glass and someone brushed my door; thus person breaking glass probably one of household.'* What on earth is that?"

"Part of the campaign against Felicia," said Susan. "It was evident from the first that there was a deliberate and very cruel campaign in progress against Felicia. The glass broken, her flowers dying always (William had said, she told me, something about acid in the water), her kitten, the knitting—it was all part of the plot. Go on."

" *'Why is Felicia the focus of attack?'* Obviously someone wanted her either to do something that she had to be forced to do, or wanted her out of the way entirely."

"Both," said Susan and shivered.

" *'Gladstone has a roving eye.'* "

"Kisses maids," said Susan. "Kisses anything feminine in a uniform."

"Did he—" said Jim, threatening.

"Slightly," said Susan, and added hurriedly: "The whole thing, though, was centered about the Easter devil."

"The *what!*" said Jim.

She told him, then, the whole story.

"So you see," she said finally. "It seemed to me that this was the situation. Mrs. Denisty ruled the household, controlled the purse strings, and was against divorce. Someone was deliberately playing on Felicia's nerves by threatening her with the Easter devil and by contriving all sorts of subtle ways of persecution. In this campaign the murder of the butler began to look like nothing more than an incident, for evidently the campaign was continuing. Then, when I found that the bridge had been tampered with (you can see for yourself tomorrow)—there's a place where it is quite evident; the nails holding the planks there in the middle have been taken out and then replaced. It would have been a very bad fall, for it's just over the deepest point of the ravine—and I realized that owing to the French lessons Felicia would have been the first to cross the bridge in the morning, was, in fact, the only one in the household who crossed it daily and at a regular time. I knew thus that the campaign against Felicia had already reached its climax once, and yet had been, for some reason, interrupted.''

"Then you think William was murdered because he saw too much?"

"And because he would have told. And his necessary murder, of course, delayed the plot against Felicia. Delayed it until the murderer realized that it could be used as a tool."

"Tool?"

"A reason for what was to appear to be Felicia's suicide."

Jim looked at the paper and read: " *'Dorothy inquires about William; Dorothy seems sincere only when she talks of Mother Denisty ruling the house. Why? Dorothy hints that Mother Denisty knows something of William's murder. Why? Is this smoke screen or sheer hatred of Mrs. Denisty? Dorothy nervous and quick-spoken until I lead her to spot where William was killed; is then poised and calm. Dorothy hints at Felicia becoming suicide. Why?'* "

"Exactly," said Susan. "Why, if not because she's keenly interested in the police inquiry—because she resents Mrs. Denisty's influence, and thus in some way Mrs. Denisty must have opposed Dorothy's own purposes—because she knows too much of the murder herself to permit herself to be anything but extremely guarded and careful in speech and manner when the subject is brought up. When you add up everything, there's just one answer. Just one pattern in which everything fits. And the knitting brought Dorothy directly into it again; that is, none of the family could have pulled out the knitting, the image didn't do it, I felt sure Felicia hadn't, and that left only Dorothy who was free to come and go in the house. But Gladstone pretended publicly that he wasn't afraid of the image, and told Felicia privately that he *was* afraid of it. Believed in its power for evil. You see, Gladstone had to make an issue of something. So he chose the Easter image. It was at the same time a point of disagreement between him and Felicia and a medium through which to work upon Felicia—it's nothing but a painted piece of wood—but I don't like it myself,'' said Susan. "He couldn't have chosen a better tool. But it was Dorothy who murdered and was ready to murder again.''

"Then Gladstone—''

"Gladstone wanted a divorce, but wanted to drive Felicia to ask for it herself, owing to his mother's feeling about divorce. Dorothy had to be in the conspiracy, for she was strongly and directly concerned. But there was this difference: Gladstone (who must have thought he had hit on an exceedingly ingenious plan) only wanted to induce Felicia to leave him. *But Dorothy had other plans.* It wasn't fear that Felicia saw in her eyes: it was hate. I knew that when she talked to me of Felicia's possible suicide. There was the strangest impression that she was paving the way, so to speak; it was then that I realized Felicia's danger. Yet I had no proof. It was, as I said, altogether intangible. Nothing definite. Except, of course, the bridge. If I'd had only one real, material clue I shouldn't have worried so. The footsteps on the bridge, though, were a help, because then I had a link between Dorothy and Gladstone, and I hadn't had that—except intangibly—up till then. But I also realized then that he must have told Dorothy the things Felicia had said to me, that Dorothy would realize that it was dangerous to permit Felicia to talk and that Dorothy would probably act at once. Would carry out the plan that had once been interrupted.''

"But you were not sure of this. You had no proof.''

"Proof?'' said Susan. "Why, no, there was no proof. And no evidence. But I would not have dared deny the evidence of my— intangibles.''

Jim grinned rather apologetically at her. "After all," he said, "there's plenty of proof now. They think Dorothy intended to kill Felicia and leave the gun with Felicia's fingerprints on it, thus indicating suicide and also that Felicia had shot the butler herself—hence her possession of the gun, hence also the suicide. Remorse. Of course, there were a hundred ways for Dorothy to have secured the gun."

He paused and looked thoughtfully and soberly into the fire.

"Intangibles," he said presently. "But not so darned intangible after all. But all the same, young woman, you are going to get the worst scolding you ever had in all your life. The *chance* you took—" He stopped abruptly and looked away from Susan, and Susan smoothed back her hair.

"Yes," she said in a small voice. "But I've got to go back there."

"Go back!" cried Jim Byrne explosively. "There?"

"Yes, I forgot to burn the Easter image," said Susan Dare.

The dog grunted and stretched. The fire was warm, the house at peace, the woman at home where she ought to be, and she hadn't seen the scratch on his nose after all.

But the Patient Died

LAWRENCE G. BLOCHMAN

⟡

Critic Anthony Boucher once noted that Lawrence G. Blochman "has single-handed created enough series detectives to fill an anthology by themselves." One of the best known is the first pathologist detective in crime fiction, Dr. Daniel Webster Coffee of Pasteur Hospital in fictional Northbank, New York. Coffee, who appears in the novel Recipe for Homicide *(1952) as well as in numerous short stories for magazines such as* Collier's, *was the character upon which the television series* Diagnosis: Unknown *was based. The Coffee stories have been collected in* Diagnosis: Homicide *(1950) and* Clues for Dr. Coffee *(1964). In "But the Patient Died," the pathologist helps a surgeon colleague determine why an apparently healthy young woman died following a routine appendectomy.*

THE SURGEON hesitated in the doorway of the pathology laboratory as if he dreaded to cross the threshold. His hand trembled when he lit a cigarette, waiting for the pathologist to look up from his microscope.

Dr. Daniel Webster Coffee, however, continued to peer intently through the twin lenses. The handiwork of the staff surgeons of Pasteur Hospital was going through the daily wringer, and Dr. Coffee was busy handing out good and bad marks, according to what he found in the tissue of a score of tonsils, appendices, and other discarded bits of human anatomy that came to him from the operating rooms.

"Appendix—normal," Dr. Coffee was dictating to his chief technician who sat beside him. "No inflammation, no congestion. Damn it, Doris, that's half a dozen normal appendix sections I've seen this week." He bent his mop of sandy hair closer to the microscope. His lower lip protruded indignantly. "Whose case is this, Doris? If it's that dollar-grabbing society butcher from the Heights, again, I'll—"

Doris Hudson interrupted the pathologist. She nodded to the surgeon in the doorway as she said: "I think Dr. Andrews wants to speak to you."

Dr. Coffee uncurled his long legs from around the legs of the chair and stood up. He held out a big, fur-knuckled hand. "Hello, Andy," he said. "What's on your mind?"

There was obviously something very much on Dr. Andrews' mind. His young face was gray with worry and his lips were taut. "Could I see the pre-operative lab reports on the Baron case again, Dan?" he asked. "That's Mrs. Harriet Baron."

"Why, sure. Doris will get them. Trouble?"

Dr. Andrews nodded. "She died," he said. "Just now. Went out like a light. I can't understand it."

"Too bad, Andy."

"She was a beautiful thing, Dan." Dr. Andrews seemed to be

[98]

talking to himself reproachfully. "Young. Long golden hair. Married only a year. . . ."

"Harriet Grey Baron," announced Doris Hudson, handing a card to Dr. Coffee.

"You know I never send a patient to the operating table, Dan," said Dr. Andrews, "unless the lab says she's ready for surgery. I didn't overlook anything, did I? No mistake?"

Dr. Coffee scanned the report. Blood count . . . Kahn test . . . Urinalysis . . . Coagulation time . . . Vitamin K estimation . . . The young surgeon was thorough, all right. He had asked for practically every test in the book.

"Looks okay to me, Andy. What happened?"

"I wish to God I knew." Dr. Andrews made a helpless gesture. "It was a simple operation—an old appendix. I've done dozens and dozens, and never lost a patient before."

"Did she die under the anaesthetic?"

"No, she'd come out of it. Then she began to sink. She died while I was giving her plasma. The incision was bleeding some, so I thought maybe I'd misread your report on coagulation time, or a vitamin K deficiency, but—I can't understand it."

"Will the relatives authorize an autopsy?" Dr. Coffee asked.

"The family's in the waiting room. I haven't told them yet. I wanted to get hold of myself first."

"We can send one of the internes," Dr. Coffee said.

"No, Dan. It's my case. I ought to face the family."

"I'll go with you," said Dan Coffee—and was immediately surprised at himself. He had always cherished the pathologist's insulation from difficult contact with bereaved relatives. Aside from the challenge of unexplained death, however, he liked Dr. Andrews a lot—and Dr. Andrews was in trouble.

It was always tough for a surgeon to lose a patient, and for Dr. Andrews, just out of the Army and established in Northbank only a few months, it was doubly tough. Not that Northbank was more intolerant or impulsive in its judgments than any other city of a hundred thousand population. Northbank rather prided itself on its culture and civic broad-mindedness. Northbank was proud of its fine modern school buildings, built by politically-influential contractors whose profits would have guaranteed its underpaid teachers a living wage for a decade. Northbank was proud of its handsome residential district on its scenic Heights, and a little ashamed—every few years at flood-time—of its rickety slums on the river shore below the high-water mark. It was proud of its Municipal Auditorium and its symphony orchestra, of its country clubs and golf courses, of its parks and playgrounds, of the richness of its surrounding farmlands which fed its growing food-canning industry. It was proud of its liberalism when the cannery workers elected a socialist to the City Council, although slightly deaf to the new councilman's cry that the municipal hospital reeked of formaldehyde, graft, and poverty. After all, Northbank's private hospitals were modern and progressive and attracted skilled physicians and surgeons. Northbank, in a word, put great value on success, and might not take kindly to a young surgeon who had lost one of his first cases in a new town. . . .

"Come on, Andy," said Dr. Coffee. "Let's go."

The waiting room in the surgical wing of Pasteur Hospital was very much like a hundred other waiting rooms in a hundred other hospitals in the American Middle West. The last cheerless light of the setting sun filtered through the many windows to scatter shadows over the impersonal neatness of the wicker furniture and the potted rubber plants. The false casualness of visitors awaiting word of life or death made subdued voices as hollow as the fierce efforts at concentration of those who pretended to read.

The surgeon and the pathologist approached a group of four people in the far corner of the room. All four were young, although one of the two women—the one in the fur jacket—had managed, with the aid of cosmetics and *haute couture*, an air of worldly wisdom beyond her years. The other woman was quite plain, but her unadorned freshness breathed pleasant, friendly candor. One of the men was brashly and blankly handsome, with an expensive, tweedy aura about the studied carelessness of his sports clothes. The other man wore a sailor's uniform; there was a petty-officer's rating on his sleeve. They sat in pairs, separated by an empty chair on which the sailor had thrown his flat hat and pea-jacket.

"Mr. Baron," said Dr. Andrews, "I'm afraid I have bad news for you."

The handsome, tweedy young man stood up. So did the plain-looking girl with the white scarf around her light brown hair. The girl said: "You can't mean, Doctor, that my sister is—" She choked on the last word.

The tweedy young man merely looked blank.

"She's gone, Margery," said Dr. Andrews to the girl in the white scarf. "She went very quickly, just a few minutes ago."

The tweedy young man shook his head as though he did not understand. His expression did not change. He said: "My wife . . . ?"

Margery sobbed. The sailor got awkwardly to his feet and put a timid hand on her shoulder.

The woman in the fur jacket crossed her silken legs and opened her suède bag. The emerald-cut diamond on her right hand sketched an arc of cold fire as she raised a fragrant wisp of lace to dab at her long, dark eyes.

There was a moment of tense silence. It was a strange, unreal silence, yet the tenseness was almost tangible as it permeated the little group like a turgid cloud of noxious vapor. Dr. Coffee thought: This is not the dumb, incredulous silence of sudden grief. There is something more here—hate, perhaps, or suspicion, or even some unnatural exultation masquerading as stunned, wordless sorrow.

". . . my sympathy . . ." Dr. Andrews was saying softly, sincerely.

Dr. Coffee scarcely heard the surgeon's words. He was trying to analyze the uneasy currents of human emotion swirling around him. He did not like what he felt, but he could not tell why. He looked from face to face, from mask to mask. That was it; they *were* masks: the tragi-comic mask of the husband, with its frozen handsomeness unable to comprehend the finality of death, unable to register anything except its own charm; the alabaster mask of sheer, abstract beauty of the woman in the fur jacket, a tragic mask as impersonal in its beauty as death itself; the bronzed mask of classic comedy that the sailor wore, a mask of clumsy tenderness clumsily fumbling with the brutal fact of a warm, kindred spirit grotesquely and senselessly wounded; even little sister Margery was wearing a mask, a tear-stained mask of indecision which was neither stricken child nor bewildered woman.

"But you said it was such a simple operation," the husband mumbled. His limpness bumped the chair next to the woman in the fur jacket and jelled into a sitting posture.

"Let me explain," said Dr. Coffee. "I'm pathologist at this hospital, and, in a way, just as much responsible for what has happened to Mrs. Baron as Dr. Andrews. You don't know me, because the pathologist works backstage. But my laboratory has checked every phase of Mrs. Baron's condition. I'm sure you won't find much comfort in it now, but I think you should know that Mrs. Baron couldn't have been in more competent hands than Dr. Andrews'."

The woman in the fur jacket gave a short, brittle, bitter laugh. "That's an old one," she said. "The operation was successful, but the patient died."

"Mrs. Baron's death is just as mysterious as it is tragic," Dr. Coffee said. "Mr. Baron, will you give permission for an autopsy which may clear up the mystery?"

Baron was sitting with his head in his hands. Without looking up, he said: "No. You've done plenty already. Let her alone now. Don't touch her."

"But, Mr. Baron, you consented to an operation. An autopsy is just another operation, in a way."

"No," the husband repeated.

Dr. Andrews said: "Margery, you want to know why your sister didn't pull through, surely. You'd consent to an autopsy."

The girl with the white scarf around her hair opened her lips but did not speak. She turned her blue eyes toward the sailor, as though seeking an answer in the jutting angle of his square, tanned jaw. Whatever she saw there seemed to frighten her. Her eyes widened. Then her lips closed again with some new-found strength. She was no longer plain-looking. She was suddenly mature, resolute, even beautiful with the beauty of character.

"If Jerry says no," she said quietly, "I think you should respect his wishes."

"In that case," said Dan Coffee, "I shall advise Dr. Andrews to refuse to sign the death certificate."

Baron's head bobbed up belligerently from his hands. "What does that mean?" he demanded.

"In event of unexplained death, the law of this state requires that the Coroner be notified. The body cannot be released to you until the Coroner is satisfied as to the cause of death. He will probably order an autopsy."

"I think that's cruel," Margery said. There was no anger in her voice. "At least you'll let us see Harriet?"

"Naturally," said Dr. Andrews. "If you'll come with me—"

"Wait a minute." The sailor's raised elbow intercepted the surgeon. "Don't the family rate just one cry in private?"

The dead woman's sister closed her eyes and leaned her head against the sailor's shoulder. "Oh, Steve!" she whispered.

On the way back to the pathology laboratory, Dr. Coffee asked Dr. Andrews: "Who's the dame with the dead foxes and the ice cube? I've seen her somewhere before. Is she another sister?"

"Diana Price," Dr. Andrews replied, "is a girlhood chum. Went to some Eastern finishing school with Mrs. Baron. Career woman. When the Price family moved to California, Diana stayed here and opened her own real estate agency. She's made quite a bit of money and evidently spends it all. Café society."

"Something's wrong with her," Dr. Coffee said. "Did you notice the skin around her eyes? And her lips?"

"I couldn't see beyond the Helena Rubenstein layer," said Dr. Andrews.

"What does Baron do for a living?" Dr. Coffee asked.

"Stocks and bonds. Customers' man, I think. Dan, is the Coroner going to do us any good?"

"I think so."

"Of all the coroners I ever knew," said Dr. Andrews, "about one in ten was capable of performing an intelligent autopsy."

"Make it one in twenty," said Dr. Coffee. "Our local boy is one of the other nineteen. Dr. Thomas Vane, Northbank County Coroner, is just beginning to accept the idea that some diseases are caused by bacteria, and I doubt if he believes in viruses. But he has one great advantage: He's lazy."

"You mean he'll let you do the autopsy?"

"If I work it right," said Dr. Coffee.

Doris Hudson was lifting a steel rack of slides from a xylol bath as the two doctors entered the laboratory. She wiped her fingers on a towel, brushed a tendril of dark hair from her forehead, and smiled. She was tall and slim and wore her white smock as though it had been designed by Schiaparelli.

"Your wife called, Dr. Coffee," she said. "She asked me to remind you that your Aunt Mary is coming for dinner. She said to tell you to be on time because she finally got her hands on some of those Delmonico cuts you've been demanding for so long—the thickest, most magnificent steaks in Northbank since Pearl Harbor. And she said please not to bring along any homework in Mason jars, on account of Aunt Mary's finicky appetite."

"Thanks, Doris," Dr. Coffee said. "Will you call the police station for me? I want Lieutenant of Detectives Max Ritter."

An instant later Dr. Coffee was speaking into the phone. "Hello, Max," he said. "Dan Coffee. We've got something here at the hospital which may be something for you, or it may be nothing. Anyway, I want to make a coroner's case of it. . . . Well, a woman died mysteriously after an operation, and the relatives refuse permission for an autopsy. . . . That's right, Max—not quite kosher. Think the Coroner will insist on doing the autopsy himself? . . . That's right, Max, it's Wednesday—the Coroner's pinochle night. . . . The woman's name was Harriet Grey Baron. She—Oh, you do, eh? . . . Sailor? Yes, there was a sailor here today. . . . You do? . . . Okay, Max, I'll be waiting for you."

Dr. Coffee grinned as he hung up. "Max is bringing the Coroner personally—just to watch. The Coroner won't stay long."

"What did he say about a sailor?" Dr. Andrews asked.

"Let me tell you about Ritter," said Dr. Coffee. "Max is a Northbank boy—son of a junk dealer. He had to leave high school in his third year—father died and he had a mother and sister to support—but he's smart as a Quiz Kid. Worked up from flatfoot to be youngest lieutenant in the detective bureau."

"And the sailor?"

"I'm coming to that. Max says he went to high school with a boy named Steve Forest who was engaged to marry Harriet Grey when he went to war. Three years in the Navy, two in the Pacific. Max says Steve Forest just came home a few days ago."

"And found his fiancée married to Mr. Jerry Baron?"

Dan Coffee nodded. "Coming to the autopsy, Andy?"

"I'll be there," said Dr. Andrews.

Coroner Thomas Vane was a large, florid, triple-chinned gentleman who seemed to swim in the floodlighted glare as he entered the white-tiled autopsy room. He was a head shorter and two paunches thicker than the slight, dark, curly-haired lieutenant of detectives who accompanied him. The Coroner shook hands with Dr. Andrews, then waved away the white gown and rubber gloves that Dr. Coffee offered him.

"This is your party, Coffee," he said. "And what's the idea, anyhow, of calling me in a case like this, when you've got a whole hospital full of doctors to sign the certificate?"

"Unexplained death, Coroner," said Dr. Coffee. "You authorize me to go ahead?"

"Sure, go ahead." The Coroner's bald pate gleamed rosily as

he nodded. "But I think you're wasting your time and mine."

Dr. Coffee said nothing, but his underlip protruded. He glanced at the golden hair cascading over one end of the stainless-steel table in a frozen torrent. Then he picked up his scalpel.

"Great stars!" he said a moment later. "Look at this."

Dr. Andrews grimaced. "Good lord!" he exclaimed. "The poor girl bled to death internally."

"Just as I thought," said the Coroner. "Surgical shock and internal hemorrhage." He winked at Dr. Coffee. "Nothing criminal here. Nobody to blame. I'll just sign the death certificate."

"Don't you want to wait till I've finished?" Dr. Coffee asked.

"Not necessary," said the Coroner. "I'll leave the certificate with you. I've got to run along. Glad to've met you, Andrews."

When the Coroner had gone, Lieutenant of Detectives Max Ritter asked: "Why did she bleed to death, Doc?"

"I won't know for a few hours yet," Dan Coffee said. "I've got to take samples of the blood to my lab. But it's homicide, Max."

"Why, Doc?"

"Lab tests showed Mrs. Baron in good physical shape this morning," Dan Coffee said. "Her blood clotted in the normal time of three minutes. A few hours later her blood just wouldn't clot at all, so that she bled to death despite a technically perfect operation. I've got to find out what happened to her in those few hours."

"I think I get the idea," Max Ritter said. "Somebody put drops in her Ovaltine."

"Possibly," said Dr. Coffee. "Or she was given something hypodermically. It may have been a nurse's error."

"You can rule out the nurse's error," said Dr. Andrews. "I gave her the pre-operative morphine myself. I'm sure it was correct."

"Look, Doc," said Max Ritter. "Why don't I do a little leg work while you make with the test tubes? Maybe Doc Andrews can give me a list of people who saw Mrs. Baron today."

Dr. Andrews obliged with the names of the nurses, an interne,

Jerry Baron, Margery Grey, and Diana Price. He did not know the name of the sailor, but Ritter said it was Steve Forest.

"How late do you think you'll be cooking with the Bunsen burner tonight, Doc?" Ritter asked.

"Probably until around midnight," said Dr. Coffee.

"I'll drop in," said the detective.

The hush of night had settled over the surgical wing of Pasteur Hospital. An occasional nurse moved silently down the corridor in response to the mute appeal of a red call light. Somewhere behind a closed door a patient moaned in his sleep. A sleepy orderly pushed an empty stretcher cart past the door of the pathology laboratory.

Inside the laboratory there was no sound except the sibilant breath of the Bunsen burner and the faint tinkle of thin glass as Dr. Coffee bustled among his flasks and beakers. He replaced a test tube of pinkish liquid in its rack and took up another tube. He added a colorless solution, drop by drop, counting the drops. He shook the tube and chuckled to himself. Then he said aloud: "It checks. I was right. It checks."

"What checks, Doctor?" said a pleasant feminine voice behind him.

Dan Coffee turned, startled. "Oh, hello, Doris," he said. "Why aren't you home in bed?"

Doris Hudson placed a paper bag and a cardboard container on the pathologist's work bench. "I thought you could use a trained lab technician," she said, "and also some coffee and a sandwich. You always forget to eat—even when there's steak for dinner."

"Great stars!" Dr. Coffee looked at his watch. "I was supposed to go home for dinner tonight, wasn't I?"

"I phoned your wife," Doris said. "I told her you'd been detained by an important autopsy."

"Thanks, Doris. Was she furious?"

"She never gets furious any more. She was as sweet and resigned as usual, and a little wistful over the prospect of entertaining your Aunt Mary for a whole evening. Aren't you going to eat your sandwich?''

"Sure," said Dr. Coffee. He shook the test tube again.

"It's corned beef on rye. Sorry it's not Delmonico steak. What checks, Doctor?''

"I've been titrating against Mrs. Baron's blood with protamin sulphate," said Dr. Coffee. "I've found heparin."

"Heparin? Isn't that what they use in blood transfusions?''

"Sometimes, to prevent clotting. Heparin is a powerful anti-clotting agent.''

Dr. Coffee was unwrapping his sandwich when the door opened, and Margery Grey came in. She was dressed in black. The bloom was gone from her cheeks. She was very pale, and seemed much older. She leaned against the doorjamb, breathing rapidly.

"They've arrested Steve Forest," she said when she had caught her breath. "Nobody will tell me where he is. I've got to find him. Where's Lieutenant Ritter?''

Dr. Coffee shook his head. "Why do you come here, Miss Grey?''

"I've looked everywhere else. Anyhow, you started all this. You brought in the police. Why did you do it, Doctor? Why?''

"Because your sister was murdered, Miss Grey," said Dr. Coffee. "Deliberately, cleverly, and diabolically murdered.''

"But how, Doctor?''

"With an injection of heparin that made her bleed to death after her operation.''

"Steve Forest didn't do it." Margery Grey looked Dan Coffee squarely in the eye.

"Did Lieutenant Ritter arrest him for murder?''

"No, he . . . Lieutenant Ritter said he was arresting Steve for obstructing justice and destroying evidence.''

"What evidence, Miss Grey?''

"Well, when Lieutenant Ritter came to our house, Steve and I were going through poor Harriet's things. We were tearing up some old letters Steve wrote to Harriet from the Pacific, when he was still engaged to marry her. The Lieutenant said we were destroying incriminating evidence. Maybe some of the letters did *seem* incriminating. . . ."

"Did Steve ever threaten to kill your sister?"

"Well, in one letter, the one he wrote just after Harriet threw him over to marry Jerry, Steve said he'd strangle Harriet with his bare hands if he ever saw her again . . . but that was a year ago, and—Oh, I don't know, Doctor, but if *I* wanted to kill somebody in anger, or for revenge, or because I hated them for hurting me . . . Well, I think I'd want them to know I was doing it, to hear what I had to say. But the way you explain it, whoever killed Harriet planned it carefully so he'd never be found out. It just couldn't have been Steve. It couldn't."

"How can you be so positive, Miss Grey?" Dr. Coffee asked.

"Because . . ." The girl's voice faded almost to a whisper. "Well, because Steve didn't love Harriet any more. He told me so. When he came back and saw her again, he knew it was all over."

"And he loves you now?" suggested Dr. Coffee.

Margery Grey blushed. It was the first time Dr. Coffee had seen a woman blush in years. Doris Hudson never blushed; she merely made wisecracks to cover up embarrassment. And Mrs. Coffee hadn't blushed since the first years of their marriage—not for ten years at least. But Margery was very pink as she said:

"I can't answer that. I don't know—truly. But I do know that I love Steve—terribly, more than I could ever tell you or him or anybody. I've always loved him, even when he was in love with Harriet, before he went to war, when I was just the dirty-nosed kid sister with her hair in braids. And I've got to help Steve. Where is he?"

"You'll have to ask the police," said Dr. Coffee. "My only function in this matter is to report scientific facts. If your friend Steve—Here's Lieutenant Ritter now."

Max Ritter kicked the door shut behind him with his heel. He pushed his gray felt hat to the back of his head and sat on the edge of a desk. "Hello, Beautiful," he said. "Why don't you make yourself very scarce and invisible? I want to talk to Doc Coffee."

"If it's about Steve Forest, I'm not leaving," Margery said.

"Let her stay," said the pathologist.

"Okay." Ritter shrugged. "What's the score now, Doc? Did you find out what hit the lady?"

"Yes," said Dr. Coffee. "It was heparin."

"Could she swallow heparin without tasting it?"

"She didn't swallow it, Max. It must have been injected, because heparin disintegrates in the stomach. As a matter of fact, I found three needle marks in Mrs. Baron's arm. One was obviously the point at which blood was taken for the lab tests this morning. The second was made by the pre-operative opiate. The third must have been the heparin."

"Wouldn't it take savvy to needle in the heparin?" Ritter asked.

Dr. Coffee shook his head. An intravenous injection, he explained, would act more quickly, but ten c.c.'s of heparin, even injected into a muscle, would completely destroy the power of the blood to form clots after about half an hour. Moreover, the surgeon wouldn't notice it during the operation, because he would clamp hemostats on the blood vessels before they even started to bleed. But afterward, when the incision was closed . . .

"Steve didn't do it," said Margery Grey.

"Didn't he?" said Max Ritter. "He was a pharmacist's mate, first class, in the Navy. He'd know about heparin and how to handle a hypodermic. And listen to this, Doc." Ritter took some letters from his pocket.

"I told Dr. Coffee about the letters," said Margery.

"Here's one they didn't get to tear up," the detective continued. " 'And if I was in Northbank tonight, instead of out here on the other side of the world, I'd like nothing better than killing you with my own hands. Yes, you and that hairless lapdog you say you love so much.' Looks like Steve wasn't fooling."

"Steve hadn't the chance to do anything to Harriet, even if he'd wanted to," Margery said. "He came to the hospital with me."

"Now, Beautiful, don't try to change your story. You told me he brought flowers and you left your sister's room to get a vase to put the flowers in. So Steve was alone with your sister for at least three minutes."

"He did have the opportunity, then," said Dr. Coffee.

"Opportunity," said Ritter, "*and* a hypodermic. Look what I found in the pocket of his pea-jacket." There was a gleam of glass and chromium as the detective produced a syringe from a manila envelope. The syringe was empty, and the needle was snapped off close to the nose. "Any way of telling what was in this baby?"

"Certainly," said Dr. Coffee. "Doris will make a solution from inside the barrel, and we'll titrate for heparin. Hello! This is one of our hypos. See? The name of the hospital is stamped in the ring at the top. Maybe I'd better see if I can find something on the outside, too. Doris, give me a camel's hair brush."

Carefully the pathologist ran the tip of the tiny brush around the circular crevices between the metal mountings and the glass cylinder of the syringe. With infinite pains he dusted the grooves onto a thin rectangle of glass the size of two postage stamps. He slipped a thinner and smaller square of glass on top of the first. Then he stepped to his microscope and sat down. For two silent minutes he twisted the focusing knob.

"Max," said Dr. Coffee at last, "what did Steve Forest say when you found the syringe in his pea-jacket?"

"He couldn't explain how it got there. He said he didn't even know it was in his pocket." Ritter sighed. "Doc, it's no fun putting the pinch on a guy I went to school with, particularly when I'll probably catch hell from my chief for sticking my long eagle beak into something that ain't even officially a crime. Wait till Captain Hall reads the Coroner's report on this. Boy, boy!"

There was another long silence while Dr. Coffee shifted the

glass slide under the nose of the microscope. Then he asked:

"Max, are there swans in the islands of the Pacific?"

The detective cocked his head to one side and stared at the pathologist as if questioning his sobriety.

Dr. Coffee continued to squint into his microscope.

At nine-thirty the next morning Dr. Dan Coffee paused opposite the blackboard in the main corridor of the surgical wing to read the list of operations chalked up for the day. A dull day was in prospect for the pathology lab; routine tests. Dr. Coffee proceeded to his laboratory around a jog in the corridor. He said good morning to Doris Hudson, took off his jacket, and had one arm into his white coat before he saw Lieutenant Max Ritter sitting on his desk, smoking a cigarette.

"Hi, Doc," Ritter said. "You're late."

"I stopped off at Northbank College on my way down," said Dr. Coffee. "I wanted to talk to the professor of ornithology—about swans."

"Swans!" the detective echoed. "Say, what the hell is all this bird talk, Doc?"

"Maybe nothing," said Dr. Coffee. "Anything new, Max?"

"Plenty," Ritter replied. "Last night while I was working on Steve Forest, a couple of my boys were keeping tabs on the Widower Baron. They waited outside the Midtown Mortuary Chapel while he was fixing up a nice funeral for his wife. They followed him to a Southside bar where he met the lush and lovely Diana Price. Mr. Baron and Miss Price drowned their sorrow in two-three drinks and then departed, with my boys right behind. The bereaved husband drove the sorrowing Miss Price to her home on the Heights. My boys report that two minutes later a light went on in Miss Price's bedroom."

"Was Baron with her?" Dr. Coffee asked.

"With her? He was way ahead of her," Max Ritter said. "I'm sorry I can't give you a complete blow-by-blow report, but my boys say that after one minute and twenty seconds of the first round, Miss Price broke the clinch, went to her own corner, and pulled down the shade."

"Very interesting," said Dr. Coffee. "Particularly for Steve Forest."

"I don't say this gives Steve an out," Ritter said, "but a grief-stricken widower who makes like a tomcat on the night his beloved wife conks out sure as hell better think up some good answers. Look, Doc, I asked the boys to bring Jerry Baron up here. Also the Price dame, Margery Grey, and Steve Forest, but separate. I hate moving in on you like this, Doc, but—"

"I guess I invited you to this one," Dan Coffee said.

"If that tightwad City Council would come through with a few nickels for a police lab, I wouldn't have to bother you," the detective continued. "There's nothing like a little high-class science to scare hell out of a wrong guy. He thinks he's pulled off the smartest job in the books, but when he finds that a smarter guy can put a little blood in a bottle, add a drop of this and that, with maybe a dash of Worcester sauce, and come up with all the answers—well, it knocks 'em."

"Let's get Dr. Andrews in on this, too," said the pathologist. "After all, it was his patient."

"Sure, get Doc Andrews, if he'll help bust this open in a hurry," Ritter said. "Because . . . Well, to tell the truth, Doc, I ain't on this case officially any more. In fact, I was yanked off it this morning with pinwheels and Roman candles. Captain Hall says, 'The case is closed. It shouldn't never of been opened. The Coroner says the Baron dame died from surgical shock.' So I says, 'But Doc Coffee claims it's a plain case of homicide.' Then the Captain blows his top. 'Listen,' he says. 'Are you taking orders from me or from that quack up at Pasteur Hospital? Now lay off.' They're all afraid of hurting the Coroner's feelings, specially in an election year."

"I didn't know Captain Hall was even interested in politics," Dr. Coffee said.

"He ain't," said Ritter. "But he's got a wife and four kids, and he wants to keep on being friends with the Chief of Police. The Chief ain't only his boss; he's a political buddy of the Coroner's.''

Dr. Coffee frowned. "But if you're off this case, Max—"

"Look, Doc, today's my day off." Max Ritter grinned. "And if I want to work at my hobby of cracking homicide cases on my own time, nobody can say anything as long as I use your lab for headquarters, and as long as I can prove the Coroner is wrong." The grin vanished. "Say, Doc, you ain't going to let me down? You'll make an honest woman of me?"

"I'm sure we're right, Max," Dr. Coffee said.

The little laboratory was crowded. Doris Hudson was as busy as a bird dog in an aviary, shooing plainclothesmen off the centrifuge, the microtome, and the electric oven in which she was melting paraffin. She had already moved the more fragile glassware and perishable specimens to bacteriology next door.

Dr. Coffee was re-appraising the four people he had met in the waiting room the evening before. He was contrasting the bland, smiling, freshly shaven Jerry Baron with the tousled and bewhiskered Steve Forest who had slept in his clothes at the police station and looked it. Margery Grey seemed not to have slept at all. Diana Price looked impeccable and imperturbable. Dr. Coffee glanced at her suède handbag, and then at the smaller bag of woolen broadcloth in Margery's lap. He wondered if Max was going to crack this alone, or if science would have to step in.

Max Ritter spoke briefly and somewhat ungrammatically about the miracles of science in crime detection. He asked Dr. Coffee to explain how he had discovered that Harriet Baron had bled to death as the result of an injection of heparin.

"So you see, folks," Ritter said when the pathologist had concluded, "it ain't possible to hide anything from the doctor. Does anybody want to come clean now, or do we have to sweat it out?"

There was no response.

"Okay, so we get to work," said Ritter. "When your father

died last year, Beautiful—I mean, Miss Grey—you and your sister Harriet came into quite a piece of change, didn't you?"

"Father left us a considerable estate, yes," Margery said.

"Who gets Harriet's share now? Jerry Baron?"

"Unless my sister changed her will in the last month or so," Margery replied, looking at the floor, "the estate was to go into a trust fund. Jerry was to get the income from it as long as he didn't remarry."

Dr. Coffee was watching Diana Price. He saw her pause in the act of lighting a cigarette. She stared hard at Jerry Baron across the flame of her lighter.

Dr. Coffee leaned forward suddenly to whisper to Doris Hudson: "Doris, go ask the head nurse to come in here."

"Miss Grey," Max Ritter went on, "did your sister know that Jerry Baron was two-timing her with Diana Price?"

"She knew . . . Well, everybody knew that Jerry and Diana were quite close before he married Harriet," Margery said. "She—"

"Now, see here," Baron interrupted. "This is all a lot of nonsense. Diana and I are very old friends."

"Not so old you don't have young ideas," Ritter said. "What were you two up to last night?"

"I don't know what you mean," said Baron blandly.

"Oh, come, Jerry," said Diana Price. "Let's not go through the motions of protecting my reputation. I told you we were being followed last night."

"Ain't it true, Baron," Ritter pursued, "that you wanted to get rid of your wife so you could marry Miss Price?"

"Of course it's not true."

"Didn't you ask your wife for a divorce? And didn't she refuse to give it to you?"

"I never asked Harriet for a divorce," Baron said. "I didn't want a divorce. I loved Harriet."

"But now that you're a free man, I guess you figure on marrying Diana Price, don't you, Baron?"

"Why, no," said Baron. He smiled blankly. "I have no intention of remarrying."

Dr. Coffee was watching Diana Price again. He saw a faint ripple run along her pointed jaw. Her eyes changed expression.

"One more question, Baron," said Ritter. "Were you alone with your wife yesterday, shortly before the operation?"

"No," said Baron.

"Why, Jerry darling, you forget," said Diana. Her voice, too, had changed. It was metallic now, higher pitched, almost shrill. "You were alone with Harriet when I arrived. Remember?"

"That's right, I guess I was," Baron admitted. "I was with Harriet when Dr. Andrews gave her a hypo. When he left, I stayed alone with Harriet until Diana came. By that time Harriet was getting pretty dopey, so Diana and I went to the waiting room."

"Right to the waiting room? Both of you?"

"Yes," said Diana.

"Well, yes," said Baron. "Diana went to the powder room on the way, but she joined me a couple of minutes later."

"So you had plenty of time, Baron, to give your wife a shot of heparin before Diana arrived," Ritter said. "And while she was in the powder room, you slipped the hypo in the pocket of Steve Forest's pea-jacket in the waiting room."

"I did nothing of the kind," Baron protested.

"Okay, Clam," said Ritter. "I guess Doc Coffee has ways of getting the truth out of you. What about it, Doc?"

"I think it would help clear up matters," said Dr. Coffee, "if Miss Price would submit to an A–Z test."

Diana Price stiffened in her chair. "I? An A–Z test? Why?" she demanded haughtily.

"To confirm—or disprove—what the naked eye seems to tell me about you," said Dr. Coffee. "From certain external symptoms which are not completely reliable, I should say you were about two months pregnant, Miss Price. Shall we make a test?"

"Decidedly not." Diana spoke through lips that were tight against her teeth. "Not only is your proposal insulting, but I can't see that it has any bearing on poor Harriet's death."

"I can," said Dr. Coffee. "If the father of your unborn child was in no hurry to divorce his wife to marry you, you may have taken other steps to secure his freedom. Oh, hello, Miss Toms."

Doris Hudson had just returned to the laboratory with the head nurse. Dr. Coffee addressed the buxom woman in white: "Miss Toms, you know Miss Price, don't you?"

The head nurse nodded pleasantly. "Indeed I do. Miss Price was one of our most faithful Nurses' Aids during the war. She hasn't been quite so faithful recently, although she did come around again last week."

"Last week? In uniform? On a regular tour of duty?"

"She put in a full afternoon. Miss Price has always shown a great interest in her work," said the head nurse. "Are we going to see you more often now, Miss Price?"

Diana's only reply was a slight contraction of her nostrils.

"Did Miss Price ever assist at a blood transfusion," Dr. Coffee asked, "one at which heparin was used?"

"Let me see. . . . Yes, I believe she did."

"So she would have access to the hospital's heparin and hypodermic syringes," Dr. Coffee said. "Dr. Andrews, do you remember when Mrs. Baron made up her mind to be operated?"

"I'd been urging the operation for the past month, after she'd had a slight flare-up of a chronic condition," Dr. Andrews said. "But she made her decision only ten days ago. She came to my office with Miss Price and told me she'd talked things over with her husband and decided to have the appendix out."

"Ten days ago. And three days later, Miss Price came to the hospital in her old role of Nurses' Aid to filch a syringe full of heparin." Dr. Coffee turned abruptly to Diana. "Miss Price, you didn't go to the powder room when you left Mr. Baron for a moment yesterday afternoon. You returned to Mrs. Baron's room, because you knew she was alone and so drowsy from drugs that she would not realize that you were injecting heparin into her arm."

"Oh, stop it, Doctor." Diana was desperately jocular, but her smile stuck to her teeth. "Lieutenant Ritter just said it was Jerry who put the hypodermic in poor Steve's pocket."

"Max was mistaken," said Dr. Coffee gravely. "I have evidence to show that the hypodermic was carried in a woman's handbag before it went into Steve Forest's pocket. Max, would you please confiscate Miss Grey's handbag—and Miss Price's? I want the compacts—and the powder puffs."

Max Ritter pounced on the two handbags, and Dr. Coffee held his breath. If the powder puffs were alike, he was sunk.

Margery Grey's compact was small and square. The powder puff was a tiny pad of plush. Diana Price's big round tortoise-shell compact contained a large feathery puff. Dr. Coffee breathed again. He said:

"Last night I made a microscopic examination of the dustings from under the metal parts of the syringe found in Steve's pocket. I found particles of rice powder and feather fragments. The feather fragments have been positively identified as swans'-down. The best powder puffs, like Miss Price's, are made of swans'-down.

"Max, I guess you can consider that fragment of swans'-down as a feather in your cap. You can count on my testimony later, but right now I've got all of yesterday's operations to diagnose. So if you could move your three-ring circus out of my lab . . ."

For several seconds no one spoke. The only sound in the laboratory was a long sigh as Margery Grey buried her face in the rumpled bosom of Steve Forest's jumper. Then Max Ritter put his hand on Diana's shoulder.

"Diana baby," he said, "let's us go down to the detective bureau and watch Captain Hall's face when we tell him how you and the Coroner both slipped up on a few drops of blood."

A moment later Dr. Andrews said: "Dan, I can't begin to thank you. I'm sorry it turned out to be such nasty business. You know, for a minute I was almost sorry for Diana Price—when she first realized she'd planned the nearly perfect crime for nothing, that her poor dumb playboy wasn't going to marry her anyhow, and she tried to pin it all on the handsome brute."

"I might have been sorry," said Dr. Coffee, "if she hadn't tried to involve the sailor."

The phone rang and Doris Hudson answered.

"There's one thing I'd like to ask," said Dr. Andrews. "About those visual symptoms of second-month pregnancy—just what are they, Dan?"

Dr. Coffee laughed. "Unless you take the lady's clothes off," he said, "there aren't any, except occasionally a slight thickening of the lips, the nostrils, and the skin around the eyes. But you know as well as I do that's nothing to go on. I just made up that part to get Diana's reaction. Who was it, Doris?"

"Your wife," Doris Hudson said. "She wanted to know if you'd be home for dinner. She has a duck."

"Great stars! It's nearly noon and look at that stack of slides. I'll be there till Christmas."

"Roast duck, stuffed with wild rice, and basted with brandy and bitter-orange peel. Your favorite duck, Mrs. Coffee says. I told her you'd be home for dinner," said Doris. She sat down beside the microscope and opened her notebook.

The Problem of the Covered Bridge

EDWARD D. HOCH

*Dr. Sam Hawthorne is the quintessential country doctor of the
early part of this century: folksy, wise, and a friend to all and
sundry in his rural environment. He also happens to be a whiz
at solving the most amazing "impossible crimes," such as the
one in this story—a strange wintry disappearance that seems to
defy rational explanation. Edward D. Hoch is a master of this
type of detective story—and a number of other types as well. He
has published some 650 stories over the past thirty years, one of
which, "The Oblong Room," won a Mystery Writers of America
Edgar in 1968. He is also the editor of the acclaimed annual
anthology* Year's Best Mystery and Suspense Stories.

YOU'RE ALWAYS hearin' that things were better in the good ol' days. Well, I don't know about that. Certainly medical treatment wasn't better. I speak from experience, because I started my practice as a country doctor up in New England way back in 1922. That seems a lifetime ago now, don't it? Heck, it *is* a lifetime ago!

"I'll tell you one thing that was better, though—the mysteries. The real honest-to-goodness mysteries that happened to ordinary folks like you an' me. I've read lots of mystery stories in my time, but there's never been anything to compare with some of the things I experienced personally.

"Take, for instance, the first winter I was up there. A man drove his horse and buggy through the snow into a covered bridge and never came out t'other end. All three vanished off the face o' the earth, as if they'd never existed!

"You want to hear about it? Heck, it won't take too long to tell. Pull up your chair while I get us—ah—a small libation."

I'd started my practice in Northmont on January 22, 1922 (the old man began). I'll always remember the date, 'cause it was the very day Pope Benedict XV died. Now I'm not Catholic myself, but in that part of New England a lot of the people are. The death of the Pope was a lot bigger news that day than the openin' of Dr. Sam Hawthorne's office. Nevertheless, I hired a pudgy woman named April for a nurse, bought some second-hand furniture, and settled in.

Only a year out of medical school, I was pretty new at the game. But I made friends easily, 'specially with the farm families out along the creek. I'd driven into town in my 1921 Pierce-Arrow Runabout, a blazin' yellow extravagance that set my folks back nearly $7,000 when they gave it to me as a graduation gift. It took me only one day to realize that families in rural New

England didn't drive Pierce-Arrow Runabouts. Fact is, they'd never even seen one before.

The problem of the car was solved quickly enough for the winter months when I found out that people in this area lucky enough to own automobiles cared for them during the cold weather by drainin' the gas tanks and puttin' the cars up on blocks till spring arrived. It was back to the horse an' buggy for the trips through the snow, an' I figured that was okay by me. In a way it made me one of them.

When the snow got too deep they got out the sleighs. This winter, though, was provin' unusually mild. The cold weather froze over the ice on Snake Creek for skatin', but there was surprisin' little snow on the ground and the roads were clear.

On this Tuesday mornin' in the first week of March I'd driven my horse an' buggy up the North Road to the farm of Jacob an' Sara Bringlow. It had snowed a couple of inches overnight, but nothin' to speak of, and I was anxious to make my weekly call on Sara. She'd been ailin' since I first come to town and my Tuesday visits to the farm were already somethin' of a routine.

This day, as usual, the place seemed full o' people. Besides Jacob and his wife there were the three children—Hank, the handsome 25-year-old son who helped his pa work the farm, and Susan an' Sally, the 16-year-old twin daughters. Hank's intended, Millie O'Brian, was there too, as she often was those days. Millie was a year younger than Hank, an' they sure were in love. The wedding was already scheduled for May, and it would be a big affair. Even the rumblings 'bout Millie marryin' into a non-Catholic family had pretty much died down as the big day grew nearer.

"'Lo, Dr. Sam," Sally greeted me as I entered the kitchen.

I welcomed the warmth of the stove after the long cold drive. "Hello, Sally. How's your ma today?"

"She's up in bed, but she seems pretty good."

"Fine. We'll have her on her feet in no time."

Jacob Bringlow and his son entered through the shed door,

stampin' the snow from their boots. "Good day, Dr. Sam," Jacob said. He was a large man, full of thunder like an Old Testament prophet. Beside him, his son Hank seemed small and slim and a bit underfed.

"Good day to you," I said. "A cold mornin'!"

"'Tis that. Sally, git Dr. Sam a cup o' coffee—can't you see the man's freezin'?"

I nodded to Hank. "Out cuttin' firewood?"

"There's always some to cut."

Hank Bringlow was a likeable young chap about my own age. It seemed to me he was out of place on his pa's farm, and I was happy that the wedding would soon take him away from there. The only books an' magazines in the house belonged to Hank, and his manner was more that of a fun-lovin' scholar than a hard-workin' farmer. I knew he and Millie planned to move into town after their marriage, and I 'spected it would be a good thing for both of 'em.

Millie always seemed to be workin' in the kitchen when I made my calls. Maybe she was tryin' to convince the family she could make Hank a good wife. By the town's standards she was a pretty girl, though I'd known prettier ones at college.

She carefully took the coffee cup from young Sally an' brought it to me as I found a place to sit. "Just move those magazines, Dr. Sam," she said.

"Two issues of *Hearst's International?*" It wasn't a magazine frequently found in farmhouses.

"February and March. Hank was readin' the new two-part Sherlock Holmes story."

"They're great fun," I admitted. "I read them a lot in medical school."

Her smile glowed at me. "Mebbe you'll be a writer like Dr. Conan Doyle," she said.

"I doubt that." The coffee was good, warming me after the cold drive. "I really should see Mrs. Bringlow an' finish this later."

"You'll find her in good spirits."

Sara Bringlow's room was at the top of the stairs. The first time I went in, back in January, I found a weak, pale woman in her fifties with a thickened skin and dulled senses, who might have been very close to death. Now the scene was different. Even the room seemed more cheerful, an' certainly Sara Bringlow was more vividly alive than I'd ever seen her. Sittin' up in bed, with a bright pink shawl thrown over her shoulders, she welcomed me with a smile. "See, I'm almost all better! Do you think I can git up this week?"

Her illness today would probably be classed as a form of thyroid condition called myxedema, but we didn't use such fancy words back then. I'd treated her, an' she was better, an' that was all I cared about. "Tell you what, Sara, you stay in bed till Friday an' then you can get up if you feel like it." I winked at her 'cause I knew she liked me to. "If truth be known, I'll bet you been sneakin' out of that bed already!"

"Now how would you know that, Doctor?"

"When Sally met me at the door I asked how you were and she said you were up in bed but seemed pretty good. Well now, where else would you be? The only reason for her sayin' it like that was if you'd been up and about sometime recently."

"Land sakes, you should be a detective, Dr. Sam!"

"I have enough to do bein' a doctor." I took her pulse and blood pressure as I talked. "I see we had some more snow this mornin'."

"Yes indeed! The children will have to shovel off the ice before they go skatin' again."

"The wedding's gettin' mighty close now, isn't it?" I suspected the forthcomin' nuptials were playin' a big part in her recovery.

"Yep, just two months away. It'll be a happy day in my life. I s'pose it'll be hard on Jacob, losin' Hank's help around the farm, but he'll manage. I told him the boy's twenty-five now—got to lead his own life."

"Millie seems like a fine girl."

"Best there is! Catholic, of course, but we don't hold that

again' her. 'Course her folks would rather she married Walt Rumsey on the next farm, now that he owns it an' all, but Walt's over thirty—too old for a girl like Millie. I 'spect she knowed that too, when she broke off with him."

There was a gentle knock on the door and Susan, the other twin, came in. "Momma, Hank's gettin' ready to go. He wants to know about that applesauce for Millie's ma."

"Land sakes, I near forgot! Tell him to take a jar off the shelf in the cellar."

After she'd gone I said, "Your daughters are lovely girls."

"They are, aren't they? Tall like their father. Can you tell them apart?"

I nodded. "They're at an age where they want to be individuals. Sally's wearin' her hair a mite different now."

"When they were younger, Hank was always puttin' them up to foolin' us, changin' places and such." Then, as she saw me close my bag, her eyes grew serious for a minute. "Dr. Sam, I *am* better, aren't I?"

"Much better. The thickenin' of your skin is goin' away, and you're much more alert."

I left some more of the pills she'd been takin' and went back downstairs. Hank Bringlow was bundled into a fur-collared coat, ready for the trip to Millie's house. It was about two miles down the windin' road, past the Rumsey farm and across the covered bridge.

Hank picked up the quart jar of applesauce and said, "Dr. Sam, why don't you ride along with us? Millie's pa hurt his foot last week. He'd never call a doctor for it, but since you're so close maybe you should take a look."

Millie seemed surprised by his request, but I had no objection. "Glad to. I'll follow you in my buggy."

Outside, Hank said, "Millie, you ride with Dr. Sam so he doesn't get lost."

She snorted at that. "The road doesn't go anywhere else, Hank!"

But she climbed into my buggy an' I took the reins. "I hear tell you've got yourself a fancy yellow car, Dr. Sam."

"It's up on blocks till spring. This buggy is good enough for me." Mine was almost the same as Hank's—a four-wheeled carriage with a single seat for two people, pulled by one horse. The fabric top helped keep out the sun and rain, but not the cold. And ridin' in a buggy during a New England winter could be mighty cold!

The road ahead was windin', with the woods on both sides. Though it was nearly noon, the tracks of Hank's horse an' buggy were the only ones ahead of us in the fresh snow. Not many people came up that way in the winter. Before we'd gone far, Hank speeded up and disappeared from sight round a bend in the road. "Hank seems so unlike his pa," I said, making conversation.

"That's because Jacob is his stepfather," Millie explained. "Sara's first husband—Hank's real father—died of typhoid when he was a baby. She remarried and then the twins were born."

"That explains the gap."

"Gap?"

"Nine years between Hank and his sisters. Farm families usually have their children closer together."

Hank's buggy was still far enough ahead to be out of sight, but now the Rumsey farm came into view. We had to pause a minute as Walt Rumsey blocked the road with a herd of cows returnin' to the barn. He waved and said, "Hank just passed."

"I know," Millie called back. "He goes so fast we can't keep up with him."

When the cows were gone I speeded up, still following the track of Hank's buggy in the snow. As we rounded the next corner I thought we'd see him, 'cause the road was now straight and the woods on both sides had ended. But there was only the covered bridge ahead, and the empty road runnin' beyond it to the O'Brian farm.

"Where is he?" Millie asked, puzzled.

"He must be waitin' for us inside the bridge." From our angle we couldn't yet see through it all the way.

"Prob'ly," she agreed with a chuckle. "He always says that covered bridges are kissin' bridges, but that's not true at all."

"Where I come from—" I began, and then paused. The interior of the bridge could be seen now, and no horse an' buggy were waitin' inside. "Well, he certainly went in. You can see the tracks in the snow."

"But—" Millie was half standing now in her seat. "Something's there on the floor of the bridge. What is it?"

We rode up to the bridge entrance and I stopped the horse. There were no windows cut into the sides of this covered bridge, but the light from the ends and from between the boards was enough to see by. I got down from the buggy. "It's his jar of applesauce," I said. "It smashed when it fell from the buggy."

But Millie wasn't lookin' at the applesauce. She was starin' straight ahead at the unmarked snow beyond the other end of the fifty-foot bridge. "Dr. Sam!"

"What is it?"

"There are no tracks goin' off the bridge! He came into it, but he didn't leave it! Dr. Sam, *where is he?*"

She was right, by gum! The tracks of Hank's horse an' buggy led into the bridge. Fact is, the damp imprint of the meltin' snow could be seen for several feet before it gradually faded away.

But there was no horse, no buggy, no Hank Bringlow.

Only the broken jar of applesauce he'd been carrying.

But if he hadn't disturbed the snow at the far end of the bridge, he must be—he *had* to be—still here! My eyes went up to the patterned wooden trusses that held the bridge together. There was nothing—nothing but the crossbeams and the roof itself. The bridge was in remarkably good shape, protected from weathering by its roof. Even the sides were sturdy and unbroken. Nothin' bigger than a squirrel could've fit between the boards.

"It's some sort of trick," I said to Millie. "He's got to be here!"

"But *where*?"

I walked to the other end of the bridge and examined the un-marked snow. I peered around the corner o' the bridge at the frozen surface of Snake Creek. The skaters had not yet shoveled off the snow, and it was as unmarked as the rest. Even if the horse an' buggy had passed somehow through the wooden floor or the sides o' the bridge, there was no place they could've gone without leavin' a mark. Hank had driven his buggy into the bridge with Millie an' me less than a minute behind him, dropped his quart jar o' applesauce, and vanished.

"We've got to get help," I said. Instinct told me I shouldn't disturb the snow beyond the bridge by goin' forward to Millie's house. "Wait here an' I'll run back to Rumsey's farm."

I found Walt Rumsey in the barn with his cows, forkin' hay out of the loft. "'Lo, Doc," he called down to me. "What's up?"

"Hank Bringlow seems to have disappeared. Darnedest thing I ever saw. You got a telephone here?"

"Sure have, Doc." He hopped down to the ground. "Come on in the house."

As I followed him through the snow I asked, "Did Hank seem odd in any way when he went past you?"

"Odd? No. He was bundled up against the cold, but I knew it was him. I kept my cows to the side o' the road till he passed."

"Did he say anything?"

"No, just waved."

"Then you didn't actually see his face or hear his voice?"

Walt Rumsey turned to me. "Wa-el, no. But hell, I've known Hank mosta my life! It was him, all right."

An' I s'pose it had to be. No substitution o' drivers could've been made anywhere along the road, and even if a substitution had been made, how did the substitute disappear?

I took the phone that Walt Rumsey offered, cranked it up, and asked for the Bringlow farm. One of the twins answered. "This is Dr. Sam. We seem to have lost your brother. He didn't come back there, did he?"

"No. Isn't he with you?"

"Not right now. Your pa around?"

"He's out in the field somewhere. You want Momma?"

"No. She should stay in bed." No need to bother her yet. I hung up an' called the O'Brian farm with the same results. Millie's brother Larry answered the phone. He'd seen nothin' of Hank, but he promised to start out on foot toward the bridge at once, searchin' for buggy tracks or footprints.

"Any luck?" Rumsey asked when I'd finished.

"Not yet. You didn't happen to watch him after he passed, did you?"

Rumsey shook his head. "I was busy with the cows."

I went back outside and headed for the bridge, with Rumsey taggin' along. Millie was standin' by my horse an' buggy, lookin' concerned. "Did you find him?" she asked.

I shook my head. "Your brother's on his way over."

While Rumsey and I went over every inch of the covered bridge, Millie simply stood at the far end, watchin' for her brother. I guess she needed him to cling to just then. Larry O'Brian was young, handsome, an' likeable—a close friend of both Hank Bringlow an' Walt Rumsey. My nurse April told me that when Walt inherited the farm after his folks' death, both Larry and Hank helped him with the first season's planting. She'd also told me that despite their friendship Larry was against Hank marryin' his sister. P'raps, like some brothers, he viewed no man as worthy of the honor.

When Larry arrived he had nothing new to tell us. "No tracks between here an' the farm," he confirmed.

I had a thought. "Wait a minute! If there aren't any tracks, how in the heck did you get over here this mornin', Millie?"

"I was with Hank at his place last night. When the snow started, the family insisted I stay over. We only got a couple of inches, though." She seemed to sense an unasked question, and she added, "I slept with the twins in their big bed."

Larry looked at me. "What d'you think?"

I stared down at the smashed quart of applesauce which everyone had carefully avoided. "I think we better call Sheriff Lens."

Sheriff Lens was a fat man who moved slowly and thought slowly (Doctor Sam continued). He'd prob'ly never been confronted with any crime bigger than buggy stealin'—certainly nothin' like the disappearance from the covered bridge. He grunted and rasped as he listened to the story, then threw up his hands in dismay. "It couldn'ta happened the way you say. The whole thing's impossible, an' the impossible jest don't make sense. I think you're all foolin' me—maybe havin' an April Fool joke three weeks early."

It was about then that the strain finally got to Millie. She collapsed in tears, and Larry and I took her home. Their pa, Vincent O'Brian, met us at the door. "What is this?" he asked Larry. "What's happened to her?"

"Hank's disappeared."

"Disappeared? You mean run off with another woman?"

"No, nothin' like that."

While Larry helped Millie to her room, I followed Vincent into the kitchen. He wasn't the hulkin' ox of a man that Jacob Bringlow was, but he still had the muscles of a lifetime spent in the field. "Hank wanted me to come along," I explained. "Said you'd hurt your foot."

"It's nothin'. Twisted my ankle choppin' wood."

"Can I see it?"

"No need." But he pulled up his pants leg reluctantly and I stooped to examine it. Swellin' and bruisin' were pronounced, but the worst was over.

"Not too bad," I agreed. "But you should be soakin' it." Glancing around to be sure we weren't overheard, I lowered my voice and added, "Your first thought was that Hank Bringlow had run off with another woman. Who did you have in mind?"

He looked uneasy. "Nobody special."

"This may be serious, Mr. O'Brian."

He thought about it and finally said, "I won't pretend I'm happy about my daughter marryin' a non-Catholic. Larry feels the same way. Besides, Hank fools around with the girls in town."

"For instance?"

"For instance Gert Page at the bank. Wouldn't be surprised he run off with her."

I saw Millie comin' back downstairs and I raised my voice a bit. "You soak that ankle now, in good hot water."

"Has there been any word?" Millie asked. She'd recovered her composure, though her face still lacked color.

"No word, but I'm sure he'll turn up. Was he in the habit of playin' tricks?"

"Sometimes he'd fool people with Susan an' Sally. Is that what you mean?"

"Don't know what I mean," I admitted. "But he seemed anxious for you to ride with me. Maybe there was a reason."

I stayed for lunch, and when no word came I headed back to town alone. The Sheriff an' some others were still at the covered bridge when I rode through it, but I didn't stop. I could see they'd gotten nowhere toward solvin' the mystery, and I was anxious to get to the bank before it closed.

Gert Page was a hard-eyed blonde girl of the sort who'd never be happy in a small New England town. She answered my questions 'bout Hank Bringlow with a sullen distrust she might have felt towards all men.

"Do you know where he is, Gert?"

"How would I know where he is?"

"Were you plannin' to run off with him before his marriage?"

"Ha! Me run off with him? Listen, if Millie O'Brian wants him that bad, she can have him!" The bank was closin' and she went back to countin' the cash in her drawer. "B'sides, I hear tell men get tired of married life after a bit. I just might see him in town again. But I sure won't run off with him and be tied to one man!"

I saw Roberts, the bank's manager, watchin' us and I wondered why they kept a girl like Gert on the payroll. I 'spected she was most unpopular with the bank's lady customers.

As I left the bank I saw Sheriff Lens enterin' the general store across the street. I followed and caught him at the pickle barrel. "Anything new, Sheriff?"

"I give it up, Doc. Wherever he is, he ain't out by the bridge."

The general store, which was right next to my office, was a cozy little place with great wheels of cheese, buckets o' flour, an' jars o' taffy kisses. The owner's name was Max, and his big collie dog always slept on the floor near the potbellied stove. Max came around the counter to join us and said, "Everyone's talkin' about young Hank. What do you think happened?"

"No idea," I admitted.

"Couldn't an aeroplane have come over an' picked up the whole shebang?"

"I was right behind him in the buggy. There was no aeroplane." I glanced out the window and saw Gert Page leavin' the bank with the manager, Roberts. "I hear some gossip that Hank was friendly with Gert Page. Any truth to it?"

Max scratched the stubble on his chin and laughed. "Everybody in town is friendly with Gert, includin' ol' Roberts there. It don't mean nothin'."

"I guess not," I agreed. But if it hadn't meant anything to Hank Bringlow, had it meant somethin' to Millie's pa an' brother?

Sheriff Lens and I left the general store together. He promised to keep me informed and I went next door to my office. My nurse April was waitin' for all the details. "My God, you're famous, Dr. Sam! The telephone ain't stopped ringin'!"

"Hell of a thing to be famous for. I didn't see a thing out there."

"That's the point! Anyone else they wouldn't believe—but you're somethin' special."

I sighed and kicked off my damp boots. "I'm just another country doctor, April."

She was a plump jolly woman in her thirties, and I'd never regretted hirin' her my first day in town. "They think you're smarter'n most, Dr. Sam."

"Well, I'm not."

"They think you can solve this mystery."

Who else had called me a detective that day? Sara Bringlow? "Why do they think that?"

"I guess because you're the first doctor in town ever drove a Pierce-Arrow car."

I swore at her but she was laughin' and I laughed too. There were some patients waitin' in the outer office and I went to tend to them. It was far from an ordinary day, but I still had my practice to see to. Towards evening, by the time I'd finished, the weather had turned warmer. The temperature hovered near 40 and a gentle rain began to fall.

"It'll get rid o' the snow," April said as I left for the day.

"Ayah, it'll do that."

"Mebbe it'll uncover a clue."

I nodded, but I didn't believe it. Hank Bringlow had gone far away, and the meltin' snow wasn't about to bring him back.

The telephone woke me at four the next mornin'. "This is Sheriff Lens, Doc," the voice greeted me. "Sorry to wake you, but I gotta bad job for you."

"What's that?"

"We found Hank Bringlow."

"Where?"

"On the Post Road, about ten miles south o' town. He's sittin' in his buggy like he jest stopped for a rest."

"Is he—?"

"Dead, Doc. That's what I need you for. Somebody shot him in the back o' the head."

It took me near an hour (Doctor Sam went on) to reach the scene, drivin' the horse an' buggy fast as I could over the slushy country roads. Though the night was mild, the rain chilled me to the bone as I rode through the darkness on that terrible mission. I kept thinkin' about Millie O'Brian, and Hank's ma only just recoverin' from her lengthy illness. What would the news do to them?

Sheriff Lens had some lanterns out in the road, and I could see their eerie glow as I drove up. He helped me down from the buggy an' I walked over to the small circle of men standin' by the other rig. Two of them were deputies, another was a farmer from a nearby house. They hadn't disturbed the body—Hank still sat slumped in a corner o' the seat, his feet wedged against the front o' the buggy.

I drew a sharp breath when I saw the back of his head. "Shotgun," I said curtly.

"Can you tell if it happened here, Doc?"

"Doubtful." I turned to the farmer. "Did you find him?"

The man nodded and repeated a story he'd obviously told 'em already. "My wife heard the horse. We don't git nobody along this road in the middle o' the night, so I come out to look around. I found him like this."

In the flare of the lantern light I noticed somethin'—a round mark on the horse's flank that was sensitive to my touch. "Look here, Sheriff."

"What is it?"

"A burn. The killer loaded Hank into the buggy an' then tied the reins. He singed the horse with a cigar or somethin' to make it run. Could've run miles before it stopped from exhaustion."

Lens motioned to his deputies. "Let's take him into town. We won't find nothin' else out here." He turned back to me. "At least he's not missin' any more."

"No, he's not missin'. But we still don't know what happened on that bridge. We only know it wasn't any joke."

The funeral was held two days later, on Friday mornin', with a bleak winter sun breakin' through the overcast to throw long March shadows across the tombstones of the little town cemetery. The Bringlows were all there, 'course, and Millie's folks and people from town. Afterwards many of us went back to the Bringlow farm. It was a country custom, however sad the occasion, and many neighbors brought food for the family.

I was sittin' in the parlor, away from the others, when the bank manager, Roberts, came up to me. "Has the Sheriff found any clues yet?" he asked.

"Nothin' I know of."

"It's a real baffler. Not just the *how*, but the *why*."

"The *why*?"

He nodded. "When you're goin' to kill someone you just do it. You don't rig up some fantastic scheme for them to disappear first. What's the point?"

I thought about that, and I didn't have a ready answer. When Roberts drifted away I went over to Sara Bringlow and asked how she was feelin'. She looked at me with tired eyes and said, "My first day outta bed. To bury my son."

There was no point arguin' with a mother's grief. I saw Max bringin' in a bag of groceries from his store and I started over to help him. But my eye caught somethin' on the parlor table. It was the March issue of *Hearst's International*. I remembered Hank had been reading the Sherlock Holmes story in the February and March issues. I located the February one under a stack o' newspapers and turned to the Holmes story.

It was in two parts, and called *The Problem of Thor Bridge*. Bridge?

I found a quiet corner and sat down to rea1.

It took me only a half hour, and when I fir ished I sought out Walt Rumsey from the next farm. He was s andin' with Larry O'Brian on the side porch, an' when he saw me comin' he said, "Larry's got some good bootleg stuff out in his buggy. Want a shot?"

"No, thanks, Walt. But you can do somethin' else for me. Do you have a good stout rope in your barn?"

He frowned in concentration. "I s'pose so."

"Could we ride over there now? I just read somethin' that gave me an idea how Hank might've vanished from that bridge."

We got into his buggy an' drove the mile down the windin' road to his farm. The snow was melted by this time, and the cows were clustered around the water trough by the side of the barn. Walt took me inside, past empty stalls an' milk cans an' carriage wheels, to a big shed attached to the rear. Here, among assorted tools, he found a twelve-foot length of worn hemp.

"This do you?"

"Just the thing. Want to come to the bridge with me?"

The ice of the creek was still firm, though the road had turned to mud. I handed one end o' the rope to Rumsey and played out the other end till it reached the edge of the frozen creek. "What's this all about?" he asked.

"I read a story 'bout a gun that vanished off a bridge by bein' pulled into the water."

He looked puzzled. "But Hank's buggy couldn'ta gone into the crick. The ice was unbroken."

"All the same I think it tells me somethin'. Thanks for the use o' the rope."

He took me back to the Bringlow house, puzzled but unquestioning. The mourners were beginning to drift away, and I sought out Sheriff Lens. "I've got an idea about this mystery, Sheriff. But it's sort of crazy."

"In this case, even a crazy idea would be welcome."

Jacob Bringlow, tall and unbent from the ordeal of the funeral, came around the corner o' the house with one of the twins. "What is it, Sheriff?" he asked. "Still searchin' for clues?"

"We may have one," I said. "I got an idea."

He eyed me up an' down, p'raps blamin' me for what happened to his stepson. "You stick to your doctorin'," he said with a slur, and I knew he'd been samplin' Larry's bottle. "Go look at my wife. She don't seem right to me."

I went inside and found Sara pale and tired-looking. I ordered her up to bed and she went without argument. Max was leavin', and so was the O'Brian family. The banker had already gone. But when I went back on the porch, Jacob Bringlow was still waitin' for me. He was lookin' for trouble. Maybe it was a mixture of grief and bootleg whiskey.

"Sheriff says you know who killed Hank."

"I didn't say that. I just got an idea."

"Tell me. Tell us all!"

He spoke loudly, and Larry O'Brian paused with Millie to listen. Walt Rumsey came over too. In the distance, near the buggies, I saw Gert Page from the bank. I hadn't seen her at the funeral, but she'd come to pay some sort of last respects to Hank.

"We can talk about it inside," I replied, keepin' my voice down.

"You're bluffin'! You don't know a thing!"

I drew a deep breath. "All right, if you want it like this. Hank was reading a Sherlock Holmes story before he died. There's another one he prob'ly read years ago. In it Holmes calls Watson's attention to the curious incident of the dog in the night-time. I could echo his words."

"But there was no dog in the night-time," Sheriff Lens pointed out. "There's no dog in this whole danged case!"

"My mistake," I said. "Then let me direct your attention to the curious incident of the cows in the daytime."

It was then that Walt Rumsey broke from the group and ran towards his buggy. "Grab him, Sheriff!" I shouted. "He's your murderer!"

I had to tell it all to April, back at my office, because she hadn't been there and wouldn't believe it otherwise. "Come on, Dr. Sam! How did the cows tell you Walt was the killer?"

"He was bringin' them back to the barn, across the road, as we passed. But from where? Cows don't graze in the snow, and their waterin' trough is next to the barn, not across the road. The only possible reason for the cows crossin' the road in front of us was to obliterate the tracks of Hank's horse an' buggy.

"Except for those cows, the snow was unbroken by anything

but the single buggy track—all the way from the Bringlow farm to the covered bridge. We know Hank left the farm. If he never reached the bridge, whatever happened to him had to happen at the point where those cows crossed the road.''

"But the tracks to the bridge! You were only a minute behind him, Dr. Sam. That wasn't long enough for him to fake those tracks!"

I smiled, runnin' over the reasonin' as it first came to me. "Roberts the banker answered that one, along with Sherlock Holmes. Roberts asked *why*—why did the killer go to all that trouble? And the answer was that he didn't. It wasn't the killer but Hank Bringlow who went to all the trouble.

"We already knew he'd fooled people with his twin sisters, confusin' their identities. And we knew he'd recently read *The Problem of Thor Bridge*, which has an impossible suicide of sorts takin' place on a bridge. It's not too far-fetched to imagine him arrangin' the ultimate joke—his own disappearance from that covered bridge.''

"But *how*, Dr. Sam?" April wanted to know. "I read that Sherlock Holmes story too, an' there's nothin' in it like what happened here.''

"True. But as soon as I realized the purpose o' those noonday cows, I knew somethin' had happened to those tracks at the barn. And only one thing could've happened—Hank's buggy turned off the road and went *into* the barn. The tracks from the road to the bridge were faked.''

"How?" she repeated, not yet ready to believe a word of it.

"*When* is the more important question. Since there was no time to fake the tracks in the single minute before we came along, they had to have been done earlier. Hank and Walt Rumsey must've been in cahoots on the scheme. Walt went out that mornin', after the snow had stopped, with a couple o' old carriage wheels linked together by an axle. On his boots he'd fastened blocks o' wood a couple o' inches thick, with horse-shoes nailed to the bottoms.

"He simply trotted along the road, through the snow, pushin' the pair o' wheels ahead of him. He went into the bridge far enough to leave traces o' snow, then reversed the blocks o' wood on his boots and pushed the wheels back again. The resultin' tracks looked like a four-footed animal pullin' a four-wheeled buggy.''

"But—'' April started to object.

"I know, I know! A man doesn't run like a horse. But with practice he could space the prints to look good enough. And I'll bet Hank an' Walt practised plenty while they waited for the right mornin' when the snow was fresh but not too deep. If anyone had examined the tracks o' the horse carefully, they'd've discovered the truth. Careful as he was, Walt Rumsey's prints comin' back from the bridge woulda been a bit different, hittin' the snow from the opposite direction. But they figured I'd drive my buggy up to the bridge in his tracks, all but obliteratin' them, which is what I did. They couldn't really be examined then.''

"You're forgettin' the broken jar o' applesauce,'' April said. "Don't that prove Hank was on the bridge?''

"Nothing of the sort! Hank knew in advance his ma planned to send the applesauce to Mrs. O'Brian. He prob'ly suggested it, and he certainly reminded her of it. He simply gave Walt Rumsey a duplicate jar a day or two earlier, an' it was that jar Walt broke on the bridge. The jar Hank was carrying went with him into Walt's barn.''

"What if it hadn't snowed that mornin'? What if someone else came along first to leave other tracks?''

I shrugged. "They would've phoned one another and postponed it, I s'pose. It was only meant as a joke. They'd have tried again some other day, with other witnesses. They didn't really need me an' Millie.''

"Then how did it turn from a joke into murder?''

"Walt Rumsey had never given up lovin' Millie, or hatin' Hank for takin' her away from him. After the trick worked so well, he saw the perfect chance to kill Hank and win her back. Once I knew he was in on the trick, he had to be the killer—else why was he keepin' quiet 'bout his part in it?

"Hank had hidden his horse an' buggy in that big shed behind the Rumsey barn. When we all went back to town, an' Hank was ready to reappear an' have a good laugh on everyone, Walt Rumsey killed him. Then he waited till dark to dispose of the body on the Post Road. He drove the buggy part way, turned the horse loose to run, and walked home.

"This mornin' after the funeral I made an excuse of wantin' a piece of rope so I could see the inside of Rumsey's barn again. He had spare carriage wheels there, and the shed was big enough to hold a horse an' buggy. That was all the confirmation I needed."

April leaned back and smiled, convinced at last. "After this they'll probably give you the Sheriff's job, Dr. Sam."

I shook my head. "I'm just a country doctor."

"A country doctor with a Pierce-Arrow car!" . . .

"That's the way it happened, back in '22. I've often thought I should write it up now that I'm retired, but there's just never enough time. Sure, I've got other stories. Lots of 'em! Can I get you another—ah—small libation?"

Hurting Much?

CORNELL WOOLRICH

According to an old saw, "No man is a hero to his dentist." The detective in this typically harrowing Woolrich thriller, however, proves that axiom wrong, and in very convincing fashion. Cornell George Hopley Woolrich (1903–1968) was a tragic figure who lived most of his life in New York City hotel rooms, both alone and with his domineering mother. The sense of unfulfillment and doom that plagued him throughout his life is one of the reasons he was able to depict terror in his fiction with such striking authenticity; no writer past or present rivals him in the evocation of such dread and suspense as can be found in The Bride Wore Black (1940), Phantom Lady (1942, as William Irish), and his many other novels and short stories.

THERE WAS another patient ahead of me in the waiting room. He was sitting there quietly, humbly, with all the terrible resignation of the very poor. He wasn't all jittery and alert the way I was, but just sat there ready to take anything that came, head bowed a little as though he had found life just a succession of hard knocks. His gaze met mine and I suppose he could tell how uncomfortable I was by the look on my face but instead of grinning about it or cracking wise he put himself out to encourage me, cheer me up. When I thought of this afterward it did something to me.

"He not hurt you," he murmured across to me confidentially. "Odder dantist say he very good, you no feel notting at all when he drill."

I showed my gratitude by offering him a cigarette. Misery loves company.

With that, Steve Standish came in from the back, buttoning his white jacket. The moment he saw me, professional etiquette was thrown to the winds. "Well, well, Rodge, so it's finally come to this, has it? I knew I'd get you sooner or later!"

I gave a weak grin and tried to act nonchalant. Finally he said in oh, the most casual manner, "Come on in, Rodge, and let's have a look."

I suddenly discovered myself to be far more considerate of others than I had hitherto suspected. "This—er—this man was here ahead of me, Steve." Anything to gain five minutes' time.

He glanced at his other patient, carelessly but by no means unkindly or disdainfully. "Yes, but you've got to get down to your office—he probably has the day off. You in a hurry?" he asked.

"Thass all right, I no mine, I got no work," the man answered affably.

"No, Steve, I insist," I said.

"Okay, if that's the way you feel about it," he answered genially. "Be right with you." And he ushered the other patient inside ahead of him. I saw him wink at the man, but at the moment I didn't much care what he thought of my courage. No man is a hero to his dentist.

And not long afterward, I was to wonder if that little attack of "cold feet" hadn't been the luckiest thing that ever happened to me.

Steve closed his office door after him, but the partition between the two rooms had evidently been put in long after everything else in the place. It was paper-thin and only reached three-quarters of the way up; every sound that came from the other side was perfectly audible to me where I sat, fidgeting and straining my ears for indications of anguish. But first of all there was a little matter of routine to be gone through. "I guess I'll have to take your name and pedigree myself," Steve's voice boomed out jovially. "It's my assistant's day off."

"Amato Saltone, plizz."

"And where do you live, Amato?" Steve had a way with these people. Not patronizing, just forthright and friendly.

"Two twanny Thirr Avenue. If you plizz, mista."

There was a slight pause. I pictured Steve jotting down the information on a card and filing it away. Then he got down to business. "Now what seems to be the trouble?"

The man had evidently adjusted himself in the chair, meanwhile. Presumably he simply held his mouth open and let Steve find out for himself, because it was again Steve who spoke: "This one?" I visualized him plying his mirror and maybe playing around with one of those sharp little things that look like crochet hooks. All at once his voice had become impatient, indignant even. "What do you call that thing you've got in there? I never saw a filling like it in my life. Looks like the Boulder Dam! Who put it in for you—some bricklayer?"

"Docata Jones, Feefatty-nine Stree'," the man said.

"Never heard of him. He send you here to me?" Steve asked sharply. "You'd think he'd have decency enough to clean up his own messes! I suppose there wasn't enough in it for him. Well, that headstone you've got in there has to come out first of all, and you just pay me whatever you can afford as we go along. I'd be ashamed to let a man walk out of my office with a botched-up job like that in his mouth!''

The next thing that came to my ears was the faint whirring of the electric drill, sounding not much louder than if there had been a fly buzzing around the room over my head.

I heard Steve speak just once more, and what he said was that immemorial question of the dentist, ''Hurting much?'' The man groaned in answer, but it was a most peculiar groan. Even at the instant of hearing it, it struck me there was something different about it. It sounded so hollow and far away, as though it had come from the very depths of his being, and broke off so suddenly at the end.

He didn't make another sound after that. But whatever it was, it had taken more than a mere twinge of pain to make him groan like that. Or was it just my own overwrought nerves that made me imagine it?

An instant later I knew I had been right. Steve's voice told me that something out of the ordinary had happened. ''Here, hold your head up so I can get at you,'' he said. At first jokingly, and then—''Here! What's the matter with you?'' Alarm crept in. ''Wake up, will you? Wake up!'' Alarm turned into panic. ''Rodge!'' he called out to me.

But I was on my feet already and half across the waiting room, my own trivial fears a thing of the past. He threw the door open before I got to it and looked out at me. His face was white. ''This fellow—something's happened to him, he's turning cold here in the chair and I can't bring him to!''

I brushed past him and bent over the figure hunched in the chair. Horrible to relate, his mouth was still wide open. I touched his forehead; it was already cooler by far than the palm of my hand, and clammy to the touch. I tried to rouse him by shaking him—no good—then felt for his heart. There was no heartbeat any more. Steve was on the other side of him, holding his dental mirror before the open mouth. We both watched it fascinatedly; it stayed clear as crystal.

"He's gone," I muttered. "What do you make of it?"

"I'm going to try oxygen," Steve babbled. He was hauling down a big, clumsy-looking cylinder from a shelf with jerky, spasmodic movements that showed how badly shaken he was. "You'd better send in a call for an ambulance—hurry!"

The phone was outside in the waiting room; that didn't take any time at all. When I came back there was a mask over the man's face and a tube leading from his mouth to the cylinder. Steve was just standing there helplessly. Every few seconds he'd touch a little wheel-shaped valve on the cylinder, but the indicator showed that it was already as wide open as it could go. "Keep your hand on his heart," he said to me hoarsely.

It was no use. By the time the ambulance doctor and a policeman got there, Steve had taken the tube out and turned off the oxygen.

The ambulance doctor took one look as he came in and then told us what we already knew. "All up, eh?" he said. He then stretched the man out on the floor, with the help of the cop, and began to examine him. I cleared out of the room at this point and sat down to wait outside—fully imagining I was being bighearted and staying on of my own free will to brace Steve up instead of going somewhere more cheerful. It would all be over in another five or ten minutes, I thought unsuspectingly, and then maybe Steve and I had better go and have a drink together someplace.

The patrolman came out to me and asked if I'd been in there when it happened. I told him no, I'd been out here waiting my turn. I was about to add for no particular reason that I was a very good friend of Steve's and not just a stray patient, when things began to happen rapidly.

So far everything had been routine on their part. But now the ambulance doctor finished his examination and came out, kit in hand, Steve trailing after him. What he had to say was to the policeman, not to Steve at all. "It wasn't his heart," he said. "Better phone Headquarters and tell the coroner to come up here. He might want to bring a couple of the boys with him."

"What's up?" Steve tried to sound casual but he wasn't very good at it. The cop was already at the phone.

"Not natural causes at all," the doctor said grimly. He wouldn't say anything more than that. The shrug he gave plainly meant, "It's not my job." I thought he looked at Steve a little peculiarly as he closed the door after him.

The cop became noticeably less friendly after that; he remained standing to one side of the door and had a watchful air about him. Once when Steve made a move to go back into the outer room, his upper lip lifted after the manner of a mastiff with a bone and he growled warningly, "Take it easy, fellow."

They didn't take long to get there, the coroner and "a couple of the boys." They looked more like high-powered real estate agents to me, but this was the first time I'd ever been in the same room with a detective.

"What's up?" began one of them, lingering with us while the coroner and his pal went inside.

Steve told him the little there was to tell; the man had climbed into his chair, Steve had started to drill, and the man had gone out like a light. No, he'd never treated him before, never even laid eyes on him until five minutes before he'd died.

That was all there was to this first session—a harmless little chat, you might call it. The cop went back to the beat, a stretcher arrived, and poor Amato Saltone departed, his troubles at an end. Steve's, though, were just beginning—and possibly mine with them. The second detective came out with the coroner, and the atmosphere, which hadn't been any too cordial, all at once became definitely hostile.

"Cyanide of potassium," snapped the coroner. "Just enough to kill—not a grain more, not a grain less. I pumped his stomach, but the traces were all over the roof of his mouth and the lining of his throat anyway." And he too departed.

The second detective held the inner door open and said,

"Come inside, Dr. Standish." It wasn't said as politely as it reads in print.

I've already mentioned that every word spoken could be heard through or over the partition. But I was only allowed to hear the opening broadside—and that was ominous enough. "Where do you keep your cyanide, Dr. Standish?"

As soon as he realized what the acoustics of the place were, the detective who had remained with me immediately suggested, with heavy emphasis, "Let's just step out in the hall."

After we'd been standing out there smoking a while, Steve's office phone rang. My guardian took it upon himself to answer it, making sure that I came with him, so I had a chance to overhear the wind-up of Steve's quizzing. The call itself was simply from a patient, and the detective took pains to inform her that Dr. Standish had canceled all appointments for the rest of the day.

I didn't like the way that sounded; nor did I like the turn the questioning had taken.

"So a man that's going to commit suicide goes to all the trouble of having a cavity filled in his mouth just before he does it, does he?" Steve's interrogator was saying as we came in. "What for—to make himself beautiful for St. Peter?"

Steve was indignant by now. "You've got a nerve trying to tack anything on me! He may have eaten something deadly outside without knowing it and then only got the effects after he was in my chair."

"Not cyanide, pal—it works instantly. And it isn't given away for nothing either. A fellow of that type would have jumped off a subway platform, it's cheaper. Where would he have the money or drag to buy cyanide? He probably couldn't even pronounce the name. Now why don't you make it easy for yourself and admit that you had an accident?"

Steve's voice broke. "Because I had nothing to do with it, accidentally or otherwise!"

"So you're willing to have us think you did it purposely, eh? Keenan!" he called out.

We both went in there, Keenan just a step in back of me to guide me.

"There's no trace of where he kept it hidden, but it's all over his drill thick as jam," Keenan's teammate reported. He detached the apparatus from the tripod it swung on, carefully wrapped it in tissue paper, and put it in his pocket.

"I'm going to book you," he said. "Come on, you're coming down to Headquarters with me."

Steve swayed a little, then got a grip on himself. "Am I under arrest?" he faltered.

"Well," remarked the detective sarcastically, "this is no invitation to a Park Avenue ball."

"What about this fellow?" Keenan indicated me. "Bring him along too?"

"He might be able to contribute something," was the reply.

So down to Headquarters we went and I lost sight of Steve as soon as we got there. They kept me waiting around for a while, then questioned me. But I could tell that I wasn't being held as an accessory. I suppose my puffed-out cheek was more in my favor than anything else—although why a man suffering from toothache would be less likely to be an accessory to murder than anyone else I failed to see. They didn't even look to see if it was a phony; for all they knew I could have had a wad of cotton stuffed in my mouth.

I told them everything there was to tell, not even omitting to mention the cigarette I had given the man when we were both sitting in the waiting room. It was only after I'd said this that I realized how bad it sounded for me if they cared to look at it that way. The cyanide could just as easily have been concealed in that cigarette. Luckily they'd already picked up and examined the butt (he hadn't had time to smoke more than half of it) and found it to be okay. Who says the innocent don't run as great a risk as the guilty?

I told them all I could about Steve and as soon as I was cleared and told I could go home, I embarked on a lengthy plea in his defense, assuring them they were making the biggest mistake of their lives.

"What motive could he possibly have?" I argued. "Check up on him, you'll find he has a home in Forest Hills, two cars, a walloping practice, goes to all the first nights at the theater! What did that jobless Third Avenue slob have that *he* needed? Why, I heard him with my own ears tell the guy not to be in a hurry about paying the bill! Where's your motive? They came from two different worlds!"

All I got was the remark, Why didn't I join the squad and get paid for my trouble, and the suggestion, Why didn't I go home now?

One of them, Keenan, who turned out to be a rather likable sort after all, took me aside and explained very patiently as to a ten-year-old child: "There's only three possibilities in this case, see? Suicide, accidental poisoning, and poisoning on purpose. Now your own friend himself is the one that has blocked up the first two, not us. We were willing to give him every chance, in the beginning. But no, he insists the guy didn't once lift his hands from under that linen apron to take the stuff himself—to take it out of his pocket and pop it in his mouth, for instance. Standish claims he never even once turned his back on him while he was in the chair, and that the fellow's hands stayed folded in his lap *under* the bib the whole time. Says he noticed that because everyone else always grabs the arms of the chair and hangs on. So that's out.

"And secondly he swears he has never kept any such stuff around the place as cyanide, in any shape or form, so it couldn't have got on the drill by accident. So *that's* out too. What have you got left? Poisoning on purpose—which has a one-word name: murder. That's all today—and be sure you don't leave town until after the trial. You'll be needed on the witness stand."

I spent the rest of the night with a wet handkerchief pasted against my cheek, doing some heavy thinking. Every word Steve and the victim had spoken behind the partition passed before me in review. "Where do you live, Amato? Two-twanny Thirr Avenue, mista." I'd start in from there.

I took an interpreter with me, a fellow on my own office staff who knew a little of everything from Eskimo to Greek. I wasn't taking any chances.

There seemed to be dozens of them; they lived in a cold-water flat on the third floor rear. The head of the clan was Amato's rather stout wife. I concentrated on her; when a fellow has a toothache he'll usually tell his wife all about it.

"Ask her where this Doctor Jones lived who sent him to Standish."

She didn't know, Amato hadn't even told her what the dentist's name was. Hadn't they a bill from the man to show me? (I wanted to prove that Amato had been there.) No, no bill, but that didn't matter because Amato couldn't read anyway, and even if he had been able to, there was no money to pay it with.

If he couldn't read, I persisted, how had he known where to find a dentist?

She shrugged. Maybe he was going by and saw the dentist at work through a window.

I went through the entire family, from first to last, and got nowhere. Amato had done plenty of howling and calling on the saints in the depths of the night, and even kept some of the younger children quiet at times by letting them look at his bad tooth; but as for telling them where, when, or by whom it had been treated, it never occurred to him.

So I was not only no further but I had even lost a good deal of confidence. "Docata Jones" began to look pretty much like a myth. Steve hadn't known him, either. But the man had said Fifty-ninth Street. With all due respect for the dead, I didn't think Amato had brains enough to make up even that little out of his head. I'd have to try that angle next, and unaided, since Amato's family had turned out to be a bust.

I tackled the phone book first, hoping for a short cut. Plenty of Joneses, D.D.S., but not a single one on Fifty-ninth. Nor even one on Fifty-seventh or Fifty-eighth or Sixtieth, in case Amato was dumb enough not even to know which street he'd been on. The good old-fashioned way was all that was left.

I swallowed a malted milk, tied a double knot in my shoelaces, and started out on foot, westward from the Queensboro Bridge. I went into every lobby, every hallway, every basement; I scanned every sign in every window, every card in every mail box. I consulted every superintendent in every walk-up, every starter in every building with an elevator, every landlady in every rooming house.

I followed the street west until it became fashionable Central Park South, then farther still as it turned into darkest San Juan Hill, giving a lot of attention to the Vanderbilt Clinic on Tenth Avenue, and finally came smack up against the speedway bordering the Hudson, with my feet burning me like blazes. No results. No Dr. Jones. It took me all the first day and most of the second. At 2 P.M. Thursday I was back again at the Bridge.

I got out and stood on the corner smoking a cigarette. I'd used the wrong method, that was all. I'd been rational about it, Amato had been instinctive. What had his wife said? He was going by and most likely saw some dentist working behind a window and that decided him. I'd been looking for a dentist, he hadn't—until he happened on one. I'd have to put myself in his place to get the right step.

I walked back two blocks to Third Avenue and started out afresh. Amato had lived on Third Avenue, so he had probably walked all the way up it looking for work until he got to Fifty-ninth, and then turned either east or west. West there was a department store on one side, a five-and-ten and a furniture store on the other; they wouldn't interest him. East there was a whole line of mangy little shops and stalls; I turned east. I trudged along; I was Amato now, worrying about where my next dollar was coming from, not thinking about my tooth at all—at least, not just at that moment.

A shadow fell before me on the sidewalk. I looked up. A huge, swaying, papier-mâché gold tooth was hanging out over the doorway. It was the size of a football at least. Even Amato would have known what it was there for. Maybe he'd got a bad twinge just then. The only trouble was—I'd seen it myself yesterday, it was almost the first thing that had caught my eye when I started out. I'd investigated, you may be sure. And the card on the window said *Dr. Carter*, as big as life. That was out—or was it? Amato couldn't read; "Carter" wouldn't mean any more to him than "Jones." But then where had he got "Jones" from? Familiar as it is, it would have been as foreign to him as his own name was to me.

No use going any farther, though. If that gold tooth hadn't made up Amato's mind for him, nothing else the whole length of the street could have. I was on the point of going in, for a quick once-over, but a hurried glance at my own appearance decided me not to. Serge business suit, good hat, dusty but well-heeled shoes. Whatever happened to Amato, if he *had* gone in there, wasn't likely to happen to anyone dressed the way I was. If I was going to put myself in his place, I ought to try to look like him. And there were a few other things, too, still out of focus.

I jumped in a cab and chased down to Headquarters. I didn't think they'd let me see Steve, but somehow I managed to wangle it. I suppose Keenan had a hand in it. And then too, Steve hadn't cracked yet; that may have had something to do with it.

"What enemies have you?" I shot out. There wasn't much time.

"None," he said. "I never harmed anyone in my life."

"Think hard," I begged. "You've got to help me. Maybe 'way back, maybe some little thing."

"Nope," he insisted, "my life's been a bed of roses until the day before yesterday."

"Let's skip that and look at it the other way around. Who are your friends—outside of myself?"

He ran over a list of names as long as a timetable. He left out one, though. "And Dave Carter?" I supplied. "Know him?"

He nodded cheerfully. "Sure, but how did you know? We

used to be pretty chummy. I haven't seen him in years, though—
we drifted apart. We started out together, both working in the
same office I have now. Then he moved out on me—thought he
could do better by himself, I guess."

"And did he?"

"He hit the skids. All the patients kept on coming to me, for
some reason, and he just sat there in his spic-and-span office
twiddling his thumbs. Inside of six months the overhead was too
much for him and here's the payoff: he ended up having to move
into a place ten times worse than the one he'd shared with me.
What with one thing and another, I lent him quite a bit of money
which I never got back."

"Did he turn sour on you?"

"Not at all. Last time I saw him he slapped me on the back
and said, 'More power to you, Stevie, you're a better man than I
am!' "

"In your hat!" I thought skeptically. "When was the last time
you saw him?"

"Years back. As a matter of fact, I clean forgot him until
you—"

I stood up to go without waiting for him to finish. "Excuse the
rush, but I've got things to do."

"Dig me up a good lawyer, will you?" he called after me.
"Price no object."

"You don't need a lawyer," I shouted back. "All you need is a
little dash of suspicion in your nature. Like me."

I got Keenan to take me in and introduce me to the chief. The
chief was regular, but a tough nut to crack. Still he must have
been in good humor that day. If he reads this, no offense meant,
but the cigars he smokes are awful. I had a proposition to make
to him, and two requests. One of them he gave in to almost at
once—loving newspapermen the way he did. The other he said
he'd think over. As for the proposition itself, he said it wasn't so
hot, but to go ahead and try it if I felt like it, only not to blame
anyone but myself if I got into trouble.

From Headquarters I went straight to a pawnshop on Third Avenue. It was long after dark, but they stay open until nine. I bought a suit of clothes for six bucks. The first one the man showed me I handed back to him. "That's the best I can give you—" he started in.

"I don't want the best, I want the worst," I said, much to his surprise. I got it all right.

From there I went to a second pawnshop and purchased what had once been an overcoat. Price, four-fifty. The coat and suit were both ragged, patched, and faded, but at least the pawnbroker had kept them brushed off; I fixed that with the help of a barrel of ashes I passed a few doors away. I also traded hats with a panhandler who crossed my path, getting possession of the peculiar shapeless mound he had been wearing on his head.

I trundled all this stuff home and managed to hide it from my wife. In the morning, though, when she saw me arrayed in it from head to foot, she let out a yell and all but sank to the floor. "Now never mind the hysterics," I reproved. "Papa knows just what he's doing!"

"If this has anything to do with Steve, you're a day late," she told me when she was through giggling. "They've dismissed the case against him." She held out the morning paper to me.

I didn't bother looking at it; in the first place, it was one of the two requests I'd made at Headquarters the night before; in the second place, it wasn't true.

Keenan was waiting for me on the southwest corner of Fifty-ninth and Second, as per agreement. Anyone watching us would have thought our behavior odd, to say the least. I went up to him and opened my mouth as if I were Joe E. Brown making faces at him. "It's that tooth up there, that molar on the right side. Take a good look at it." He did. This was for purposes of evidence. "Got the picture?" He nodded. "I'm going in now, where that gold tooth is, halfway down the block. Back in half an hour. Wait here for me and keep your fingers crossed."

This statement wasn't quite accurate, though. I was sure I was going in where the gold tooth was, but I wasn't sure I was coming back in half an hour—I wasn't sure I was coming back at all, any time.

I left him abruptly and went into the office of Dr. David Carter. I was cold and scared. The accent bothered me too. I decided a brogue would be safest. No foreign languages for me. Carter was a short, dumpy little man, as good-natured and harmless-looking as you'd want. Only his eyes gave him away: slits they were, little malevolent pig eyes. The eyes had it; they told me I wasn't wasting my time. The office was a filthy, rundown place. Instead of a partition, the dental chair was right in the room, with a screen around it. There was an odor of stale gas around.

My feet kept begging me to get up and run out of there while I still had the chance. I couldn't, though; Keenan was waiting on the corner. I wanted to keep his respect.

Carter was standing over me; he didn't believe in the daily bath, either. "Well, young fellow?" he said sleekly. I pointed sorrowfully at my cheek, which had been more or less inflated for the past three days. The pain had gone out of it long ago, however. Pain and a swelling rarely go together, contrary to general belief.

"So I see," he said, but made no move to do anything about it. "What brings you here to me?" he asked craftily.

"Sure 'tis the ellygant gold tooth ye have out, boss," I answered shakily. Did that sound Irish enough? I wondered. Evidently it did.

"Irishman, eh?" he told me, not very cleverly. "What's your name?"

"McConnaughy." I'd purposely picked a tongue-twister, to get the point across I was trying to make.

He bit. "How do you spell it?"

"Sure, I don't know now," I smiled wanly. "I nivver in me life learned to spell." That was the point I was trying to make.

"Can't read or write, eh?" He seemed pleased rather than disappointed. "Didn't you ever go to school when you were a kid?"

"I minded the pigs and such," I croaked forlornly.

He suddenly whipped out a newspaper he'd been holding behind his back and shoved it under my nose. "What d'you think of that?" It was upside down. He was trying to catch me off guard, hoping I'd turn it right side up without thinking and give myself away. I kept my hand off it. "What do it say?" I queried helplessly.

He tossed it aside. "I guess you can't read, at that," he said. But the presence of the newspaper meant that he already knew Steve was back in circulation; the item had been in all of them that morning.

He motioned me to the chair. I climbed into it. I was too curious to see what would happen next to be really frightened. Otherwise how could I have sat in it at all? He took a cursory glance into my mouth—almost an absent-minded glance, as if his thoughts were really elsewhere. "Can you pay me?" he said next, still very absent-minded and not looking at me at all.

"I'll do me best, sorr. I have no job."

"Tell you what I'll do for you," he said suddenly. "I'll give you temporary relief, and then I'll send you to someone who'll finish the job for you. He won't charge you anything, either. You just tell him Doctor Smith sent you."

My heart started to go like a triphammer. So I was on the right track after all, was I? He'd picked a different name this time to cover up his traces, that was all.

He got to work. He pulled open a drawer and I saw a number of fragile clay caps or crowns, hollow inside and thin as tissue paper. They were about the size and shape of thimbles. I could hardly breathe any more. Steve's voice came back to me, indignantly questioning Amato: "Looks like the Boulder Dam . . . some bricklayer put it in for you?"

He took one of these out and closed the drawer. Then he opened another drawer and took something else out. But this time I couldn't see what it was, because he carefully stood over it with his back to me. He glanced over his shoulder at me to see if I was watching him. I beat him to it and lowered my eyes to my lap. He closed the second drawer. But I knew which one it was: the lower right in a cabinet of six.

He came over to me. "Open," he commanded. My eyes rolled around in their sockets. I still had time to rear up out of the chair, push him back, and snatch the evidence out of his hand. But I wasn't sure yet whether or not it *was* evidence.

Those caps may have been perfectly legitimate, for all I knew; I was no dentist. So I sat quiet, paralyzed with fear, unable to move.

And the whole thing was over almost before it had begun. He sprayed a little something on the tooth, waxed it with hot grease, and stuck the cap on over it. No drilling, no dredging, no cleansing whatever. "That's all," he said with an evil grin. "But remember, it's only temporary. By tomorrow at the latest you go to this other dentist and he'll finish the job for you."

I saw the point at once. He hadn't cleaned the tooth in the least; in an hour or two it would start aching worse than ever and I'd *have* to go to the other dentist. The same thing must have happened to Amato. I was in for it now! "Don't chew on that side," he warned me, "until you see him." He didn't want it to happen to me at home or at some coffee counter, but in Steve's office, in Steve's chair!

Then he gave me the name and place I was to go to. "Standish, Twenty-eight and Lexington, second floor." Over and over again. "Will you remember that?"

That was all I needed—I had the evidence against him now. But I didn't make a hostile move toward him; instead, I stumbled out into the street and swayed toward the corner where Keenan was waiting for me. Let the cops go after him. I had myself to worry about now. I was carrying Death in my mouth. Any minute, the slightest little jolt—

Keenan had been joined by a second detective. They both came toward me and held me up by the elbows. I managed to get my mouth open and Keenan looked in. "Get the difference?" I gasped.

"It begins to look like you were right," he muttered.

He phoned the chief at Headquarters and then got me into a taxi with him. The second man was left there to keep an eye on Carter and tail him if he left his office.

"What're you holding your mouth open like that for?" he asked me in the cab.

"A sudden jolt of the taxi might knock my teeth together," I whispered. I had seen how thin those caps were.

We raced down Lexington and got out at Steve's office. Steve had been rushed up there from the detention pen in a police car, along with the chief himself and two more detectives. He had to have facilities if he was going to save me from what had happened to Amato.

"He's got the evidence," Keenan informed them as I pointed to my mouth. "In there," I gasped, and my knees buckled under me.

Steve got me into the chair. Sweat broke out on his face after he'd taken one look at Carter's work, but he tried to reassure me. "All right, all right now," he said soothingly. "You know I won't let you down."

He looked around at them. The chief had his usual rank cigar in his mouth, which had gone out in the excitement. One of the others held a pipe between his clenched teeth.

"Where's your tobacco pouch?" asked Steve hoarsely. "Let me have it, I'll get you a new one."

The lining was thin rubber. He tore that out, scattering tobacco all over the floor. Then he held it up to the light and stretched it to see if there were any holes. Then, with a tiny pair of curved scissors, he cut a small wedge-shaped hole in it. "Now hold your mouth wide open," he said to me, "and whatever you do, don't move!" He lined the inside of my mouth with the rubber, carefully working the tooth Carter had just treated through the hole he had cut, so that it was inside the rubber. The ends of the rubber lining he left protruding through my lips. I felt as if I were choking. "Can you breathe?" he said. I batted my eyes to show him he could go ahead.

He thrust wedges into my cheeks so that I couldn't close my jaws whether I wanted to or not. Then he came out with a tiny mallet and a little chisel, about the size of a nail. "I may be able to get it out whole," he explained to the chief. "It's been in less than half an hour. Drilling is too risky."

His face, as he bent over me, was white as plaster. I shut my eyes and thought, "Well, here I go—or here I stay!" I felt a number of dull blows on my jawbone. Then suddenly something seemed to crumble and a puff of ice-cold air went way up inside my head. I lay there rigid and—nothing happened.

"Got it!" Steve breathed hotly into my face. He started to work the rubber lining carefully out past my lips and I felt a little sick. When it was clear he passed it over to the detectives without even a look at its contents, and kept his attention focused on me. "Now, watch yourself—don't move yet!" he commanded nervously. He took a spray and rinsed out the inside of my mouth, every corner and crevice of it. "Don't swallow," he kept warning me. "Keep from swallowing!" Meanwhile, Keenan, his chief, and the others had their heads together over the spread-out contents of the little rubber lining.

Finally Steve turned off the water and took the pads away from my gums. He sat down with a groan; I sat up with a shudder. "I wouldn't want to live the past five minutes over again for all the rice in China!" he admitted, mopping his brow.

"Packed with cyanide crystals," the chief said. "Go up there and make the pinch. Two counts, murder and attempted murder." Two men started for the door.

"Top drawer left for the caps, bottom drawer right for the cy," I called after them weakly and rather needlessly. They'd find it, all right.

But I was very weary all at once and very much disinterested. I stumbled out of the chair and slouched toward the door, muttering something about going home and resting up. Steve pulled himself together and called me back.

"Don't forget the nerve is still exposed in that tooth of yours.

I'll plug it for you right this time." I sat down again, too limp to resist. He attached a new drill to the pulley and started it whirring. As he brought it toward me I couldn't help edging away from it. "Can you beat it?" He turned to Keenan, who had stayed behind, and shook his head in hopeless amazement. "Takes his life in his hands for a friend, but when it comes to a little ordinary drilling he can't face it!"

The Memorial Hour

WADE MILLER

><

Wade Miller was the pseudonym of San Diego writers Robert Wade and Bill Miller, who also wrote as Whit Masterson, Dale Wilmer, and Will Daemer. (When Miller died suddenly in 1961, Wade continued to produce crime fiction under the Masterson name and also under his own name, abandoning the other pseudonyms.) Much of the Wade Miller output was in the hardboiled vein—the Max Thursday private eye novels, for instance, among them such titles as Guilty Bystander *(1947) and* Shoot to Kill *(1951)—but they also wrote straight suspense stories, offbeat crime fiction, tales of adventure, and humorous mysteries. "The Memorial Hour" is, appropriately, psychological suspense featuring psychiatrist John Kermit Conover; it is also one of Wade and Miller's most accomplished short stories.*

JACKIE, to my annoyance, made his first appearance in my office at three o'clock on a Thursday afternoon.

For the past year I had kept that particular time open for meditation since it was the hour that my wife Helen met her death in the automobile accident. Not even my receptionist knew that these weekly periods were memorial in nature; I let her believe I was taking a mental coffee break.

Nor was this a deception, for a psychiatrist can only absorb so much of other people's problems before he feels the need to clear his mind. And in the year since Helen died, I had been working very hard—burying my sorrow in my practice so to speak.

Consequently, I was disturbed to see a new patient usurping the hour that I considered my own private affair. Though I had no choice but to make the best of it, I intended to reprimand Linda, my receptionist, for her thoughtlessness with the appointment book. As it turned out, I became so caught up in the abnormality of the case that I never did correct her.

My new patient, a virile young man, acted as if he realized his presence was unwelcome. He slouched in the big leather chair opposite me, fixed his eyes on the wall above my head, and read aloud my credentials in a mocking voice. " 'Know all men by these presents that John Kermit Conover, having completed the studies prescribed by law . . .' Oh, surely that must give you godlike powers, Dr. Conover."

"Not at all." No need to take offense; many frayed personalities react defensively to the analyst at first. "The diplomas merely demonstrate that I've had some seven years of certain special training. I'm only another man, like yourself."

"No," he said quickly. He was strangely anxious. "No, we can't be anything alike." In appearance, at least, he was right. He had the smooth athletic grace of youth, the good looks of health and eagerness, and he seemed expensively well-dressed, while I . . . well, I am now fifty-three, as conservative and quiet and gray as my office walls.

"Suppose we begin with your name," I suggested.

He relaxed into his former arrogance. "Jackie Newman?" he asked with a smile. I had no doubt that it was fictitious, not that this would be especially unusual. "You call me Jackie. I'm afraid we're going to see a lot of each other."

"All right, Jackie. I hope I may be able to help you. However—"

"Look, you've got it framed there on the wall that you're a psychiatrist. You solve people's problems, don't you?"

"Not exactly. Everyone must solve his own problems. My job is to help you uncover and understand what your problem really is. Then you supply the therapy."

"Oh, nice setup," Jackie snorted. "You get the fee while I do the work."

"It's significant that you look at it that way. Do you often have feelings of being cheated?" He stared at me angrily but didn't answer. "You see, as a detached observer, I'm frequently able to detect what the patient is too emotionally bound up in to see for himself. Then I'm able to help."

Jackie dropped his head. "You can't help me," he muttered. "Nobody can. I already know what is wrong with me."

"Then let's talk about it."

"I'm afraid," he said simply. His face, free of the taut lines of arrogance, turned soft and childlike. "Unless something stops me, I know I'm going to do something bad."

"How do you mean—bad?"

"You know." His right hand twitched in a small clawing gesture. "Something violent—hurt somebody."

I reassured him that the urge to violence is imbedded in us all. It is better that the patient not think himself wholly unnatural. "Now, have you ever done anything violent, Jackie?"

"No. Not yet. But lately—well, I've been taking things, stealing . . ."

"What sort of things?"

He folded his arms, as if hugging something tightly against his chest. "Oh, things." He kept his eyes on the upright desk pen in front of me. "Nothing I actually need. But I wanted to—I get this wanting feeling inside that makes me keep taking them, more all the time."

I tried to probe deeper but with no results. What were his emotions at the time of the act? How did he feel about it afterward? I knew that the nature of the stolen objects would provide a key to his compulsion, but Jackie kept sliding away from the subject. "I'm not worried about the stealing!" he finally burst out petulantly. "It's the other thing—what I told you before."

"You believe that theft is the stepping stone to something worse, is that it?"

"Well, I keep getting urges, like I was foaming inside. Like just taking things isn't enough. Like there's something even better I could do."

"Can you give me an example?"

All he gave me was a knowing smile. Nor would he admit to any dreaming, when I took that tack. Psychiatry is the only branch of medicine where the patient will conceal his symptoms, hide them even from himself. But the outstanding fact that Jackie had come to me at all was encouraging, so I said, "Let's go about it another way. Tell me about yourself."

He related his history with some pride. It was a rambling discourse and the more I heard, the more dead certain I became that he was making it up as he went along. Although totally alone in the world now, he claimed to have come from a wealthy family upstate, to have served with distinction in the Army—"I got the Purple Heart twice"—and, following this, to have pursued several vocations, among them automobile racing and uranium prospecting. In view of his youth, his story sounded somewhat incredible.

He must have sensed my disbelief because he broke off abruptly. "How do you like it so far?" he demanded. "Are you jealous?"

"Let's say that you've raised certain questions in my mind."

"Well, they'll have to wait," he said brusquely, and rose. "Either I'll see you next week or I won't. I'm like that."

Not until after Jackie was gone did it occur to me that I'd failed to tell him that this particular appointment hour was inconvenient. Then, examining my own reactions, I decided that my omission was intentional: I wanted Jackie to return. He displayed, bad manners and all, possibilities that gripped my interest beyond the cloudy merits of his case.

My receptionist came in. "Doctor, Mrs. Greer has canceled out on her four o'clock. Some unexpected company. She hoped you wouldn't mind."

"It suits me fine," I told her. "That last patient gave me a splitting headache."

"I'll get you some aspirin," she said, instantly solicitous. I often wondered what prompted Linda to choose to work for a psychiatrist; she is such a completely uncomplicated personality. A pretty brunette, her buxom femininity and animal vitality sometimes struck me as incongruous amid the neuroses and psychoses of my practice, as if she were moving cheerily among the dead. Yet she was efficient enough and though not a graduate nurse, she fulfilled many of a nurse's functions. "By the way, Doctor, I was wondering—since we don't have anybody else coming in today—if I could get away a little early. It's our anniversary and Ed and I were planning to have dinner in town and maybe go to a show."

"Anniversary? Has it been a year already?"

"No, just six months." Linda giggled. "It probably sounds silly to you—but we're still so darn thrilled about being married . . ."

"Don't apologize for being happy," I said. "So few people are."

I thought about Jackie quite a bit during the next week, though I was by no means sure I would ever see him again. However, he appeared on schedule the following Thursday. This time he was sullen and less communicative, except to admit that he was still stealing "things."

In his depressed state he had either forgotten or discarded his previous account of his life; what little he would tell of his background varied greatly from before but sounded to me more probable. The one solid nugget of information I uncovered was that Jackie had briefly attended the same university as I, but I was unable to exploit this common experience to establish the rapport I desired.

He had quit school out of boredom, and he mumbled something about the girls there that I didn't catch and he wouldn't repeat. It included the phrase "sweaters and bare legs," and I surmised privately that his trouble was sex-centered but he wouldn't respond to that line of questioning either. Nor would he speak at all of the seven-year period following college, muttering, "Why talk about it? It's all over." Or—his favorite form of dismissal—"It isn't important."

The consultation left me somewhat despondent, partly the gloomy contagion of his own mood but mostly because I felt I was getting nowhere.

Yet the following week Jackie surprised me by bringing with him in a shopping bag the articles he had stolen. They bore out my first theory as to the center of his trouble. The "things" turned out to be brassieres—most of them fancy with lace or bright in color—and he was compulsively explicit as to when and where he had taken each one. Some had come from clotheslines in various parts of the city, but many of them were new with price tags still attached.

"Why are you telling me this today when you wouldn't before?" I asked.

"Because I'm finished." Jackie was jubilant, pacing back and forth excitedly, refusing to settle in the patient's chair. "I'm not going to steal any more of them. It's just a matter of deciding to exercise self-control."

"Have you ever considered—despite this theft aberration, which is minor—that you might be under too complete control?

That you might be hiding from yourself something of real importance?''

He turned to me with a hurt expression. ''You don't think I am cured.''

''You may be. But it's seldom that easy, Jackie.''

''You'll see,'' he promised, earnest as a five-year-old. ''I brought this stuff up here so you could give it back to the people I took it from.''

I agreed, though I knew it was an impossible task. To return all that stolen lingerie to its rightful owners would provoke questions that I wouldn't be able to answer. So I simply pressed the shopping bag into the bottom drawer of one of the filing cabinets that stood in the anteroom to my office, intending to dispose of its contents at a more convenient time.

Linda discovered Jackie's loot before I remembered to do so, however. When I entered my office one morning, she was standing in the anteroom, peering astonished into the shopping bag. ''Doctor, what on earth are these things?''

I explained, telling her a little about the patient but without mentioning his name of course. She laughed. ''Isn't that ridiculous? Stealing stuff like this!''

''To you, perhaps,'' I said, a trifle annoyed. ''But I can assure you it's deadly serious to him. Somewhere there is a deep and terrible rift in his personality.''

Jackie never mentioned the brassieres again and as far as I could tell his thefts had stopped. He proudly gave the credit to his new-found ''self-control'' but it seemed to me that his interests had merely passed on to other, and possibly more sinister, areas. Whereas he still refused to fill in the seven-year gap in his life, he suddenly began talking at great length about women he knew, or had known. All of them, according to him, fell over themselves with eagerness to win his favors.

Finally, as both his loquacity and the affairs became repetitious, I suggested that he might be indulging in fantasy.

Jackie laughed heartily. ''I told you that you were jealous of me, didn't I? Just because I've got what it takes. Here you're supposed to treat me and you don't even see how stodgy you yourself are."

I said gently, "You may not believe it, but I was young once myself."

"Not really, I'll bet. I'll bet you always had your nose buried in some book. I'm different. Why, before I quit college . . ." And he was off again, describing with relish an erotic and possibly fictitious escapade. On the other hand, it was also conceivable that he was telling the truth; he was both handsome and aggressive enough. There was always that nagging doubt in my mind as I tried to pin down which was the real Jackie.

Interspersed with his amorous reminiscences was an infrequent moment of insight into Jackie's present activities. I learned that he had bought a pair of binoculars and was spending much of his time in the big park near my office. He was watching people—he called it "studying" them.

"Nothing wrong with that," he said when I questioned him about it. "I'm expanding myself. Have to share the world with my fellow human beings, so I might as well get acquainted with them." He gave me a quick crooked grin. "The other day I watched your Linda, sitting on the grass, eating lunch out of a paper sack. I guess she was tanning her legs. Pretty jazzy for you, having something built like that around the office all day."

It was poor clinical practice but I had to become stern with him at that point. "Linda's an extremely nice girl and happily married. You'd better forget about Linda."

Jackie only smirked. In his exhilarated moods he enjoyed trying to put me on the defensive, to reverse momentarily our relationship. But he was indignant when I suggested he give me the binoculars. He flatly refused. Yet, although I didn't press the point, at the conclusion of the session I discovered that he had left them behind on my desk. I stored them away with the stolen lingerie in the filing cabinet.

During the next few weeks the collection grew steadily. Detailed drawings and floor plans of buildings, maps and written schemes for various adventures upon which he had decided to embark. Most of these were juvenile fancies but I was concerned with the recurring motif of aggression. And no matter how fanciful, all these plans represented sex substitutes—as did his actions at this time—and I was faced with the increasingly difficult job of separating what Jackie actually did from what he claimed he had done.

First, he mentioned smashing a few windows here and there. Then he recounted entering some empty houses under construction in a new tract. From this he passed on to breaking into occupied dwellings, mostly apartments in the downtown section where women lived alone. These illegal entries were accomplished in the early morning hours and he would, he claimed, creep into the bedroom and watch the sleeping woman for a while and then stealthily depart without awakening her.

"Aren't you afraid of being caught?" I asked him.

"I'm not afraid of anything," he boasted. Most of the time he was openly scornful of his fellow human beings, particularly those in authority, such as the police—or me, whom he also equated with authority. Yet Jackie occasionally underwent periods when he would draw up solemn "commandments" for virtuous living which he soon broke or evaded.

I began watching the newspapers to see if any of his presumed exploits were mentioned. They were not, but this didn't necessarily prove anything one way or the other. Breaking windows— or even knocking down a little girl on a lonely street, as he claimed to have done once—was probably too minor to make the papers.

Then one day I saw an item that sent a chill through me. A divorcee, returning home late one evening, surprised a prowler in her bedroom. They scuffled, and she was wounded in the shoulder, apparently with an ice pick. Her assailant had fled.

I felt an icy certainty that Jackie was the attacker. As he had feared from the first, he was progressing steadily from small aberrations to larger horrors. And it troubled me constantly that

I could find no way to get inside him and discover the truth about him.

Sure enough, Jackie described the attack at our next Thursday afternoon consultation. He was pale and frightened of what he had done. His hand shook as he turned over to me the ice pick that he said was the weapon. Then I was faced with a terrible dilemma, undoubtedly the most tortured problem of my career. On one hand, it seemed plain that Jackie Newman was dangerous to society and it was my duty to turn his case over to the police. On the other hand, before me sat a patient in agony whom police methods could neither help nor cure. While over all, like a fog, lay the vast complication that Jackie might just as easily have read the same news story as I and fitted it neatly into his own life picture. So wherever the truth lay hidden, there also was my duty.

Linda noticed my extreme depression. "Doctor, you've been working much too hard. Why don't you get away for a while? A vacation would do you good."

"I'd like to, Linda, but I'm afraid this is no time for it. I'd be afraid I was running away. There's a case I have to see through."

"Oh, surely it could spare you for a week."

"Not this patient. I'm hoping I can pin it down to hysterical fantasy—that the patient's sustained emotional conflict is causing him to retreat from his real self. But so far I can't get through to the *actual* patient, as it were."

I had made my decision. Jackie was my responsibility. I was aware that I must avoid the professional trap of becoming too absorbed in my patient, lest I identify with him rather than remaining in detachment. Already, I felt, I was showing an unwarranted fatherly concern.

I found hints of other dangers too, both to myself and to others. Jackie was evidencing classic symptoms of megalomania of which the ultimate expression, of course, is murder. He now talked about going armed "because my life is in danger"— though, as far as I could tell, he did nothing about this. He finally admitted to nightly dreaming—dreams of himself as the master criminal, of manipulating vast conspiracies, of running rampant in a big black car.

His periods of contrition were less frequent and he became more openly suspicious of me and my methods, ironically at precisely the time when he needed me more than ever. When I suggested the use of Pentothal to aid us in getting at the roots of his psychosis, Jackie flatly refused.

He scowled when I asked his reasons. "You know why."

"Not when it might help. Pentothal merely relaxes the mind's subconscious defenses. That's why it's sometimes called the truth serum." I explained the value of confession in insight therapy. "Almost all of us practice some form of confession as a natural safety valve. A child uses his mother, a husband his wife or vice versa . . . why, before my wife died, I often made her my confessor to get rid of whatever repressions I might have."

Once again Jackie's refuge lay in trying to turn my words against me. "People confess because they're afraid, right?"

"That's a very rough generalization."

"Why don't you admit that you had to make a full report every night to your wife because you were afraid of her?"

"Because it wouldi_'t be true."

"There's the mind's subconscious defenses speaking," Jackie scoffed. "*You're* the one who needs the truth serum, Doctor. Maybe you'd find out things. Like maybe these meditation periods that I've been butting into are really celebrations that your wife is dead, and now you're free."

"Free to do what?" I inquired wearily. My headaches were beginning earlier these days.

"Free to hire that bosomy brunette, for one thing. Your wife wouldn't have let you play games like that in her day, would she?" It struck me that even Jackie's grins and grimaces were becoming more depraved as time went by. "I study people, too, Doctor. I know what goes on."

Linda. Jackie's thoughts revolved more and more about Linda

these days. His growing interest in my young receptionist seemed to me like an ominous line on a fever chart, climbing steadily upward.

At first, there had been only veiled remarks which led to more open discussion, no matter how I attempted to discourage the subject. Then began the letters—long pencil-scrawled communications addressed to her, warped forms of ordinary love letters that were born in indecency and grew into obscenity. But none of them was mailed or delivered to her; each was handed over to me first and was added to Jackie's dossier, which by now was rather extensive. Furthermore, Jackie made no effort to approach Linda personally, perhaps because I warned him severely against any such attempt.

I also warned Linda, but more obliquely. I mentioned that there seemed to be a rash of prowlers molesting women these days, adding lightly, "But I don't imagine your Ed leaves you by yourself very much, Linda."

She laughed. "I'll say not. Ed's home every evening. I keep telling him I didn't get married to be alone."

I was relieved. With her husband to protect her at home and with me to keep a sharp eye on her during office hours, I didn't believe that Linda was in any particular danger even if Jackie should prove to be a violent case. I was still convinced that he was an hysterical fantast, a half-personality living in a dream-world of juvenile aspirations and compulsive lies.

Then, for a time, we seemed to make real progress. Jackie reverted to his earlier desire to be helped. Although he sat puzzled and uncommunicative, he listened attentively to me. He continued to make his sweeping resolutions for better behavior but now he apparently kept most of them. He confessed to prowling aimlessly through the city streets at night but without the accompanying acts of petty vandalism. He admitted that he still experienced the same wild urges but now he took a morose pride in standing up to them. Most significant of all, he didn't speak of Linda as frequently, and he wrote no more erotic letters.

For the first time I began to believe that the battle had turned, that Jackie was going to come home to himself.

One Thursday afternoon he appeared in a highly agitated state. For a full half hour he sat fidgeting in the big leather chair, saying nothing, not looking at me. All at once he blurted, "Worthless little tramp—she deserves anything that happens to her!"

I knew instinctively whom he meant but I had to be sure. "Linda?"

"Oh, I see things. Last night, through her window, she and that stupid ape she's married to. Kissing and hugging and fooling around—not even decent enough to pull down the blinds."

"Jackie, you promised—"

"It makes you sick." His hands were clenched together in fury. "Her trotting around in just her slip and that moron grinning at her while all the time it should have been me in there." He added incongruously, "They had steak for dinner, too."

I listened despondently as Jackie raged on, describing in painful detail the actions of Linda and her husband. He had spent the entire evening crouched on the fire escape outside their apartment, watching and listening. Finally I interrupted him.

He didn't act as if he heard me. "Her slip, it had a lace heart over the left breast. The prettiest thing you ever saw—so pretty it made you want to tear it."

"Jackie, listen to me! This has got to stop!"

He looked sly. "I didn't do anything. Why are you getting so excited?"

I said angrily, "What you did was bad enough!" I had to make an effort to calm myself. "You're intelligent, Jackie—you know yourself where this sort of behavior is leading you. I've believed that, between the two of us, we could solve your problems. But any future actions of this sort and I'll be forced to get outside help."

He rose and came to stand over me, eyeing me oddly. "But I don't think you really want to cure me, Doctor. I think you rather enjoy me."

Then he left.

I spent the rest of his consultation hour staring at the telephone, wondering again if I should call the police and put an end to the whole business. But I couldn't bring myself to lift the receiver. One more conference, I decided; then I'll know for sure. And I was absolutely certain, without reason, that Jackie would return.

He came back on schedule the following Thursday, his manner serenely confident. I was concealing my own nervousness. I said, "Jackie, have you been thinking about our previous conversation?"

He smiled as he walked around my desk to stand over me again. "Oh, yes."

"Then I gather that you've come to some decision."

"Yes, I've finally made up my mind. I'm going to reform— right afterward."

"Afterward?" It hurt my neck to look up at him. "After what?"

"After I take care of Linda. That's what I've needed all along to get the evil out of my system. Then I'll be able to be good forever and ever." His voice rang with relief and boyish exuberance. "It's such a simple cure."

I could scarcely believe I'd heard his fantastic suggestion. "Jackie," I whispered, "this is all wrong. How can you even think of—"

"Just this one last bad thing," he announced. A trace of saliva gleamed in one corner of his mouth. "Then everything will be finished. You know I *have* to do it, Doctor. So you call her in here and let me get it over with." He began to unbutton his shirt.

"No!" I said. "This has gone far enough! Sit down and make yourself think how impossible this is!"

"But it'll be so easy. I'm stronger than you are. And we're all alone in here."

That much was true. At this moment Jackie was the master. But I made a last plea. "Jackie, at least think what you're doing to yourself! Think of the consequences! Think what they'll do to you!''

"I've got to find peace," he said solemnly. "They'll understand that when I tell them. Now let's see—where did we put that ice pick?"

I found myself unable to move. Through a faint haze I watched him pull open the filing cabinet drawer and rummage for the ice pick. I understood exactly what he intended to do, but I was powerless to interfere. As in a nightmare, I seemed to have no conscious will of my own. Jackie dominated everything. I saw him push the buzzer to summon Linda and I waited for the terrible act that was to come.

The door opened and she appeared, a smiling healthy picture of normality in her white uniform. "Yes, Doctor?"

"Come all the way in," Jackie said huskily. "I've been waiting a long time."

She took a step forward, then her eyes widened incredulously as Jackie prowled toward her. "What's the matter?" she asked, backing away. "What are you doing with that ice pick?"

She screamed as Jackie sprang at her, hugged her close, then began tearing at the open throat of her uniform. She was stronger than Jackie had expected—she was fighting for her life. She got hold of his right wrist and with both hands held the sharp spike away from her breast while Jackie's free hand pounded her face and clawed at her dress. And through it all I remained paralyzed with horror, watching the brutal assault.

Linda, writhing to escape, slipped and sprawled to the floor at Jackie's feet. Jackie bared his teeth in a wild outburst of triumph. He raised the ice pick for the final blow. Linda shrieked for mercy, calling his name.

But it was not Jackie's name she called. It was my name.

"Doctor Conover!" she screamed. "For God's sake, don't kill me!"

Abruptly the piercing headache clamped down on me again and I was no longer a spectator to attempted murder. I was the attacker. I stared down in horror at the ice pick in my hand, at

Linda huddled at my feet. Not Jackie Newman but Dr. John Kermit Conover.

I was Jackie.

No wonder that I had been so completely absorbed in his "case," since it was my own. Linda, screaming my name, had broken through the barrier of my lifelong repressions and I could see the terrible significance of the identity I had invented, the "new man" I longed to be.

Jackie—everything I never was. Now I could look back on my empty life—the vise of early marriage at college, the seven years of medical training under the spur of Helen's ambition. Not even Jackie, the amoral dream figure of myself, had been willing to speak of those seven years. "He" had not been afraid of the truth. I hated Helen. I was glad she was dead. But she died too late for me to change my life and enjoy my new freedom.

Standing there, shaking with the pain of revelation, I wasn't aware that Linda had scrambled away. She came back quickly with half a dozen men from the surrounding offices. They approached me cautiously but they had nothing to fear. I dropped the ice pick and fell to my knees before them.

And now I sit here in a strange locked room, awaiting the tenth—or is it the hundredth?—visit by a trio of men who will question me about the rift in my personality. I know all the words. Hysterical fantasy . . . self-suggestion . . . sustained emotional conflict . . . It doesn't matter. Jackie will never return.

And neither will I.

Guilty Witness

MORRIS HERSHMAN

✳

On the surface, the life of a pharmacist may seem to be pretty innocuous and mundane. But don't tell that to Stanley Krane, the protagonist of "Guilty Witness," especially not after you've turned the last surprising page of this little slice out of Stanley's life. Morris Hershman, in a professional writing career that has spanned close to forty years, has published many fine criminous stories and novels, among the latter such titles as Target for Terror *(1967).*

'BY, HONEY," my wife said.

" 'By. See you in the place at one o'clock."

I walked slowly down three flights of stairs, out of the building and across the street, finally stopping under a neon sign: EXPRESS PHARMACY.

My name appeared on the store window in trembling gold flake above the words: *Notary Public: Stanley Krane, Ph.G.*

I went into my usual routine, first noticing that the garbage had been taken away. I opened the two working locks and the token lock that a child could handle whether it had a key or not. Once inside, I shut off the burglar alarm at the right of the phone booths, took the small carton of postage stamps from its nightly hiding-place between the legs of a full-sized cotton display rack, and switched on the fluorescence near the counter. The Express Pharmacy was open for business.

The day started out badly. A kid rushed in to ask if I kept triangular bandages. I sold aspirins and a comb.

At half past ten Mrs. Verber came in. She lived in the same apartment house I did, but my wife and I were on 3A and she lived on the ground level. She was always running after one of her three kids and shouting she'd send them away to the devil. It didn't help much.

She was a sickly-looking woman with tea-colored hair and wore dirty-lensed glasses that made her eyes look as if they were winking at you. If anybody had told me she was going to commit murder, I'd have laughed.

Today she bought a small box of "exorbitant cotton" and then asked: "Did you get the carton for me that I asked you about day before yesterday?"

"Sure," I said, going into the back room and coming out with a large empty carton. In the summer, when customers are going to the country on vacation, I can't find enough empties; in the winter I can't get rid of them fast enough.

Mrs. Verber said thanks and that it would be just right for holding her books and asked: "Doc, what do you have for bruises? My girl couldn't come this week and I was waxing the floor and slipped. So help me, Doc, I'm black and blue all over."

"A shame," I said, as if it hadn't happened before. The truth of it was that her husband, a slight, blondish girl-chaser who dropped into the store every so often to cash a check or make out a money order, had handed her another beating last night. Her shrieks had caused my wife and me, on the third floor, dozens of sleepless nights over the last couple of years.

I gave her Burow's solution. When she put it away in her shopping bag she had a look on her face that I'd never seen there before.

By twelve-thirty I must have talked to forty customers and forty-one salesmen when my wife came down with the lunch plates wrapped in last week's newspapers.

"Mrs. Verber was in for Burow's," I told her, sitting down at the prescription counter while the dishes emerged from their covering.

"I can't stand that woman," she said vindictively. "If I were married to Amelia Verber, I'd beat her up day and night." My wife always takes the man's side in a family argument.

"Amelia's a pest, but she doesn't deserve that kind of treatment. Why on earth does she stay with Verber at all?"

"She knows a good meal-ticket when she finds one," my wife snapped. Then her voice softened. "Ben Verber sticks it out for the children's sake."

I didn't believe that for a second, but I let it go.

"The two of them probably hate each other," I said thoughtfully. "The setup's going to explode one of these days."

The Verber business exploded late that night.

I'd been awakened by some kind of noise, and I switched on my reading-lamp.

"What's going on?" I asked sleepily.

"Sounds like a woman," my wife said. She was standing in

her bare feet when she thrust her head out the window, the heels of her hands touching its ledge.

"There are lights on in the Verber apartment," she reported. "Dining-room, probably."

"Verber's busy with his favorite indoor sport," I yawned.

"He must have a good reason."

Downstairs, the screaming was cut short. There was a moment of shocked stillness around us. My wife and I looked at each other. Something . . . something—

Thock! And again, *Thock!*

My wife looked tense. "He must be killing her."

"Maybe she's getting a little of her own back." . . .

She came into the store next morning at nine o'clock, excited and a little worried, the glasses, down to the tip of her nose, making her a dead ringer for Andy Clyde.

While I was wrapping the merchandise for her ("I'm goin' to the supermarket now and they'll think I stole the six jars of baby food"), I asked her casually: "How's Mr. Verber?"

I'd completely forgotten last night's troubles, but I was surprised by the way she acted. Her face turned a dirty yellow and the bills in her hand slid to the floor. She bent down for them and she was down a long time, as if telling herself to be calm.

She finally straightened up to her full five-nine, then handed over the money and said: "My husband's all right."

"Working, I hope."

"Sure. He's got to live, don't he?"

I hadn't seen the Verbers for a couple of weeks when I asked my wife if she knew anything about them.

She shook her head slowly. "I've run into Amelia in the butcher shop, trying to get first-cut veal; but nobody's seen Ben Verber for two weeks, not since the last time he used her for a punching bag. Not that I blame him for that, of course."

"Well, he's got a job. He doesn't hang around the building much."

"Maybe." She bit at the knuckle of her index finger. "But

there are other things, little things. The children are more spoiled than ever, nowadays. Verber could control them, but now they're becoming unbearable."

I looked up from the eighteen capsules I was working on. "Positive proof, by heavens."

"When I went into the bank yesterday, I ran into Amelia asking somebody to help her fill out a withdrawal slip."

"Most people need money at some time or other."

She let that pass. "Amelia and I have the same girl to help us, you know. Well, the other day Florence, the girl, told me that Mrs. Verber had said not to come again. She was completely satisfied with the work, but she couldn't afford it. And this is the season when Verber, who works in the garment center, should be making money hand over fist."

I threw out an explanation. "Maybe she's saving up to buy a car, for instance. She'd be glad to break every bone in her body and live on stale bread and water if she could have a car and show it off to the neighbors."

"She isn't economizing that much," my wife answered. "She's picked up a brand-new habit, too, smoking two packs of cigarettes a day. A nervous habit if ever there was one."

"Look here, honey, what's the point? There might be a good reason why Verber's not around. Maybe he's got a deadline to meet and he has to work such long hours it doesn't pay for him to sleep at home. I had an uncle—"

"But I haven't told you the worst of it," she cut in. "You know that the hall phone is on the second floor. Yesterday I heard it ring when I was coming down with your lunch. I answered, and the voice on the other end said: 'I want to talk to Ben Verber, apartment 1A. Tell him it's his boss.' I didn't want to leave the phone in case some hell-raising kids came along and hung it up, so I called out his name. A minute later, she came up the stairs. I told her the call was for her husband. 'He's working,' she said. 'I'll take it myself.'

"I started downstairs, but I couldn't help listening. She was shrieking: 'You won't go bankrupt because my husband didn't come in for two weeks.' She listened. 'That's too bad,' I heard her flaring out. 'My husband will find himself a job somewhere else.' "

A well-paying job. The kids were running wild. She was lying, economizing, making withdrawals from the bank, and smoking like a chimney.

My wife and I looked at each other. It grew mighty cold in the store all of a sudden. I looked away from her and realized why. I was shivering.

The wife insists on our having two afternoons out every week, so I have a part-time clerk. Part-time because, though I'm not a miser, the notion of paying two dollars an hour for work I myself would have been glad to get twenty years ago for fifty cents makes my blood turn to water.

On this Tuesday afternoon (the clerk comes in on Tuesday and Thursday) we were upstairs. As soon as I closed my eyes to take a nap, the doorbell rang. My wife pattered over to it from the bathroom.

"Why, no," I heard her saying, "I didn't complain to the Board of Health." The man said something in a shaky murmur. My wife answered and the door was closed softly. "Let's go into the dining-room. My husband's asleep, you'll have to be quiet."

At that, I got out of bed, opened the door, and walked into the dining-room. I knew I'd recognized the man's voice, too, and I'd been right.

"I didn't know you'd switched jobs, Harrison. The last I heard you were a detective second grade."

He stood up, grinning sheepishly. "Of all the apartments in this building, Doc, I might'a known I'd get caught in yours."

I grinned back now. We knew each other slightly. We belonged to the same chess club and met there every so often. He had two small girls and he'd buy baby goods from me, at a hefty discount, of course. By way of returning the favor he'd sometimes leave me a ticket to some police charity affair. Then when the official department ticket-seller had come and gone, seeing that I'd already kicked in, Harrison would reclaim the ticket and tell his boss he hadn't been able to get rid of it.

Now, giving him a careful eye, I asked: "What are you doing in my apartment?"

"I've had an anonymous phone tip"—he glanced at my wife—"about a Mrs. Amelia Verber. You know her, don't you, Doc? Small, stupid-looking woman built like a brick—" he glanced again at my wife. "Anyhow, she isn't what you'd call a beauty."

I grunted. I could guess who'd been giving helpful hints to hard-working cops. When my wife takes sides on an issue, there's no mistaking it.

To keep from showing how mad I was I said: "Come into the bedroom," and when Harrison had stepped in first, I closed the door on my wife.

We sat down, each on a bed, and talked in hushed voices. "Did you find anything?" I asked.

"Uh-uh." Harrison is a tall guy whose frontal baldness makes his combed hair look like two thirds of a pie. "Don't think I haven't been working at it or that a car with two men in it isn't standing in front of the building to see if she tries a getaway."

"Amelia Verber? A getaway?"

"Trouble is, you can't tell where you are with that woman even though she doesn't hide her feelings. I got the strong impression she was scared of something, her eyes popping with fear. Whether it's because her laundry hasn't come back yet or because she knocked off her husband, it's hard to say."

That was the first time the possibility had been mentioned to me, and I blanched. "What do you think?"

"It could be. Verber hasn't been at his job for two and a half weeks. The only withdrawals from their joint bank account in that time have been made by her."

"Exactly as if Verber had run out with one of his girl friends and left her to support the kids."

"Maybe, but the woman's hiding something. Because, y'see, if she really did knock him off, we'll be up against a tough problem: what did she do with Verber's body?"

I was dumfounded. "You mean she cut him in pieces, that sort of thing?"

Harrison looked annoyed. "I'd bet my last cent that she hasn't got the nerve. Of course I gave her apartment the once-over in the role of Board of Health inspector looking for a crummy waterpipe, and I'll swear she hasn't got a dead man in it."

"Then she must have gotten him out of there some way." I had just about accepted the fact of Verber's being dead.

"I asked a lot of neighbors on that. No soap."

"Middle of the night?"

"She hasn't bought, hired, or borrowed a car recently, take it from me. Besides, can you imagine Amelia Verber going out in the middle of the night and carrying her husband's dead body in a valise?"

"Well then, where is it?"

I said earnestly: "Harrison, the sooner you get to the bottom of this, the better. Maybe she's done something to her husband" (I could imagine my wife listening outside the door and sneering), "but if it's a mistake, she's having an unbearable time."

"Doc, the pain's unbearable," Mrs. Verber was saying.

She'd come in on Wednesday afternoon with a prescription that called for phenobarbital. She needed it. Her eyes were flickering more than usual and her straggly hair was fixed like a cruller on the back of her head. Every second or so she puffed at the cigarette between her thumb and forefinger.

"What's the medicine for?" she asked me, as a lot of people do, checking up on their doctor to make sure he hasn't given them vitriol as he'd probably like to.

"The medicine's a tonic," I said, keeping the truth from her because I didn't know how she'd take it.

"They got to build me up like I was a housing project," she snorted. "How much'll it be, Doc?"

I decided to charge her eighty-five cents. It wasn't as if she passed any other drugstores on her way home.

She agreed to the price and asked me to send up the medicine in the evening.

"Glad to." I smiled.

Well, you know how it goes in a store. Things happen. She'd come in during the afternoon. In the evening my wife decided to take in a show with one of her girl friends, and I wouldn't let the delivery boy near the register to take care of trade. It turned out to be one of those nights on which everybody wants to wait for a prescription, and while those people are sitting around, others come in and ask for items you happen to be out of so that you have to send the delivery boy to your competitors to oblige with whatever is needed.

At closing time, half past eleven, I remembered my promise to Mrs. Verber. The kid had left twenty minutes ago, and besides she lived in my house; I'd have to bring it over myself. I hoped I wouldn't find her asleep, but to judge from the medicine, she hadn't been getting much sleep lately.

Two policemen sat in a car in front of the house, their eyes glued on the entrance. I guessed they'd been put there to keep Mrs. Verber worried.

She answered the door to my knock, dressed in a red-white bathrobe. Her hair was loose down the back of her neck; I doubt if she'd slept at all. We whispered together so as not to disturb the children.

Framed in the doorway, I could see most of the apartment. The children were sleeping in the living-room, and in the bedroom I saw by the light from an old-fashioned fixture that only one side of the double bed had been slept in.

Mrs. Verber went to a closet in the foyer at her right, where I saw on the hat ledge a gigantic valise and near it a higgledy-piggledy collection of books and pamphlets of all kinds. One of them thudded to her feet as I watched. She didn't move to pick it up.

She found the money and, slamming the closet door behind

her, paid me by carefully counting out two quarters and thirty-five pennies.

"Thanks a lot, Doc. G'night."

I walked up the three flights of stairs to my apartment and stumbled into bed. I thought of Mrs. Verber's having killed her husband. The neighbors must have made it clear by this time that they knew what'd happened. I didn't think, somehow, in spite of her often-mentioned stupidity, that she'd been fooled by Harrison in the part of Board of Health inspector. She must have seen the car standing smack in front of her window, too. As soon as Harrison figured out what she'd done with the body of her girl-chasing husband, he'd take her downtown and keep her there.

And since nobody had seen her trying to get rid of any bulky object—in fact, she couldn't possibly have managed it—the dead man was hidden somewhere in the apartment. Cold logic.

But Harrison had said: "I'll swear she hasn't got a dead man in it," meaning in the apartment.

No, Harrison was wrong. I'd seen so many stories about how hard it is to get rid of a body, I was surprised that looking for Ben Verber's was a lot like looking for a needle in a haystack.

I thought it over carefully, getting the whole situation clear in my head, weighing pros and cons, and just as I had given it up and decided to get some sleep, the answer came to me.

On Thursday morning, over the phone, Harrison told me he'd come down to the store a little later. He didn't think I could give him much in the way of help.

The clerk, who was supposed to come in at one-thirty, reached the store promptly at two, and when I had shown him which prescriptions to fill and was ready to leave, Harrison was in the store.

We walked outside to the park benches and sat down with my wife, who couldn't have been dragged away by anything less than a couple of strong-minded elephants.

I started by saying, "I think I know where she's hidden the body."

"Think?" Harrison's eyebrows almost jumped into his hairline, while my wife looked sore because I hadn't already told her what was on my mind.

"Here's the idea," I went on. "You've got some kids of your own, Harrison. Do you live in a semi-private house or a tenement?"

He shrugged. "Tenement. Why?"

"Just this. When your kids were very small, where did you keep their baby carriages?"

"Same place everybody else did." He glanced covertly at my wife, oozing sympathy for her through the pores. "Downstairs in the cellar where the janitor lets people keep all sorts of odds and ends."

Suddenly he jumped to his feet. He was breathing loudly. His face colored and his eyes were like saucers on a spotless tablecloth.

"She got an empty carton from the store because she wanted to get rid of some books," I went on, "but when I took medicine over to her house last night, the carton wasn't there and I saw books piled one on top of another on a closet shelf."

Harrison was silent.

"You couldn't have known about it," I said graciously. "What we both should have known right off is that it couldn't be in the apartment."

"Why not?"

"She'd never keep it so near the children."

Harrison ballooned his cheeks and then let out the air with a rush. "We'd better take a look at that carton. . . ."

We found it easily enough in the cellar near the janitor's rooms, the three of us and the two plain-clothes men from the car.

It had formerly held six dozen boxes of Kleenex and the wholesaler had scrawled "Express Pharmacy" clearly on the sides with a black pencil. Mrs. Verber had tied it with hemp, and the janitor told us she'd asked to leave it there on the day after Verber's disappearance. We didn't want the janitor to tell everybody in the building what he'd seen, so Harrison took him along with us.

There was a chance, in spite of Harrison's confidence, that the books I'd seen were just the overflow and that the carton in front of us was full of others. He sighed.

The atmosphere in the dank, filthy place wasn't the sort to make anybody want to stay here. Nobody expects an apartment-house cellar to be the showplace of the nation, of course, but the smells here and the almost certain knowledge of what was inside the box made us all hurry.

Two quick slashes with Harrison's pocketknife cut the rope and left it dangling on the floor. He breathed on the blade before pushing it back in its proper groove. Then his gaze returned to the carton and he moved to open it.

Feet on his chest. Red, red pajamas. A thin blondish fellow looking as if he'd been caught asleep and was too tired to get up. At least half of his face looked that way; the other half had been smashed in.

We'd all been sure the man was dead, so there should have been nothing to make a fuss about. I guess we'd all left logic pretty far behind. The detectives pushed out their lips and drew them back in again; the janitor's hands were in front of him as if for protection; my wife murmured over and over again: "I knew she'd done it. I knew that all the time."

There was a sound back of us, the cellar door opening slowly: a half inch, three quarters, an inch, the squeaky door twanging against our taut nerves. We didn't have to turn around. We stood and waited. Even Harrison, who was experienced, who must have arrested dozens of women in his time, had to run his tongue over dry lips.

She didn't hesitate at the sight of a cluster of people around her husband's impromptu grave. She must have known she couldn't run away now, that she didn't have a chance in the world.

I turned to look. She was walking toward us, her body straight and firm. She was dressed a little more quietly this time. Her hair was done in the same way I'd seen it last night, hanging down her back like so many strands of rope. She didn't wear make-up, but in this darkened cellar she might have passed for a handsome woman.

It was odd how she controlled the scene, as if we'd jump when she told us to and not before. We did. The moment she stopped in front of Harrison, we seemed to come alive.

"You said you were from the Board of Health. I was afraid of you, but I didn't know why."

You could almost see her mind working. Suddenly. Like the snap of her fingers. They couldn't prove it. They didn't know who'd killed him. She could say the carton had disappeared, it had been stolen, this wasn't the same box; she could say anything.

"I don't know what happened. I didn't put him there. You don't think *I* put him there. I wouldn't kill my own husband. I *loved* my husband."

Silence.

"I suppose it's useless. You're all against me. You wouldn't believe my story. They were always on his side. They figured I was just the woman he married. For money, maybe.

"I meant it when I said I loved him. That's one of the reasons why I put him down here. I couldn't leave him in the house and I didn't know what to do. I had the carton, so I put him in that. I liked to think he was close to me. I used to come down here every day, walk over and just stand looking down at him 'cause I wanted him close to me. I was so scared that some day I'd come down and find he was gone.

"He wasn't so bad, really. We used to have our fights once in a while and I even thought of getting a divorce. But it never lasted. We'd make it up, get together somehow, be right back where we started from. Like a second honeymoon.

"I don't remember when I first noticed it. He turned a lot nastier than he'd ever been. He'd get sore for no reason at all.

Once I met him coming out of a candy shop. I asked him what he'd been doing in there. I had a right to know, didn't I?

"But he pushed me; he said, 'Get out of the way, you,' as if I was a total stranger. I knew what it was then. I'd seen it happen before. It'd all be over in a couple weeks. He'd be sorry, you know, the way men are when an affair goes up in smoke, and I'd be in seventh heaven. Until the next one.

"I didn't mind the candy. He always bought 'em candy. The woman would tell her husband she'd bought it herself and everybody'd be happy. Except me.

"This time he was sticking to the same woman for months and months. I was worried. That night I wasn't able to sleep, so I went out for a walk. When I got back he was home from work. He was in the bedroom, trying to jam all his clothes in a valise.

" 'I'm going to her,' he said when I asked him what he was up to. 'We're finished, you and me.'

" 'Where you going?' I said.

" 'Out o' the country. Tropics, maybe. She'll come with me.'

" 'What about the kids?'

" 'Let 'em go to work or something. I don't know. I'm no millionaire. I can't support you and the kids and Dorothy.'

"Dorothy. That was her name, Dorothy. He couldn't support his own children on account of he had to support her.

"I killed him. I couldn't do anything else."

Large fat tears rolled down her cheeks, but she didn't make a sound. Finally she clenched and unclenched her fists and drew back her lips in a snarl.

"But I know who it was this time. I know for sure. I was chasing one of the boys up the stairs like I always do and I saw the box of chocolates delivered. She isn't going to get away with it, I promise you. I'll kill her like I killed Ben."

She stiffened and shrieked, her eyes glinting, her teeth bared as she jerked away from Harrison, long fingernails outstretched, and before any of us could make a move she was scratching, screaming, kicking, clawing at *my wife!*

The Doctor Takes a Case

GEORGE HARMON COXE

✳

*What connection can there possibly be between the murder of a
private detective and the apparently natural death of an elderly
millionaire? Discovering the answer is the task delegated to
medical examiner Paul Standish, and it takes all his forensic
skills to do so. George Harmon Coxe (1901–1984) began writing
stories for pulp magazines such as Black Mask in the 1930s, and
during his fifty-year career he became known as a craftsman of
the detective story. In addition to Paul Standish—who appeared
in a series of short stories in Collier's and other magazines in the
1940s and 1950s—Coxe created a number of colorful series char-
acters, among them news photographers Flash Casey and Kent
Murdock, and private eye Jack Fenner.*

IF IT HAD not been for the initiative of Lieutenant Ballard of the central office, and the usual amount of luck so essential to the successful solution of any homicide, it is unlikely that anyone would have associated the murder of Max Pell, private detective, with the death of James Cooper, aristocrat, who died in bed from apparently natural causes.

Not even Dr. Standish would have known, though he was the medical examiner and had inspected the body of Pell which had been found slumped over his office desk with two bullets in his chest. For the autopsy confirmed the cause of death, and when a copy of his report had been duly sent to the District Attorney, Standish anticipated no further connection with the case.

Until the following noon, that is, when, after two solid hours of ministering to office patients, Mary Hayward, his nurse, opened the door, closed it quietly and leaned against it. She brushed a wisp of medium-blond hair back from her young forehead and fixed narrowed green eyes upon him.

"Lieutenant Ballard is here," she said in a voice that relegated the lieutenant to the ranks of undesirable visitors. "I told him he'd have to wait."

Standish gave her a crooked grin because he recognized the tone and the censure it implied. In the year that Mary had served him as nurse, secretary, and Girl Friday she had made plain her disapproval of his work as medical examiner and she resented especially the demands Lieutenant Ballard made upon his time.

"He said it was about the Max Pell case," she said. "Shall I tell Mrs. Taylor to come in?"

"Mrs. Taylor?" Standish said with some annoyance. "She had no appointment."

"She came before the lieutenant." Mary's smile was smug. "Also she is wealthy. She has rich friends."

Standish sighed aloud, but Mary was gone, and so he smiled for Mrs. Taylor, who was a plump forty and very chic, and prepared himself for a story he often heard from women who had too much money and too much leisure. But while he listened politely with his ears he thought mostly about Lieutenant Ballard and Max Pell, and when he had ushered his patient to the door after prescribing certain mild dietary changes, he pressed the buzzer to summon Mary. She came in a moment later with Ballard, a solid-looking man in his late thirties with a neat and well-dressed look about him and keen gray eyes that were seldom still.

Usually he kidded a little with Mary, knowing how she felt about him; this time, however, he looked a little worried. He made no reply when Mary pointedly reminded Standish that this was his afternoon for golf, but waited patiently for her to leave.

"What about Pell?" Standish said when Ballard sat down. "I thought you'd have that one all wrapped up by now."

"Hah!" said Ballard with feeling. "I got one lousy lead, and I'm sort of afraid of that. I get it this morning when I go to Pell's bank to check on his finances and they tell me a deposit has come in by mail. It's postmarked 6 P.M. last night and is a check for four hundred and some dollars made out to Pell and signed by James Cooper."

Standish sat up slowly, dark eyes thoughtful as he considered this name, which had been synonymous with the growth and prosperity of the city since its earliest days. "The West Side Cooper?" he said, still a little incredulous and knowing now why Ballard looked worried. "Did you ask him about the check?"

"I went out there."

"What did he say?"

"He didn't say." Ballard tipped one hand, let it fall. "He's dead. Died between eight and ten this morning, the doc says. From spontaneous cerebral hemorrhage."

"What doctor?"

"Lanning. A young guy. About your age."

Standish did not know Lanning, but he had heard of him. He

knew also that James Cooper was close to seventy, had nearly died a few months back from a stroke or heart attack—he could not remember which—and was considered a semi-invalid whose death at any time would surprise no one.

"Was Lanning with him when he died?"

"No." Ballard shook his head. "But he's been attending the old man for months. There were two grandsons," he said, as though this was important. "One's still in Germany with the occupation forces; the other was lost in the Pacific. His widow, Louise, has been living with the old man. Also a guy named Dwight Morley, a nephew."

Ballard put a slip of paper on the desk, added a smaller slip. The larger of these was a statement from Max Pell and as Standish glanced at it he saw that it represented seven days' work at twenty-five dollars a day, a four-day hotel bill with the word "Green" in parentheses beside it, and an item for a hundred and forty-odd dollars for railroad, Pullman, meals and tips.

"I found the bill in Cooper's desk while I was nosing around," Ballard said. "This thing"—he touched the smaller slip, a Pullman stub from Chicago to New York—"I found in Pell's pocket last night."

"No one at the house knows anything about it?" Standish watched Ballard shake his head. "And what do you want me to do?"

"Well—I thought maybe you'd want to do a p.m."

Paul Standish lit a cigarette and one hand continued to play with his lighter, snapping the little arm that covered the wick up and down. He didn't know he was doing it, for this was a habit he practiced when he was thinking hard, or when his thoughts were a long way off.

"I doubt it, Tom," he said. "From what I've heard old Cooper was overdue."

Ballard combed his sandy hair with his fingers and watched Standish somberly, finding him a lean, hard-boiled man with good bones in his jaw and a way of holding himself that suggested an innate competence and a nice co-ordination of mind and muscle. He had an easy, unaffected manner, providing you did not try to push him around, and Ballard, having no desire to do so, cleared his throat and said, "Well, will you go out to the house with me and have a look?"

"Is the body still there?"

"Lanning had signed the death certificate but I asked him not to move the old man until I'd talked to you." Ballard stood up. "He didn't like it much, Lanning I mean."

Standish thought regretfully of the afternoon of golf he was not going to get. He rose, knowing what he was going to do would prove unpleasant for everyone, but recognizing also an obligation of his own. "Yes," he said. "I'll have a look."

The Cooper home stood well back on a two-acre plot, a Tudor-type structure of stone and timber, much of it vine-covered, and a colored houseman in a linen coat took Ballard and Standish to a second-floor suite where Dr. Lanning and a dark-haired young woman were waiting.

Lanning was tall, blond, and efficient-looking. He introduced himself to Standish, his annoyance at Ballard clearly demonstrated by the way he ignored the lieutenant, and then presented the woman, who was Louise Cooper, widow of the grandson lost in the war, a slenderly rounded girl of twenty-five or so with black hair and a clear ivory skin.

"In here, Doctor," Lanning said before Standish could more than glance about the book-lined room. "It's utter nonsense, of course, but if the lieutenant wants to be difficult we might as well get it over."

Standish stepped into the adjoining bedroom, Ballard following, his face pink, but saying nothing. Lanning picked up a manila folder containing his history of the case and gave it to Standish. "As you will see from that," he said, "Mr. Cooper's death was merely a question of time. He had an enlarged heart, high blood pressure, an arteriosclerotic condition . . ."

Standish did not hear the rest of it because he was verifying the statements from the records. When he had satisfied himself, he pulled down the sheet and made a cursory inspection of the body, finding no mark or sign of violence upon it. Covering it he glanced at the bedside table and noticed the sleeping pills. Lanning, as though reading his mind, said, "If you're wondering about an overdose, the answer is no. I brought that bottle of fifty the day before yesterday and only two are gone, one for last night and one for the night before." He eyed Ballard with disdain. "As for anyone committing a murder—and that's what you're suggesting, isn't it?—when the man had no more than a few months to live, if that, it's ridiculous."

Standish intervened by asking Lanning the facts of Cooper's death and what he learned did not help Ballard's theory. Cooper had taken his sleeping pill at nine-thirty the night before as was his custom. At eight that morning the houseman came in to raise the shades and on doing so had heard Cooper mumble something and thought he was talking in his sleep. Since he was under orders to leave after raising the shades and let Cooper get up when he felt like it, the houseman had gone out and not until ten o'clock, when he came back to see why Cooper hadn't ordered breakfast, did he discover that the man was dead.

Standish nodded and returned to the sitting room. When Louise Cooper did not glance up from her chair but continued to stare listlessly out the window, he examined the room, noticing now that the books which lined the nearby wall were nearly all detective stories. There were some reference volumes on the bottom shelf, books on criminology, legal medicine, police practice and toxicology; and because he still could not make up his mind about Cooper and wanted time to think, he spoke about them.

"He must have been quite a detective-story fan."

"He was," Louise Cooper said. "It was about the only pleasure he had left."

She glanced from Lanning to Ballard, and Standish had a moment to study her and see how very attractive she was in spite of the tired lines about her mouth and eyes. Then, as she seemed about to continue, the door opened and a man entered, a slim, thin-faced man of thirty-five or so, with sparse brown hair and glasses. When he was introduced as Dwight Morley, Standish knew this was the nephew Ballard had spoken of.

If Morley was at all upset by what had happened he gave no sign of it, but glanced casually at Standish and asked bluntly if there was to be an autopsy. When Standish said he did not know, Morley shrugged and his mouth was thin.

"It's a lot of nonsense," he said. "The old boy simply died in his sleep and anyone who says different is crazy—not that he didn't pick a good time for it."

He was staring at Lanning as he spoke and Standish, seeing that look and the way the woman's mouth tightened, felt a sudden tension in the room where none had been before. Ballard, too, sensed the undertone of animosity and resentment in the words, for he said, "A good time for who, Mr. Morley?"

"I was thinking of Dr. Lanning," Morley said. "Mr. Cooper was about to make a change. He was dissatisfied with the doctor's work."

"That's a lie," said Lanning, his blond face flushing.

"Possibly a good time for Louise too," Morley said, as though he had not heard. He took off his glasses to clean them and blinked pale, myopic eyes. "Cooper didn't approve of the Doctor's relations with Louise," he said.

"And what were those relations?" Ballard asked.

"We were in love," the girl said simply. Then, her head up and sparks in her eyes, she faced Morley. "You should be ashamed," she said. "Not once did you try to make things pleasant for him, not once would you read to him or . . ."

"That trash?" Morley waved his glasses to indicate with scorn the detective books. "I should say not."

"And so I had to, night after night, because I knew if I didn't no one would."

"You don't have to feel so noble about it." Morley put on his glasses and his voice remained sardonic. "I noticed it didn't take you long to start painting your nails again."

Dr. Lanning spoke under his breath and stepped towards

Morley, his jaw hard and eyes stormy. Ballard, taking no chances, moved in front of him and Lanning stopped.

"Take it easy," Ballard said.

Louise Cooper had her head down and Standish could see her face working. She looked at her red-painted nails. "Yes," she said in a small voice. Then, lifting her glance, speaking more to herself than anyone in the room, she said, "He didn't like painted nails. He spoke about it the day after I came nearly a year ago and so I wore them plain. Then this morning . . ." She hesitated, a catch in her voice. "Oh, what difference does it make? You wouldn't understand."

Standish cleared his throat. He still did not know what he should do, but thinking of the old man in the other room and hearing now this bickering and recrimination, he felt a little sick inside and wanted only to get out. He nodded at Ballard and the lieutenant said, "What about it?"

"I'll have the body removed to the morgue."

"But look here." Lanning spoke quickly, his eyes resentful. "You've seen the record. You've no reason to doubt me as the attending physician just because some private detective no one ever heard of was murdered last night."

"Mr. Cooper heard of him," Ballard said.

"If you insist on performing an autopsy . . ." Lanning began.

"I didn't say that," Standish cut in. "I want to make a more thorough examination and I can do it better at the morgue. I'll let you know if there's to be an autopsy . . ."

Dr. Standish played no golf that afternoon. When he had made further inspection of the body at the morgue without finding any sign of violence he came back to the office and sat at his desk, harried by his thoughts and by the things Lieutenant Ballard and Mary Hayward had to say.

Ballard came in at three. "I talked to the Cooper lawyer," he said. "Frank Alson. He's burning at the idea of a p.m. but he told me about the will and all three of them had sweet motives."

"You're figuring the girl too?" Standish asked.

"I'm figuring everybody and you know it," Ballard said and went on to elaborate. "Morley and the girl cut in for a third of about two million bucks and the grandson in Germany gets the other third. I talked to the servants and Morley was right when he said the old man had trouble with Lanning over the girl."

He pulled out the Pullman stub he had found in Max Pell's pocket. He said he'd learned that Dr. Lanning came from Chicago and had gone to school there, coming here after his Army service because he had an uncle in town who was retiring from practice. "So Lanning was in a spot to marry a third of two million dollars," he said, "and that's a motive, son."

"What about the girl?"

Ballard consulted his notes. He said the girl was from Oklahoma City and had met young Cooper at a U.S.O. dance while he was serving as an instructor to Navy fliers at Norman. Later when Cooper knew he was going to sea he married Louise and she continued to live there until he was reported killed off Okinawa in the summer of '45.

"Then she came to live with the grandfather," Ballard said. "Been here ever since."

"She and Morley didn't get along."

"Because she said he started making passes at her after she'd been there a couple of months." Ballard scowled. "That Morley," he said. "I don't know. He's a writer, so he says. Got a lot of books I never heard of and is writing something that's supposed to remake the world his way. He's been living with the old man for five years and the servants could never figure why the old guy put up with him. But he did. Morley stands to get a third of that dough, and if old Cooper got wind of something and put Max Pell checking up on him . . ." He did not finish the thought. He leaned forward. "Something about the set-up smells, Doc," he said. "What about an autopsy?"

Dr. Standish lit a cigarette and worried his lighter, his eyes darkly brooding because he could no longer evade the issue. He knew that in a legal sense he was within his rights to perform or order an autopsy; he remembered the phrasing of the law and knew that it was his opinion and his alone that determined whether an autopsy should or should not be done. He knew, too, that there were other than legal considerations.

"Frank Alson is the Cooper lawyer," he said. "He carries a lot of weight in town. If I do a p.m. and find out Cooper died as Lanning says he died . . ."

"Alson will sure throw that weight around," Ballard finished.

"Yeah," he said, and stood up. "I guess he could make it tough for a young guy like you." He hesitated, put on his hat, gray eyes steady. "It's up to you, Doc."

Standish sighed and his grin was humorless. "Get out," he said. "Beat it. I'll do your p.m. tonight."

Paul Standish had cause to view with doubt his decision several times before the afternoon was over. He had to listen to Lanning's protests; he had to listen to Frank Alson, who not only protested but threatened certain reprisals when he realized that Standish would not change his mind.

"I can't stop you," Alson said, "but if you're wrong I can promise you more publicity than you ever had in your life—all of it bad."

Mary Hayward added her arguments to the others when she learned what had happened and what Standish intended to do. Normally her manner during office hours was one of strict formality but occasionally she scolded and bullied him with the proprietary intensity of a woman in love, though it was unlikely that she had ever admitted such an interest, even to herself. She had argued before that he should give up his work as medical examiner, stating that he would be much farther ahead if he put the same amount of time and effort on his own practice. She said so now.

"I think you're crazy," she said quite honestly, "to risk your future just because Lieutenant Ballard has some silly hunch."

Dr. Standish wondered about this after Mary had gone, his mind going inevitably back to old Doc Lathrop who, in those tough early days when Standish had first hung out his shingle, had suggested that he might like an assistant medical examiner's

job on a fee basis. "You'll get a real chance to know anatomy,"
Lathrop said. "It might be something you'd like."

Standish found that Lathrop was right. The fees paid his office
rent and the knowledge gained helped him to save lives in the
Pacific. Coming back to find Lathrop overworked and ready for
retirement it had seemed natural enough to accept the full responsibility for the office, and though there had been times
when he questioned the wisdom of his decision, he had never
seriously considered giving up this work. That his own interest
in crime might have influenced him was something he would
have quickly denied.

Now he found himself wishing he had taken Mary's advice
and in the hours that followed he found little comfort in the
knowledge that he was doing his duty as Doc Lathrop had taught
him. Not until eleven o'clock that night, when the autopsy was
over and certain photographs had been taken, was he able to
relax and find some measure of pride and satisfaction in what he
had done. For he knew in the end that Lieutenant Ballard's suspicions were well founded. James Cooper had indeed died of a
hemorrhage but not, as Lanning had maintained, a spontaneous
one brought on by natural causes. Cooper had been murdered.

The city maintained an office for its medical examiner on the
second floor of the mortuary and adjoining this was a conference
room. Here, at nine-thirty the next morning, Dr. Standish made
known his findings to Lieutenant Ballard and those he had
summoned.

Dwight Morley sat indolently in his chair at one end of the
yellow-oak table, his myopic eyes veiled but suspicious. Louise
Cooper, in a simple black dress that accented her paleness and
made her brown eyes enormous, sat at one side and next to
her was Dr. Lanning, his mouth sullen and gaze hostile as
he watched Standish remove some 8" × 10" prints from an
envelope.

Standish gave it to them straight, and without preliminaries.
He said Lieutenant Ballard's suspicions had been confirmed. He

said James Cooper had been murdered, though this was no reflection on Lanning's diagnosis, since the type of wound would be clinically undetected.

"Given the same case history, I would have made the same diagnosis," he said. "It took an autopsy to reveal the truth."

Lanning reached for the photographs, stared at one and then another, his mouth white. Louise Cooper sat perfectly still, eyes wide and incredulous as she watched Lanning. Dwight Morley shifted in his chair.

"What *was* the cause of death?"

"Cooper was stabbed," Standish said. "With a thin round instrument like an awl or an ice pick. Stabbed here," he said and put a finger in front of and slightly above his ear. "The autopsy showed the brain wound and when we shaved the hair we photographed the point of entry. Not over three-sixteenths of an inch in diameter," he said, "with a minute scratch an eighth of an inch from that."

He rose, collected his photographs and handed them to Ballard, his lean face grave, his gaze steady as he studied those around the table.

"He died yesterday morning," he said, "but in my opinion he was stabbed the night before after the sleeping pill had taken effect. A younger man might have lived for days with that sort of wound, but in Mr. Cooper's condition, death came more quickly."

"But"—Dwight Morley swallowed before he could continue—"there was no blood."

"A drop or two possibly," Standish said, "which the killer wiped away some time before morning." He walked to the door, thanked them for coming. "I'll make my report and send a copy to the District Attorney," he said to Ballard and with that the lieutenant jumped up and followed him into the hall, asking the others to remain.

"Now what, Doc?" he said.

"Look for an ice pick or an awl, preferably one that has a

rough spot in the metal that crimps the handle to the blade.''

"Sure." Ballard scowled. "But what do you think? You must have some ideas. You generally do."

"I'm all out of ideas." Standish fashioned a wry grin. "You wanted an autopsy . . . You had an idea Max Pell's murder was hooked up with Cooper and it looks as if you were right. Anyway now you've got another murder. That's what you wanted, wasn't it?"

Ballard looked hard at him, half closing one eye. "Just like that, huh?" he said.

Standish pretended he didn't hear. "My job is to determine the *cause* of death," he said. "You and the D.A. are supposed to take it from there, and you know it."

Ballard accepted the decision because there was nothing he could do about it, but as the day wore on Dr. Standish found it hard to sit back and do nothing. It was all right while he was busy with an office full of patients; it was all right when Ballard came in at noon with an ice pick which he had found in the Cooper kitchen and which had the proper length and the required rough spot on the metal crimping to match the photograph. But when he had a chance to think over the things Ballard said, the seeds of worry grew like weeds in the fertile soil of his imagination.

For Ballard was concentrating on Dr. Lanning and his reasons seemed sound. "He's going to marry one third of two million bucks," Ballard said. "To stop him the old man was going to fire him and maybe—I admit I'm guessing on this—cut the dame off. Max Pell was in Chicago checking on something and Lanning came from Chicago. . . . Also," he said, "Lanning had the sort of knowledge a guy would need to think up a murder like that. He never dreamed there'd be a p.m. and there wouldn't have been if it hadn't been for you stringing along with me."

Standish made no comment then and for the next two hours busied himself with a paper he was to read that evening at a dinner given by the State Medical Association. Then, with this out of the way, doubt and uncertainty again began to crowd his mind and, not telling Mary Hayward where he was going, he drove to the Cooper home.

There he talked to the houseman and servants; he inspected again the old man's suite and took a quick look at Dwight Morley's bedroom and study. When he returned to the office he telephoned a local travel agency, then called a friend of his saying he would be unable to attend the dinner and asking him to read the paper he had prepared.

Mary Hayward, overhearing part of this conversation, was shocked and upset. She demanded to know why, but instead of answering her Standish telephoned Ballard and asked about Dr. Lanning.

"Still think he's your boy?" he asked. "Have you booked him?"

"Not yet," Ballard said and wanted to know why Standish asked. "I thought you weren't interested."

Standish ducked that one. He said he'd been thinking things over. "I think you've got the wrong man," he said. "I don't know whether I can prove it or not. I'm not even sure I can . . ."

Ballard cut him off with a growl. He had worked with Paul Standish often enough to respect his intelligence and ability. In the past the doctor's knowledge and shrewd observations had helped break other murders and Ballard was not the sort of officer who, once he had settled on a suspect, became blind to other aspects of a case.

"Never mind the prologue," he said. "All I want to know is, will you try—and what do you want me to do?"

Standish told him without elaborating his own theory and when he hung up he found Mary Hayward standing before him, her arms folded across her young breasts and her green eyes severe.

"So that's the reason you can't give your speech?"

Standish had a hard time meeting her gaze. He tried to pretend it was not important. "It'll probably be a lousy dinner anyway. . . . Look," he said in a gesture of peace, "I should be back by seven. We'll go out somewhere and get a steak."

"No," said Mary, "we will not." Then, because she had the impetuous directness of youth and because the things Standish said and did were so important to her, she continued her scolding without shame.

"I should think it would be enough, the chance you took performing the autopsy," she said. "You stuck your neck clear out to there and you got away with it. I guess it's a good thing you did," she added with some reluctance, "and I can understand that because you felt it was your duty. But this other—well, you've said yourself your job was to determine the *cause* of death and if you go up there trying to be a detective when you're not supposed to, instead of going to that dinner, then all I can say is that you're just"—she groped for a word and found it—"just grandstanding."

Standish pushed back his chair and stood up, his eyes averted so she could not see the hurt and disappointment mirrored there.

"You're probably right, Mary," he said quietly.

"But you're going."

"Until I'm sure about Dr. Lanning. I'm sort of responsible for putting him on the spot. Maybe he's guilty; maybe Ballard can prove it. But if he's not, and he gets involved and arrested, it will ruin his career whether he's guilty or not. . . . You can leave those letters I dictated on the desk," he said, "and I'll sign them when I get back. There's no need for you to wait."

There was a police car parked in the Cooper driveway and when Dr. Standish went upstairs he found Lieutenant Ballard waiting with a police photographer and a plain-clothes man. The photographer was setting up his equipment under the suspicious gaze of Dwight Morley, but Louise Cooper watched without interest and Dr. Lanning, who had been sitting on the arm of her chair, stood up when he saw Standish, surveyed him disdainfully, spoke coldly.

"What is this?" he demanded. "Are you taking over the functions of the detective bureau, Standish? Because if you are . . ."

Ballard interrupted, his voice steady. "I'd take it easy if I were you, Dr. Lanning. I'm the guy that thinks maybe you're guilty, not the Doctor. He took the trouble to come up here to see if he could prove I was wrong."

Lanning said, "Oh." He sat down again, glanced uncertainly about. Then, some of his defiance and bluster remaining, he said, "What makes you think I didn't kill him, Standish?"

"I don't think you would have used that ice pick," Standish said. "It came from downstairs, from a kitchen drawer. I doubt if you'd even know it was there and . . ."

"I didn't."

". . . I don't think you'd have used it anyway, unless you were trying to pin the job on someone else, because you have instruments of your own that would have done just as well—as a matter of fact," he said, "I doubt if any doctor in his right mind would be stupid enough to kill in that fashion. A smart attending physician could take the life of a man in Mr. Cooper's condition by simpler methods and without fear of post-mortem findings."

"I thought of that but . . ." Lieutenant Ballard paused, his gaze troubled, "Max Pell had a Pullman stub from Chicago," he said. "Lanning came from Chicago."

"What I want to know," Dwight Morley said, pointing at the photographer, "is what this fellow is supposed to be doing."

No one answered him. The others were watching Standish and he said, "All that stub proves is that Pell *passed through* Chicago. The hundred and forty-odd dollars he had on his bill suggests that he went a lot farther than Chicago. I checked with a travel agency. For that money a man might go twice that far. Maybe to Oklahoma. Pell wrote the word 'Green' opposite his hotel charge. There is a Hotel Green in Oklahoma City."

He turned on Dwight Morley. "You want to know what he's doing?" He indicated the photographer. "He's going to take some pictures of that bottom shelf and the reference books

Cooper kept there. I came up here this afternoon and checked on your library; I notice you go in for Proust and Thomas Mann and Marx and Krafft-Ebing.''

"I damn well don't read this junk.''

"Somebody did,'' Standish said. "Somebody took a particular interest in this book.'' He pointed to a heavy volume of legal medicine. "It's been used recently because the top of it is clean and the adjoining volumes have a thin coating of dust; that's what we're going to photograph first.''

He took a breath and said, "I've got a copy of that book in my office; most medical examiners have. It's printed on heavy coated stock, the kind that takes fingerprints well. We'll photograph page 412, I think. Because on that page is a picture of a man who died like Cooper died. It shows the tiny little hole the ice pick made, a hole covered by hair that went undetected until the autopsy. I think the fingerprints we'll find on that page will match yours, Mrs. Cooper.''

For three seconds the room was still. No one moved. Then Lanning jumped up, his face stiff. "No!'' he said. "Now wait!''

Standish ignored him. He took one look at Louise Cooper's drawn, gray face, saw the approaching hysteria in her hot, bright eyes and went on, his voice direct, controlled.

"We might even find the answer for those red nails you were in such a hurry to paint,'' he said. "There wasn't much blood, was there? A drop or two which you wiped from the wound. But there was a little blood on the weapon and maybe your luck turned bad. You didn't get the blood on your fingers or nails where you could wash it off, you got a drop or so inside the nail, in the quick, where it wouldn't wash off and where you couldn't dig it out without making the quick bleed.''

He said, "When the lieutenant came I guess that stain worried you some—until you realized that no one would notice it if you painted your nails.'' He glanced at Ballard, and Ballard was watching the woman and Standish said, "A microscopic analysis will tell us if I'm right about that and . . .''

He had no chance to finish. The hysteria and panic he had

seen growing in the woman's eyes took command. She came out of the chair with catlike quickness, whirling away from the still incredulous Lanning and turning towards the door.

Standish made no move to stop her. He recognized this wild desire to escape as the instinctive, animal-like reaction of one whose mind no longer functions properly and let Ballard and the plain-clothes man deal with it. Then, seeing the look of shock and horror on Lanning's face, he knew that it was the young doctor and not the woman who would most need help and sympathy.

Mary Hayward was waiting when Doctor Standish returned to his office at seven-thirty; so were three reporters and a photographer who had heard about the autopsy. They wanted to know details and asked if he had any ideas about the murderer.

Standish said he had no comment. He said he had given a full report to the District Attorney and that any statement would have to come from him. "If you're interested in the police angle," he said, "why don't you talk to Lieutenant Ballard? I understand he made an arrest just a few minutes ago."

The gentlemen of the press got out fast and when Mary closed the door Standish went into his office, put his hat on the desk and sank gratefully into the chair. Mary came in and sat down opposite him; after a moment she said, her voice ashamed, "And I thought you were grandstanding. I'm sorry."

Standish glanced at her, finding a spot of color in the tawny smoothness of each cheek and seeing now the concern in her eyes. He told her to forget it, understanding her apology, and because he felt so weary and beaten and empty inside he said no more but sat motionless until she rose and went to the small refrigerator and began to take out ice. She put this into a glass, added Scotch and water and handed it to him.

"Take it," she said. "I guess a doctor has a right to a drink after a day's work, just like anyone else. . . . Would it help any to talk about it?"

Standish drank gratefully. Before he knew it he was answering questions, and presently Mary had the whole story. Then, arranging her hands in her lap, she sighed, an undertone of chagrin still lingering in her voice.

"And if you hadn't gone, the lieutenant would have arrested Lanning."

"I guess he would," Standish said. "But not for long. When he got around to figuring out the Pullman fare and one thing or another he would have had to let him go. But it would have been tough on Lanning. . . . It's still tough," he said heavily. "In a different way."

"For a while," Mary said. "Until he realizes how lucky he is. Until he understands how it might have been if he had married her . . . Why?" she asked presently. "Why did she do it?"

"She was a bad one," Standish said. "She ran away from home as a kid and got in trouble with some guy and wound up in reform school. Later she married a soldier and when he went overseas she made the mistake of marrying young Cooper without getting a divorce. She got by for nearly a year with the old man but he got wind of something and sent Max Pell west to check up on her and Pell got the goods. That's why the old boy had a row with Lanning. He wanted to break up the affair without telling Lanning the truth and when Louise saw she was going to get kicked out without a dime she made up her mind to do something about it before Cooper called in his lawyer. She'd spent a lot of time reading about crime to the old boy and she got the idea on how to kill him from that book on legal medicine. After that she simply walked in on Pell and shot him and walked out. If it hadn't been for Ballard finding Cooper's check she would have gotten away with it."

He drained his glass, put it aside, and with it he somehow put aside his weariness. He did not know whether it was the drink or the talking he had done which was responsible, but he felt immeasurably better. When he found Mary watching him and remembered her warm friendly ways he recognized the emptiness inside him for what it was and sat up.

"Look," he said. "I'm hungry." He shook his finger at her,

continued with mock severity. "It's not often I issue a second invitation to dinner but this time . . ."

"I accept," said Mary, her voice relieved. "I'm starved."

She stood up and Standish rose with her. When he saw her smile and the sudden radiance in her eyes he felt his own grin come and knew that everything was going to be all right again.

Miracle of the
Fifteen Murderers

BEN HECHT

✣

*"Miracle of the Fifteen Murderers" is an offbeat, ironic, and ul-
timately quite moving story of the last dramatic meeting of a
group of eminent doctors calling themselves The X Club. Like
much of Ben Hecht's fiction, it expresses what, for its time
(World War II), were rather iconoclastic views. Hecht
(1894–1964) published a large body of work during his lifetime,
including some 25 novels, 250 short stories, and 20 plays;
among the last were such famous works, coauthored with
Charles MacArthur, as The Front Page (1928) and Twentieth
Century (1933). Among his criminous works are the collection of
stories Actor's Blood (1936) and the novel I Hate Actors!
(1944)—both of which display a somewhat antagonistic attitude
toward thespians.*

THERE IS ALWAYS an aura of mystery to the conclaves of medical men. One may wonder whether the secrecy with which the fraternity surrounds its gathering is designed to keep the layman from discovering how much it knows or how much it doesn't know. Either knowledge would be unnerving to that immemorial guinea pig who submits himself to the abracadabras of chemicals, scalpels, and incantations under the delusion he is being cured rather than explored.

Among the most mysterious of medical get-togethers in this generation have been those held in New York City by a group of eminent doctors calling themselves The X Club. Every three months this little band of healers have hied them to the Walton Hotel overlooking the East River and, behind locked doors and beyond the eye of even medical journalism, engaged themselves in unknown emprise lasting till dawn.

What the devil had been going on in these conclaves for twenty years no one knew, not even the ubiquitous head of the American Medical Association, nor yet any of the colleagues, wives, friends, or dependents of The X Club's members. The talent for secrecy is highly developed among doctors who, even with nothing to conceal, are often as close mouthed as old-fashioned bomb throwers on their way to a rendezvous.

How then do I know the story of these long-guarded sessions? The answer is—the war. The war has put an end to them, as it has to nearly all mysteries other than its own. The world, engaged in reexamining its manners and its soul, has closed the door on minor adventure. Nine of the fifteen medical sages who comprised The X Club are in uniform and preside over combat zone hospitals. Deficiencies of age and health have kept the others at home—with increased labors.

"Considering that we have disbanded," Dr. Alex Hume said to me at dinner one evening, "and that it is unlikely we shall ever assemble again, I see no reason for preserving our secret.

Yours is a childish and romantic mind and may be revolted by the story I tell you. You will undoubtedly translate the whole thing into some sort of diabolical tale and miss the deep human and scientific import of The X Club. But I am not the one to reform the art of fiction, which must substitute sentimentality for truth and Cinderella for Galileo.''

And so on. I will skip the rest of my friend's all-knowing prelude. You may have read Dr. Hume's various books, dealing with horseplay of the subconscious. If you have, you know this bald-headed master mind well enough. If not, take my word for it, he is a genius.

There is nobody I know more adept at prancing around in the solar plexus swamps out of which most of the world's incompetence and confusion appear to rise. He has, too, if there is any doubt about his great talent, the sneer and chuckle which are the war whoop of the super-psychologist. His face is round and his mouth is pursed in a chronic grimace of disbelief and contradiction. You can't help such an expression once you have discovered what a scurvy and detestable morass is the soul of man. Like most subterranean workers, my friend is almost as blind as a bat behind his heavy glasses. And like many leading psychiatrists, he favors the short and balloon-like physique of Napoleon.

The last dramatic meeting of The X Club was held on a rainy March night. Despite the hostile weather, all fifteen of its members attended, for there was an added lure to this gathering. A new member was to be inducted into the society.

Dr. Hume was assigned to prepare the neophyte for his debut. And it was in the wake of the round-face soul fixer that Dr. Samuel Warner entered the sanctum of The X Club.

Dr. Warner was unusually young for a medical genius—that is, a recognized one. And he had never received a fuller recognition of his wizardry with saw, axe, and punch hole than his election as a member of The X Club. For the fourteen older men who had invited him to be one of them were leaders in their various fields. They were the medical peerage.

This does not mean necessarily that any layman had ever

heard of them. Eminence in the medical profession is as showy at best as a sprig of edelweiss on a mountain top. The war, which offers its magic billboards for the vanities of small souls and transmutes the hunger for publicity into sacrificial and patriotic ardors, has not yet disturbed the anonymity of the great medicos. They have moved their bushels to the front lines and are busy under them spreading their learning among the wounded.

The new member was a tense and good-looking man with the fever of hard work glowing in his steady dark eyes. His wide mouth smiled quickly and abstractedly, as is often the case with surgeons who train their reactions not to interfere with their concentration.

Having exchanged greetings with the eminent club members, who included half of his living medical heroes, Dr. Warner seated himself in a corner and quietly refused a highball, a cocktail, and a slug of brandy. His face remained tense, his athletic body straight in its chair as if it were poised for a sprint rather than a meeting.

At nine o'clock Dr. William Tick ordered an end to all the guzzling and declared the fifty-third meeting of The X Club in session. The venerable diagnostician placed himself behind a table at the end of the ornate hotel room and glared at the group ranged in front of him.

Dr. Tick had divided his seventy-five years equally between practicing the art of medicine and doing his best to stamp it out—such, at least, were the impression of the thousands of students who had been submitted to his irascible guidance. As Professor of Internal Medicine at a great Eastern medical school, Dr. Tick had favored the education-by-insult theory of pedagogy. There were eminent doctors who still winced when they recalled some of old bilious-eyed, arthritic, stooped Tick's appraisals of their budding talents, and who still shuddered at the memory of his medical philosophy.

"Medicine," Dr. Tick had confided to flock after flock of students, "is a noble dream and at the same time the most ancient expression of error and idiocy known to man. Solving the mysteries of heaven has not given birth to as many abortive findings as has the quest into the mysteries of the human body. When you think of yourselves as scientists, I want you always to remember that everything you learn from me will probably be regarded tomorrow as the naive confusions of a pack of medical aborigines. Despite all our toil and progress the art of medicine still falls somewhere between trout casting and spook writing."

"There are two handicaps to the practice of medicine," Tick had repeated tenaciously through forty years of teaching. "The first is the eternal charlatanism of the patient who is full of fake diseases and phantom agonies. The second is the basic incompetence of the human mind, medical or otherwise, to observe without prejudice, acquire information without becoming too smug to use it intelligently, and most of all, to apply its wisdom without vanity."

From behind his table Old Tick's eyes glared at the present group of "incompetents" until a full classroom silence had arrived, and then turned to the tense, good-looking face of Dr. Warner.

"We have a new medical genius with us tonight," he began, "one I well remember in his pre-wizard days. A hyperthyroid with kidney disfunction indicated. But not without a trace of talent. For your benefit, Sam, I will state the meaning and purpose of our organization."

"I have already done that," said Dr. Hume, "rather thoroughly."

"Dr. Hume's explanations to you," Tick continued coldly, "if they are of a kind with his printed works, have most certainly left you dazed if not dazzled."

"I understood him quite well," Warner said.

"Nonsense," Old Tick said. "You always had a soft spot for psychiatry and I always warned you against it. Psychiatry is a plot against medicine."

Dr. Hume smiled archly at this.

"You will allow me," Tick went on, "to clarify whatever the learned Hume has been trying to tell you."

"Well, if you want to waste time." The new member smiled nervously and mopped his neck with a handkerchief.

Dr. Frank Rosson, the portly and distinguished gynecologist, chuckled. "Tick's going good tonight," he whispered to Hume.

"Senility inflamed by sadism," said Hume.

"Dr. Warner," the pedagogue continued, "the members of The X Club have a single and interesting purpose in their meeting. They come together every three months to confess to some murder any of them may have committed since our last assembly.

"I am referring, of course, to medical murder. Although it would be a relief to hear any one of us confess to a murder performed out of passion rather than stupidity. Indeed, Dr. Warner, if you have killed a wife or polished off an uncle recently and would care to unbosom yourself, we will listen respectfully. It is understood that nothing you say will be brought to the police or the A.M.A."

Old Tick's eyes paused to study the growing tension in the new member's face.

"I am sure you have not slain any of your relatives," he sighed, "or that you will ever do so except in the line of duty. The learned Hume," he went on, "has undoubtedly explained these forums to you on the psychiatric basis that confession is good for the soul. This is nonsense. We are not here to ease our souls but to improve them. Our real purpose is scientific. Since we dare not admit our mistakes to the public and since we are too great and learned to be criticized by the untutored laity and since such inhuman perfection as that to which we pretend is not good for our weak and human natures, we have formed this society. It is the only medical organization in the world where the members boast only of their mistakes.

"And now"—Tick beamed on the neophyte—"allow me to define what we consider a real, fine professional murder. It is the killing of a human being who has trustingly placed himself in a doctor's hands. Mind you, the death of a patient does not in itself spell murder. We are concerned only with those cases in which the doctor by a wrong diagnosis or by demonstrably wrong medication or operative procedure has killed off a patient who, without the aforesaid doctor's attention, would have continued to live and prosper."

"Hume explained all this to me," the new member muttered impatiently and then raised his voice. "I appreciate that this is my first meeting and that I might learn more from my distinguished colleagues by listening than by talking. But I have something rather important to say."

"A murder?" Tick asked.

"Yes," said the new member.

"Very good," he said. "We shall be glad to listen to you. But we have several murderers in the docket ahead of you."

The new member was silent and remained sitting bolt upright in his chair. It was at this point that several, including Hume, noticed there was something more than stage fright in the young surgeon's tension. The certainty filled the room that Sam Warner had come to his first meeting of The X Club with something violent and mysterious boiling in him.

Dr. Philip Kurtiff, the eminent neurologist, put his hand on Warner's arm and said quietly, "There's no reason to feel badly about anything you're going to tell us. We're all pretty good medical men and we've all done worse—whatever it is."

"If you please," Old Tick demanded, "we will have silence. This is not a sanatorium for doctors with guilt complexes. It is a clinic for error. And we will continue to conduct it in an orderly, scientific fashion. If you want to hold Sam Warner's hand, Kurtiff, that's your privilege. But do it in silence."

He beamed suddenly at the new member.

"I confess," he went on, "that I'm as curious as anybody to hear how so great a know-it-all as our young friend Dr. Warner could have killed off one of his customers. But our curiosity will have to wait. Since five of you were absent from our last gathering, I think that the confessions of Dr. James Sweeney should be repeated for your benefit."

Dr. Sweeney stood up and turned his lugubrious face and shining eyes to the five absentees.

"Well," he said in his preoccupied monotone, "I told it once, but I'll tell it again. I sent a patient to my X-ray room to have a fluoroscopy done. My assistant gave him a barium meal to drink and put him under the fluoroscope. I walked in a minute later and when I saw the patient under the ray I observed to my assistant, Dr. Kroch, that it was amazing and that I had never seen anything like it. Kroch was too overcome to bear me out. What I saw was that the patient's entire gastro-intestinal tract from the esophagus down was apparently made out of stone. And as I studied this phenomenon I noticed it was becoming clearer and sharper. The most disturbing factor in the situation was that we both knew there was nothing to be done. Dr. Kroch, in fact, showed definite signs of hysteria. Even while we were studying him the patient showed symptoms of death. Shortly afterward he became moribund and fell to the floor."

"Well, I'll be damned," several of the absentees cried in unison, Dr. Kurtiff adding, "What the hell was it?"

"It was simple," said Sweeney. "The bottom of the glass out of which the patient had drunk his barium meal was caked solid. We had filled him up with plaster of Paris. I fancy the pressure caused an instantaneous coronary attack."

"Good Lord!" the new member said. "How did it get into the glass?"

"What, if anything, was the matter with the patient before he adventured into your office?" Dr. Kurtiff inquired.

"The autopsy revealed chiefly a solidified gastro-intestinal tract," said Sweeney. "But I think from several indications that there may have been a tendency to pyloric spasm which caused the belching for which he was referred to me."

"A rather literary murder," said Old Tick. "A sort of Pygmalion in reverse."

The old professor paused and fastened his red-rimmed eyes on Warner.

"By the way, before we proceed," he said, "I think it is time to tell you the full name of our club. Our full name is The X-Marks-the-Spot Club. We prefer, of course, to use the abbreviated title as being a bit more social-sounding."

"Of course," said the new member, whose face now appeared to be getting redder.

"And now," announced Old Tick, consulting a scribbled piece of paper, "our first case on tonight's docket will be Dr. Wendell Davis."

There was silence as the elegant stomach specialist stood up. Davis was a doctor who took his manner as seriously as his medicine. Tall, solidly built, gray-haired and beautifully barbered, his face was without expression—a large, pink mask that no patient, however ill and agonized, had ever seen disturbed.

"I was called late last summer to the home of a workingman," he began. "Senator Bell had given a picnic for some of his poorer constituency. As a result of this event, the three children of a steamfitter named Horowitz were brought down with food poisoning. They had overeaten at the picnic. The Senator, as host, felt responsible, and I went to the Horowitz home at his earnest solicitation. I found two of the children very sick and vomiting considerably. They were nine and eleven. The mother gave me a list of the various foods all three of them had eaten. It was staggering. I gave them a good dose of castor oil.

"The third child, aged seven, was not as ill as the other two. He looked pale, had a slight fever, felt some nausea—but was not vomiting. It seemed obvious that he too was poisoned, but to a lesser degree. Accordingly I prescribed an equal dose of castor oil for the youngest child—just to be on the safe side.

"I was called by the father in the middle of the night. He was alarmed over the condition of the seven-year-old. He reported that the other two children were much improved. I told him not to worry, that the youngest had been a little late in developing food poisoning but would unquestionably be better in the morning, and that his cure was as certain as his sister's and brother's. When I hung up I felt quite pleased with myself for having anticipated the youngest one's condition and prescribed the castor oil prophylactically. I arrived at the Horowitz home at noon the next day and found the two older children practically recovered. The seven-year-old, however, appeared to be very sick indeed. They had been trying to reach me since breakfast. The child had 105° temperature. It was dehydrated, the eyes sunken and circled, the expression pinched, the nostrils dilated, the lips cyanotic, and the skin cold and clammy."

Dr. Davis paused. Dr. Milton Morris, the renowned lung specialist, spoke.

"It died within a few hours?" he asked.

Dr. Davis nodded.

"Well," Dr. Morris said quietly, "it seems pretty obvious. The child was suffering from acute appendicitis when you first saw it. The castor oil ruptured its appendix. By the time you got around to looking at it again, peritonitis had set in."

"Yes," said Dr. Davis slowly, "that's exactly what happened."

"Murder by castor oil," Old Tick cackled. "I have a memo from Dr. Kenneth Wood. Dr. Wood has the floor."

The noted Scotch surgeon, famed in his college days as an Olympic Games athlete, stood up. He was still a man of prowess, large-handed, heavy-shouldered, and with the purr of masculine strength in his soft voice.

"I don't know what kind of a murder you can call this," Dr. Wood smiled at his colleagues.

"Murder by butchery is the usual title," Tick said.

"No, I doubt that," Dr. Morris protested, "Ken's too skillful to cut off anybody's leg by mistake."

"I guess you'll have to call it just plain murder by stupidity," Dr. Wood said softly.

Old Tick cackled.

"If you'd paid a little more attention to diagnosis than to shot-putting you wouldn't be killing off such hordes of patients," he said.

"This is my first report in three years," Wood answered modestly. "And I've been operating at the rate of four or five daily, including holidays."

"My dear Kenneth," Dr. Hume said, "every surgeon is entitled to one murder in three years. A phenomenal record, in fact—when you consider the temptations."

"Proceed with the crime."

"Well"—the strong-looking surgeon turned to his hospital colleague, the new member—"you know how it is with these acute gall bladders, Sam."

Warner nodded abstractedly.

Dr. Wood went on. "Brought in late at night. In exteme pain. I examined her. Found the pain in the right upper quadrant of the abdomen. It radiated to the back and right shoulder. Completely characteristic of gall bladder. I gave her opiates. They had no effect on her, which, as you know, backs up any gall bladder diagnosis. Opiates never touch the gall bladder."

"We know that," said the new member nervously.

"Excuse me," Dr. Wood smiled. "I want to get all the points down carefully. Well, I gave her some nitroglycerine to lessen the pain then. Her temperature was 101. By morning the pain was so severe that it seemed certain the gall bladder had perforated. I operated. There was nothing wrong with her damn gall bladder. She died an hour later."

"What did the autopsy show?" Dr. Sweeney asked.

"Wait a minute," Wood answered. "You're supposed to figure it out, aren't you? Come on—you tell me what was the matter with her."

"Did you take her history?" Dr. Kurtiff asked after a pause.

"No," Wood answered.

"Aha!" Tick snorted. "There you have it! Blind man's buff again."

"It was an emergency." Wood looked flushed. "And it seemed an obvious case. I've had hundreds of them."

"The facts seem to be as follows," Tick spoke up. "Dr. Wood murdered a woman because he misunderstood the source of pain. We have, then, a very simple problem. What besides the gall bladder can produce the sort of pain the eminent surgeon has described?"

"Heart," Dr. Morris answered quickly.

"You're getting warm," said Wood.

"Before operating on anyone with so acute a pain and in the absence of any medical history," Tick went on, "I would most certainly have looked at the heart."

"Well, you'd have done right," said Wood quietly. "The autopsy showed an infarction of the descending branch of the right coronary artery."

"Murder by a sophomore," Old Tick pronounced wrathfully.

"The first and last," said Wood quietly. "There won't be any more heart-case mistakes in my hospital."

"Good, good," Old Tick said. "And now, gentlemen, the crimes reported thus far have been too infantile for discussion. We have learned nothing from them other than that science and stupidity go hand in hand, a fact already too well known to us. However, we have with us tonight a young but extremely talented wielder of the medical saws. And I can, from long acquaintance with this same gentleman, assure you that if he has done a murder it is bound to be what some of my female students would call 'a honey.' He has been sitting here for the last hour, fidgeting like a true criminal, sweating with guilt and a desire to tell all. Gentlemen, I give you our new and youngest culprit, Dr. Samuel Warner."

Dr. Warner faced his fourteen eminent colleagues with a sudden excitement in his manner. The older men regarded him quietly and with various degrees of irritation. They knew without further corroboration than his manner that this medico was full of untenable theories and half-baked medical discoveries. They had been full of such things themselves once. And they settled back to enjoy themselves.

There is nothing as pleasing to a graying medicine man as the opportunity of slapping a dunce cap on the young of science. Old Tick, surveying his colleagues, grinned. They had all acquired the look of pedagogues holding a switch behind their backs.

Dr. Warner mopped his neck with his wet handkerchief and smiled knowingly at the medical peerage. What he knew was that this same critical and suspicious attention would have been offered him were he there to recite the tale of some miraculous cure rather than a murder.

"I'll give you this case in some detail," he said, "because I think it contains as interesting a problem as you can find in practice."

Dr. Rosson, the gynecologist, grunted, but said nothing.

"The patient was a young man, or rather a boy," Warner went on eagerly. "He was seventeen and amazingly talented. In fact, about the most remarkable young man I've ever met. He wrote poetry. That's how I happened to meet him. I read one of his poems in a magazine and, by God, it was so impressive I wrote him a letter."

Dr. Kurtiff frowned at this unmedical behavior.

"Rhymed poetry?" Dr. Wood asked, with a wink at Old Tick.

"Yes," said Warner. "I read all his manuscripts. They were sort of revolutionary. His poetry was a cry against injustice. Every kind of injustice. Bitter and burning."

"Wait a minute," Dr. Rosson said. "The new member seems to have some misconception of our function. We are not a literary society, Warner."

"I know that," said Warner, working his jaw muscles and smiling lifelessly.

"And before you get started," Dr. Hume grinned, "no bragging. You can do your bragging at the annual surgeons' convention."

"Gentlemen," Warner said, "I have no intention of bragging. I'll stick to murder, I assure you. And as bad a one as you've ever heard."

"Good," Dr. Kurtiff said. "Go on. And take it easy and don't break down."

"I won't break down," Warner said. "Don't worry. Well, the patient was sick for two weeks before I was called."

"I thought you were his friend," Dr. Davis said.

"I was," Warner answered. "But he didn't believe in doctors."

"No faith in them, eh?" Old Tick cackled. "Brilliant boy."

"He was," said Warner eagerly. "I felt upset when I came and saw how sick he was. I had him moved to a hospital at once."

"Oh, a rich poet," Dr. Sweeney said.

"No," said Warner. "I paid his expenses. And I spent all the time I could with him. The sickness had started with a severe pain on the left side of the abdomen. He was going to call me but the pain subsided after three days, so the patient thought he was well. But it came back after two days and he began running a temperature. He developed diarrhea. There was pus and blood, but no amoeba or pathogenic bacteria when he finally sent for me. After the pathology reports I made a diagnosis of ulcerative colitis. The pain being on the left side ruled out the appendix. I put the patient on sulfaguanidine and unconcentrated liver extract and gave him a high protein diet—chiefly milk. Despite this treatment and constant observation the patient got worse. He developed generalized abdominal tenderness, both direct and rebound, and rigidity of the entire left rectus muscle. After two weeks of careful treatment the patient died."

"And the autopsy showed you'd been wrong?" Dr. Wood asked.

"I didn't make an autopsy," said Warner. "The boy's parents had perfect faith in me. As did the boy. They both believed I was doing everything possible to save his life."

"Then how do you know you were wrong in your diagnosis?" Dr. Hume asked.

"By the simple fact," said Warner irritably, "that the patient died instead of being cured. When he died I knew I had killed him by a faulty diagnosis."

"A logical conclusion," said Dr. Sweeney. "Pointless medication is no alibi."

"Well, gentlemen," Old Tick cackled from behind his table,

"our talented new member has obviously polished off a great poet and close personal friend. Indictments of his diagnosis are now in order."

But no one spoke. Doctors have a sense for things unseen and complications unstated. And nearly all the fourteen looking at Warner felt there was something hidden. The surgeon's tension, his elation and its overtone of mockery, convinced them there was something untold in the story of the dead poet. They approached the problem cautiously.

"How long ago did the patient die?" Dr. Rosson asked.

"Last Wednesday," said Warner. "Why?"

"What hospital?" asked Davis.

"Saint Michael's," said Warner.

"You say the parents had faith in you," said Kurtiff, "and still have. Yet you seem curiously worried about something. Has there been any inquiry by the police?"

"No," said Warner. "I committed the perfect crime. The police haven't even heard of it. And even my victim died full of gratitude." He beamed at the room. "Listen," he went on, "even you people may not be able to disprove my diagnosis."

This brash challenge irritated a number of the members.

"I don't think it will be very difficult to knock out your diagnosis," said Dr. Morris.

"There's a catch to it," said Wood slowly, his eyes boring at Warner.

"The only catch there is," said Warner quickly, "is the complexity of the case. You gentlemen evidently prefer the simpler malpractice type of crime, such as I've listened to tonight."

There was a pause, then Dr. Davis inquired in a soothing voice, "You described an acute onset of pain before the diarrhea, didn't you?"

"That's right," said Warner.

"Well," Davis continued coolly, "the temporary relief of symptoms and their recurrence within a few days sounds superficially like ulcers—except for one point."

"I disagree," Dr. Sweeney said softly. "Dr. Warner's diagnosis is a piece of blundering stupidity. The symptoms he has presented have nothing to do with ulcerative colitis."

Warner flushed and his jaw muscles moved angrily.

"Would you mind backing up your insults with a bit of science?" he said.

"Very easily done," Sweeney answered calmly. "The late onset of diarrhea and fever you describe rules out ulcerative colitis in ninety-nine cases out of a hundred. What do you think, Dr. Tick?"

"No ulcers," said Tick, his eyes studying Warner.

"You mentioned a general tenderness of the abdomen as one of the last symptoms," said Dr. Davis smoothly.

"That's right," said Warner.

"Well, if you have described the case accurately," Davis continued, "there is one obvious fact revealed. The general tenderness points to a peritonitis."

"How about a twisted gut?" Dr. Wood asked. "That could produce the symptoms described."

"No," said Dr. Rosson. "A volvulus means gangrene and death in three days. Warner says he attended him for two weeks and that the patient was sick for two weeks before he was called. The length of the illness rules out intussusception, volvulus, and intestinal tumor."

"There's one other thing," Dr. Morris said. "A left-sided appendix."

"That's out, too," Dr. Wood said quickly. "The first symptom of a left-sided appendix would not be the acute pain described by Warner."

"The only thing we have determined," said Dr. Sweeney, "is a perforation other than ulcer. Why not go on with that?"

"Yes," said Dr. Morris. "Ulcerative colitis is out of the question, considering the course taken by the disease. I'm sure we're dealing with another type of perforation."

"The next question," announced Old Tick, "is, what made

the perforation?''

Dr. Warner mopped his face with his wet handkerchief and said softly, "I never thought of an object perforation."

"You should have," Dr. Kurtiff smiled.

"Come, come," Old Tick interrupted. "Let's not wander. What caused the perforation?"

"He was seventeen," Kurtiff answered, "and too old to be swallowing pins."

"Unless," said Dr. Hume, "he had a taste for pins. Did the patient want to live, Warner?"

"He wanted to live," said Warner grimly, "more than anybody I ever knew."

"I think we can ignore the suicide theory," said Dr. Kurtiff. "I am certain we are dealing with a perforation of the intestines and not of the subconscious."

"There you are, Warner," Old Tick said. "We've narrowed it down. The spreading tenderness you described means a spreading infection. The course taken by the disease means a perforation other than ulcerous. And a perforation of that type means an object swallowed. We have ruled out pins and chicken bones. Which leaves us with only one other normal guess."

"A fish bone," said Dr. Sweeney.

"Exactly," said Tick.

Warner stood listening tensely to the voices affirming the diagnosis. Tick delivered the verdict.

"I think we are all agreed," he said, "that Sam Warner killed his patient by treating him for ulcerative colitis when an operation removing an abscessed fish bone would have saved his life."

Warner moved quickly across the room to the closet where he had hung his hat and coat.

"Where you going?" Dr. Wood called after him. "We've just started the meeting."

Warner was putting on his coat and grinning.

"I haven't got much time," he said, "but I want to thank all of you for your diagnoses. You were right about there being a catch to the case. The catch is that my patient is *still alive!* I've been treating him for ulcerative colitis for two weeks and I realized this afternoon that I had wrongly diagnosed the case—and that he would be dead in twenty-four hours unless I could find out what really was the matter with him."

Warner was in the doorway, his eyes glittering.

"Thanks again, gentlemen, for the consultation and your diagnosis," he said. "It will enable me to save my patient's life."

A half hour later the members of The X Club stood grouped in one of the operating rooms of St. Michael's Hospital. They were different-looking men from those who had been playing a medical Halloween in the Walton Hotel. There is a change that comes over doctors when they face disease. The oldest and the weariest of them draw vigor from a crisis. The shamble leaves them and it is the straight back of the champion that enters the operating room. Confronting the problem of life and death, the tired, red-rimmed eyes become full of greatness and even beauty.

On the operating table lay the naked body of a Negro boy. Dr. Warner in his surgical whites stood over him, waiting. The anesthetist finally nodded. The dark skin had turned ashen and the fevered young Negro lay unconscious.

The fourteen members of The X Club watched Warner operate. Wood nodded approvingly at his speed. Rosson cleared his throat to say something, but the swift-moving hands of the surgeon held him silent. No one spoke. The minutes passed. The nurses quietly handed instruments to the surgeon. Blood spattered their hands.

Fourteen great medical men stared hopefully at the pinched and unconscious face of a colored boy who had swallowed a fish bone. No king or pope ever lay in travail with more medical genius holding its breath around him.

Suddenly the perspiring surgeon raised something aloft in his gloved fingers.

"Wash this off," he muttered to the nurse, "and show it to the gentlemen."

He busied himself placing drains in the abscessed cavity and then powdered some sulfanilamide into the opened abdomen to kill the infection.

Old Tick stepped forward and took the object from the nurse's hand.

"A fish bone," he said.

The X Club gathered around it as if it were a treasure indescribable.

"The removal of this small object," Tick cackled softly, "will enable the patient to continue writing poetry denouncing the greeds and horrors of our world."

That, in effect, was the story Hume told me, plus the epilogue of the Negro poet's recovery three weeks later. We had long finished dinner and it was late night when we stepped into the war-dimmed streets of New York. The headlines on the newsstands had changed in size only. They were larger in honor of the larger slaughters they heralded.

Looking at them you could see the death-strewn wastes of battles. But another picture came to my mind—a picture that had in it the hope of a better world. It was the hospital room in which fifteen famed and learned heroes stood battling for the life of a Negro boy who had swallowed a fish bone.

Doctor's Orders

JOHN F. SUTER

✵

This potent vignette mixes crime and obstetrics in a most unusual fashion, and packs quite a wallop in its final lines. You won't soon forget it. Likewise superb are West Virginian John F. Suter's other stories for such periodicals as Ellery Queen's Mystery Magazine and Alfred Hitchcock's Mystery Magazine, many of which have also been anthologized.

THIS PAIN, the pain is everywhere. No, not everywhere, but I throb in the places where there is no real pain. And now it is only an ache and an exhaustion, but it seems as if there is no time, no space, nothing but this. But I am a little stronger than I was. So little. But I am stronger. I have to get well. I intend to get well I will get well.

"Mr. Shaw, I think she'll come out of it all right. As you know, it was either your wife or the baby, for a while. But she's improved, I assure you. Of course, there will always be that weakness which we can't correct."

"I understand. Just to have her well again is all I care about."

I had better open my eyes. Jeff isn't here. I can't sense him. But I can stand the white room now. I no longer have a wish to die. Even though he didn't live. I could grieve and grieve and grieve, and I wanted to when Jeff first told me. But there is no strength in that sort of grief. I will get well.

"You did tell her that the baby died?"

"Yes, Doctor. It was hard for her to take at first. Very hard. Then I told her that it had been a boy. That pleased her, in spite of—of what happened."

There. The world is back. So much sunshine in the room. So many flowers. I wonder if Jeff—

"Did you tell her that the child is already buried?"

"Not yet. If you're sure that she's stronger, I'll tell her today."

"You don't think she'll hold it against you for going ahead with the funeral, Mr. Shaw?"

"Jessie is very level-headed, Doctor. She'll understand that we couldn't wait. And—if you don't think it's out of style to say so—we love each other."

I'm sure Jeff has done whatever is best. If only it—he—had lived until I could have seen him . . . How long have I been here? Where is Jeff? Is he being sensible, as I begged him to be? Is he at work, so that he won't endanger his job, the job that's so important to him? Oh, I do love him, and I do so want to give him fine children.

"Perhaps, then, Mr. Shaw, it would be better for you to tell her the rest of it than for me to do it. It might be easier for her to believe someone who loves her. Sometimes the patient thinks the doctor doesn't know as much as she herself does."

"That part won't be easy."

I hope the children will look like Jeff. I'm not ugly, but I'm so—plain. Jeff has the looks for both of us. That's one of the reasons they all said he was only after my money. But he's refused to let me help him. He's independent. He keeps working hard managing the sporting-goods department, when neither of us would ever have to work again, if we didn't want to. I must get well, for his sake. I will get well.

"Easy or hard, Mr. Shaw, it has to be done. Someone has to tell her. It will come best from you. She must never try to have a child again. Never. It will kill her. Make no mistake about it— having another child will kill her."

"I'll take the responsibility, Doctor. You needn't say a thing to her. I think I can convince her. Perhaps I can even persuade her to move away for a while, so that old associations won't keep haunting her."

I'm glad that I made my will in Jeff's favor before I came to the hospital. He doesn't know about it, and it wasn't necessary, as it turned out. But I'm glad. He's been so good to me that now I'm sure of him . . .

The door swung inward, silently. She turned her head,

slowly, and a tired smile crept across her white face. A tall young man with crinkled blond hair was in the doorway.

"Jeff."

He was at her bedside, kissing her palm. "Jessie."

When they both could speak, she gripped his fingers. "Jeff, I've been lying here thinking. Everybody has troubles of some kind or other. We can overcome this. I'm going to get strong, fast. Then we're going to have another baby, just as quickly as we can. Aren't we?"

He smiled proudly. The truth was exactly the right answer.

"We certainly are, sweetheart. We certainly are."

The Splinter

MARY ROBERTS RINEHART

＞◇＜

Veterinary medicine is an intriguing offshoot of the mainstream
medical world, and most vets care as much for their "patients"
as the family doctor does for his. In fact, the hero of this story,
Dr. Mitchell, has been heard to say that he likes some dogs better
than some people—and in this investigation of the disappearance of the young owner of one of his patients, he finds out why
he feels that way. Mary Roberts Rinehart (1876–1958) is best
known for her romance and romantic suspense novels—among
them The Circular Staircase (1908), The Red Lamp (1925), and
The Yellow Room (1945)—but she was also a prolific writer of
short stories, publishing nine collections of varying types. In
"The Splinter" she shows not only her skill at characterization
but also her mastery of the tale of straight detection.

THE DOORBELL roused young Doctor Mitchell from an exhausted nap on the old sofa in his office. It also set off a series of yaps and squeals from the dogs in the hospital behind him, and he waited for the third peal of the bell before he grunted and got up. There was something urgent about the last one, as though someone was practically leaning against the bell. It annoyed him. For the past three days and nights, along with other men, he had ranged the wooded hills behind the town, looking for a lost child. Now he was stiff and tired.

"What the hell!" he muttered, as the bell rang again.

He limped to the street door and flung it open with unreasonable fury.

"Look," he began, "get your finger off that thing and . . ."

He stopped abruptly. A small and rather frightened boy was standing there. In the early morning light he looked pale, and the freckles on his face stood out distinctly.

"Can I come in, mister?" he said. "I don't want anybody to see me."

Mitchell stepped aside and the boy darted into the office. Only then did Mitchell realize that the boy was carrying a small dog, and that he looked a little frightened.

"Sit down, son," he said. "Got your dog there, I see. Well, that's my business. What's wrong? Eat something he shouldn't?"

The boy sat down. He looked rather better now. A little of his color had come back.

"He's not mine," he said. "I guess you could say I stole him."

But Mitchell had recognized the dog by that time. He stared at the boy.

"That's Johnny Watson's dog, Wags," he said. "Let's hear about it. Why did you steal him?"

"I had to," the boy said, as if that explained everything, and then he sat very still.

Mitchell inspected the lad gravely. It was Johnny Watson for whom he and the posse of citizens had been searching. At first, the search had been more or less desultory, for Johnny was known to have a roving foot. At the age of seven he had already set a local record for the number of times he had been missing, but previously he had always come home of his own accord or been discovered and brought back.

Usually, Johnny's excursions were brief. He was picked up and returned home within a few hours. But this time was different. The entire town knew that he always took his dog with him, and on the evening of the day he disappeared a deer hunter found the dog up on Bald Hill, a mile or so back of the town, and carried him down. Carried him, because the dog was too lame and exhausted to walk.

The hunter took him to the police station in the county courthouse, and the chief of police sent for the boy's aunt, a Mrs. Hunt, with whom he lived.

"This Johnny's dog?" he asked.

She eyed the tired little creature without pleasure.

"I suppose it is," she said. "You can keep him. I don't want him. If you ask me Johnny's been kidnaped."

"Kidnaped? What for?" the chief snapped. "He hasn't any money, nor have you, Hattie. Don't be a fool. And you're taking the dog back, whether you want him or not."

That was the evening of the first day, but by the end of the second the town began to rouse. People were talking, for everybody knew Johnny, with his wide blue eyes and his endearing grin. Everybody knew Wags too, and when another day had gone by, a posse was formed to search the hills. No Johnny was found, however. Now he had been missing for five days, and hope had practically been abandoned.

Knowing all this, Doc Mitchell eyed the boy who was holding Johnny's dog in his arms. The youngster was nine, possibly ten, a well-built sturdy lad with a tousled head and a pudgy nose.

"All right," Mitchell said. "So you stole him. I suppose you had a reason. Better be a good one, son."

"I think Mrs. Hunt wants him to die," he said simply. "She keeps him tied in the yard day and night, in the cold. And he's lame, too. His foot's awful sore."

Carefully he put the dog on the floor, and Mitchell saw that he was standing on three legs.

"Why on earth do you think she wants him to die?" he asked sharply.

"All the kids think so, mister," the boy said quietly. "They think she knows where Johnny is, and she doesn't care if he's found or not."

"That's a pretty bad thing to say," Mitchell snapped. He got up and lifted the dog. He was thin, and one paw was badly swollen; but he seemed to realize he was in friendly hands, and wagged his stubby tail.

"Hello, Wags," the young veterinary said. "In a bit of trouble, eh? Want me to look at it?" He glanced at the boy, who looked more cheerful.

"I thought if you would fix his foot, and maybe hide him here for a while, I'd pay for him. I've got two dollars."

Mitchell smiled.

"Let's not bother about that just yet," he said. "I like dogs, and I've always got one or two free boarders around the place. Anyhow, Wags and I are old friends. Johnny used to bring him in now and then. Want to stick around while I look at the foot?"

"I'd like to, if it's all right with you."

Mitchell took the boy to the small operating room, and as he prepared the table he learned who he was. His name was Harold Johnson, but he was usually called Pete. He lived in the house next to the Hunt place, and he knew Johnny well and liked him. Mitchell eyed Pete.

"Have the kids got any idea where Johnny went?" he said casually. But to his surprise the boy's face went suddenly blank.

"No, sir," he said flatly. "Only Wags kept trying to get up into the hills, before she tied him."

Mitchell did not press the subject. He picked up the dog and put him on his side on the table. Wags did not move. It was as though he knew something good was going to be done to him, and except for a low whine he was quiet while Mitchell examined the paw.

"Looks like he's got something in it," he said. "I'll have to open it, son. Want to hold him while I get after it?"

"Yes, sir. I'd like to."

Looking down at him, Mitchell had an absurd desire to pat the boy's hair, which needed cutting and had a cowlick to boot. He restrained himself and picked up a scalpel.

"Better not look," he said. "It'll take only a couple of seconds." And a few moments later, "All over, son. Now let's see what we found."

What he drew out with the forceps was a long wooden splinter, and Pete gave him a sickly grin.

"So that's what it was," the boy said, and letting go of the dog found a chair and sat down.

Mitchell held the splinter up and examined it, and he rather thought the dog looked at it too. At least he raised his head. Then he dropped it back again and closed his eyes.

"Looks as though this came off a board somewhere," he said. "No houses up in the hills, are there? Nobody lives there that I know of."

Pete didn't know. Except for visits to a picnic ground not far away, the town children were not allowed in the hills. There were stories of bears, and one had been shot there not too long ago. Pete was looking better now, but he waited until Wags had been put into a cage before he came out with what was in his mind.

"Look, mister," he said. "Maybe Johnny comes back, or maybe he doesn't. But could you keep this a sort of secret? Mrs. Hunt could have me arrested."

"Why wouldn't Johnny come back? Any place we could have missed looking for him?"

Pete looked unhappy.

"I guess not, if he was where you could see him," he said.

"What does that mean?" Mitchell asked sharply. But Pete slid off his chair and picked up his cap.

"That's just talk," he said. "And thanks a lot. It's time I went home for my breakfast."

Mitchell watched the boy leave. He was a likable kid, he thought. But before he went upstairs to his apartment for a shower he called Joe, his assistant, into his office.

"We've got a new boarder," he said. "He needs sleep right now, but when he wakes up give him a good feed. And if anyone inquires for him we haven't got him."

"What's the idea?" said Joe. "We got him and we ain't got him. We got plenty, Doc, without stealing them."

"He's Wags, Johnny Watson's dog," Mitchell said. "And I wish to God he could talk. He knows something, Joe."

Joe looked startled.

"You think he knows where the boy went, Doc?"

"I think he knows where the boy is. That may be something different. And stop calling me 'Doc.' "

The next morning, after coffee in his apartment upstairs, Mitchell made his rounds of his small hospital, doing dressings, putting a new cast on the broken leg of a Great Dane, inspecting a blue Persian cat who had had difficulty with her first litter of kittens, and feeding a banana to a small chimp left there by a traveling carnival. Johnny Watson had loved the chimp. The last time he had been in they had been sitting together, and the boy had had his arms around the small ape.

It made Mitchell feel a little heartsick to remember.

By noon he took off his professional coat and dressed for the street, and soon after he was in the office of the chief of police.

The chief looked tired.

"Look, Doc," he said, "I hope this is important. I ain't as young as I used to be, and this last three days have about finished me. All I want is to get home and soak in a hot bath."

Mitchell nodded.

"Maybe it's important, maybe not, Chief," he said. "You

know these hills pretty well. Any cabins in them?"

"Cabins? No, not that I know of. Hunters who go in there use tents. Was a bunk-house on Bald Hill for workers in the old quarry about twenty years ago, but they moved out after the highway was finished. Only a ruin now. Roof's fallen in." He eyed Mitchell curiously. "Why? We searched the quarry and the bunkhouse too, what's left of it. Combed the whole place. The boy's not there."

"That's not far from where the dog was found, is it?"

"Still got a bee in your bonnet, Doc, haven't you?" the chief said quizzically. "Yep. Used to be a road up there to the quarry, but it's gone now. Only a sort of track. Dog was near it, all tuckered out."

Mitchell lit a cigarette and smoked it absently.

"That's a mile or so away," he said. "What was the dog doing there?"

The chief grunted.

"Chasing a squirrel or a rabbit, and got lost. That's easy."

Mitchell got up.

"It's too easy, Chief," he said. "Why did the boy keep running away? Got any ideas about it? I suppose a psychiatrist would say there was a reason for it."

"I'm no psychiatrist," the chief said, yawning. "I'm only a cop. How the hell should I know?"

Mitchell persisted. "What about the Hunt woman? Think she had anything to do with it? Was she good to the boy?"

The chief looked indignant.

"Now look," he said, "I've known Hattie Hunt all my life. She's pretty well on in years to raise a kid. But she fed him and took care of him. She did her duty to him, and that's a fact."

Mitchell was thoughtful.

"Orphan, wasn't he?"

"Yep. Plane crash. Both parents killed. Damned lucky for the boy he wasn't with them. The father had the promise of a job on the Coast, and during a stopover in Nebraska the kid fell and broke his leg. They had to leave him in a hospital in Omaha, so when the authorities found the mother's purse in the wreck, with a letter in it from Hattie, they notified me and sent me the letter. I told Hattie, and she went out and got him. Got the dog too. Seems a nurse in the hospital gave it to him. Pretty hard on the old girl, if you ask me."

"Where did all this happen?"

"Somewhere out near Omaha, I forget the place."

"You still have the letter?"

The chief stared at him.

"Look, Doc," he said. "That's three years ago, and what the hell has it got to do with the boy's disappearance?"

"Only what I said—that it's queer for a child to keep running away time after time."

"You get them now and then," the chief said indifferently. "Kids with a wandering foot." He grinned. "Lots of dogs do that too, don't they? Only they usually have a damn good reason!"

This small jest seemed to please the chief; he got up and straightened himself with a grunt.

"I'm going home and get a hot bath and a decent meal for a change," he said. "But maybe I do have the letter. I'll see."

He went stiffly to an ancient wooden file in a corner and fumbled with one of the drawers lettered H, from which he took out a pair of bedroom slippers and a soiled shirt, which last he greeted with pleasure.

"So that's where the damned thing was," he said, gratified. "If you'd heard my wife going on about it you'd have thought I was involved with another woman. Well, let's see."

In due time he located a folder and brought it back to the desk. The letter H seemed to cover a number of things, from a stolen horse to a prescription for falling hair; but at last he produced a letter and passed it triumphantly to Mitchell. It had come from the Police Department of Omaha, Nebraska, and was a brief description of the parents' death and the boy's situation. Enclosed was the letter from Mrs. Hunt to the dead woman. It was not a particularly affectionate one.

Dear Emily, it said. *In answer to your request I can only say I am totally unable to help you. As you know I objected and still object to your marriage. Aside from that I have barely adequate means to live on, and your suggestion that I help you because you have a child is outrageous. That is your fault and your husband's responsibility. Certainly not mine.*

There was no closing—it was merely signed Hattie Hunt, and the writing was small and crabbed. Mitchell handed back the letter, but made a note of the date of the one from the Omaha police. The chief watched him with amusement.

"So what?" he said. "There was a receipt from the hospital in the purse too, so they located the boy and Hattie went West and got the kid. Only thing she objected to was the dog, but Johnny wouldn't let go of him. Raised hell when she tried to leave him behind. Maybe you can understand that, Mitch. You must like dogs, to be in your business."

"I like them better than some people," Mitchell said drily.

He left soon after that, feeling a little foolish. All he had was a dog with a sore paw, a rather large splinter from a board of some sort, and a boy named Pete who almost certainly believed Johnny was dead. Still, that in itself was curious. Children did not usually think in such terms. However, what with radio and television these days . . .

That afternoon Mitchell put the splinter from Wags' paw under his microscope and examined it carefully. It was pine, he thought, from an old piece of pine board, and of course there were a dozen explanations for it. Only one thing was sure. It had been in the dog's foot for several days, to have caused the fester it had.

What had Pete meant about the Hunt woman? Mitchell knew her merely by sight, a dour-looking woman of sixty or thereabouts, always shabbily dressed in rusty black, and with a hard unsmiling face. Not the loving sort, to judge by her letter, and that was an understatement if he ever heard one. But it was a long way from murder. And why murder anyhow? What possible motive would she have for getting rid of the boy?

He sat back, considering. Up to the finding of Wags on Bald

Hill, Johnny's disappearance had been regarded as one of his normal wayward excursions. It was only afterwards that things looked ominous, since boy and dog were inseparable, and then search parties had started out. Maybe the kids had something, he thought, and after some hesitation he wrote out and telephoned a night letter to the police in Omaha, wording it carefully because of the local operator.

"Seven-year-old boy named John Watson missing here. Was injured in accident your neighborhood three years ago and taken to hospital your city. Possibly trying to make his way back. Be glad of any details of said accident and name of hospital. Please wire collect."

He gave his name and address, and was rewarded by the warmth in the night operator's voice after she read it back to him.

"You know," she said. "I never thought of that. I'll bet that's just what Johnny's doing."

"It's a possibility, anyhow," he said. "Just keep it to yourself, will you? I don't want to hurt the chief's feelings."

"That old blabbermouth!"

Mitchell made his final rounds at ten o'clock that night, and Wags seemed comfortable. He decided to walk off his uneasiness, and it was a half hour later when he found himself near the Hunt property. It stood back from the street, as did the other houses in the vicinity, and in the moonless night it looked dark and gloomy, a two-story frame building once white and now a dirty gray against its background of low hills. It was unlighted save for a dim glow from a rear window—the kitchen, he thought—and rather amused at himself, he turned in and went quietly to the back of the house.

Seen through a window, the kitchen proved to be empty and he was about to leave when he became aware of a small figure beside him.

"She's out looking for Wags," Pete whispered. "She's gone up the hill with a flashlight. Why would she think he goes up there? It's kinda funny, isn't it?"

"I wouldn't know, son," Mitchell said frankly. "It's pretty rough going. I'll wait here a while, so you'd better go home. You don't want your mother coming out after you, do you?"

Left alone, the young doctor watched the hill behind the house, but no light appeared, and after a few minutes he stepped onto the porch and tried the kitchen door. It was unlocked, and with a prayer that Pete was not watching he stepped inside. It was a dreary room, floored with old linoleum, and with a tin coffee pot on a rusty stove. It looked as though little cooking was done there, and with a final look at the hillside he moved into the house itself.

He had no flashlight, but by using a match here and there he got a fair idea of the rooms. They showed neatness but a sort of genteel poverty, and even in the basement there was no sign of a board from which Wags could have got the splinter. Only on the second floor did he find anything odd. If Johnny Watson had ever lived there there was no sign of it. Just one room, obviously Mrs. Hunt's, showed any signs of occupancy. The others were bleak and empty, even to the closets.

It seemed incredible that the boy's room should be empty. Had she sent him away, *clothes and all?* It was the only explanation he could think of, and he began to think his previous apprehension might have been absurd. Nevertheless, he was infuriated—remembering the long hard search and the anxious town, while in all probability she had known all along where the boy was.

He got out of the house just in time. There was a light coming down the hill. It came steadily to the edge of the woods. Then whoever carried it stopped and extinguished it. Mitchell slid around the corner of the house and waited until, by the light from the kitchen window, he recognized Mrs. Hunt. She was in a heavy coat, with a handkerchief tied over her head, and at the foot of the steps he confronted her. He could hear her gasp as he greeted her.

"Good evening," he said. "Sorry if I frightened you. I was taking a walk, and I saw your light in the woods. Nothing wrong, is there?"

For a moment she could not speak. She had obviously been badly scared, and she dropped the flashlight, as though she could no longer hold it. When he picked it up she made no move to take it.

"Who are you?" she said. "Whoever you are you've no business here. What are you doing—spying on me?"

"Not at all." His voice was casual. "I thought someone might be in trouble. My name's Mitchell—Doctor Mitchell. If you're all right I'll be going on."

But she had recovered by that time and eyed him suspiciously.

"So that's who you are!" she said angrily. "Maybe you know where my dog is. Maybe that boy next door stole him and took him to you. If you've got him I want him back, or I'll make plenty of trouble."

He laughed.

"That's rather fantastic, isn't it?" he said. "Why should the boy do anything like that? Was the dog sick?"

She ignored that, sitting down abruptly on the kitchen steps, and Mitchell held out the flashlight to her. In doing so he snapped the light on, and he had a momentary glimpse of her. Wherever she had been she had had no easy time. The heavy coat had accumulated considerable brush and pine needles, and below it her stockings were torn to rags. She looked exhausted too, her elderly face an ugly gray. He cut off her protests as he gave her the flashlight.

"If it's Johnny's dog you're talking about," he said, "I'd be a little slow about accusing this boy, whoever he is. Any kid who knew Wags—and a lot of them did—might have taken him."

She seemed to be thinking that over. Then she got up and climbed the steps.

"Well, let whoever has him keep him," she said. "I don't like dogs. I never did."

It was no use going on, he realized, and she ended the conversation by going into the house and slamming the kitchen door. In a sense he felt relieved. If she had sent the boy away he was probably all right, and with this hope, and because he was tired from the days of searching, Mitchell slept rather late the next morning.

The answer from Omaha arrived at noon that day. It was fully detailed, having been sent collect, and it verified the airplane crash and the deaths of the Watsons; also the boy's broken leg and his having been claimed by a relative named Mrs. Hunt. It added something however which puzzled him. It said: *Left for East by car.*

He wandered in again to see the chief that afternoon. Evidently his wife had taken him in hand, for the chief wore a clean shirt and even a necktie. He was in a bad humor, however.

"Now see here, Doc," he said, "the Johnny Watson case is closed, and I'm damned glad of it. Unless," he added suspiciously, "you've got the dog. In that case you're under arrest, and no fooling."

Mitchell managed to look surprised.

"Dog?" he said. "What dog?"

"All right, so you haven't got him," the chief growled. "Probably chewed the rope and got away. What brings you here anyhow?"

"I just had an idea," Mitchell said. "What would you do with a kid you didn't want? How would you get rid of him? By car?"

The chief eyed him.

"Well, God knows there are times when I could spare some of mine," he said. "What are you talking about? The Hunt woman didn't get rid of Johnny. You can bet on that. She had nothing to gain by it. Besides, she has no car, if that's what you mean, and couldn't drive it if she had one."

Mitchell was puzzled as he left. How could Mrs. Hunt have spirited Johnny away?—if she had done so. Not by bus, or train, that was sure. Both trainmen and bus drivers knew the little blond boy and his dog by sight. Yet the empty room in the Hunt house certainly meant she did not expect him back. There was only one other explanation—and that was one he did not have to accept.

As a result he motored into the city that afternoon, carrying the splinter from Wags' foot in a cellophane envelope, and went to the crime laboratory at police headquarters. After a long delay he got to a technician and had it put under a microscope, where a young man in a white coat worked over it.

"Nothing very interesting about it," he said after a time. "Looks like blood and pus on it, if that's what you want."

"No. I want to know about the splinter itself. What is it?"

"Pine," said the laboratory man. "Probably came off a board. Apparently been varnished at one time. Mean anything to you?"

"Not unless I can find where it came from," Mitchell said grimly, and took his departure.

Down on the street he stood by his car and wondered what else he could do. After all, the youngster had been gone before, although never as long as this. And there was no real reason to believe this was not simply another runaway. All Mitchell had was a small boy's belief something had happened to Johnny, a dog with a splinter which might have come from anywhere, and a woman who apparently did not expect the child to come back.

So strongly was all this in his mind that he was not really surprised to see her in person. She did not notice him, but she had come out of a garage across the street, and it seemed so strange a place for her to be that he waited until he saw her take the bus back home before he went in himself.

There were a couple of chauffeurs loafing there, and somewhere in the back an employee was working on the tube of a tire. In a corner was a small glass-enclosed office with a clerk at a desk, and after looking about Mitchell went in there. The man looked up annoyed, after making an entry in a ledger, and Mitchell's voice was apologetic.

"Sorry to bother you," he said, "but I was to take my aunt home in my car. I'm afraid I missed her. Elderly woman in black."

The clerk nodded.

"You missed her all right, brother," he said. "At least it sounds like her."

Mitchell nodded.

"I try to keep an eye on her," he said. "She's peculiar at times. She wasn't trying to buy a car, was she?"

"Buy a car!" The clerk grinned. "She's had an old second-hand one here in dead storage for three years. Never took it out, but comes in now and then to pay her storage bill. Name's Barnes. That right?"

"Not my aunt, then," Mitchell said, and was about to leave when the man spoke again.

"Funny thing about this old dame," he said. "Keeps it here all that time, and now she wants it. Came in ten days ago or so and ordered it put in condition in a hurry. Then never showed up again until today!"

"Did she say when she wanted it?" Mitchell hoped his voice was steady. "Might be my aunt after all. She gets ideas like that."

"No. Just wanted it ready. Said she might need it soon. That's all."

Mitchell went rather dazedly into the street. Some things were clear, of course. What had happened to the car in which she had brought the boy East, for instance. And she had meant to use it again a few days ago, only Wags had been found and as a result the search had been started. She had not dared make a move then, but that either the boy or his body was hidden away somewhere Mitchell no longer doubted, and his blood froze as he considered the possibilities.

Why had she wanted to get rid of the child? And why had the body not been found? She gained nothing by his death, if that was what had happened. Or did she? Some inkling of the truth stirred in him, and it frightened him with its implications. As soon as he got home he called the hospital in Omaha and listened with interest to the reply.

"Caused some excitement, I suppose?" he said.

"What do you think?" said the remote voice.

That afternoon for the first time he really believed Johnny Watson was dead. It was without any enthusiasm that he received Joe's report on Wags.

"Foot's fine," Joe said. "Only he ain't too happy, Doc. He ain't eatin' right, for one thing. I gave him a mess of good hamburger today, and he just looked at it."

"I'm going to need him tonight, Joe," Mitchell said. "I'll carry him if I have to, but you don't know where he is. Get that?"

Joe looked bewildered.

"That woman, she's raisin' hell about him," he said dolefully. "You want to get into trouble?"

"Very likely," Mitchell said drily. "I don't know just when I'll be taking him, but I have an idea where he wants to go."

At 6 o'clock—supper time in the town—he called Pete on the phone and asked him if Pete was busy that night. When the boy said he was not, only some homework, Mitchell said he had a job for him.

"I want to know if Mrs. Hunt leaves her house tonight," he said. "Can you do it? And if she does will you telephone me at once?"

"Sure. That's easy," Pete said excitedly.

"All right. Only don't try to follow her. Just call me up here. I'll be waiting."

Nothing happened that night, however, and the next day was endless. Mitchell did his usual work without enthusiasm, and late in the afternoon dropped in on a harassed police chief, who scowled when he saw him.

"If it's about the Watson kid," he said sourly, "why don't you mind your own business, which is dogs?"

Mitchell grinned and lit a cigarette.

"All right," he said. "Now I'll ask you one. Where up in the hills would the dog Wags get a splinter of varnished wood in his foot?"

"Well, for God's sake!" the chief exploded. "Where does any dog pick up a splinter?"

"It lamed him so badly he couldn't walk. Remember where he was found. The fellow who found him had to carry him back to town. Remember that?"

"It just occurs to me," the chief said suspiciously, "that you know too damned much about this dog. How'd you learn about a splinter?"

"I took it out of his foot," Mitchell said, and slammed out of the office.

He expected trouble after that, but evidently the chief was not interested. At 6 o'clock Pete called up to say he would be on the job again that night, if it was okay. Mitchell said it was certainly okay with him, and rang off grinning. But after that the evening seemed endless. He stayed near the telephone, trying to read a copy of *Veterinary Medicine*, but when by 9 o'clock there was no message from Pete he finally called the boy's home. Pete, however, was not there, and his mother was worried.

"He left quite a while ago," she said. "I don't know what got into him. I was using the phone about the young people's meeting at the church, and he acted very excited. Then when I finished he was gone."

"He didn't say where he was going?"

"No. But he said if you called I was to tell you somebody had started up the hill. I wasn't really listening. Only he knows he isn't allowed up there, and it's too late for him to go to the movies."

Mitchell was sure where Pete had gone, and he felt a cold chill down his spine. How long had he been gone? And what would happen if he overtook the Hunt woman? She must be desperate by this time, if what Mitchell believed was true. Wherever Johnny was hidden, alive or dead, she would be on her way there now, and Pete was not safe in the hands of a half-crazed woman.

He never remembered much that followed. He must have picked up Wags and got into his car, and some time later he was climbing through woods and dense underbrush, using his flashlight cautiously. But it seemed an interminable time and an endless struggle when, with the dog in his arms, he saw a light moving slowly, ahead and above him.

The dog saw it too and whined, and Mitchell put a hand over

his muzzle. After that he was even more cautious, climbing carefully and without his flash. Once he fell headlong and almost lost the dog.

It seemed an hour or more before he reached the edge of the clearing on Bald Hill and stopped. Mrs. Hunt was there, near the ruined bunk-house, sitting as though exhausted on a fallen timber, and his heart contracted sharply as he saw that she held a long-handled spade in her hands.

There was no sign of Pete, but Wags had recognized the place. He gave a short sharp bark and leaped out of Mitchell's arms. In a second he had shot past the woman and was scratching furiously at the door of a small shack adjoining the bunk-house. The woman leaped to her feet and caught up the spade.

"You little devil!" she said hoarsely. "Just stay there till I get you."

Then Mitchell heard Pete's shrill young voice from somewhere among the trees.

"Don't you touch him," he screamed at her. "Let him alone. And I'm getting the police. You're a bad wicked woman."

From the stirring in the underbrush Mitchell realized that Pete was running down the hill, and drew a long breath. The woman seemed stunned. She barely noticed him as he approached her.

"All right," he said. "Where is he, Mrs. Hunt?"

She did not speak, but after a moment she raised a heavy hand and pointed to the shack near the bunk-house, where the dog was scratching wildly at an improvised door of old pine boards. And where a little boy inside was calling weakly:

"Hello, Wags," he said. "I knew you'd come back."

Early the next morning Mitchell sat in the chief's office, looking smug.

"So you combed the whole place!" he said. "Why on earth didn't you look in that shack?"

"Why the hell should I?" the chief said irritably. "It was boarded up and bolted on the outside. The boy couldn't lock himself in from the outside, could he? Why didn't he yell?"

"Probably afraid it was her," Mitchell said. "He was always afraid of her. That's why he kept running off. Or he may have been given a dose of sleeping pills. I don't suppose we'll ever know. But I imagine she didn't mean to do anything drastic in the beginning. Maybe take him by car to the Coast and get rid of him in a home, or something of the sort. But when she learned from the insurance company a day or so ago that she had to produce a body or wait seven years for the money . . ."

"Money! What money?"

"Oh, didn't I tell you?" Mitchell said, as if surprised. "His parents took out airplane accident insurance before they left Omaha, naming the boy as beneficiary. Twenty-five thousand each. It didn't cost much. And the company paid it to Johnny in the hospital, with your friend Hattie as guardian, or something like that. I imagine," he added smoothly, "that fifty thousand dollars has been eating her heart out. She's his only relative."

"Are you saying she meant to *murder* him?" the chief said incredulously.

"I am. Only you'll never jail her. She'll go to an institution somewhere."

He ignored the chief's shocked face and dropped something on the desk.

"You might like to have this," he said. "It's the splinter that saved Johnny Watson's life."

He left the chief staring at it in complete bewilderment and drove back to his hospital, where Joe eyed him skeptically, his torn clothes, his dirty face, and unshaven jaw.

"Must have had a big night, Doc," he said. "How's the other fellow?"

"Doing fine in the hospital," Mitchell said cheerfully. "How's Wags?"

"Looks like he's had a big night too," he said. "But he's sleepin' fine."

"Good for him," Mitchell said, and went upstairs.

Downstairs it was feeding time, with the usual pandemonium of whines and barks, and he was reminded of the talk he had had with the chief of police a day or so ago. He had said then that he liked some dogs better than some people, and all at once he knew why.

Sound Alibi

JACK RITCHIE

✳

Between 1953 and 1983, Jack Ritchie (1922–1983) published several hundred short stories. His smoothly flowing narratives, in which not a word is wasted, earned him a reputation as one of the best mystery story writers of our time. A number of these tales have been collected in A New Leaf and Other Stories (1971), and his "For All the Rude People" is considered a minor classic. While the doctor in this story is murdered at its outset, Ritchie characterizes him in a very few paragraphs as someone for whom we can feel sympathy; thus we are pleased to find that his avocation—which is very close to his vocation—proves helpful in exposing his killer.

DR. MCLANE put his hand on the phone. My eyes narrowed. "Just what the devil do you think you're doing?"

"I'm going to call the police. I have no intention of being blackmailed."

"You're not thinking, Doctor," I snapped. "It's hardly intelligent for one of our most eminent heart specialists to ruin his career for the relatively small sum of five thousand dollars."

Dr. McLane was a tall, dry man with graying hair. "I'm not stupid enough to believe that giving you the money will be the end of it. You'll be back again and again."

That was quite true, but I wasn't going to admit it. "Doctor, I'm not a greedy man. Five thousand will be quite sufficient."

He studied me for a few moments. "Just how did you happen to find out about me?"

I smiled. "We are both specialists in our own fields, Doctor. You have probably listened to a hundred thousand heartbeats and they have told you many things. I too listen, and study, and investigate. These are the attributes of a good lawyer, and for appearance's sake at least, I maintain an office."

I permitted myself to relax a bit, enough to needle him by asking, "You served three years, didn't you? Larceny, wasn't it?"

He flushed angrily. "That was over thirty years ago and I was innocent."

I clicked my tongue. "Come now, Doctor. Does that really make any difference? The point is that you are a former convict. I don't think your patients will like that."

He kept his eyes on me and when he finally spoke his voice was tired. "You are quite right. My innocence and all the rest of it make no difference now."

His face was lined. "I am a collector of heartbeats. As you said, I have listened to a hundred thousand of them." He smiled faintly. "I have listened to mine too. It is not important to me now what the world or anyone in it thinks of me. I have less than two months to live, even if I am careful.''

He lifted the phone from the cradle. "I believe I'll be helping the other unfortunates whom you must be victimizing.''

My temper erupted. This stupid old man could spoil everything for me—the work of years. My hand closed on a heavy ashtray.

He was dialing when I struck. He staggered and dropped the phone. I hit him again and again until he collapsed to the floor.

I stood over him, cursing, watching the rug darken with his blood. When I realized the seriousness of what I had done, my anger was gone and fear had taken its place. I knelt beside the doctor and lifted his wrist. There was no pulse.

I stood up and automatically returned the phone to its cradle.

I started for the door, but stopped abruptly before I reached it. Running away would do no good. There was Collins, Dr. McLane's secretary, to be considered. He had just been leaving for the day when I had rung the doorbell.

I took out my handkerchief and wiped my forehead. I couldn't run. Something else had to be thought of.

I moved restlessly about the large cluttered living room. The door at one end opened to a medium-sized study whose walls and ceiling were covered with acoustical tiles. A large desk and two filing cabinets occupied one side of it. One wall was devoted to shelves containing hundreds of phonograph records. A walnut-colored record player was near the desk.

I stared at the walls as an idea slowly formed. Putting that idea to work would be tricky, but it seemed to me the only possible way out.

I went to the phone and dialed Walt Matson at his home. When he answered, I gave him Dr. McLane's address. "I want you over here right away. Now don't give me any excuses.''

His voice was querulous. "I can't do that. I got a meeting to address tonight.''

I gripped the phone. "I'm not asking you to come, Walt. I'm telling you.''

"But this meeting's important."

"In that case," I said, speaking clearly, sharply, "I guess a lot of people will be interested in knowing that the honorable Walter Matson, Chairman of the City Council, has his finger in the pie every time the city buys a piece of property."

There was a long pause and then Matson said, "I'll be there."

I cut the connection and immediately dialed Mona Saunder's number. She put up a stubborn front too, but I had a few sentences for her that made her change her mind.

The next twenty minutes were painfully long. I kept glancing at my watch. Finally at eight-thirty, I heard the front doorbell ring.

I made certain it was Mona Saunders before I opened the door.

Her eyes were hostile; impatience and anger were in her movements. "Just what are you up to now?" she demanded. "I told you I can't get any more money right now. Not a cent."

Walt Matson's car pulled up behind Mona's at the curb, and I waited at the door.

He was a big man running to fat and his face was red with annoyance. "What the hell is it this time? I told you not to push me too far."

I led them both into the living room. They stopped short when they saw Dr. McLane's body.

Walt's face went white, but Mona didn't appear to be disturbed. It wasn't the first time she'd seen a murdered man. She glanced at me. "What is this all about?"

"You two are going to be my alibi."

Walt's eyes widened. "I can't do anything for you. I'm sorry— but I can't cover for murder."

"You don't have a choice," I said, with a great show of calm. "You're accustomed to the pleasure of the good things of life. So I don't think you'll like what they put on the trays at Joliet. If I sink, I'll pull both of you down with me."

Mona's eyes wandered back to the body for a moment. She was in her late twenties, slim, and though there was a hardness in her she could conceal it when it suited her purpose. She came to the point. "What are we supposed to do?"

I went to the far end of the living room and opened the door. "This is the doctor's study. All three of us were in here when the doctor was killed."

Mona smiled thinly. "Why were we in that room? I imagine the police might want to know."

I rubbed at the tightness in my neck as I thought it out. "According to the newspapers, McLane's been campaigning for another hospital to be built on the north side."

I paced the room. "Mona, you came to me with an offer to contribute money to the doctor's fund."

Mona's laugh was forced and bitter. "That's a good one. Why Wayne wouldn't give me a cent now. Even for something like that."

"I don't care whether he would or he wouldn't. The point is you thought you could persuade him to. You thought if you could arrange all the details, he'd kick in the cash. That's because you know your husband's a nice guy underneath all that money he's got."

I resumed my pacing. "Because I'm a lawyer, you wanted me to arrange the details. I was to get in touch with Dr. McLane and arrange an appointment. You wanted to meet him."

I stopped in front of Walt. "I got you here because you're a city official. I suggested to the doctor that it would be wise to consult you about the best location for the hospital."

I rubbed my forehead hard, remembering Collins, Dr. McLane's secretary, who probably arranged all the doctor's appointments. "Neither of you had a formal appointment. I just phoned both of you, after speaking to Dr. McLane."

Walt's jowls quivered nervously as he nodded his head.

Mona's eye glittered. "It looks to me like this time we've got the cards. This is your turn to crawl for favors."

I smiled tightly. "I don't have to crawl, Mona. What ever gave you that idea? I can always remind the police to dig up your first husband's body. The one, you recall, who had no money and wouldn't give you a divorce when you met Wayne."

She thought that over, then nodded tightly. "We'll have it your way," she said.

"All right," I said. "Now listen. We were all about to go into the study when the front doorbell rang. Dr. McLane excused himself; he was going to answer it. He told us to go on into the study and wait for him there. We went into the study and closed the door. Remember that. We closed the door."

I took a deep breath, let it out . . . "Now we don't know who rang the doorbell. We didn't see him or her. We conducted small talk among ourselves for about twenty-five minutes and then we began to wonder what was keeping the doctor."

"Finally you, Walt, opened the door to the living room and all three of us saw the body at the same time. None of us was ever alone with the doctor. Even for a second after he left to answer the doorbell. That's our story and nothing more. The less we say, the fewer mistakes we're likely to make."

Walt's fleshy face was moist. "Don't you think we should have heard something? At—at least the body falling?"

I shook my head. "No. We were in the study and the door was closed. That room is soundproof or practically soundproof. If we'd have heard any noise, the police will want to know why we didn't rush out and get a look at the murderer."

They had no more questions or suggestions.

I picked up the phone and dialed the operator. "Will you please connect me with the police? This is an emergency."

Sergeant Harrison watched the body being carried out in a wicker basket. "It's surprising," he said, "that none of you heard anything. I should think one of you would have heard a cry, or the sound of the doctor falling."

Mona shook her head. "No. We heard nothing."

Harrison turned to Dr. McLane's secretary. "And you're certain the doctor had no enemies?"

Collins was a small diffident man. The police had brought him to the house shortly after their arrival. He shook his head.

"Dr. McLane was well liked by all who knew him."

Harrison nodded absently. "It must take a lot of presence of mind to kill a man while there are three people in the next room."

I tried to keep the impatience out of my voice. I'd already provided him with an answer twice before. "If we didn't hear anything," I said, "then it follows that most likely the murderer couldn't hear us. He must have thought the doctor was alone in the house."

Harrison had gray hair and light blue eyes that at times appeared almost vague. He moved to the study door. "I'd like to have all of you come in here." He turned to one of the uniformed men. "When I close the door, drop one of those book ends on the floor a few times."

We filed into the study and Harrison closed the door. After a few moments, we heard a dull thud from the next room.

Harrison looked at me. "Apparently this room isn't as soundproof as you seem to think."

I forced a smile. "You forget, Sergeant, we were in here talking. That might have had something to do with our not hearing anything."

The noise came again and this time it had been in the middle of my last sentence.

"Sergeant," I said, "you're assuming Dr. McLane cried out or dropped heavily to the floor. Maybe that wasn't the case at all."

That should have ended it, but Walt was too nervous to think clearly. "The phonograph was playing," he blurted out. "That's why we didn't hear any noise."

I had difficulty concealing my anger. The damn fool. The more there was to our story, the more chance there would be to find flaws in it. But he had committed us, and I had to back him up.

"Yes," I said. "I forgot about that. The phonograph was playing. It was playing when we entered the study."

Harrison smiled thoughtfully at the ceiling. "Wasn't it difficult to discuss anything with that thing going?"

I stifled my irritation. "It was playing softly. More or less background music."

There was a flicker in Collins' eyes. He opened his mouth as though to say something and then hesitated.

Harrison spoke to me. "I suppose you couldn't remember what records were playing?"

I shook my head. "No."

Mona took my cue. "Neither can I, Sergeant. I haven't much of an ear for music."

When I spoke again, my irritation showed. "What difference does it make?"

Harrison smiled. "I don't know that it makes any difference at all. I just like to round up as many facts as possible."

Walt moistened his thick lips. "I think it was classical music."

It was difficult for me not to glare at him, at his perspiring flabby face.

Collins cleared his throat. "Dr. McLane had a large collection of what are generally termed classical records. He preferred that type of music."

Harrison walked to the record player and lifted the lid. "There aren't any records in this machine now."

I breathed heavily. "I must have put them back on the shelves after the last one played. Maybe I shouldn't have done that, considering you think them so important. But I did. Is that a criminal offense?"

Collins smiled faintly. "Dr. McLane had quite an extensive collection of classical records, but he didn't keep them in this room."

My temper got out of hand again. "Just what do you call all of these!"

Collins moved to the record racks. His eyes traveled along a shelf and he made a selection. "I think this one should be particularly appropriate. Dr. McLane was a collector, but a rather unique one. His collection was more than a hobby; it was part of his work."

He put the record on the machine and switched it on. "This particular record is entitled 'Dr. James McLane.' "

I listened to the strange thumping for a few seconds and suddenly, with a stab of panic, I realized what I was hearing.

Collins indicated the shelves. "Dr. McLane was a heart specialist and he collected heartbeats. These are the records of his patients, of famous men, of animals, of himself."

I looked at Mona and Walt. Walt would be the first to crack. And I could see it in Mona's eyes that she wasn't thinking of me and my troubles anymore. She was thinking about her first husband and what she would tell the police concerning his death.

Harrison smiled as he watched me. And there was no sound in the room, but the beating of a dead man's heart.

Paint Doctor

JOE L. HENSLEY

⋇

*The hero of this story is an unusual sort of medical man: a law
student whom the navy perversely trained as a pharmacist during World War II. Joe L. Hensley himself is a lawyer, and in
"Paint Doctor" he shows great insight both into points of international law and the compassionate administration of medicine. His excellent suspense novels featuring attorney Donald
Robak—among them* Deliver Us to Evil *(1971),* Legislative Body
(1972), and A Killing in Gold *(1978)—draw upon his experience
in the Indiana General Assembly. A collection of his short stories,* Final Doors, *was published in 1981.*

THE LETTER arrived at Henderson's law office on a dull fall day. It was a substantial letter covered with bright, Japanese stamps. Sam Henderson took it from his secretary. When she was gone he opened the letter and found one sheet of paper inside folded around another sealed envelope. The second envelope was marked: *To be opened when I die*, then signed, *Iwo*. Henderson hefted it, tempted a little because he was and always had been a curious man and because he'd not heard from Iwo for a long time. He regretfully, finally, put it aside.

The single sheet contained only a few lines:

Paint Doctor,

I write you from a hospital. People look at me and we smile, but I know I am sick. Should I die, you may then read the letter I enclose herewith. My family and hopefully some part of my countrymen join me in thanking you for the years of life you gave me.

Iwo

Henderson read the note several times, examined the sealed envelope once more, held it up to the light, but could make nothing out, then put it in a drawer and locked it there.

He sat back in his chair, remembering, thinking back to an old, almost forgotten war.

It had been half a lifetime since Henderson had first seen Iwo, Colonel Iwo.

Then, Henderson had been a Chief Pharmacist flown to Santuck Island on a PBY seaplane to replace an independent duty corpsman who'd come down with filariasis, so that everything south of his navel had suddenly swollen to alarming size. The plane flew Henderson in and the anonymous corpsman out on the same flight from and to Guam.

Henderson found himself being welcomed, if that was the appropriate word for it, in the steaming heat of a bomb-damaged concrete wharf by three marines—a captain, a gunny sergeant, and a corporal.

"Get the new Chief's seabag, Corporal King," the captain ordered crisply. He received Henderson's salute and wiped ineffectually at his sweaty forehead in return. "It's cooler here after dark," he apologized. "I'm Captain Azus." He indicated the gunny sergeant. "Sergeant Donnelly." He gave Henderson an intent, appraising look. "The General asked them to send someone who could play bridge. Do you play bridge?"

"I'd be rusty," Henderson said.

Sergeant Donnelly smiled. "If you can count honor points, you're a better man than the inept lad you replaced."

Henderson examined the three marines. They all looked tough, competent, and battle proven. "Third Division?"

Captain Azus nodded. "Sure. Real Jap eaters. Come on now. We'll show you your quarters and you can get settled in, Chief. The prisoners will be with you for sick call at eight in the morning. There are some things General Kershand will want you to know about our routine before then."

"Routine?" Henderson asked, not understanding.

"Yes. There's this program the General has set up. Your part in it is that if a prisoner complains of hurting outside then you paint the sore spot with Merthiolate. If he hurts inside you give him two A.P.C.'s. That's all."

"Someone could die," Henderson said uncertainly, not liking the instructions.

"Several of our people did," Sergeant Donnelly said, still smiling, but not so much now. "Eleven of them. We believe they were mostly downed flyers. Maybe there'd have been a survivor or two off a tin can that went down six months ago in the narrows. We think the prisoners you'll be treating under our orders killed those eleven." He nodded. "General Kershand doesn't want things made easy for them. And we think they're healthy enough. They get lots of sun and exercise." He smiled once more, this time without humor.

"You mean they killed our people during the war?"

"Not exactly. Say, instead, right at the end of it, executed them, Samurai sword stuff. All the bodies were found in a common grave inside the prisoners' compound. Without their heads. We're still looking for the heads." Donnelly nodded seriously. "Every time we get even a hint about those heads I go dig another hole. It's become a game. I've maybe dug fifty holes so far without success."

"I see."

"The Japs you'll be treating are the prime murder suspects, Colonel Iwo and his four top aides. Some people don't think we can break them. We think we can. We think we can get enough on them to hang them all. Our methods are our business. General Kershand wants nothing to interfere." He nodded. "God help you if you get in the way, Chief."

Henderson had two large tents, both with raised plywood floors. One was a hospital tent, the other, situated behind it, was for storage and sleeping. The hospital tent was well equipped for a corpsman on independent duty without a medical officer. There was a complete pharmacy, an autoclave, surgical instruments, and even a small, portable X-ray machine.

He settled in. He was twenty-eight years old and his enlistment would end in December. His course was set: He'd go back to the States for one final year of law school. But first there'd be a few months of Santuck Island to endure.

Don't rock the boat, he told himself.

He began to unload his seabag. He put extra socks, skivvies, and khakis in an empty locker. Up the way, through a net window, he could see the marine encampment. It wasn't very large. Beyond that there would be the tents of the surrendered Japanese, thousands of them.

Henderson made himself be only mildly curious about Santuck Island. Since Guadalcanal he'd seen a dozen islands. Now he was tired of islands and atolls, glad the war was done, ready to go home. He'd seen good men die, young, bright men. Five

Japanese prisoners meant little to him. He told himself he was only mildly curious about them because he'd be treating them.

He went through the marine chow line and stoically ate what they gave him. He then returned to his tents, unpacked the rest of his gear, and the few tattered law books he'd carried for almost four years.

When darkness came the marines came to his tent.

There were three of them again, Captain Azus, Sergeant Donnelly, and one new one. They came into the light of his tent, closing the screen quickly behind them against the darting, whirring night moths. They stomped and smiled.

"Get the cards," Azus said. "They're in that drawer." He pointed. He nodded at the man Henderson had not seen before. "This here's General Kershand."

Henderson snapped to attention.

"You needn't do that, son," the one star General said gently. "I read your records this afternoon. You were at the Canal with the First Divisions like me and Azus and Donnelly. You probably hate Japs as bad as we do." He stepped into the light. His hair was white and cut very short. He was thin and small and old, but he exuded energy. Henderson knew of him. A tough man. Mean.

There couldn't be more than a few hundred marines on Santuck Island. Not enough for a General to command. Henderson had a moment of intuition.

"The prisoners?" he asked. "You're here because of them?"

General Kershand took no offense. "I know the Japanese. I know how to deal with them. So I was sent." He smiled. "Long days. A lot of questions, but not enough answers yet. So get the cards and let's play bridge. A tenth of a cent a point. I'll take your part if you don't trust yourself to gamble. The last corpsman didn't."

"I'll gamble."

General Kershand nodded approvingly at him. "Show him what we brought, Donnelly."

Donnelly handed Henderson a small sack. Inside there were a

dozen eggs, a loaf of bread, and a quarter pound of butter.

"Put those in your reefer. After three rubbers we'll cook them up on your hotplate." He gave Henderson a grin. "The General gets you. Captain Azus and I are partners from way back."

Henderson nodded. A square table was pushed into the circle of light. The cards were dealt.

Henderson was at first nervous and cautious. He soon found that none of the other three were truly expert bridge players. They all three played similarly, wide open, psych bids, doubles and redoubles, daring leads, very cutthroat. Of the three, General Kershand was the most daring, the most unorthodox.

Henderson adapted. He had, in undergraduate and law school, played duplicate and regular contract bridge with able players. For a long time he'd teamed with a sarcastic man who was a life master and very good. The man, in their partnership, had incessantly smoked black cigars, used foul language, and been completely intolerant of error. Henderson was rusty, but the game soon returned, in all its intricacies, to him.

With only fair cards he and the General whomped the other two. Four dollars plus apiece.

Over eggs and toast running with butter Henderson asked diffidently, "I'd like to hear more about the island."

"Why?" General Kershand asked.

"Curiosity. And I have to treat the prisoners."

The General held up a warning hand. "Stay shy of it, Chief. They had no mercy for our people and now must be shown none in return. You will treat them within my rules. Soon, when there's a bit more evidence, our legal people will come in, relieve me, then fly them back to Japan for trial."

"Yes, sir. I see," Henderson said, not seeing at all.

"We've a dozen Japanese soldiers who'll testify to seeing Iwo and the rest enter into the prisoner compound the day after Hiroshima. We've got statements from two enlisted Koreans who dug the burial hole that morning. We can't yet put Samurai swords in the prisoners' hands. But one of them will break, one of the five. I know the Japs. One will want to live."

"The heads are the peculiar thing," Captain Azus said. His face was shadowed, out of the light. "No one but those five can tell us where the heads went. But soon, with luck, we'll know that also. If we had the heads, we might be able to identify the victims individually through service dental charts. We know you were in law school, and so you know it could make for an easier trial."

The General frowned at Henderson. "Forget your law school for now. Remember only that this is our business and particularly my business, son. You paint them and pill them. Anything more has to clear through me, and *it won't*. It's my job to make their lives intolerable until one of them breaks. We'll run them, grill them, run them some more. Not much sleep and not much food. And then they have the added burden of Iwo."

"What about Iwo?" Henderson dared to ask.

"You'll soon see." The General scraped at the rest of his eggs. "It's you and me against these two young bandits from now on. You're a cautious player, but a good one." He gave Henderson an approving look. "Take more chances."

In the morning Henderson found out about Iwo. Two battle-garbed guards escorted four trotting prisoners, all of the procession quick stepping along. The four prisoners were slowed because they carried a stretcher. The fifth prisoner rested on the stretcher.

Outside the guards lined the sweaty prisoners up. One marine stayed on guard. The other brought the prisoners in, one by one.

The Japanese were short, dour men. They looked tired, ill at ease, stretched to the breaking point. They smelled of fish and sweat and dirt. None of the four who'd borne the stretcher spoke English. All had nicknames given them by the guards.

"This one's called Squirrel," the guard intoned. "The last doc always gave him two A.P.C.'s."

Henderson nodded and obeyed his instructions. He pilled two, Squirrel and Ace, then painted two, Eddie and Wing.

"You'll have to come outside for the other one," the guard

said apologetically. "He won't get up so the others have to carry him." He winked. "I think it's getting to the place where they're damned tired of it."

Henderson went outside. The fifth man lay in the stretcher smiling a little, looking up at the hot blue sky.

"New doctor," he said conversationally.

"I'm Chief Henderson. You must be Colonel Iwo."

"No talking to him," one of the guards warned harshly. "He can talk to you, but the rules are you say nothing back."

Henderson nodded.

Iwo smiled even more. One thin hand unbuttoned a faded shirt, very dirty, devoid of any insignia of rank. His chest, on both sides, was painted red.

"Hurt chest," he explained. "Air raid. Your flying bastards."

Henderson bent forward to inspect. The smell made him almost gag. Iwo was gaunt and each bone showed. There was a peculiar, small lump on the right side at collar bone level. Henderson touched it gently.

"Paint me," Iwo commanded softly. "Paint me, Doctor. Do your part in this slow ritual you make us die by."

Henderson hesitated and then dutifully painted fresh Merthiolate over the man's upper chest. When he was done, at command, the other four, Squirrel, Ace, Eddie, and Wing hoisted Iwo and began their trot back to their compound. The trailing guard lifted his rifle to Henderson and grinned.

"Thanks, Doc. See you tomorrow."

Henderson adopted a routine. Each morning, first off, he would solemnly attend to the prisoners, never varying their treatment. Later in the day he'd hold sick-call hours for the marines. There he could use his considerable medical skills. He treated everything from persistent ear fungus and heat rashes to occasional broken bones. Only when something seemed beyond him did he consign a patient to the daily Guam plane and the hospital there.

Once, years before, Henderson had complained when the Navy sent him to hospital corps school, ignoring his legal background. It had done no good. So, that failing, he'd become expert, made the Navy way his way, and survived.

After sick call he'd loll the rest of the day away, reading books from the small camp library, or studying his few precious law books.

At nights, almost every night, he played bridge with the same foursome. To the great delight of General Kershand, despite the fact that Henderson continued to play his conservative game, he and Henderson won consistently.

Henderson would have been content except for the prisoners. It made him feel unsure participating in a nullity.

"Why do the guards bring the prisoners at all?" he inquired after a game one night.

Captain Azus answered. "Geneva Convention, Chief. Prisoners are entitled to medical attention." He smiled. "The Japs winked at it. We've learned what we're doing here from the enemy. Cruelty brings cruelty. So medical attention means what we decide, not what they expect and want."

"The war's over," Henderson said reasonably.

"Not yet. Not for those who did what was done here."

Henderson shook his head. "It worries me. I think there may really be something wrong with Colonel Iwo."

General Kershand shook his head. "He's faking and the others are helping him. That's why we make them carry him with them every place they go. Iwo presented his sword to me at the surrender, all very correct and ceremonial then. When the bodies were found he took to bed."

"I'd like to X-ray him," Henderson said.

General Kershand shook his head. "No way."

"If you ordered it and I found nothing, then that could hurt him at a future trial."

"I won't change the way we're doing things. One of those men will break if things continue as they are now. We run them and question them. They only sleep two hours at a stretch. Then we start on them again. Stop being a lawyer." He shook his head. "No way."

In deep night, soon after, there came to be a way. Henderson was shaken awake by Captain Azus.

"Come with me, Henderson. Now! There's hell to pay."

Henderson pulled on rumpled khakis and got into the Captain's Jeep. They jolted down a rusty road at an excessive speed and parked near a small, barbed-wire enclosure. Flashlights picked them up, beckoned them on.

"This way. This way."

Four prisoners, Squirrel, Ace, Eddie, and Wing, lay bloodily dead in a large single tent in the center of the enclosure. The fifth prisoner, Colonel Iwo, bled sluggishly from his wrists. Henderson ignored the dead and examined Iwo. The cuts were straight, but not, hopefully, deep enough.

"They all cut their wrists," Azus said, somehow scandalized about it. "God knows where they got a razor. We check them all the time. They passed it on, one to another. Iwo was last. Maybe he chickened out. The others cut groins too. He didn't."

"Get him to my tent. I'll sew him up and start plasma," Henderson said. "He's lost a lot of blood. He's weak and could die also."

Captain Azus nodded agreement. "The General isn't going to be happy about this. A lot of us are going to catch hell."

Henderson directed the shaken guards in loading Iwo into the Jeep. He kept pressure on the wrist cuts, stopping the bleeding. Iwo sat in the seat with his head back, looking up curiously at the night sky, his eyes open.

"Paint doctor," he said softly. "Damn paint doctor. Let me die. Then all this will be done."

"No," Henderson said firmly.

In the tent he sewed the cuts together and gave Iwo plasma, one unit, then another. When blood pressure and pulse were more normal he wheeled the X-ray unit into place and X-rayed

Iwo's chest. The guards watched curiously, making no protests.

General Kershand stomped angrily in as Henderson was reading the wet film.

"Four dead men," he said savagely. "This bastard the only one left." He shook his head. "And I find you violating my express orders."

"Yes, sir. I'm sorry, sir. Could I ask you if when he surrendered his sword to you at the ceremony did he make a big thing out of it? Did he draw it, flourish it, lift it, swing it?"

"He gave it to me. That's all." The General shook his white head. "I'd put you in the brig if I had anyone else to treat this murdering Jap. I may do that yet."

"Yes, sir," Henderson continued. "I was wrong, but the pain for him must have been excruciating." He pointed at the X-ray. "His collarbone's splintered on the right side. You can see the break and the calcification around it. The edges don't meet well. If he tried doing much, even now, he might cause the fracture to compound, come through the skin. And there are, at my count, at least four rib fractures on his left side, probably more. Our last bombing raid on Santuck—was it before or after Hiroshima?"

"I'd guess before. After the bomb at Hiroshima everything stopped in this area." General Kershand drew closer to the X-ray film, frowning at it.

"This man didn't cut off any heads with that shoulder."

"This is none of your affair," General Kershand said coldly. "This man is your enemy. You're not his lawyer. Whether he wielded a sword or not, he was in command of this island. He participated."

"General, with all respect, this man will eventually be tried by lawyers, defended by other lawyers. Without someone around to put the sword in his hand or the words of command in his mouth, he's not going to be found guilty."

"Perhaps. That's conjecture."

Henderson nodded surely.

"They've beaten me, then," General Kershand said softly. "They died to beat me."

Henderson sensed the same thing. He nodded.

The General looked away and then back. He smiled sourly. "My recollection is you're due out in December, Henderson. You've probably cost yourself some added time tonight. With four dead and Colonel Iwo in the shape he's in, my job here's done. I'm going to fly back to Guam with you and Iwo." He stopped for a moment, thinking. "Maybe there'll be a decent bridge game there for an old plunger who's about to retire." He nodded. "You argue Iwo's case with the legal people there. You show your X-rays to the doctors."

"Yes, sir," Henderson said. "I will."

"Why, Henderson? Why bother with an animal like him?"

Henderson thought for a moment. "Perhaps because what we were doing was no more right than what Colonel Iwo was accused of doing. Also, because I was curious. Mostly because he tried hard to die with the others, to cheat us also. His cuts are straight. There are no hesitation marks. He just couldn't get pressure enough on the blade to get the job done. He was so weak he never got to his groin area. Maybe the razor was dull. But if he couldn't commit suicide, he logically couldn't lop off heads with a Samurai sword."

The man on the cot moaned. They both watched as he awoke and stared about him. He pulled weakly at the bandages on his wrists, but they were secure.

"Paint doctor," he called. "Damn paint doctor."

"More than that," General Kershand said. He shook his head and went out into the night.

The obituary made the front page. It recounted Iwo's accomplishments as a Japanese statesman, as a leader of the diet or legislature, as a cabinet member. The story said the sane world had lost a sane, reliable friend. There was even, Henderson found, a long, complimentary, even flowery, editorial about Iwo inside.

Henderson unlocked the drawer and opened the second letter:

Dear Paint Doctor,

What I did, during the war years, seemed right to me then. Things I did then are abhorrent to me now.

Thank you for helping me. What your people did to me and the others attempting to obtain our confessions was also a wrong. I am glad I did not die. Perhaps I am now innocent as once I was guilty.

One of your prisoners, the last one, broke my collarbone. The rib injuries did occur during an earlier air raid.

My family died at Hiroshima. With strong drugs and hot anger all things become possible. When it was over I alone weighted the sack of heads and dropped them secretly in Santuck Bay.

Iwo

Henderson read the letter without surprise or regret. He put it back in the drawer when he was finished. A few days later he remembered it, took it out, read it once more, then burned it.

The Other Side of the Curtain

HELEN McCLOY

✧

Not a great deal is known about dreams; they are a shadowy area to which psychiatrists must apply highly subjective interpretations. But when the patient of the unnamed doctor in this haunting tale refuses to listen to his suggestions, there is really little he can do to help her. Helen McCloy frequently writes of psychiatric matters: she has published a series of twelve suspense novels featuring Paris- and Vienna-trained Dr. Basil Willing, among them Dance of Death (1938), The Goblin Market (1943), The Long Body (1955), and Mr. Splitfoot (1968). During her forty-year career she has written both formal mysteries and the type of psychological suspense found in "The Other Side of the Curtain."

FACE TO FACE with the doctor, Letty hesitated. "It seems such a little thing, but it . . . bothers me."

"A dream?"

She nodded. "For the last eight months."

"Always the same dream?"

Her glance strayed from the doctor's face to his severely impersonal office. "It begins in all sorts of ways—different scenes, different situations. Sometimes there are policemen. Sometimes a courtroom. But it always works around quite plausibly to the same ending. I seem to be walking down a long empty corridor in an eternal twilight. Suddenly I come to a curtain hanging across the passage, blocking my way. It's only cloth. I could push it aside and go on. But I don't. I stand still within a few feet of it. And then I begin to be afraid.

"The curtain is dark. It hangs in deep, inverted folds, motionless, as if it were carved in stone. There is not a breath of air, but after a few moments the folds begin to ripple and the curtain bellies toward me. Then I know that there is something behind the curtain. Not someone—something. Something unspeakable. The essence of all terror and all evil. That's when I want to run away. Just as I would if I saw a tidal wave sweeping toward me and knew I had only a few seconds to reach high ground. I make a frantic effort to turn and run. But my feet are lumps of lead. They won't move. Panic mounts from my heart to my brain. I can't think. But there is worse to come. Some force outside myself—invisible and irresistible—lifts my feet from the ground and sets me floating giddily toward the curtain and . . . whatever lies on the other side . . .

"Honestly, doctor, I don't believe I could bear it if I didn't know all the time that I was dreaming."

The doctor's interest quickened. "You know that you are dreaming? While the dream is going on?"

"Of course. Don't you? Doesn't everybody?"

[282]

"No. That's what makes a nightmare terrifying to most people. They think it's real while it's going on. But you actually dream that you are dreaming?"

"Yes." Letty was disturbed. "Am I . . . different? I always know it isn't real. Even when the terror is throttling my heart, there is a tiny, detached voice at the back of my mind which keeps saying: *Don't be afraid. It's only a dream.*

"That small, sensible voice is the one thing that makes it bearable . . . until I'm lifted into the air, like a toy balloon that has slipped its tether, and wafted against my will toward the curtain. That's when it becomes unbearable."

"But you do bear it." The doctor smiled. "Because you have to."

"Oh, no." Letty smiled back. "I don't have to. And I don't."

"What do you mean?"

"I wake myself. I concentrate my whole attention on the tiny voice that whispers: *It's only a dream.* I answer it and say: *Then wake up. You can if you really want to. You can escape this terror by the simple act of waking. Open your eyes—quick! Before it's too late. Before you reach the other side of the curtain. . . .*

"You see," Letty went on earnestly, "I can't get away by running, but I can get away by waking. My body won't obey, but my mind will. And mental escape is just as good as physical escape—in a dream. I can't move from one place to another, but I can move from one state of consciousness to another. I summon all my force of will, all my power of concentration, to wake myself. I make a mental effort, that is curiously like a physical effort. Something clicks and—I'm awake. The dream shimmers a moment. Then it's gone. And that saves me."

"From what?"

"From . . . the other side of the curtain."

"Why not wake yourself sooner? When you first begin to dream?"

"I wish I could. But I can't do it until the urge to escape becomes almost unbearable. Even then I can only do it by making a great effort of will—an exhausting effort that leaves me weak and panting when I wake . . . You do believe me?''

"Why not?" He shrugged. "All the evidence we have about dreams is necessarily subjective. I've heard of people who pinch themselves to make sure they're not dreaming. I've always wondered why it never occurs to them they may be dreaming that they are pinching themselves. . . . You have no motive that I can see for . . . embroidering. Some elements of your dream are common enough—the compulsion, the floating . . . But there's one detail that you've omitted."

"I've told you everything."

"Not one thing." His voice dropped to a quiet, suggestive tone. "What is on the other side of the curtain?"

"I don't know." Letty paled. "I don't want to know. I only know that it's horrible and—it has been there, waiting, for a long time."

"Waiting for what?"

"For me."

"Have you any idea what would happen if you refrained from using this power to wake yourself? If you simply let yourself be wafted through the curtain?"

She shook her head.

"Why not try it?"

"I couldn't. You don't know what you're asking."

"But it's only a dream," he reminded her quizzically.

"It's easy to say that—here in the daylight with you. But in that gray twilight where I am all alone . . . The urge to escape is overwhelming."

"If you didn't will yourself to wake up, it might prove interesting psychologically. It might help me to help you."

"I couldn't." Letty was trembling. "I know that if I saw what is on the other side of that curtain I would . . . die . . ."

"Yet you haven't the slightest idea what is there?"

"No. I have no idea of its shape or color, its function or meaning. I know only one thing: it's something I must never know. Something I must escape."

"Will you promise me one thing?" He was playing with a pen on his desk. "If ever you do go beyond the curtain in this dream, will you let me know what you find there?"

"But I never will," said Letty quickly. "I shall always wake myself in time."

His glance considered her with a scientist's patient, impersonal curiosity. "Hasn't it occurred to you that you may lose this power of waking yourself?"

"Oh, no!" It was a cry of despair.

"I've known only one other person who had this power—a fellow student at medical school. He lost it when he was about thirteen—at puberty. He had it all through childhood. Then it faded."

"I'm twenty-nine." Letty's voice faltered. "Did he—your friend—see behind the curtain?"

"He didn't dream about a curtain. And after he lost the power, he no longer had nightmares. But you may."

"Doctor, you've got to help me," insisted Letty. "I must get rid of this dream before I lose the power to wake myself. Why do I have this particular dream? That's what I came to find out."

"Let me ask you a question." He paused, seeming to choose his words with care. "If you know while you are dreaming that the whole experience is nothing but a dream—why are you so afraid?"

Letty's glance shifted from his direct gaze. "I don't know. Dreams aren't logical."

"Life is not logical," returned the doctor. "So few people—so few scientists realize that. But dreams are logical. In their own way. Because, like logic, they are products of the human mind in its pure state—untrammeled by the limits of matter, space and time . . . I think I know why you feel so intensely in this dream even while you are realizing it is a dream and nothing more."

"Why?"

"Because the source of the fear is not in the dream itself but in your waking life. The curtain in the dream is only a symbol—a shadowy reflection of something real which you fear when you are awake. Waking or dreaming, you know subconsciously that the fear is real. That's why the fear persists even in the dream when you know that the curtain symbolizing the fear is only part of an illusion."

"But there is no fear in my waking life!" cried Letty. "Only in my dreams."

The doctor was skeptical. "Nothing comes out of the mind that has not once gone into it. It can't create. It only reflects. Every dream images waking experience. Fear, shame, guilt are things we repudiate or repress in the waking state. So they reappear in our dreams disguised as symbols. Analysis might reveal what source of fear you are repressing in your real life. Once we dug that up, you would be rid of your dream."

"That's Freudian, isn't it?" Letty's whole body seemed to recoil fastidiously. "I really don't care for the theories of Dr. Freud. And I have never had any occasion to fear a curtain in real life."

The doctor realized he had lost a patient. He was sorry because her case had roused his curiosity. No doubt she had hoped for a simple panacea: *Eat less meat. . . . Take more exercise. . . .* But he couldn't help her that way. The preliminary physical examination had shown nothing wrong organically. . . . He was too curious to let her go without a few more questions.

"You may have forgotten the occasion. Or, more likely, the curtain is just a symbol. But the fear itself is real. What are you afraid of, Mrs. Jason?"

"Why . . . nothing . . ." All her openness was gone now. She was like one of those flowers that curls and closes every petal tightly at the first chill of sunset. "I am perfectly happy. I have no shameful past, no frustrated ambitions. I'm not afraid of anything."

"Then you are more fortunate than most," said the doctor with irony. "No financial worries?"

"No. My father left me an income that averages eight thousand a year. In a small town like Brookfield, that's ample."

"Happily married?"

"Yes, indeed." Her eyes brightened, her cheeks grew a shade pinker. "Only two months ago."

"And how long have you had this dream?"

"I told you. It began about eight months ago."

"Did anything particular happen to you about eight months ago?"

She answered promptly. Too promptly. "No. Nothing at all."

"You have many friends in Brookfield?"

"Oh, yes. My mother's and father's friends. My own school friends."

"And your husband's friends, too, no doubt?"

"Not so many. He only came to Brookfield a year ago. He doesn't know many people there."

"His profession?"

"He's an artist. But he hasn't been able to do much painting this last year because he's been having trouble with his eyes."

So he married a local heiress, thought the cynical doctor.

Innocently Letty shattered this hypothesis. "When I said I had eight thousand a year I forgot Ralph's six thousand. We're really quite comfortable on our combined incomes." She rose, pulling on gloves. "Thank you for letting me take up so much of your time. It's been a relief to talk."

A relief from what? He closed the door of the outer office regretfully. A pity most people thought their petty privacies more important than science. Analysis still had to overcome prejudice today, just as dissection did two hundred years ago. If only we could have "mind-snatching" like the old "body-snatching" . . .

The nurse-receptionist was busy with a card file on her own desk. He tossed the case card he was holding onto her blotter. "Put this in the inactive file. The lady won't be back. Acute case of well-bred reticence complicated by a Puritanical conscience."

"Something bothering that Puritanical conscience now?" The nurse picked up the card. "*Mrs. Ralph Jason* . . . Where have I heard that name before?" A startled look came into her eyes. "Why, that woman can't be Mrs. Ralph Jason. She's dead."

The doctor seemed indifferent. False names were not too uncommon with a certain type of inhibited patient. "How do you know Mrs. Ralph Jason is dead?"

"There was something about her in the papers. She was the wife of an artist living in Brookfield and she committed suicide. I noticed the name Jason at the time because I'd just been reading *Hercules, My Shipmate*, Golden Fleece and stuff."

"When was this?"

"Let me see. About eight months ago."

"Then this must be the second Mrs. Jason." The doctor pursed his lips. "I wonder . . . "

"What do you wonder, doctor?"

His eyes looked far away. "Just what is on the other side of that curtain. In her next dream she may find out . . ."

Letty seemed to be sitting in an armchair, dozing before her own fire. As usual in dreams, the scene appeared slightly out of focus. A scene shot from an erratic camera angle, revealing unfamiliar aspects of familiar objects. The room looked so long, as if one must travel an interminable distance to reach the hall archway at the other end. The ceiling seemed so high, so deep in shadow. Why was this half-imagined, half-remembered facsimile of the room so distorted by her dream-mind? Could it be the projection of some emotional disturbance?

Beyond the wavering circle of firelight, the pale green walls looked gray in the gloom. Even the vivid, jade green of the rug was subdued to a dull olive. Jagged shadows moved against the walls in silent mimicry of the crackling flames.

As space was enlarged, time was delayed. Seconds seemed to pass slowly as minutes. As if the clockwork of the universe was running down, slackening almost imperceptibly, spacing each successive tick farther from its fellow; a leisurely unwinding of the coils of life and matter, a gradual resolution of all things into their component electrons that could end only in a universal stillness, darkness, and coldness.

When her hand reached for a cigarette it seemed to move with ponderous deliberation. When she struck a match the instant between friction and flash stretched agonizingly until she was not sure the flash would come at all and felt achievement when it did.

Even Ralph's face looked different across the hearth with his eyelids closed and his head resting against the back of the winged chair. Was it the oblique angle that made his chin look longer and harder, his mouth closer and narrower? Or was it the absence of the eyes, sealed under smooth, motionless lids? Open, the eyes were so jewel-bright, such an odd shade of sea green, they distracted you from his other features. Subtract them, and his chin and mouth leaped into sudden prominence, suggesting unsuspected traits of character.

But then it was not the real Ralph sitting across this dream hearth. It was a mere shadow of the living Ralph—an image reflected in the dark, still pool of her sleeping mind and distorted, like the room. Withdrawn, impersonal—as if some barrier lay between them . . .

The sudden peal of the doorbell ripped through silence. Ralph's eyelids lifted. This was the smiling face she knew so well. She had an odd sense of recognition and relief. *Hello, Ralph, I'm glad you're back. Where were you a moment ago? Not here in this point of space-time with me . . .*

Her glance followed his to the clock. Five minutes after eleven. Too late for ordinary callers in Brookfield.

His lean body rose out of the chair in sections like a straightening jackknife. How faithfully her fertile dream-memory reproduced his every gait and gesture, all shaped and colored cunningly as life itself—all done in a flash. A few strides took his long legs down the room, through the archway. She heard the click of the hall switch, the grate of the door latch, the creak of a hinge. Then the mutter of a strange voice. Ralph's answer was pitched higher. "Why, of course. I can't imagine . . . but won't you come in?"

Lights blazed overhead. The walls seemed to leap toward her, the ceiling dropped, the whole room shrank. Fire-glow and dancing, attendant shadows were wiped out as if they had never existed. She felt constricted, almost imprisoned in this cube of harsh, yellow light the room enclosed. A fly in amber. Some instinct of self-defense rather than courtesy made her rise and turn toward the archway, her back to the fire. She wished to look her fate in the face and meet it standing.

They did not look like messengers of fate, the two men following Ralph through the archway. Either one could have served for the figure of John Q. Public in a political cartoon. The first was a stranger. Where had her dream-mind found the material for this animated mask? Some particular face, noticed briefly in a crowd, forgotten consciously, stored up unconsciously? Or was it a synthetic composite of all the strange faces she had ever seen? It must be one or the other. *Nothing comes out of the mind that has not once gone into it.* . . . Someone had told her that quite recently. . . .

It was a flat, meaty face. The gray hair looked thin and greasy, but the brows were still black, thick and bristling. An isolated tuft sprouted between the brows. The eyes were dogged and weary. Not intelligent. The eyes of a man who worked hard at some routine job.

The other man she recognized. Who could forget that albino rabbit face? The nibbling, pink mouth, the white-lashed, pink eyes that blinked so rapidly? She had seen him only for a moment this afternoon, loitering in a doorway when she left the doctor's office, standing beside another man whose face was hidden. And she had only noticed him then because she had a vague feeling she had seen him or someone like him once before, long ago . . . How like the vagrant dream-mind to conscript the face of an utter stranger, glimpsed so fleetingly on a city street, and introduce him into this dream-world. The dream-mind always seized upon some tiny incident of the day as raw material for that night's dream, the way a nesting bird seizes whatever lies at hand—a scrap of thread or paper—and builds it into the twig fabric of its nest. But unlike the bird, the dreamer could magnify his material, constructing a whole personality

out of a half-remembered face or a whole dramatic sequence out
of a half-realized sensation . . .

Ralph was speaking. "Letty, this is Captain Crane and Mr.
Mather. Gentlemen, my wife."

Captain Crane? An Army officer in mufti? Or a veteran who
insisted on using a military title in civil life? From a great distance she seemed to hear her own voice: "Won't you sit down?"

She was in her own armchair, profile to the fire, hands clasped
in her lap. Ralph was on the arm of his chair, filling his pipe.
Crane and Mather sat side by side on the little sofa. Crane leaned
back as if he were tired. Mather took pains to sit on Crane's right,
perching gingerly as if he were embarrassed.

Ralph turned toward Letty, speaking slowly and distinctly.
"Captain Crane is from the Police Department."

Silence came with the shock of a loud explosion. Police Department. POLICE DEPARTMENT . . . The words seemed to re-
verberate down the deepest tunnels of her mind, growing louder
instead of fainter as they receded. . . .

"He has a few questions to ask."

"A parking ticket?" Her voice cracked.

"No, Mrs. Jason." Crane turned to look at her gravely.
"Doubtless you recall that eight months ago your husband's first
wife, Olivia Jason, died of atropine poisoning."

"Atropine sulphate," put in Mather quietly.

Letty bowed because she could not speak. The flare of a match
masked Ralph's face. Mather's eye caught Letty's. Hastily he
looked in another direction. Who was Mather? Why was he
here? He was past the retirement age of the Police Department.
He was fat and out of condition. He was timid. Even the illogical
dream-mind weaving this fantasy could not have cast him for
the role of another policeman. . . .

"The coroner's jury brought in a verdict of suicide." Crane's
voice went on colorlessly. "For several reasons. Olivia Jason was
a cripple. A motor accident had crippled her while Ralph Jason
was driving. She blamed him for this and for the fact that inter-

nal injuries made it impossible for her to have a child. These things preyed on her mind. The coroner's verdict took all of them into consideration when it brought in a verdict of suicide while of unsound mind."

I must say something, thought Letty. But her tongue was stiff, her throat dry. In her own ears her heartbeats throbbed loudly as if magnified by a microphone.

"The police accepted that verdict at the time, but—" Crane looked directly at Letty. "One thing troubled us, even then. We were unable to trace any purchase of atropine to Olivia Jason."

"That isn't strange." Ralph had taken his pipestem out of his mouth. "Atropine sulphate occurs in several patent medicines. In this state they can be bought without a prescription. There are dozens of druggists in Brookfield and its suburbs. Each one has hundreds of customers. Why would any one druggist remember a single customer who made a single purchase of eyedrops?"

Crane pounced. "Why eyedrops, Mr. Jason? Atropine also occurs in rhinitis tablets and some ointments."

"Well, any of those." Ralph's lips closed over the pipestem.

Slowly Crane's head swung back toward Letty. "Olivia Jason couldn't drive at all. Even on crutches she could only walk a short distance. Alone, she could not have gone far beyond her own neighborhood. And she would hardly take anyone with her when she was buying poison for the purpose of suicide. A druggist might remember a crippled customer when he would forget others. Especially if he knew the cripple by sight. And all the druggists in Olivia Jason's neighborhood did know her by sight. She pestered all of them for some soporific that would ease the pain of her crippled legs."

At last Letty managed to speak. "I see."

"Do you?" A touch of sarcasm in Crane's voice. "Since the police accepted the verdict of the coroner's jury there have been two new developments which I would like you to explain—if you can."

Suddenly Letty was cold with that cold which seems to come

from within, seeping out through blood vessels and tissue until, last of all, the skin itself is clammy.

Inexorably Crane went on: "First, you have married Ralph Jason. Second, we have traced a purchase of eyedrops containing atropine to you. A purchase that occurred a few days before Olivia Jason's death."

Letty tightened her clasped hands. This was nightmare. Sooner or later it would end as all her nightmares did—the corridor—the curtain—paralysis—a slow, ineluctable drift toward the curtain—and whatever lay on the other side. The tiny voice at the back of her mind was whispering: *Don't be afraid. It's only a dream.* Mentally she answered as she always did: *Then wake up. You can if you really want to. You can escape all this terror by the simple act of waking. Open your eyes—quick— before you reach the other side of the curtain. . . .*

Desperately she gathered her forces for the supreme mental effort that was so like a physical effort. But this time nothing happened. Her will slacked with a sudden, sickening limpness and the dream held. She couldn't quite achieve that oddly mechanical click that would release her from horror and put her back in her own bed between cool sheets, with Ralph beside her and maple leaves sighing in the dark beyond the open window. . . . The doctor's voice came back to her: *You may lose this power of waking yourself. . . .* Had she lost the power so soon? Could it be that those words of the doctor, so carelessly uttered, were acting now on her subconscious mind like a post-hypnotic suggestion, inhibiting that power to wake herself at will? But she wouldn't be able to bear it when she came to the curtain. If she couldn't wake then she would . . . die . . .

"Why shouldn't Letty buy eyedrops? Lots of people do." That was Ralph's voice, but less firm than usual.

Does he . . . doubt me? The thought pierced Letty's heart like a knife. *Even in a dream I can't bear to have Ralph doubt me. Why should my own subconscious mind torture me by inventing such a dream? Nothing comes out of the mind that has not once gone into it. . . . Have I had the idea that I might be accused of Olivia's murder all along, in the waking state, ever since her death? And that Ralph might suspect me? Of course, I have never allowed myself to think of such things consciously but . . . what has been going on in my subconscious mind all these months, since Olivia died? Something like this?*

Captain Crane answered Ralph quietly. "Lots of people buy eyedrops who have something the matter with their eyes. Usually iritis when the drops contain atropine. Sometimes keratitis. We have examined the record of a medical examination given to Letty Jason when she was still Letty Knowles and applied for overseas service with the OWI during the war. Her eyes were normal then." He turned back to Letty. "Mrs. Jason, have you developed iritis or keratitis in the comparatively short time since then? If so, the fact can be established very simply by your submitting to an oculist's examination."

Letty heard her own voice, low and shaking. "My eyes are still perfectly normal."

"You don't have to answer him, dear!" That was Ralph.

"I have to warn you that anything you say may be used in evidence against you?" Letty's voice rose shrilly over the cliché. Then she laughed. "Is that it, Captain Crane?"

"I'm afraid it is, Mrs. Jason." To her amazement, she saw he was perfectly serious. "Unless you have some explanation of that purchase of atropine. I came here late this evening because I had to go through certain formalities first in order to secure a warrant for your arrest on a charge of murder in the first degree."

"Here! Wait a minute!" Ralph's pipe clattered on the hearthstone. He was on his feet, his green eyes fever-bright, his thin cheeks flushed an unnatural red. "You say you've traced the purchase of eyedrops containing atropine to Letty. I suppose that means some fool druggist thought he recognized her photograph after eight months. Can you do a thing like this on one flimsy identification?"

"Identification and motive and a few other things that will come out at the trial," returned Crane. "It was not an identification by photograph either." He looked at Mather. A bead of sweat gathered on Mather's forehead. "This is the druggist, Mr. Mather," went on Crane. "He identified Letty Jason this afternoon when he stood with me outside the door of a doctor's office in the city and saw her come out. He was sure of the identification then, but I brought him with me this evening so he could see her at close range and be doubly sure. We had a prearranged signal. When he sat down on my right it meant that he was absolutely sure—that I could go ahead with the arrest."

"How can he be sure?" demanded Ralph. "When he only saw her once before, for a moment, eight months ago?"

"That will come out at the trial. Every murderer makes at least one slip. Fortunately for us Mrs. Jason was in a state of agitation when she bought the eyedrops and she made her one slip then."

Ralph whirled on Mather. "Are you sure? After all these months? Do you realize what you are doing to her?"

One moment ticked away while Mather looked into Letty's eyes. Then a strange thing happened—a thing she thought characteristic of the dream-world where there is no consistency or plausibility in the way people behave. Tears gathered in Mather's pink eyes—one, then two, trickled down his quivering cheeks. He was weeping for her and weeping for himself. He was an ordinary man leading an ordinary life. Suddenly circumstances had put the power of life and death into his flabby hands. He had never borne such a responsibility. He didn't want to bear it now. But he couldn't lie. He was too simple even to think of lying. Too innocent and too frightened.

"Yes, I'm sure," he whispered hoarsely. "I remember the light, taffy-colored hair and the dark, brown eyes and the three little moles that form a triangle on her right cheek. She looked so pretty when she ran in, hurried and hatless, asking for the eyedrops . . . that summer day . . . I'm sure, but . . . Oh, God! I wish I wasn't sure! I'm so sorry . . . so very sorry . . ."

"You're sorry!" Ralph's voice was hard. "You damned sniveling sentimentalist! If you're so sorry, why in hell didn't you keep your mouth shut?"

Letty felt Ralph's hands, warm and rough, against her icicle fingers. "Don't worry, darling. We'll get the best lawyer in the city. It's all a silly mistake—circumstantial evidence. We'll find the druggist who sold Olivia the stuff if we have to hire a hundred private detectives . . ."

Captain Crane's hand touched her elbow with authority. "Ready, Mrs. Jason . . . ?"

Every time Letty raised her eyes from the concrete floor to the stone wall, the striped shadow of the barred window had moved a few more inches with the movement of the sun. The universe wasn't running down—it was running away, racing, tearing, skidding down the slope toward the abyss without a hand to stay the throttle. The world wouldn't end in universal lethargy—it would end in a cosmic crash of blast and flame. Soon the friction of this terrific speed must generate fire and the whole dizzy maze of spinning suns and planets would explode in a giant shower of sparks and cinders. Minutes were seconds, hours were minutes. Days and nights whirled by in a blur of stripes—the flicker of a picket fence seen from the window of an express train. She felt the rush of wind against her face, heard the roar of speed in her ears, faster, faster, faster . . . Impressions were a jumble of flashes, scattered and incoherent as a montage of films.

The day the lawyer came. A core of callousness sheathed in a skin of synthetic sympathy, smooth and cold. "Just one question, Mrs. Jason. Did you buy that patent eye medicine from the druggist, Mather? The whole case is going to turn on that point."

Blood drained from her face. Her swollen heart labored to expel the overload. She began to tremble—lips, hands, knees. Why did he ask? Did he know the truth?

"No," she whispered. "Oh, no."

Bleak eyes were looking at her, without sympathy, without hope. "Mather's story is . . . circumstantial. Just what did you do that afternoon of June twenty-second? Remember?"

"How can I?" Letty looked blank. "That was eight months ago."

The lawyer's mouth thinned to a harder line. "Mrs. Jason, your life depends on this. Do you understand?"

"Yes."

"Then tell me, frankly and in confidence, are you protecting anyone?"

"No. Please don't question me any more. Please."

In his eyes she saw a new-born idea quicken to life and grow. His lips scarcely moved. Perhaps he did not realize he had spoken his thought aloud. But she caught the words. And the look of contempt. "You did buy it, didn't you?"

She was nauseated by the giddy pace of time. Weeks wheeled by as swiftly as days. Yet she knew this was illusion. The whole elaborate sequence of events was doubtless taking place between two breaths drawn as she lay asleep in her own white bed in her own blue and white bedroom with the maple leaves rustling beyond the window. Hadn't it been proved that a dream involving weeks of time and a vast variety of incident could unreel its whole length in the single instant between the ringing of an alarm clock and the waking of the dreamer?

Ralph came the day before the trial. Looking in his face was like looking in the mirror her cell lacked for fear she would break it and use the splinters to slash throat or wrist. His look of thin, bloodless skin, stretched taut over unfleshed bone, must be her own look after these weeks of strain.

"We haven't been able to trace the purchase of atropine to Olivia," he said soberly. "She must have got it somewhere. I've a dozen private detectives working on it. They'll turn up something before it's too late."

"Suppose they don't." Her quiet voice seemed to startle him. Had he never really considered that possibility until now?

He glanced toward the guard and dropped his voice. "Then . . . we'll have to tell the truth."

She whispered. "Is there no other way?"

"It won't be too bad," he argued. "I had a perfectly good reason for asking you to buy those eyedrops for me. The chief point against you is the fact that you bought the drops when you didn't need atropine for your eyes. But I did need it. I've been using the drops for years. And I still do. As I told you before, we can always prove that by a medical examination of my eyes. It would be different if my eyes were normal like yours. But since I can prove that I have a mild case of chronic iritis they can't convict me on the case as it stands.''

"They couldn't convict," said Letty. "But they would suspect That's why I agreed to keep still about the eyedrops when Olivia poisoned herself with the same drug you use for your eyes. Once they knew about that, they would look for other evidence against you.''

"They could look till doomsday. They wouldn't find a thing.''

"If only there were some other way I could clear myself without involving you. The druggist who sold atropine to Olivia must exist. She couldn't walk far. She must have got the stuff in this neighborhood somehow . . . Or could she have used an old phial of your eyedrops?''

"She couldn't. There was never any left over. And I always carried the current phial in my pocket.''

"Ralph, why did Olivia choose atropine?''

"What do you mean?''

Letty mused aloud. "Atropine . . . The name comes from Atropos. Wasn't she the one among the Three Fates who snipped the thread of life with her shears? An oddly feminine figure for Death, almost domestic. The neat, industrious seamstress . . . the spinster, cutting what she had spun. Olivia was feminine, domestic. She loved to sew. And you know she hated you. Because you were driving the car when it crashed and she was crippled . . . Do you suppose she chose that particular drug as her poison deliberately because she knew that it was the drug you used for your eyes?''

"What good would that do her?''

"She hoped that you would be prosecuted for her murder.''

"Letty! Do you really think that Olivia would kill herself simply to make me suffer?"

"She hadn't much to live for. Lameness, pain . . ."

"What if she did? We can't prove it now. And, damn it, she must have got the stuff somewhere! If only we had more time to trace her movements on that day before her death when she went out alone . . ."

Letty drew a deep breath, nerving herself for the sacrifice it was so plain he expected. "Don't tell the lawyer . . . yet."

"You're quite sure you can wait? A little longer?"

"Let's leave the truth till the last moment. We'll always have it to fall back upon, if worst comes to worst. . . . Isn't there anyone else who might have poisoned Olivia? You told me once she was on bad terms with a servant. . . ."

Ralph dismissed this. "Hardly a motive for murder. What made you think of such a thing?"

"The fact that you haven't been able to trace the purchase of atropine to Olivia, with all these men working on that one point. Could it mean that she never bought the stuff at all? That someone else we haven't even suspected poisoned her under our noses?"

"She saw so few people," muttered Ralph. "Her doctor . . . her lawyer . . . and her servant . . . It doesn't seem possible . . ."

Letty's nightmares were always wintry and twilit. So she was not surprised to find the vast courtroom bathed in a melancholy, gray dusk on each day of the trial. The judge, high on his bench, was one of the archetypes characteristic of dreams. Saturn as El Greco painted him—senile and vicious, the old man of the tribe devouring his own children. Bloodshot eyes, bloodless lips, papery skin—he looked the enemy of everything that changed and therefore the enemy of life itself, the delegate of death.

But when Letty turned her eyes the other way she found no comfort. Merely tier upon tier of heads, blank and yellowish as gourds, in the shadowless light, almost as misshapen, quite as empty. Only the eyes were alive—watching her.

Like mechanical dolls the witnesses shuttled on and off the stand. Press a spring and each could squeak a few thin, metallic words. People whom Letty had hardly noticed as human beings were now determining her fate—Olivia's cook, Olivia's doctor and lawyer, Olivia's milkman and grocer, the little druggist, Mather.

Yes, I was the first Mrs. Jason's cook. Tongue like a serpent she had. I told her what I thought of her when she fired me. Nagging, selfish old thing. I didn't care if she was a cripple. I always pitied her poor husband. Yes, the second Mrs. Jason—Miss Knowles as she was then—used to come through the kitchen from the tennis court when Mrs. Jason's luncheon tray was being set out on the table. Usually tea or a glass of milk and salad and a custard . . . Yes, Miss Knowles was always running in to see if Mrs. Jason wanted anything and Miss Knowles was often passing through the kitchen alone because I'd be answering the doorbell or the telephone. She'd pass me in the front hall. I remember two times she took the tray up to Mrs. Jason alone. Right before Mrs. Jason's death, that was . . . Well, within a day or so . . .

Yes, I was the first Mrs. Jason's doctor . . .Yes, I think I may say her injuries affected her attitude toward Mr. Jason . . .

Yes, I was the first Mrs. Jason's lawyer. When they were first married she made a will leaving everything to Mr. Jason . . . About six thousand a year. She told me he had nothing of his own . . .

Yes, I'm a druggist. I prefer the word pharmacist. Mather is the name. Fred Mather . . . I'll explain how I can remember her buying the eyedrops after eight months. You see, I'd just set up in business for myself. New store and everything. I wanted trade, so I made a point of asking each woman customer for her name and address so I could send her folders and samples whenever I got in a new line of cosmetics. Mrs. Jason—Miss Knowles then—gave me her name and address. Seems funny now that she didn't think of giving a false name, but, as Captain Crane said to me, all murderers make some slip somewhere or they'd never be caught. . . .

Objection! . . . Sustained. Pray continue . . .

During the last eight months I've mailed several folders and other stuff to Miss Knowles. Then, when her marriage to this Mr. Jason was announced in the papers, I remembered her. And I remembered how I first saw her, that day she came in to buy eyedrops with atropine in them. And then I remembered reading about an inquest on an Olivia Jason who had died of atropine poisoning. Seemed sort of queer, taken altogether, so I went around to the nearest police station and told them about it . . . Oh, yes, the bottle was clearly marked: *Poison—For External Use Only* . . . No, it's not very strong . . . A one per cent solution of atropine sulphate. The dose was clearly marked, too— *One or two drops in each eye every three hours* . . . Well, a twentieth of a grain is supposed to be the fatal dose and if you drank the whole bottle that's about what you'd get . . .

Letty could no longer distinguish words. Just a humming crescendo of accusation, exquisitely titillating to the participants. The hunt was up, the hounds were in full cry, all inhibitions against cruelty resolved by the rationale of punishment—the one thing that makes it possible for sadists to live comfortably in an organized society.

Now Ralph was on the stand. Letty could tell by the look of her own lawyer that Ralph's testimony had not helped. Somehow, for all his good intentions, the prosecutor had trapped him into several damaging admissions—the unhappiness of his first marriage and his utter failure to trace Olivia's purchase of atropine. But after all, how could he deny these things under oath when so many other witnesses had testified to them already?

Court is adjourned . . .

Letty faced her lawyer, again. His face was serious now and, for the first time, compassionate. As if he felt she were already judged and doomed. As if justice could do no more and the time for mercy had come.

"Mrs. Jason, if you know of anything further in your own defense, it must come out now. This is your last chance. So far everything has been against you."

"You mean—there's no hope of my being acquitted?"

"None whatever."

Letty expelled her breath in a great sigh. "As a last resort—call my husband to the stand again."

"Why?"

"You'll find out when you call him."

"That won't do, Mrs. Jason. I can't question him intelligently unless I know what I'm questioning him about. I'm surprised your husband hasn't come forward before now—if he knows anything that would clear you. Or did he advise you to wait till the last minute?"

"No, no. I advised him."

"Why?"

"I was afraid of . . ."

"Of what?"

"It's simple, really. Ralph and I were driving together that afternoon of June twenty-second, the day before Olivia killed herself. Ralph had to stop to fix the car—something wrong with the carburetor. I got out and strolled around. He asked me to stop in a drugstore and get this patent thing for him—the eyedrops. He has a tendency to chronic iritis. A medical examination of his eyes will prove it."

Her voice trailed off into silence as she saw the lawyer's expression. "You should have told me all this before. We should have had the medical examination made before the trial began. And an oculist to testify. Now there's no time, but the case is so desperate, we'll have to take a chance . . ."

It was very late now. The gray dusk was darker. Everything was dimmer. The old judge sat so still, his pallid face so expressionless, that Letty had the wild fancy he might have died there on the bench and no one had noticed the difference. All the other faces looked flat to her bemused eyes, as if they were painted on a backdrop to simulate spectators in a courtroom scene. The only living face was Ralph's as he mounted the stand again. A model witness—serious, alert, choosing each word with sober deliberation—only—he wasn't saying the right things.

"I never asked Letty, my present wife, to buy patent eyedrops for me containing atropine. Not on June twenty-second—not on any other day . . . No, I have never used eyedrops containing atropine sulphate . . . No, there is nothing the matter with my eyes. I have never had iritis, acute or chronic. A medical examination will prove the truth of that statement, I believe."

Letty's lawyer stammered, "B-but—if I call your wife to the stand and she testifies that she remembers clearly . . ."

Before the prosecutor could object to this most irregular question, Ralph had slipped in an answer equally irregular but nonetheless effective. "I have known for some time that Letty was given to . . . exaggeration, but I did not believe her capable of . . . murder."

"Your honour, I protest that—"

"Oh, boy, has he put the rope around her neck! Where's that telephone?"

"My God, wasn't he supposed to be a witness for the defense?"

"Well, what would you do if you suddenly realized right on the witness stand that your second wife must have poisoned your first wife? The minute he knew she'd suggested that line of questioning to her lawyer, he knew she was guilty and counting on his pity or gallantry to back up her cock-and-bull story. . . ."

The guard touched Letty's arm. She stood still, looking across a heaving sea of faces to Ralph's face, a little higher than the others—a face that looked suddenly cold, triumphant, and evil. No medical examination of his eyes was necessary for her. She knew he would not make this statement on the witness stand unless it could be proved. She had only had his word for the statement that the peculiar sea-green color of the iris in his eyes was the effect of iritis on eyes naturally blue. That was a symptom of the disease, she knew. But she also knew that some people are born with light green irises. There had been occasional inflammation, but that could be simulated . . . vinegar or pepper . . . She had seen him use eyedrops, but they were clear and colorless as water. They could have been water. She was no doctor. She couldn't tell by merely looking at his eyes whether he needed atropine drops or not. Until this moment she had not recalled hearing somewhere, at some time, that even the mildest case of iritis would leave the eyes dull as well as inflamed. Ralph's eyes had always been so jewel-bright. . . .

It was not only her ignorance that made her vulnerable. It was also her trust in him. The one thing that had never occurred to her was to doubt his good faith, to ask for confirmation of any statement he made. No doubt he had counted on that. When had he first told her about his sick eyes? The day after the accident that crippled Olivia . . . Accident? Of course not. Ralph had inherited Olivia's six thousand a year as he would now inherit Letty's eight thousand. No wonder Olivia had hated him—crippled, helpless, suspecting the truth, hesitating to change her will until it was too late. . . .

How did she know all this so surely? Perhaps in the inmost core of her being she had always known it and never admitted it even to herself. In her heart she had always known that he was a murderer and her own silent, unacknowledged complicity in his crime was a part of the mechanism that now condemned her to death.

She saw all this and more in one brilliant flash of realization. The events of her life were no longer in sequence but all spread out before her in one continuous pattern. Time had ceased to exist. She was seeing her whole life all at once as an entity with a shape of its own—the Long Body of the Hindus, the body that extends in the dimension of time as well as in the dimensions of space. It was all one piece, shaped from the beginning to the end where she now found herself, predetermined by a shy, lonely girlhood that was to make her in later life the easy prey of a plausible adventurer. She had wanted to be fooled because it was so pleasant to be fooled by Ralph. And now that pleasant fooling had brought her to the foot of the scaffold.

The horror that had lain waiting in ambush for her behind the symbolic curtain of her other nightmares was simply herself—her own life seen as an integral whole, the Long Body that few mortals can bear to look upon. For the truth about Ralph and Olivia was a part of that ultimate self which she had always suspected, and never admitted in the waking state. Which in other dreams she had masked with a symbolic curtain and fled by willing herself awake . . .

Wake . . .

She didn't have to bear this horror. There was one way she could escape from the whole thing—by waking. It didn't matter whether the jury acquitted her or not. It didn't matter whether the judge condemned her or not. It didn't matter whether Ralph betrayed her or not. For this was only a dream. All these people—judge, jury, Ralph himself—were not real. They were only dream images in her own mind. Even the stone wall of the prison cell that felt so solid under her fingertips was a dream image, too, more intangible than a shadow. She had only to wake and everything would go on just as it had before. . . .

She and Ralph would laugh about this dream tomorrow at breakfast. *Ralph, I had the most impossible nightmare last night. I dreamed that you had murdered Olivia and got me accused of the murder in your place by neatly providing me with means and opportunity beforehand. You even provided me with a motive—by marrying me. And then you repudiated me on the witness stand so cleverly that no one would think for a moment we had conspired together to kill her. As of course we hadn't. I was the dupe . . . And Ralph would answer: So that's what your subconscious mind really thinks of me! Or was it the mince pie and cheese we had for dinner?*

She gathered her powers of concentration together and looked steadily at the dream courtroom telling herself to wake, straining for that mental click that would wipe out all this ugliness and restore her to her own bedroom, cool and fresh from the night wind pouring through the open windows. In another moment the whole scene should begin to shimmer and crumple as if it were all painted on gauze that was about to waver and collapse. . . .

But this time there was no wavering. Again the dream held. Even in the waking state her sense of external things had never been more vivid and detailed than it was at this moment. The nick in the prosecutor's front tooth, the bristle that sprang from a mole on the judge's chin casting a thread of shadow, the spiral paths left by fingertips on a dusty electric bulb overhead. And Ralph's supple features still twisted into a mask of shock and grief.

She could not bear to look that treachery in the face a moment longer. *You know it's only a dream! Wake up!*

Then the last veil fell. Truth stood before her, whole and hideous, the greatest horror of all.

She was awake.

She had been awake all along. From that first moment of shock when she had seemed to be dozing before the fire in a dream and Ralph had brought two strangers into the living room, her tortured mind had sustained the illusion of a dream as a refuge from terror and disillusion. That was why she had not walked down a corridor towards a curtain in this nightmare, as she did in all the others.

Other people mistook a dream for reality while they were dreaming. She had mistaken reality for a dream while she was waking. Was it so strange when reality itself had so many dream qualities? Incoherence, illogic, injustice, relativity in the duration of time, inexhaustible fertility in the invention of character and incident, the haunting sense of uneasiness, the feeling of being swept on helplessly by an inexorable current from an unknown source to an unknown destination. All she had ever known of reality was its reflection in the mind. A dream was simply a less disciplined reflection of that same reality in that same mind. Easy enough to mistake one for the other.

But this was not a dream: this nightmare was life itself.